Xin Publishing

Pawns

Clive K Semmens

Xin Publishing

Published by Xin Publishing
an imprint of Xin He Ltd.
Hill Quays
14 Commercial Street
Manchester M15 4PZ
United Kingdom

ISBN: 978-0-9564897-9-1

Foreword

A different leg of the trousers of time?

I planned the whole of *Pawns*, and wrote the first half of it, in the late 1970s. It then languished until I picked it up again in 2011. At first I considered updating the first half to take account of changes in the world in the meantime, but quickly realized that it wouldn't work.

So *Pawns*'s leg of the trousers of time had already diverged somewhat from ours at the very beginning of the book. Almost the whole of it is actually set in 1990. In Part I, the world is pretty much as one might, in the late 1970s, have expected the 1990 world to be – but not exactly as it actually was. For example, the accident at Chernobyl hadn't happened, and the Soviet Union hadn't started imploding.

From Part II onwards, the divergence is very much greater.

When I planned *Pawns*, and while I was writing the first half of it, it was, I thought, a complete story in itself. I still think it is. But while I was completing it, *Going Forth* began to form in my mind. *Going Forth* is a sequel to *Pawns,* some thirty years later.

I hope you think *Pawns* is a worthwhile read. If you do, I hope you'll read *Going Forth* – and find it worth reading as well.

Part I

Chapter 1

'... I did it my way.' End of record. Golden oldies! Bloody jukebox!

Kid feeding space invader machine in the corner. Is it war fever? Xenophobia? He can't be very good at it – putting his coins in every few minutes. Bloody thieving machine! Where's the kid get the money anyway? Poor kid must be bored silly.

In the other corner of the café: me. Watching the kid playing space invaders. My coins for each cup of tea lasting me a bit longer. Watching the back of the girl who'd put the record on. Watching the waitress – surreptitiously though: the kid is concentrating on his game; the jukebox girl is looking the other way; but the waitress looks this way from time to time. She smiles at me when our eyes meet; but it's embarrassing. So I'm pretending to read my book. Well – actually reading it, between times. But every now and then realizing that I've taken nothing in and going back a couple of pages. I wonder if anyone has noticed that I've been reading the same two pages for an hour and a half?

An old news vendor trudges into view down Market Street. Grey hat. Grey jacket. Grey trousers. Grey bag of grey papers. Even his face as grey as any I've seen. In a grey street, under a grey sky. Crosses Bridge Street by the zebra crossing and comes into the Britannia. His shoes are falling off his feet: even though he's got a job, I bet he's no better off than I am. Looks worse off.

'Tea love, ta. Two sugars.'

'Sugar's on the table again now, sir. Shortage is over, you see, and it's less work for me. Eighty pee that'll be. Thank you sir.'

'Ta lass. You don't seem overworked at the moment you know.'

'No. But you should be here in the afternoon. Two of us. Hammer and tongs.'

'Aye. Mebbe.'

The news vendor comes and sits opposite me. Perhaps he recognizes my inability to reject anyone. No reason to reject him. Lonely old codger, absolutely harmless. Just needs a bit of companionship. Not enough of that in the world. He starts to talk about his life, his job, his home. But I'm not really thinking about him: barely able to say the right things at the right time. After a while I look at my watch and excuse myself.

I expect he knows I'm only escaping, but he can't accuse me of lying. Anyway, maybe he realizes he can talk to me again, and I'll be increasingly embarrassed pretending to have somewhere to go.

Stand up, put on my coat. Catch the waitress's eye: 'See you later.'

'See you.'

Strange: that isn't embarrassing at all. Perhaps because it's clear cut: know what's going on, what's coming next. Over and out.

Over the zebra. Up Market Street. Left into Northgate. Now I'm out of sight of the Britannia: no need to look purposeful any more.

Admit it Pete: you too are bored silly. So, probably, are the jukebox girl and the waitress. Nothing to do. The lot of five million Britons. No – more. The waitress, for instance, has a job. Not one of the five million. And I bet the old news vendor is bored silly too. Bored and lonely.

A travel agent's window: bloody package tours. Half-naked models on sunny beaches. In an empty grey street under a darkening grey sky.

Mike's gone to see his parents: not back till next Thursday to sign on. Lonely – not just bored: don't want to go and see anyone, they're only acquaintances. I need friends. Mike's away.

Half-naked models on sunny beaches. Man in bright clothes leaning back on rope in impossible position on sun-soaked cliff with dizzying drop to out-of-focus below. Jumbled houses on narrow cobbled street on hill in brilliant sunshine. Drizzle starting and street lights coming on.

Left again into the arcade out of the drizzle. Mike's away and June isn't talking to me. Now there's the truth of this mood. Amazing how the mind shuts things out. Is it all over with June? Do I want her back, anyway? Hasn't this been coming for a long time? Pretty girl at the bottom of narrow cobbled street in brilliant sunshine – where? Italy? Cornwall? Haven't I been looking at other girls and thinking, for a long time? And just what has June been thinking, for a long time?

Andy's café. Bright lights. Loud music. Lots of video games. Lots of kids. Steamed up windows. Tina loves Terry in the steam. Rubbed out quick with a cardigan sleeve. A vivid green-and-red sleeve. Quick sight of a pretty face through the clear patch.

Keep on walking. Looking purposeful. Pity the Arcade's so short: drizzle again. What's up with me anyway? Doubt if 'Tina' – was that Tina? – even saw me. Why should I care what she thinks of me anyway? Still: I'm not going back into the Arcade. Nor am I going to stand in a doorway: this drizzle could go on for hours. And I'm not going home yet: I would die of boredom and loneliness. And I can't go back to the Britannia yet: the news vendor might still be there. And anyway I can't afford to spend all my time in cafés.

Pity the library's shut. Go there during the day tomorrow, Pete: it's cheaper than cafés. And you'll have to go to a café for the evening. I wonder what June's doing, thinking?

Bridge Street again – I hope the newsvendor can't see me from the Britannia! Still, it's dark out here and light in there and he isn't right by the window. Better go the other way for the moment anyhow.

Queue waiting to go into the Odeon. I wonder what's on? Don't bother to look: it's four and a half quid. Stop here on the bridge.

Wharfe Street lights on the water. Little rings in the water where the raindrops land. Dark backs of Quebec Street warehouses. Limestone parapet wet, dampening my coat sleeves.

It's raining harder now; I'll get soaked. Hope the newsvendor (Mr Grey? that's a good name) has gone: I'll go back to the Britannia.

Streetlights glistening on the surface of Quebec Street. Noise of tyres on wet road. Headlights reflecting on wet road. Over the zebra.

'Think I'll have a meal, love, please. Can't be bothered to go home and cook. Egg and chips.'

'And a tea?'

Nod.

'Two fifty-five please.'

'Ta.'

Take coat off. Sit down in a corner. Mr Grey has gone. So has the space-invader kid. Jukebox keeps looking at her watch and then down the street. Maybe she's being stood up.

Reading the same two pages again. Wishing I'd bought a paper from Mr Grey. Maybe, just maybe, there might be a job in it worth the effort of applying for.

Egg and chips. 'Ta love'. Red sauce. Can't hold the book and eat egg and chips at the same time. Watch a group of kids up Market Street, playing the fool and shouting. Two cars pass. An old van.

Young bloke running down Market Street, noisy on the wet pavement. Straight across Bridge Street – don't think he looked at all. Straight into the Britannia, up to Jukebox.

'Sorry I'm late love. Head office is snowed under with work and Sergeant Robinson's been briefing us on how to do some that they're offloading onto us. Now I know why we were given those two kid recruits to train the other week.'

'Relax love. We've time for another tea before we set off. When's the next train?'

'Not for an hour and a half. Come on, if we run we can catch this one.'

Exit young couple, fast. She sounded nicer than she looked. Wonder where they were going? Don't know the comings and goings of trains. Not used one for years.

'Another cup of tea love?'

What? I don't think that's ever happened to me before!

'No ta.'

'It's all right. It's on the house. I'm having one.'

'Oh! Okay – thanks.'

Two cups of tea.

'Mind if I join you?'

She's got more guts than I have. Or just less confused motives to get embarrassed about.

'Be my guest. Thanks for the free tea.'

'There's no-one to know. I'm quite glad you're here. I don't like being on my own in the evenings. Anyhow, I don't like to see you so depressed – it makes me depressed. You're usually so cheerful. Old Tom was quite worried about you, cutting him off like that.'

She takes more notice of people than I do. I've noticed she's a pretty girl with a warm smile. That's about all, in all the months she's been working here.

'Do you know him then?'

'Tom Green? He's a regular. He's in here as often as you are; I'm surprised you've not met before. He's a bit more talkative than you – I'd say I know him quite well.'

'I feel bad about cutting him off now. I figured I'd given him enough time not to offend him. I'd...'

'He wasn't offended. Most people scarcely give him the time of day. He was just surprised, and a bit worried about you. But you weren't giving him time, he was giving you time, Pete.'

'How'd he know I'd not be another who'd scarcely give him the time of day? Why should he be surprised? Why should he worry about me? Anyway, how'd you know my name? And what's yours?'

'You know, I do believe you're actually listening to every word I'm saying. But I can't answer six questions at once. Ask them again, one at a time!'

Laughter.

'I doubt if I can remember them exactly!' More laughter.

'I'm Cathie, anyway, for one. And, maybe you're always on your own when you come in here, but I see you around town with Mike and Jill and June, and you call each other by name. But to get back to old Tom: he knows you'd normally chat to him for an hour or more, 'cause he does talk to his mates, you know. He knew you weren't listening really, and he knew why you left. He's not stupid, you know. When you came out of Quebec Street and went down towards the canal, he shot off quick. Didn't want you to get soaked waiting to come back in here.'

God. People are more conscious than I am. I've never connected anyone I've seen around town as being the same person as 'the pretty waitress in the Britannia'; but she's even caught my name. And the old codgers' club that to me were just disconnected lonely old men needing companionship talk about me and are concerned for me.

'I didn't see – Tom? – leave. I just guessed he'd be gone by now. Where would he go to on an evening like this? I just don't understand other people's lives.'

'I reckon he thought you'd be watching for him to leave. Don't know where he'll have gone though. He won't be wandering the streets on his own, that's for sure. What will you do later on?'

What does that mean? Or doesn't it mean anything? Can't go wrong assuming it means only what it says.

'I'll walk home, read my book for a while, and then go to bed, I expect. Maybe get a paper and look at the situations vacant. What about you?'

'My dad'll come down and walk me home come closing time. If this weather clears up my little brother'll want to show me the stars; else we'll all be round the telly.'

Can't have meant anything; her evening is cut and dried.

'Does your dad walk you home every night? How old's your little brother? How much does he know about the stars?'

'You and your questions! My dad doesn't reckon it's safe for me to walk home alone. My brother's ten, and I don't know how much he knows 'cause he knows more than I do. Have you got any family?'

'Not around here. I've got an elder brother in Sheffield but the rest of the family still lives in London. Mum, Dad, little sister, one Granny still going strong.'

'What brought you up here?'

'I came to stay with my brother, looking for work. Got a job at Ripley's. Couldn't stand commuting from Sheffield so I got myself digs. Then Mike found this flat for me. If I'd still been in digs I'd have left when Ripley's went broke.'

'Have you been out of work ever since then? I was still at school then.'

'Apart from a temporary job on the canal project, yes.'

'My dad used to work at Ripley's. Twenty years. He reckons he'll never get another job. Not much work in light engineering any more. He thinks he's too old to change trades. Do you think you'll get another one?'

'Sooner or late, I hope. Scarcely keep body and soul together on today's benefits. Might go abroad. Some folks reckon it's not so bad in Germany.'

'I don't reckon much to Germany. My Uncle Jack's just got back off a temporary job on a shelter complex there. He says unemployment's as bad there as it is here, and there's a lot of violence and disruption.'

'What did your dad do at Ripley's? Maybe I know him.'

'He was in charge of the presses. Hello, I've got a customer.'

Young man in jeans and a filthy yellow jumper. Mud. Clean jeans. Very strange.

'Two teas love please. My mate's just coming. Have you anywhere we can wash?'

'Up the stairs, straight ahead. Can't do anything for your jumper, though!'

Laughter. No explanation. Couldn't really expect one, I suppose. So Cathie's dad was – is – Mr Jordan. Cathie Jordan. Cathie Jordan back behind the bar. Cathie Jordan whose dad walks her home every evening – but who is alone in the Britannia half the evening every night.

Splashing noises upstairs. Another – less muddy – young man arrives, with a blue kit bag. Sits down.

'Your mate's upstairs in the bathroom.' Cathie.

'Thank you. I'll follow him if I may. He has ordered some tea, hasn't he?'

'Yes. I'll bring you them when you come down.'

'Thanks.' Southern accent, but a precise, foreign-sounding turn of phrase. I wonder where he's from?

I wonder what time this place shuts? I've never stayed very late. Do I want to meet Mr Jordan with his daughter? Would Cathie find it embarrassing? Come on, Pete, it's you who would find it embarrassing. Shall I ask her what time she shuts? Or shall I just leave fairly soon?

Get up. Coat on. 'See you.'

'Are you going already?'

'Aye. I'll most likely be in tomorrow.'

'Okay – see you tomorrow love.'

Bloody coward Pete.

Over the zebra. Still raining, little streams down the gutters now. Up Market Street. Interesting: the gutter stream is muddy. Past the end of Northgate. All the shop lights out now. Wonder if Andy's is still open? Wonder what time the Britannia closes? Wonder what Cathie is thinking? Wonder what Mike is doing at home with his parents in Somerset? Wonder what June and Jill are doing?

Bicycle splashes past up the hill, lights flickering. Slow on the hill. Maybe dynamo slip on wet tyre. Turns left into Long Lane.

Cross the end of Long Lane. Top of the hill. Mud in the road, road works signs. Temporary traffic lights. Digger. Dark stretch of road, one street light not working. Turn right into Fieldhouse Road. Pedestrian approaching on the other side of the road, heavy man, striding out.

'Evening Pete.'

Oh. Who is it? Can't see his face with the light behind him. Voice sounds like George. What's he doing here? Hope it is George.

'Evening George.'

Hope it was George.

Quarry Road. Park Hill. Rose Lane. Walker Terrace. Number 30. Round the back through the passage. Flat 2. Fumble for keys. Let myself in. Empty. Same dreariness as when I left this morning. Unlived-in feeling. Cold. Lonely. Boring. Things not washed up. Can't be bothered to do that now; have to wait for the water to warm up. Wouldn't change the feel of the place anyway. Miss Mrs Wooller; digs in her house felt more like home than home used to. Pity the Benefit Office won't pay for digs.

Independence! A dreary flat. Still, I suppose it's less embarrassing to have my friends round here than it used to be at Mrs Wooller's. 'Cup of tea, dear? Do have one of my home-made scones.' Couldn't hold a private conversation unless she was out, which wasn't often.

Damn! Left my book at the Britannia. Hope Cathie keeps it for me. Cathie. See her tomorrow. Cathie Jordan.

Probably nothing to it. Anyway, what about June? Is it all over with her? Do I want it to be all over? Is there any chance of being just friends? It's going to be awkward with Jill and Mike otherwise. Does June want it all over? Or doesn't she know, like me? Anyway, maybe I do know: I do want it all over. I just want to be friends. I think.

What to do tomorrow? Wash up. Clean up. Wish I could afford some paint to brighten the place up! And a few big soft cushions, and a carpet. Wish I could even afford to keep the place warm! Go to the library. Join if they'll let me, and borrow some books. Britannia in the evening.

Cathie Jordan. What is she thinking? Has her dad come and walked her home yet? What is the time, anyway? Who cares? To bed.

Chapter 2

The following day I didn't wash up or clean up. I got up, and it was still raining; the flat was as dreary as ever, and I just had to get out quickly. Just grabbed a slice of bread and ate it dry as I walked down the steps into the yard. It must have been quite early; I could hear the rattle of milk bottles as I came out of the passage onto the street. Mr Wright with his old pick-up and two lads.

'Morning Pete.'

'Morning Jim.'

'Called me George last night, you know. Reckon you were miles away!'

'Sorry Jim. I don't know why, I thought it was George, you know.'

Two lads scurrying back with the empties. Off again with fresh bottles; Mr Wright turning the truck round in the end of the street.

'See you.'

'See you.'

Lads jumping into cab and truck rumbling off.

It was too early to go to the library, so I thought I'd just wander down by the river for a bit, and never mind the mud. I climbed over the low wall at the end of Walker Terrace and down the bank into the old railway cutting. Even dead, the brambles made it quite an exercise; later in the year they'd be impenetrable. But the path at the bottom along the ballast was easier than the one at the top between the brambles and the wall.

I ambled along the bottom of the cutting without really thinking about anything and without meeting a soul, just feeling very empty. And beginning to get wet and a bit cold; the drizzle seemed able to get right through my cagoule. *Condensation?* But I wasn't in a mood to care very much.

I crossed the new access track the quarry had made for itself across the line, without really noticing that someone had cut the barbed wire, or even thinking about the fact that I was trespassing. There didn't seem to be any dangerous machinery using the track at the time; that was all I cared about. Then the line came out onto an embankment, and I could see down into the quarry. I could feel the wind and I noticed that the quarry seemed to be undercutting part of the embankment further round the curve. I wondered if they had the right; but I didn't actually know whether perhaps they had bought this whole length of the line. It seemed safe enough when I got to that stretch of the embankment, but there was still a fence at the foot, and the quarry was being worked exactly to the line of the fence.

I thought, *you can't talk to June about things like that, she's not interested. Nor Jill. And Mike'll only talk when they aren't with us. I wonder if Cathie thinks about things like that? What, if anything, is happening with Cathie?*

I scrambled down the side of the embankment to cross Falls Lane where they'd demolished the bridge. *What's that noise? Ah. It's a big diesel engine being started up, probably down in the quarry.* Up onto the embankment the other side. The rain was beginning to ease off, and the sky had broken into separate tatters of cloud chasing each other across a pale grey background. In the east, over the town, there was even a shaft of sunlight bright against a bank of dark cloud on the horizon. From over there there'd be a fine rainbow over the town; I could see curtains of rain right in the light.

I'd stopped to watch the display, but then the rain hit me with a sudden squall, and I looked down the sides of the embankment for shelter, knowing already there was none. But the rain went as suddenly as it came, and then, a few moments later, I was in sunshine. Wet and happy.

Jesus, how quickly a mood can change, I thought, *an impressive display of weather, and a bit of sunshine. Bingo!*

But that made me think about moods, and why I'd been depressed, and then I got depressed again. I remembered I'd planned to clean up the flat, and wash up, and then go to the library, and then go to the Britannia. I decided I still could – only maybe miss out the cleaning and washing up until tomorrow. I walked on along the embankment in the wind and the fresh feeling after the rain. I thought, *no, better do it today; it'll only help to make you depressed again tomorrow, Pete, if it's still there.* I walked back to the gap where Falls Lane bridge wasn't. But I just couldn't be bothered to scramble down and up again; so I went to the broken edge and just stood there. *I'll have nothing else to do tomorrow, except that I'll need to go to the launderette by then; it won't fill the day, but it'll help.* Back along the embankment. Little clouds scudding northwards across a blue sky: *it's going to be a nice day.* Rabbit! Stopped again, ears up. And off again, and out of sight into the hedgerow. I wondered what was going through its mind.

I clambered through the barbed wire onto the viaduct, walked to the middle, lay down on the huge stone blocks, and wriggled under the railings until my head was over the edge. How far down to the river? I didn't know. The shadow of the viaduct fell across the falls but the locks on the canal lay in the light coming through one of the arches. Two years earlier those locks had been useless; now they were all clean concrete and new steel. I'd laboured on that job.

A small cabin cruiser putt-putted into sight from behind the paper mill. Lucky bastards! I wished I could afford to potter along the canal in something like that. I'd hoped at one time to get work on a freight barge when the canal was reopened, but I'd yet to see a single freight barge. I reckoned that the whole project was make-work and a leisure facility for the idle rich. But the depth was suitable for big stuff; pleasure boats rarely draw more than a couple of feet. Surely no-one would go to such lengths to con the public? Only a very few would realize the implications if they'd only made it three feet deep; and no-one else would listen to those few. Except those who would listen equally to the flat earth society.

I wished Cathie was there with me. *My God, I've only talked to her for a few minutes! I mustn't build this up into something it might not be!* I tried to wish June was there with me; but I didn't want her there. But it was a lovely feeling being there high up above the valley, with the sun and the shadows and everything little and sharply clear and fresh and wet far below. A lovely feeling that ached to be shared.

I didn't hear the crunching of the ballast until they were very close. 'Beautiful morning, isn't it, young man?' An elderly couple with two dogs. Didn't look the sort to be clambering through barbed wire.

'Yes. It's lovely, isn't it?' *What an inspiring conversation. Still, it signifies non-aggression.* The cold was beginning to seep through my clothes from the stone, so I wriggled back and got up. The wind on wet clothes made me shiver. I ran to the south end of the viaduct and scrambled down into the shelter on the sunny side of the embankment.

Out of the wind I felt much more comfortable, but I jogged to the edge of the valley to try to warm up. There was a broken down wall at the top of the woods and then the ground dropped away steeply among the trees. I had to pick my way carefully; in places it was quite precipitous. After a few yards I reached the first arch of the viaduct and crossed the recognized footpath that went under it.

At the bottom I climbed over the gate and onto the tow path. It was very quiet; I could hear a few birds chattering somewhere and from behind the paper mill I could hear the roar of the falls sounding just like wind in leaves. I'd not been round here for several months – not since autumn – and then the paper mill had still been working. One of the smallest and oldest in the country. And now it was starting to show signs of decay. One winter; the gutters clogged up with leaves that hadn't been cleared out in autumn, water running down the walls; doors hanging open and windows broken already. Depressing.

I had reached the first of the locks. The sun had moved round and now this side of the canal was in shadow. I walked out onto the lock gates – that pleasure boat's crew was conscientious, they'd left both sets shut – and stood in the sun, contemplating the peacefulness. I looked up at the viaduct and tried to imagine myself up there, my head sticking out like a gargoyle above the central pillar. A rather short, timid gargoyle.

Then the paper mill with the sun beginning to catch it beckoned me and I set off again. I leapt over the spillway – which was running, so much for conscientious navigators – and that set me into a run as far as the mill. I poked my head round the corner of the half-open door. There was an abominable stench. As my eyes grew accustomed to the darkness I saw two old men lying in the passageway, fast asleep. Partly not wanting to wake them up, and partly because of the smell, I decided not to go in. I walked all round the mill, edging carefully past where the building came practically to the side of the canal and the hoist jutted out like a gibbet above. Then there was a cobbled yard between the end of the mill and the foot of the viaduct, slippery in the wet. At the side of the mill a flight of stone steps with a wide stone parapet led up the outside to another door, with 'Office' in flaking paint on a piece of delaminating plywood. I climbed up, but the door had a large padlock on it. Leaning over the parapet at the top of the stairs, I could see where there had obviously been a big waterwheel at one time. From up there I could see the top of the falls around the cut-off end of a narrow embankment; and then I realized for the first time that that narrow embankment had formerly carried the feedwaters for the mill.

Back down the stairs. I finished the circuit of the mill. Then over the lane and down to the side of the river. I found a suitable rock, dry in the wind and the sun, and sat down. The sun was on the falls, and on me, and the little bridge just above the falls was dark against the cataract in the shadow of the arch of the viaduct. I felt at peace. I was warm, and beginning to dry out. Sleepy.

And still this ache to share these idyllic surroundings.

I must have dozed off for a while because the next thing I knew the shadow of a pier had come across me and I was getting cold. Now the falls were in shade and the little bridge was capped in light. I mounted the rocks on the left of the falls and slipped through the stile into the lane. Standing on top of the bridge I was back in sunshine. I stared down into the water below the bridge hoping for a sight of some fish, but saw none.

It amazed me how quickly the edge of the viaduct's shadow moved down the stonework. And suddenly the surface of the water was sparkling with light and the bottom had disappeared.

A bicycle appeared round the corner at the top of the hill, and swept down the slope. 'Morning.' 'Morning.' A rustle of displaced air and tyres on tarmac as he coasted over the hump.

He sped on down, past the mill and under the viaduct out of sight. *Nice bike.*

I debated whether to amble into town yet, and go to the library; but if I went now, I'd have to stay there most of the day, or be stuck in town with nothing to do. But I was beginning to get hungry, so I thought perhaps I'd go into town straight away, maybe buy some cheese and a packet of pressed dates, and come back here for a while; or go to the library and come back here for a bit in the afternoon. But it probably wouldn't be so nice later on, or the weather might break. But I was hungry so I set off into town and left the rest of the day to worry about itself.

I walked into town along Long Lane, because by the time I got to the end of Falls Lane, the hole in my guts was too insistent to allow me to follow the river. There was an articulated truck between the two bridges, almost blocking the lane. It had a flat tyre and there was no-one to be seen. As I climbed out of the valley, a yellow pick-up sped dangerously down the hill. The wheel in the back seemed incongruously huge.

Just past the brow of the hill I turned right down Westgate and went into Collingwood's. They weren't very busy yet and I was out through the checkout with my cheese and dates and milk in no time. I went to the bottom of Westgate, crossed Quebec street and went through the little passage through the old derelict warehouses. I sat on the huge stone sill and dangled my legs over the water. I ate my meal and basked in the sun there for a while. I could hear the buzz of town getting under way, and see the first few shoppers on Wharfe Street across the canal. But my little dead end passage was like another world. I felt as though no-one could see me, or as though if they did, they thought I was part of a fairy-tale; that there was no connection between my world and theirs. I don't think anyone but me ever used the passageway; I suspected very few other people even knew it was there. But it couldn't have been nearer the middle of Burnfield.

Tony and Steve walked down Wharfe Street. They didn't look at the backs of the warehouses, even with the sunshine on them; whoever does? So they didn't see me. I resisted the temptation to shout to them. I did that once to Mike from just there, and he looked all over for me. I couldn't stop laughing. But I didn't particularly want to talk to Tony or Steve. I wasn't in the mood for casual chat.

Somewhere I could hear a telephone ringing. A little bird darted from the sill of a door on my left to the sill of a window on my right; it too knew this side of the canal was isolated from the bustle of the town.

After a while I decided I'd go and look in the library; maybe borrow a book and go back to the falls to read. Or maybe go somewhere else out of town so as not to spoil the memory of the morning. I got up and walked back out onto Quebec Street, turned right down to Bridge Street. The Britannia beckoned to me with its promise of a cup of tea; but I'd decided not to go there until the evening. Couldn't afford to spend all my time there. My mind went back to the previous evening; Tom Green the newsvendor; wandering the streets; 'Tina Loves Terry'; and Cathie. *Cathie Jordan. Hope we get the place to ourselves again tonight. Hope I'm not making something out of nothing.*

At the library they wouldn't let me join; they said I needed some sort of identification. No, a letter addressed to me wouldn't do. No driving licence? No banker's card? No, it's no use going home and getting your Birth Certificate, it doesn't have your signature or your photograph on it, you could use anyone's.

I didn't feel like offering them my benefit card. I had the feeling there'd be some reason why that wouldn't do either, and anyway the fact that I was a claimant seemed to be none of their business. I'm sure they knew, anyway: who else of my generation would be in the library at ten thirty on a Tuesday morning?

I went in to have a look anyway, and Chris was there. I told her the ridiculous tale, and she offered to borrow a book for me if I promised to return it in time. 'You don't have to show your ticket to return books. Anyone can return them for you. They just check the date stamp in the books.' I was very grateful, and touched by her trust: if I kept the book, they'd charge her for it. But what I really wanted was to be able to borrow books in the future. When I'd found a book I wanted, and wanted to go, she'd gone. It hadn't been all that long; I wondered if she'd had second thoughts.

So I left the library bookless. I didn't want to go to the Britannia and ask for my book; I needed that as an intro for the evening. And I didn't think I could afford to buy books, and I hadn't the guts to shoplift them. So I wandered out of town, south along Bridge Street and then Wood Lane, disconsolate and wondering what to do with myself for the rest of the day.

In the usual manner, the day got on very well without any grand decisions about what I should do with myself. I just wandered around, first down by the aqueduct, and then around the steep little back streets in Raikeley. I hadn't really explored Raikeley before; I discovered the library there for the first time. I'd never thought of anywhere so small having a library. It was just a converted house in one of the two main streets; and it was closed.

'Opening hours: Monday, Wednesday and Friday, ten till three; Tuesday and Thursday, six till eight in the evening; Saturday, ten till twelve thirty.'

And just now it was Tuesday afternoon. I wondered what sort of books it had, and how many. And whether I would have been able to join easily if it had been open.

I did manage to find one of the two fish and chip shops open. There was a queue, and an old man arguing with the proprietor about his change. It was getting to be a hot day for early spring, but I didn't think it was hot enough for frayed tempers; and I couldn't tell who was in the right. Nor could I tell who won in the end. I got my chips eventually, and ate them sitting on the wall of the little cemetery on the top of the hill overlooking the village.

On the top of the hill it was quite chilly in the wind after being in the village; but the view was tremendous. There still wasn't a cloud in the sky. I stuffed my chip paper into a crack between the stones and slipped down into the shelter of the wall. The sun was nearly down to the western horizon, the moorland just south of the viaduct and the mill where I'd been in the morning.

Thinking of that reminded me of the mood I'd been in in the morning: the aches to share, the depression. None of that now: I was quite at peace in the solitude and the sun. Until that minute, not thinking about my state of mind. I knew from experience that as long as I remained unattached, I'd spend a lot of my time in moods like that, but for the moment, I was at peace. I suspected that if I managed to remain unattached, the frequency and severity of such moods would gradually diminish. But then I thought of the emptiness of the coming evening, and imagined the ache to share whatever possibilities the morning might present; and I remembered Cathie at the Britannia, and hoped she'd be there this evening.

It was really too early to go to the Britannia: I couldn't sit there for three or four hours, and anyway, I'd just had those chips. And there'd be plenty of light for an hour or so. But the cold was beginning to get through to me from the ground, and the world, lovely as it was, would be cold anywhere out of doors; and apart from wondering what to do with myself again, I seemed to be in a good mood. So I decided to go home for a couple of hours and do a bit of cleaning up. I thought I'd survive it, if I did it knowing what I was going to do for the remainder of the evening.

It wasn't easy to decide which way to get to Quarryside from Raikeley; there wasn't a direct route. I could either go back along Wood Lane into town, or along the tow path to the end of Falls Lane and across the fields; either way was a bit of a dog's leg. And I didn't particularly fancy fighting my way across the fields, with all the wet weather we'd had recently, even after the day's sun. And now I'd mapped out my evening, it was suddenly seeming rather short, what with the walk home and all. But I didn't fancy the dreary, familiar trek between town and Quarryside, not three times in one evening. So I set off down to the canal.

The sun went down behind the shoulder of the hill as I reached the tow path. There were a couple of kids playing ducks and drakes with some thick broken glass; doing surprisingly well considering the awkwardness of the angle into the water.

Despite the short supply of missiles, they cheerfully let me have a try; I couldn't make it skim at all, not even one bounce.

At Long Lane I decided to stay on the tow path and walk back along the old railway from the paper mill; the idea of the fields was becoming even less attractive with the diminishing light, and I could always cut my cleaning short by the odd half-hour. I realized that by now the library in Raikeley would be open, and that I could have spent the first part of the evening there, and then gone from there to the Britannia; but I'd keep on the way I was going now. I wondered if the kids were still there by the canal in the village, and I imagined them yelling, 'Hey, mister, you forgotten something?'

Paper mill. Twice in one day. But I didn't go back along the old railway line, I took the longer, more staid route along Falls Lane. As I was climbing Park Hill a girl I didn't know came out of Rose Lane and passed me, walking fast without looking up; I had the strong feeling she was scared of me. There were lights on in the houses, but the street lights still weren't on as I went into the passage down the side of my flat.

I'd judged my mood just about right: knowing that I was going out, doing the washing up was just a job, and I knew that with it done the flat wouldn't feel so bad when I got back later. I even cleaned down the work surface in the kitchen, and emptied the rubbish from the kitchen and the living room. But I didn't sweep up; I told myself that what was left of the evening wasn't too long to sit in a café. But I spruced myself up before I went out more than I'd done in months.

There were a few people about as I walked into town, but nobody that I had more than a passing acquaintance with. I was beginning to feel a fool, going to a rendezvous with my own imagination. I imagined Cathie cutting me off short, curtly returning my book, or even denying its existence; or giving me enough rope to hang myself, and then laughing at me. I began to think of going into Andy's and hoping that Tina might chat me up; and realizing that that was just as silly. If I went into Andy's, I'd just sit in a corner and watch the world, hoping the world wouldn't notice my immotivation.

Nothing ventured, nothing gained, I said to myself, or is it 'faint heart never won fair lady?' To the Britannia! An old man was selling newspapers on the corner of Northgate – it wasn't Tom Green – and I bought one: I needed something to occupy myself if I had to sit around for a while on my own. Over the zebra, into the café, straight up to the counter – straight up to Cathie, Cathie Jordan.

'Tea love please.'

'Hello Pete. You left your book here yesterday, you know. I hope you don't mind, I've been reading it. Here it is. Tea you said?'

'Ta. Yes. Ta.' Feeling tongue tied and going red. Spilling the tea in the saucer. Trying to carry a cup of tea, a book and a newspaper. Flustered.

Several customers. Same kid playing space invaders. Cathie Jordan, looking at me, I'm sure. Me, desperately trying not to look at her, trying to put my tea down, put my book down, put my newspaper down, drink my tea, not too fast, read my book, or perhaps read my paper.

God, am I glad June isn't here now – or Jill for that matter. Imagine if they walked in just by chance at the moment! How would I react? How am I reacting just thinking about it?

I tried to find my place in my book – and discovered that there were two bookmarks! One of them was between the pages I'd read so many times; the other was a few pages before it. In failing biro was written on the unfamiliar bookmark,

'Can I borrow it when you've finished it, please, Pete? Don't lose my place.'

I could've kissed that bookmark. But I couldn't look at Cathie. I couldn't even look at the other customers; I dreaded to think what they thought of me. I was sure my face was as red as a beetroot.

Probably they didn't even notice me. And I'm sure that if they did, they didn't understand what was going on, much less care. But I couldn't persuade myself of that at the time. So I read the next two pages about five times in the next half-hour.

Customers came and went. I heard Cathie's voice making small talk with a dozen strangers and a few regulars. No-one knew; gradually I calmed down and began to look around. The space-invader kid had gone; the juke-box was silent. There were maybe a dozen people in the café, nearly all just drinking, but an elderly couple were eating beans on toast. They were talking softly and fast between mouthfuls, and were obviously having a very earnest discussion. There was a group of four, a middle-aged couple and a young couple. I could see the young couple holding hands under the table, and the young man was quite red. He looked very like the older man, who I guessed was his father. I didn't often analyse things like that, but the co-incidence struck me and I nearly laughed aloud; and I suddenly felt a glow of sympathy for the fellow.

Cathie had her back to the café and I couldn't make out what she was doing. She appeared to be concentrating on something on a work surface, but her hands weren't moving and she seemed very still altogether. I was just realizing that maybe she was deep in thought; and that maybe I was staring at her; and that maybe she'd look up in a minute and catch me staring at her, and that therefore perhaps I'd better look away; when another customer came in and we both looked towards the door. There was nothing about the new arrival to hold my attention and I glanced back at Cathie; Cathie glanced at me at the same moment and our eyes met briefly before she began to deal with her customer. She smiled at me, and I tried to smile back; I was so self-conscious I felt I was grimacing and turning red again.

Then Cathie was serving and I was wondering how I could make my tea spin out a little longer, how long I could reasonably stay over one cup of tea with the café so unexpectedly full, and how on earth, and whether, I could face another trip to the counter to order something else, another encounter with Cathie, in front of all those people. I wasn't hungry. How can one sit in a café just drinking cup after cup of tea? What do people think?

Do people even notice? Do I notice other people sitting about for ages over cups of tea? Only when I'm killing time myself.

I was calming down again, and deciding it was time for another cup of tea. And a piece of cake. Then try to read my paper: that would need less concentration than the book, because there'd be less continuity. I got up and went to the counter.

'You don't mind waiting a minute while I do this meal, do you, Pete?'

'No, of course not.'

'Just a cup of tea, is it?' Over her shoulder.

'I'll have a bit of Battenburg as well, please.'

'Go and sit down, I'll bring it to you, it's okay.'

For some reason the situation seemed to be back in control again; I sat down and read my paper. Cathie prepared and delivered the meal, and then prepared two cups of tea and my bit of cake; I think she was going to come and sit with me. But she left one of the teas behind and just brought me mine, because yet another customer came in just as they were ready.

'God, it's busy tonight,' she whispered as she put down my things.

I looked for the situations vacant columns in my paper. There were the usual ads for the armed forces. Surprisingly, there were no adverts for jobs abroad on shelters. Noticing that set me to wondering why there should be so many foreigners here doing building work, when we were exporting labour to build shelters elsewhere, and unemployment was so high here anyway. And then I thought that of course unemployment was high elsewhere anyway; but then why did other countries want to import labour to build shelters?

Maybe, I thought, it has something to do with security: there certainly isn't much information about as to where exactly any English shelters are. Maybe the building work being done here by foreigners is really shelters, maybe they simply aren't designed to be big enough for everybody, and only certain categories of people will be able to use them. Hard cheese, everybody else.

There weren't any jobs suitable for me at all; not many altogether. I skipped through the rest of the paper, reading bits here and there, but it wasn't really very interesting. I gave it to the man at the table behind me who'd been reading it over my shoulder. He was a bit embarrassed but grateful, and we had a short discussion, notable only for its triviality, about the dreadful state of the world. After a few minutes he looked at his watch and departed. I thought of myself with Tom Green the previous evening, and suspected that this fellow too was merely escaping, and chuckled inwardly. I felt a comradely benevolence towards him, that he could hardly have suspected. If he had, I realized, he would probably have felt patronized. Also, I'd made the situation embarrassing for him in the first place, which Tom hadn't done to me.

Returning to my book, I actually managed to get into it, and was three parts finished when a touch on my shoulder alerted me. Cathie was saying that she was just closing up, her dad would be here in a minute, and she was sorry it'd been so busy and she'd not had time for a chat.

I was half across the zebra before I was fully back in the real world and realized that I'd rather rushed out, didn't know what impression I'd just given Cathie; and was half-way up Market Street before I'd realized I'd not paid for my tea and Battenburg. I looked back, thinking that here was an excuse for a quick word to clear up my abrupt exit; but the café lights were out and two people I took to be Cathie and Mr Jordan were just disappearing behind Cohen's on the corner of Market Street and Bridge Street. *There's a little clue as to where she lives, I thought, they cross the zebra and then turn down towards the canal.* Then: *some clue! That narrows it down to about a quarter of the town.* I couldn't really imagine what I'd do with the information anyway; I could always find her at the Britannia. But having had the thought, I slipped into the next phone box to look in the directory, hoping they were on the phone. No directory. So I rang directory enquiries, and felt a fool when I was told that there were two columns of Jordans, quite a lot of them in Burnfield. I didn't have the gall to push the matter, saying which quarter of Burnfield, and I felt relieved it was all so anonymous.

Back at home I tried to finish my book before I went to bed, so I could lend it to Cathie the following day; but my thoughts were going round and round and I resolved to finish it in the morning.

Chapter 3

I lay in bed for a while just listening to the wind. Then I got up, got my book, and went back to bed: it was cold in the flat. I finished the book, and then got dressed and began to collect the things together to take to the launderette. I didn't often read in bed in the mornings, and the morning had an unreal air about it as a result; I had the distinct feeling of being an independent observer, watching the world through the unfamiliar eyes of an unfamiliar body which was getting on with its unfamiliar life quite without any contribution from me.

I made myself an egg sandwich, and then set off for the launderette, black plastic bag over my shoulder like the caricature burglar. It was very blowy, and the sky was a racetrack of miscellaneous clouds against a blue background. Quite cold.

At the lauderette the price of the wash had gone up, and the time on the driers seemed to have gone down again; I had to start another tenner. There wasn't an attendant, but fortunately there was a woman with her two small children who had a screw-top jar full of coins and were quite happy to change my tenner for me. The wash had been the same price for a long time, and it surprised me to notice how strange it felt putting the extra coin in. And it took two more coins than usual to get everything dry. *Perhaps I should get a line and some pegs. In this weather things would dry in no time. And I bet it's all bull about people getting their clothes nicked.*

Back to the flat. Still early; so I did my sweeping up. Then, the weather still being dry and looking like staying that way, I decided to go to Raikeley again and see if I could join the library there.

I racked my brains for some means of identification, and finally took my benefit card, my medical card and my birth certificate. Only my benefit card carried my signature, and I hoped I wouldn't need to use it. But I had decided I didn't mind if the staff of Raikeley library knew I was a claimant, Raikeley being little and a long way away, and plenty of people knowing anyway. And I had a feeling they wouldn't be so officious there.

Old railway. Falls Lane. Tow path. Only tiny bits of broken glass left where the kids had been the night before.

They weren't so officious at Raikeley library. It was staffed by one woman of about forty, in carpet slippers and giving the impression that it was pure chance that she wasn't in curlers. She was very friendly and didn't ask for identification at all. There weren't many books in comparison to the number in Burnfield library, but they seemed to be well selected. I found a beautiful old five-volume atlas of the world, and pored over it for an hour or more. The librarian came over and looked at it with me for a while, and observed that it was rather out of date, there was a much newer one at Burnfield, but it was only a single volume, less detailed in some parts, and wasn't this a lovely book?

There was no-one else in the library at all.

The bulk of the atlas was physical maps, only a few smaller scale political maps, and I realized that only the political maps would really go out of date very much. Then I put it away and decided to go out for a while to give my eyes a rest, and get some chips, and then come back for another perusal of the shelves, and to borrow a couple of books.

Both the fish and chip shops were closed. One of them would be opening in about three-quarters of an hour, but there was a corner shop open and I bought myself a steak and kidney pie and an orange instead. I went up to the cemetery again to eat.

This time I went round the other side out of the wind, looking south away from Burnfield. Green fields below me, dotted with scattered old barns and a couple of farmhouses, and then the land rising beyond to the moors, blotches of dark green among browns and rusts and hints of purple, almost black; scattered rocks and a few sheep. A tractor pulling some kind of machinery in a little lane, the sound of its engine reaching me thinly against the wind.

Back down to the library. As I reached it, I realized my hands were sticky from the orange, and I'd have to wash them somewhere; the only place I could think of was the canal. With a wind like this my clothes would dry easily after I'd wiped my hands on them. So I carried on down through the village to the canal and lay down on the concrete and reached down into the water. It was very cold, and I pulled my hands out to rub them together, then a quick splashy rinse and a good shake. Getting up again without soiling my wet hands on the dusty concrete was quite difficult, and then I couldn't brush the dust off my clothes or wipe my hands dry on my dusty clothes. So I stood on a little bridge with my frozen hands sticking out over the parapet drying in the wind. Some ducks swam out from under the bridge and erratically made their way westwards; it occurred to me that they couldn't have been very pleased about all the new concrete canalsides.

After a few minutes my hands were dry and I brushed the dust off my clothes. They didn't come perfectly clean; it still looked as though I'd been rolling in the dirt. Which I had, of course.

In the library I found a complete set of telephone directories for the entire country, and that reminded me of the fiasco with the directory enquiries operator the night before, and I writhed internally with renewed embarrassment. I selected the Burnfield directory and found the page with Jordan on it. There were indeed two – well, one and a half – columns of Jordans, and about ten of them had Burnfield numbers; but only two of them were in the right area of town, and they were a Doctor J. N. Jordan (his, or her, surgery) and a Mrs Elsie Jordan with a posh sounding address; so I concluded that they weren't on the phone.

A little before three o'clock I selected an interesting looking book on geothermal energy and a couple of science fictions and took them to the counter; the librarian gave me a big smile and produced a little plastic card and then checked out the books with a light pen just like buying goods with a credit card in a big store. Then she gave me my card and told me to sign it soon and said she'd see me again soon. I thanked her and left, my books under my arm. Unless someone had been in early, or had nipped in and out quickly at lunchtime, I'd been the only customer all day; and she shut up shop five minutes early as soon as I left.

Strange place to have a computer check-out; I suppose they just automatically install them in all libraries now.

Walking along Wood Lane I had a good look at my new library card; it was the first thing of the kind I'd ever had. I thought about her instruction to sign it 'soon', and realized that it was a protection for me against the loss of the card. It had my name embossed on it; she must have had the embossing equipment on the premises. It seemed rather extravagant. I couldn't imagine anything simple enough to be reasonable in a place like that.

Of course I couldn't read the bar code, and there didn't appear to be any magnetic stripe anywhere; the only things I could read apart from my name were 'Burnfield District Libraries' on the front, and 'Books should be returned at the library from which they are borrowed, or renewed at any library, within three weeks' on the back. As far as I could work out, it was valid for any library in Burnfield. I decided to leave it a few days until the staff at the town library had forgotten about my attempt to join, and then try to use it there. *Maybe I should look at someone else's card first, and see if there's any difference.*

Half-way through the wood I realized that I hadn't brought my book with me to lend to Cathie, and that anyway it was still a bit early to go to the Britannia if I wanted to be there in the evening when I might be Cathie's only customer. So I scrambled down the slope between the trees to the side of the river, and followed the bank as far as the aqueduct. Then up onto the tow path to cross the river, over the fields on South Hill, across Long Lane and into the little snicket that ran up to the bottom of Quarryside. Park Hill. Rose Lane. Walker Terrace.

There was a letter from the Electricity Board threatening to cut off my supply if I didn't pay my bill – which I hadn't had yet – within seven days of two weeks ago; and then I realized that it wasn't addressed to me at all, but to Mike; and that on the outside of the window envelope he'd crossed out his own address and written mine. I wondered if he'd opened it and resealed it, or whether he'd known instantly what it was and never opened it at all. I assumed he'd paid the original bill in the meantime; but it started me wondering what had become of my bill for the quarter?

But I decided there was nothing I could do about it except wait and see; and I sat down to read about geothermal energy. There was a general chapter on 'the energy crisis' which was very pessimistic, but seemed well researched, apparently going back directly to material written by original researchers; not quoting quotes of quotes of quotes. The author was himself working in geothermal research, but the main text was quite readably presented and hung together well even skipping over the maths, much of the worst of which had been relegated to an appendix. There was a lot more use being made of earth heat worldwide than I'd realized, and the potential was apparently enormous.

After a couple of hours I needed a bit of activity, so I walked into town the long way, along the old railway and then down the embankment into Station Road when I reached the high chain-link fence closing off the main line. It was still light, and I decided to go into my canal-side retreat for a while and watch dusk gather in the town, and watch the scurryings of the townspeople at the end of their day.

When it was dark, and the streetlights had been on for a while, and activity in Wharfe Street had diminished to almost nothing, I picked up my books – Geothermal Energy and the one I was lending to Cathie – and walked back out into Quebec Street, down to Bridge Street, and over the zebra into the Britannia. I was beginning to feel very lonely; I wasn't used to spending so much of my time alone. Still, Mike would be back tomorrow.

Cathie wasn't in the Britannia; another girl was serving. I'd seen her before a few times, and the realization struck me that Cathie didn't work there every evening. I wondered where she was, what she was doing, thinking.

'Evening love. Cup of tea please.' I'd intended to have a meal and stay all evening, but now I decided I'd not stay long and I'd eat at home.

'Eighty pee, please.' Shorter than Cathie, a bit plumper, sharper looking.

I went and sat at a table by the window, facing down the hill towards the canal. I had a great aching feeling of aimlessness; but there was no feeling of insecurity or threat and the strength of the feeling was quite pleasurable in a melancholic sort of way. I felt able to sit there staring at the lights and the darkness and the looming buildings for hours. I was warmer in the Britannia than I'd been all day.

A group of kids skylarking ran down the road; a girl seemed to have got a boy's scarf. Then she rolled it into a ball and tossed it to another girl who ran back up the road. I recognized her green and red cardigan before I recognized her face; *Tina?* She was a lot younger than I'd imagined when I'd seen her in Andy's, maybe fourteen or fifteen.

They disappeared back up Bridge Street and the street was quiet again. I absent-mindedly picked up my book and let it fall open at the bookmark. I looked down to start reading, but it was the wrong book, the one I'd finished that morning; and there was Cathie's bookmark, 'Can I borrow it when you've finished it, please, Pete? Don't lose my place.'

I thought back to Sunday and my row with June; and then to seeing her in town on Monday and her pretending not to have seen me. Our few happy months before the strained weeks seemed like a different existence; even Sunday seemed remote and unreal.

And Cathie wasn't in the Britannia that night. Obviously I was going to come again the following night; but that day Mike was coming back. I didn't know what time he'd be arriving, but I did know he signed on at half past two, so I decided to meet him there. I didn't expect to have to make deliberate excuses to get to the Britannia in the evening; but anyway, Friday night would do just as well for catching Cathie again. Wouldn't it?

No it wouldn't. Anyway, there was no guaranteeing my solitude on Friday night, either, so I decided to come into the Britannia in the morning. Of course, it might very well be quite busy then, but every extra opportunity would help. And I could certainly lend her my book if she was there, anyway, and sort of keep the pot boiling.

With my thoughts chasing each other round my head, geo-thermal energy didn't get much of a chance. I spun my tea out for about an hour, then decided to patronize Andy's to the tune of a cup of tea; I could watch a different bit of the world go by for an hour before going home to make myself something to eat.

'See you.' That surprised me – I hadn't expected any acknowledgement from the other waitress.

'See you.' *She's friendlier than she looks.*

Zebra. Market Street. Northgate. Arcade. Andy's, not all steamed up. The noise hit me as I went in and I thought it was going to be too much, but I was in a very placid mood and very quickly got used to it. There were a lot of teenagers in there, but most of them were standing around the machines and there were plenty of seats. I chose one by the window and opened my book. That cup of tea lasted three-quarters of an hour. I hadn't read much, but I'd quite enjoyed listening in to the banter going on between the kids, and I got myself another cup of tea, even though I was beginning to get hungry.

'Do you play pool?' Andy – if he really is Andy – from behind the bar.

'Sometimes – I'm not very good.'

'Doesn't matter. I'm thinking of getting a table, wondered what you thought.'

'Don't know really. I suppose Mike and I might come in every now and then to play. Not very often I don't think though. Be a bit crowded wouldn't it? Be poking people in the face with cues all the time, wouldn't you?'

'Maybe.'

Jukebox competing with monotonous non-tunes from half a dozen video games. My second cup of tea lasted me half an hour and I'd had enough. Hungry.

'See you.' Thought of calling him 'Andy' and seeing what his reaction would be, but thought better of it.

'See you Pete.' Oh God, everybody knows my name. Is it a new phenomenon, or is it just that I've never noticed before?

Same old trek. Still a hole in the road and no streetlight at the top of Market Street, an eerie green glow on the dark stretch, turning suddenly red as the temporary lights changed.

Home. Fried sausage, fried egg, fried bread. Cup of tea and a slice of bread and jam; sitting in front of the gas fire and reading Geothermal Energy. Face scorching and back cold. Nearly nodded off.

Bed. Reading Geothermal Energy by table lamp. Just awake enough to turn the light out – after dozing for a bit.

Chapter 4

Thursday. Signing on day for Mike. Blowing a gale again. Spots of rain flying in the wind.

It had been very wet during the night. I was glad my flat was the ground floor of the house: most of the houses in this area of town had leaky roofs. Old Timothy upstairs was always complaining about it. Mike's flat would be very damp when he got home, especially having been empty for ten days.

As I opened the door into the living room the warmth hit me: I'd left the gas fire on all night. I'd never be able to afford the bill when it came if I did that too often, and I'd get cut off. I turned it off and wondered what I could do in there for an hour or two while the room cooled down, so as not to waste the luxury of a warm room. I got myself some cereal and went back into the living room with it instead of eating it in the kitchen as usual, and then I decided I'd catch up with my mending. I darned a few socks and put new patches on my jeans, and put the buttons back on on a couple of shirts. I looked at the crutch of my old cords, and decided that they were past repair, by me at any rate. Patching material.

Then I read Geothermal Energy for a while and had another cup of tea. By that time it wasn't so warm any more, and I started to think what I was going to do for the day. I remembered my resolution to go into the Britannia in the morning, and then to see Mike at half past two at the Employment Exchange. After that, there was no telling what might happen. If I was to be in the Britannia before it got busy for lunch, it was time I was on my way; but I still had to think of something to do for a couple of hours in the middle of the day. It looked like finding a quiet place to read; I didn't want to remind the staff at the library of my existence just yet.

Half-way down Quarry Road I realized that I'd forgotten to bring the book to lend to Cathie again, and feeling that time was tight anyway, I ran back for it. Then I ran about half the way into town, but stopped running on Fieldhouse Road so I wouldn't be out of breath by the time I got to the Britannia. The two lads I'd seen in the café on Monday night were working on the engine of the digger by the road works on Market Street. One of them looked up at me as I passed and grinned wryly,

'Bloody thing's broken down again! That's twice this week. It's just about ready for the scrap heap.'

I hoped he didn't think I was rude; I didn't stop for a moment as I wished them good luck.

Cathie was serving when I arrived, and there were three people in front of me. By the time I reached the counter there were another two behind me. Cathie was doing a meal and I was served by another girl. I'd seen her here before too, but I'd never paid much attention to café staff until the last few days. She evidently recognized me.

'Hello love. What's yours?'

'Just tea for the moment, love, ta.'

'Eighty pee.' 'Ta.'

'Ta.'

I think Cathie recognized my voice. She looked round and smiled at me, then went back to her work.

There were already quite a lot of people. I had to take one of the island tables, which I didn't like very much. I sat with my back to the door. But I could hardly sit there staring at Cathie, and with the café as crowded as it was, I didn't think I could sit for ages over a cup of tea, reading a book. So I drank my tea fairly quickly and read a page and a half, and left, hoping to be free later on. I thought maybe I'd drift past in an hour or so and go in again if it wasn't busy.

I wandered down Shipton Street to have a look in the Job Centre – it was just possible there might be some work, even if it was only labouring, or temporary, or both. But there was a look of dereliction about the place, and a smudgy pencilled note on the inside of the glass doors saying, 'This function is now carried out entirely by the Employment Exchange.' *Wonderful*. I couldn't imagine anyone wanting to go there more than the once every four weeks they had to go to sign on. An oppressive sort of place.

At least now there were only two offices they could send you back and forth between if they wanted to harass you. *Every cloud a silver lining.*

Armed Forces Recruitment Office. Plush, inviting. But someone had managed to stick a little poster on the wall above their window, that they hadn't removed yet, 'Join the Armed Forces! Travel to exotic, distant lands! Meet exciting, interesting people! And KILL THEM!' The wording was getting a bit stale with the years, but the poster had obviously not been there long. I wondered who'd put it there, and how long it would survive.

Town Hall. All the windows on the ground floor with bars, and frosted, wired glass; even so, many were cracked. First floor windows, high above the ground, large, clear and double glazed; giving a wonderful view of elaborately moulded ceilings with incongruous fluorescent lighting units. Cleaned stonework beginning to blacken again, with still-clean watercourses here and there making it look like shoddy concrete imitation.

Police station. Quite new – it had been brand new when I first came to Burnfield. Bas-relief cast concrete sculpture to a height of twenty feet, broken only by the glass-fronted foyer; topped with a glass-and-aluminium office block surrounded by a wide terrace.

On the corner of Bridge Street and Shipton Street, the Odeon. Now in four small studios. At least it hadn't been turned into a bingo parlour like so many of them. 'Man in a White Shirt', 'Hot Tip', 'After the Storm', 'Space Vampire'. I wished I could afford to see 'After the Storm': apparently it was quite something. I imagined that 'Space Vampire' would be well worth missing; but I couldn't really imagine what the other two were all about.

Too soon to go back to the Britannia. Over the wall and down onto the tow-path; I couldn't be bothered to cross Bridge Street, walk down the steps and go under the bridge. Past the backs of the Odeon, the Police station, the Town Hall, and International House. Under Shipton Street with the canal, and then up the spiral stairs onto the bridge of stairs over to the railway station. I had suddenly acquired a curiosity about when trains went where, I didn't know why. There was a poster announcing that

Burnfield was about to be electrified, and that the realignment of the track was almost complete and that soon the times to London would be cut by twenty minutes. Shame no-one could afford the tickets.

Unfortunately I couldn't afford the timetable, either. 'And that's subsidized.' No, there weren't any little leaflets of times for individual routes. 'They went out years ago.' Just wallposters, around the station. 'Or you can buy one of those to decorate your flat.' Except that they cost almost as much as the timetable.

I couldn't be bothered to memorize the wallposter; and it was by no means clear where the young couple had been going on Monday night, because they'd obviously been going to change trains somewhere and there wasn't enough information on the poster to deduce anything. Purely a mental exercise, of course, but irritating to be thwarted.

Down Station Road and back into Bridge Street, the other side of the Britannia. Which was the main point of the detour via the station: if the café was busy, I could walk straight past to go to my private alley, and not have to double back. Thinking about my motives like that was illuminating and amusing; I couldn't imagine anyone who might notice me doubling back, who wouldn't be fully aware of my aimless wanderings anyway. Or who might care.

The Britannia was busier than ever. So straight on past and up Quebec Street. Down the little passage. I sat down with my legs dangling over the water and began to read. The sun was on the pages and I had to squint. It was sheltered from the wind there, and the sun was warm on my face and hands. I shut my eyes for a few moments to relieve the glare, and lifting my head up I could see a red glow through my eyelids. Warmth.

I dozed for a few minutes, and then a cloud passed over the sun and there was a sudden chill. It was much easier to read; Geothermal Energy had a chance again. For a few minutes, until the cloud had passed.

A couple of hours passed in alternate warm dozing and chilly reading; then it was a quarter past two and time to head for the Employment Exchange. I gathered my books up under my arm and set off. Quebec Street. Water Lane. Passing the end of Beckside I saw Mike coming down with his rucksack on his back, and shouted and then waited for him.

'Hiya Pete!'

'Hiya Mike! You seen Jill yet?'

'Nope. Only just made it. I expect she'll come to the dole to meet me. Haven't you seen her?'

'You don't mean to tell me you hitched up from Somerset this morning?'

'No! I stayed at Chrissy's in Derby last night. Mind, I got down there in four and a half hours – but you can't rely on things like that. Didn't fancy being late and going through the Spanish Inquisition again. Damn nearly was, just coming from Derby.'

'Don't fancy coming into the office just now – I'll wait for you out here.'

'Okay – see you in a few minutes.'

I settled down to read again sitting on one of the benches at the top of the grass slope down to the canal.

'Hello Pete.' It was Jill. 'Waiting for Mike?'

'Yup. He went in a minute ago.'

'You don't mind if I wait with you, do you?'

'Bloody hell! When did you ever need to ask that? Who do you think I am? Lord Muck or...'

'All right! Keep your hair on. I wish I knew what was going on between you and June...'

'Sorry. I didn't mean to bite your head off. You just seemed ever so formal all of a sudden, as if you weren't one of my best friends. I wish I knew what was going on between me and June myself. She ignored me completely in the street the other day, you know.'

'You know, she says she wishes she knew what was going on too. She seems to think you want to finish with her.'

'And I get the impression she wants to finish with me. I'm not sure if I want to finish with her or not.'

'You know, that's exactly what she says. She's not sure if she wants to finish with you or not. It doesn't seem altogether passionate! But I wish you'd at least be friends.'

'Mmmm.'

Two of us, staring into the canal. Silence.

Jill reached out her hand and squeezed mine for a moment. I looked up and we exchanged smiles. Then both staring into the canal and silence again.

'Hello you two! Lost your balloon? Cheer up! What are we going to do this afternoon?' Mike came up behind the bench, put his arms round both of us and then turned to Jill and gave her a long kiss. I'd never felt awkward with them kissing before, but I did then.

'Well, what are we going to do this afternoon?' Mike.

'I don't know. I've arranged to meet June at the swimming pool at four,' Jill said, 'Why don't you two come, too? Oh, come on Pete.'

'Hey! Is there something I should know? Where is June, anyhow?'

Silence.

'You two haven't been and gone and had a row, have you?'

I didn't know what to say. Jill looked at me for a moment, then said: 'It's worse than that. Neither of them knows if they want to split up or not. And they've not talked to each other since Sunday.'

'Well you'd damn well better come to the pool with us then, Pete. Can't have cold wars. Burnfield isn't big enough.'

'Okay, okay.' I wasn't sure how I felt about it. 'Thanks for the 'lecky bill, by the way.'

At the swimming pool June seemed surprised to see me. She was friendly enough, but distant. She laughed and joked with both Jill and Mike, and I could tell that was only by an effort that Jill and Mike kept me involved at all. I felt a bit like a spare part and excused myself after only twenty minutes or so. Mike squeezed my arm under the water and said quietly, 'Okay, mate. I'll see you soon.'

I dried off and walked home, feeling wretched. I put on the gas fire and sat staring into it for ages. I thought about the many times we'd been a happy foursome. Then I thought about Cathie, but she seemed like a dream. I tried to read G.E. but it didn't seem to make any sense at all. Then I thought about

Tuesday morning, shafts of sunlight, and rain, and sun and shadow at the old mill, and aches to share; but the painful pleasure of longing had gone sour and was humiliatingly ridiculous.

But then, if longing is so ridiculous, so is feeling humiliated, and so is being depressed. But that thought didn't help much.

It was dark before I realized that the nagging pain in my stomach was hunger not emotion, or not only emotion, and that I hadn't eaten anything except a bowl of cereal all day. I tossed up in my mind between cooking myself something and walking into town and visiting the Britannia; but hunger, thrift and shyness won. Another fry-up. Then I washed up, mainly to occupy myself, not because there was any great accumulation.

By the time I'd finished I was feeling more or less on an even keel, a bit empty and melancholic, but okay; and I turned the fire off and went to bed with one of the S.F.s. It was a bit early still to be going to bed, but it was warm, and cheaper than the gas fire. I read the book from cover to cover, and it was two in the morning before I went to sleep.

Chapter 5

On Friday morning I realized that I'd made no plans at all, no arrangements with anybody, that the rest of my life was mine to do with entirely as I pleased; and it was like floating in space, forlorn. My only attachment to the world was Cathie's note to lend her my book, but after the fiasco the morning before I didn't want to get there before about half past seven in the evening. I thought that in the present circustances I'd better let Mike seek me out – I knew he would, sooner or later – rather than push myself on him; and I could see the present situation lasting quite a while. So it was obviously time to find myself some new niches.

I thought around my acquaintances, which of them I'd like to go and see. The crowd that shared the house in Anglesey Terrace, over in Shipton: Tony, Steve and Angie. I thought they'd get on my nerves. Pleasant enough, but empty-headed, and so serious about everything. Funny, how I lump them together. They must all be different, but they all seem the same to me. I wonder what they think of each other? Maybe each of them secretly thinks the other two are empty-headed and over-serious but plays the game just to keep the peace. I found the idea hilarious, and wanted to share the joke. But it would have to wait until I saw Mike. I didn't know anyone else well enough to be sure how they'd take it, or what they thought of the people in question; and it could scarcely be told without the bona fide characters. *God, if it's true, what a terrible vicious circle to be stuck in.*

Actually, it's not even true. Tony might be a bit of a bore, but he's not empty-headed. Even if he does take himself a bit too seriously.

Chris. I didn't really know her much; she hadn't been around very long. Seemed to be an intelligent lass, very self-possessed and independent. I wasn't sure whether maybe she had a job – I couldn't imagine why else she'd come to Burnfield – but if so, it certainly wasn't nine-to-five; I'd seen her at all sorts of odd places and times. Nearly always on her own. I couldn't really imagine getting very friendly with her – I couldn't imagine anyone getting very friendly with her – but I had a feeling she'd be a good person to be on good terms with. And I had an opening gambit: I wanted to look at a library ticket, and I knew she'd got one. I also had the feeling she'd understand my reason for wanting to look.

But I didn't know her exact address, only that she lived somewhere up behind the station; and I couldn't think who would know her address.

Charlie and Linda. Hadn't seen them for ages. Somehow they were a very exclusive couple, seemed to spend all their time together and not have much time for anyone else. Not having bumped into them in town for ages, I wondered if maybe they'd left Burnfield. The idea of going round and seeing if they were still there somehow didn't inspire me.

Terry and Dave. Couples again. A bit less exclusive, more inclined to involve one; but in the last few months I'd spent most of my time with Mike and Jill and June, and when I'd last seen Terry she'd almost snubbed me. I'd thought maybe they thought I'd deserted them, and perhaps I had. For livelier company. Interminable games of Monopoly, Scrabble or cards didn't inspire me much either.

And then all my old mates from Ripley's. Great folks to work with, nice to bump into in a pub or the street every now and then, but somehow not people to go visiting. Such a different perspective on life I'd almost nothing to talk to them about, except old times at work. And most of them seemed to have found jobs again somehow, or joined the Armed Forces, and wouldn't be around during the day on a Friday.

I realized what a poor selection I'd got, or it seemed poor to me at the time. I wondered whether I was being arrogant having such a poor opinion of most of my friends, and then wondered what sort of opinion they had of me. It probably wasn't any better. Bookish and stand-offish.

By the time I'd come to no conclusion at all about who to visit, or even whether to visit anyone, I'd quite automatically had my breakfast, performed my ablutions and dressed. But then my routine expired, and I still had the day to fill.

I wondered about trying to get to know some completely new people, and then wondered how to do that. Somehow that's something that just seems to happen from time to time. One changes one's haunts for some totally different reason, or someone moves into one's haunts from outside. It didn't seem to be possible to change my haunts specifically to look for new people, there had to be some other reason, or I'd notice the feeling of being an outsider, and get put off before I'd become accepted. Or perhaps if one goes somewhere simply to look for people, the obvious loneliness and aimlessness itself makes one unattractive.

I could feel another depression beginning, so I picked up the SF I hadn't read yet, and Geothermal Energy, and set off, just anywhere. At the end of the terrace, I realized I didn't know whether I'd be back at the flat before going to the Britannia in the evening, so I went back for the book for Cathie. *That's the third time in three days. Losing my marbles. Or maybe I was always like this.*

I walked up Rose Lane, over the old cutting, through the stile and up the path to the top of Rose Hill, and sat down on the big old stump in the middle of the little group of trees on the top. The wind was less than it had been in the last few days, but it was still chilly up there. There were a few clouds, but it looked likely to remain dry all day.

I stayed up there for a couple of hours, reading desultorily and gazing out over Burnfield. I could see the little cemetery above Raikeley, but the village itself was hidden behind South Hill, not much lower than where I was. On each side of South Hill the canal curved into view, and then disappeared into the industrial estate just south of Burnfield in one direction, and behind the shoulder of land overlooking the paper mill in the other. I could see the quarry, much nearer, with machinery moving in it, and the old line running in a long curve along the edge of it. I was almost in line with the embankment and the viaduct, and the track bed just seemed to set off into space across the narrow valley, a straight, horizontal line independent of the ground contours. Then, much further away still, the ground rose up behind it, still heading straight away from me in its heather-lined cutting. But it curved out of sight at the last moment, and I couldn't see the tunnel mouth. I wondered whether the tunnel was bricked up, or whether one could walk through it; I'd never been there.

Burnfield itself was mainly roofs. International House and the tower blocks on Pasture Road stood up like obelisks. The new road climbed out of the valley beyond Shipton on its monstrous embankment, hill-sized but bowling-green smooth, and then disappeared into a cutting of similar magnitude and featurelessness beyond the station.

I'd not been up early, but having read till so late the previous evening, I still felt very tired, and in the middle of the afternoon I went back to the flat for a siesta. There wasn't any mail. Timothy was just going out as I arrived. He nodded at me silently, and I wished him a good afternoon, but he didn't reply. No telling where he was going, or what he was going to do. How he filled his time was always a mystery to me.

After dozing on the sofa for a while, I decided that maybe a couple of games of something wouldn't be so bad, that I could do with some company, whoever's it might be, and that anyway maybe Terry and Dave might have some new friends it might be worth meeting. And that it wouldn't be an unreasonable route to their place to go through the maze of old streets behind the station, and maybe bump into Chris.

In the fields above the tunnel mouth, some workmen were installing a barbed-wire entanglement between the old fence and a new one right on the edge of the masonry. I asked one of them what was going on.

'Electrifying the line. They care more about young hoodlums than they do about train drivers. Some ruffian hangs a brick on a wire in front of a train, kills the driver, that's just one of those things. Now he might kill himself, that's something else altogether.'

I nearly began to argue that more innocent trespassers might be put at risk by the wires, and that in the past the amount of money needed to screen every bridge on the railway might have saved more lives spent elsewhere, while the only lives in question were one or two drivers a year, who anyway knew that

risk as one small one among many when they took the job. But I
decided that it was probably an emotional issue among
railwaymen, that he undoubtedly knew more about the statistics
than I did; and while my idea might well be right, I could
scarcely expect to convince the man and there was no point in
having a row. Instead I asked him how often drivers were killed
that way, what the voltage of the lines was, and if it was
switched on all the time or only when a train was due.

'You don't half ask a lot of questions! The voltage is twenty-
five thousand, but I don't know the answer to the others. A
driver was put in hospital at Marsden a couple of weeks ago
though.'

'Where's Marsden?'

'Just west of Huddersfield. Watch out for that roll of wire!'

I didn't bump into Chris, and Terry and Dave were out. I was
beginning to get cold, but it wasn't time to go to the Britannia
yet. I thought that maybe Smith's would be a good place to go
for a while, look at some books, get warm. I didn't have to
worry about the temptation to buy them any more: any I fancied,
I'd ask for at the library. But I didn't want to go to the library for
a day or two yet.

I bought a pen and a notebook in Smith's to write down titles;
I'd sorted out my reading for months. Every time I looked up,
there was a well-dressed man reading somewhere in the same
aisle as me; it eventually registered that he was the store
detective, and that he thought I was intending to steal
something. His professional appearance and his aimless
behaviour didn't match at all. I almost laughed at his
transparency: if it was so obvious to me, anyone to whom it
mattered would have spotted him straight away; but I stopped
myself in time. And then I thought that it would have been fine
to laugh anyway, but I couldn't laugh to order; it would have
sounded false.

Then Smith's shut and I was out on the street again. I
wandered aimlessly for a bit, beginning to feel hungry but not
wanting to go to the Britannia just yet, and wanting to eat there
rather than anywhere else. In the end I compromised and went
into Katie's for a cup of tea and a bit of apple pie, and sat there

for a while reading. I lost track of time rather and it was half past eight before I eventually made it to the Britannia. Cathie was serving, but there were quite a few people in the café.

'Hello love. Just a tea, is it?'

'No, I'll have sausage and beans, love, please. And a bit of bread. And a tea, of course.'

'That's four eighty please. How are you, anyway?'

'Not so bad. I owe you for a tea and a bit of cake the other day, you know.'

'Really? Forget it then. Here's your tea. I'll bring your meal when it's ready.'

'Thanks. I've brought that book.'

'Oh – thanks. I'd forgotten about that.'

Funny, how a casual remark quite obviously without any hidden meaning can sting. But she took the book anyway, and after she'd brought me my meal she sat down behind the counter and was reading it. The café remained quite busy all the remainder of the evening, though, and while I read quite a lot, Cathie can't have read very much, and there certainly wasn't any opportunity for us to chat. But we exchanged smiles and glances from time to time, and I felt a comradely warmth from her; and I didn't have the self-consciousness of the previous occasion. But the place was still quite full at ten o'clock, so I decided not to stay and bump into Mr Jordan.

'See you.'

'See you love.'

Chapter 6

On Saturday it was raining, but nonetheless I wanted to try Terry and Dave again, via the possibility of bumping into Chris; and failing either of these possibilities, I thought it wasn't too soon to try the library again. Maybe just spend some time there, and not try to borrow books on my card until I'd seen someone else's. Then try the Britannia again in the evening.

The route along the cutting and over the tunnel mouth didn't appeal in the wet, so I went the long way, through the middle of town. Coming down Market Street I realized it was still only about ten o'clock; rather early to go visiting. I thought of going into the Britannia, and decided it was becoming too much of a habit, a bit obvious; and decided to go into Andy's instead. Cup of tea. Changed my mind: what's wrong with being a bit obvious? You'll never get anywhere, Pete, if you aren't obvious.

So on down to the Britannia. Cheerful smile and friendly words from Cathie, but she was very busy, and there was no real contact. I didn't have a book, and anyway the place was too busy for me to sit and read; so I didn't stay long. I thought about my plan for the day, and reversed the library and the visiting: that seemed to make a lot more sense.

Passing Smith's I decided to drop in there for half an hour to amuse myself detective baiting. Having scanned every title in the place the previous day, and taken a brief look at all the interesting looking ones, I was a bit at a loss what to look at; until I hit on the idea of reading one properly. After a while the store detective disappeared, and a moment later a middle-aged woman appeared and informed me that they were a bookshop, not a library. I just put the book back and left.

Of the nine titles I'd written down in Smith's, only one was on the shelves at the library, but since I'd no intention of borrowing any yet anyway, I just sat down to read it. Maybe another day I'd ask a librarian about the others.

I read about half the book, and then put it back to look at again another day. Then I went to look for the more up-to-date, single volume atlas I'd been told about. On the first floor, in the

reference section. The reference section turned out to be much
more interesting than the ground floor. I browsed for ages before
I came to the atlases. They were not nearly as nice as the five-
volume one in Raikeley, but it was quite interesting following
the changes in the national boundaries in the Middle East by
comparing the atlases of different ages. Then I found a
Historical Atlas which did all the work for me, and the welter of
detail suddenly made the whole subject boring. I could follow
the changes of boundaries in Europe through the Napoleonic
Wars and two world wars, neatly presented side by side, page by
page; and it just wasn't interesting.

Then out, and into Scully's for a bit of cheese and some
raisins and a packet of four digestives, which I ate standing
under their awning. It was raining harder now, and I didn't
really fancy the walk out to Terry and Dave's; but I'd had
enough of the library, and I couldn't think what else to do for a
few hours.

I was soaked by the time I got there. Terry answered the door,
and I could tell by her face that she was genuinely glad to see
me. She took my coat and hung it up, and told me to make
myself comfortable in the living room while she made a cup of
tea. There was no sign of Dave. There was a wood fire burning
in a homemade hearth where I remembered a gas fire, and the
place had developed a new air of homely scruffiness.

'Sugar?' A horizontal head and two rows of finger ends round
the edge of the door.

'No ta.'

Two cups of tea, and some homemade biscuits. Terry herself
was less groomed than usual. She was wearing jeans that
weren't even crisp, and a sloppy joe that I'd last seen on Dave;
and not a trace of make-up. Only her long, sleek hair was the
same.

'I've not seen you for ages, Pete. What are you doing with
yourself these days?'

'Nothing much really. Reading, trying to keep body and soul
together, knocking about the same old haunts. What's happened
to the gas fire?'

'They cut the gas off. I couldn't afford the last bill. Dave used to have it on all the time. Good job it's an electric cooker, or I'd be really stymied. Chris helped me make the hearth though, and she's a great help with the wood: it's a lot of work fetching it, but she always helps, every week, never fail. At least I don't worry about the bill now, and I keep it warm all the time.'

'I didn't know you knew Chris. Where's Dave, though?' It had gradually been dawning on me that he'd left, but by the way she was talking, she wasn't going to mind my asking.

'I don't know where Dave is. He just didn't come home one night, and then a few days later, when I'd worried myself sick, there was this postcard from him from France, wishing me luck and saying he was sorry he'd not been able to talk about it first. Never apologized about the gas bill, though. I didn't know you knew Chris, either. We are talking about the same Chris, are we? She keeps herself to herself pretty much.'

'Sounds like her. Lives somewhere up behind the station. Only came to Burnfield a few months ago.'

We chatted for hours, and drank innumerable cups of tea, and played a couple of games of chess. I'd never played chess there before; there were always three of us. We were well matched. She didn't know the book as well as I did, but she was a natural player, and less liable to stupid errors than me. She thrashed me once, and nearly held me to a draw on the second game which I opened more cautiously.

She was quite forthcoming about herself, and her relationship with Dave, and her reaction to his departure; but I was very reticent about my relationship with June, and my friendships. But she slowly opened me up, right down to a guilt feeling about deserting old friends for new ones; and then seeking them out again when I needed them later.

She laughed at that.

'Who deserted who? Did we ever come to see you? I've been around a couple of times, just after Dave left, but you were out.'

'I suppose you're right. And I suppose I'm not often at home. Tell you what, the only way you'll ever catch me in is by prior arrangement. I'll cook a meal for both of us for Monday night. Okay?'

'That'd be great. Is it okay if I bring Chris too? We often eat together; it doesn't save any money, 'cause we splash out more on food when it's not just for ourselves, but we eat better and it's more sociable.'

About sixish she told me that she and Chris had arranged to go and see 'After the Storm' that night, and that she was going round to pick Chris up about half past six; and did I want a bite to eat with her before she went?

'No ta, I'll be on my way in a minute.' It was a convenient exit; I'd been wondering what I was going to say when I wanted to go. It sounded too daft for words to say I wanted to go and spend the evening in a café.

My coat had more or less dried out in the warm room, and it wasn't raining so hard as I walked into town. The Britannia wasn't very busy, but there were still two waitresses serving, and neither of them was Cathie. *Perhaps I should have stayed at Terry's for a bite. I'll eat at home.*

'Cup of tea and a scone, love, please.'

I was just wondering how I was going to fill Sunday, and realizing that I hadn't a great deal of reading material, when Mike came in. He got himself a cup of tea and then came and sat with me.

'You eaten yet, mate?'

'No.'

'Then how about coming round to my place in a couple of minutes? I've got enough for two of us. Jill and June have gone to the flicks. Where the hell have you been? I've been looking all over for you.'

For some reaon I didn't feel like telling him about visiting Terry. 'Just knocking about. Been in the library today, and Smith's. I've got a new game: baiting store detectives. I was up on Rose Hill most of yesterday.'

'You're a curmudgeonly old recluse, that's for sure. Don't you ever get lonely?'

'God, yes! But I'm too shy to make the first move. Especially when I'm depressed. I don't want to inflict my depression on anyone else.'

'So you stay depressed, 'cause you're lonely. What's this store detective game? Sounds risky to me.'

'You don't actually do anything. You just hang around the shop, looking furtive. After a bit you find this bloke hanging about near you, browsing, taking his time too much for someone so businesslike.'

'You amaze me, Pete, sometimes, with your innocence. That's not the store detective. That's the manager, trying to make you feel uncomfortable and leave. He knows you're not going to buy anything, or not much anyway, and you're making his shop untidy.'

'Go on! You're having me on.'

'No, straight up. The real store detective is a woman with a shopping bag, a push chair and two kids, works several shops on a timetable with others like her, and only works two days a week. Gets next to nuppence for it. And don't think innocence is any protection for you; it's their word against yours in court.'

Teas finished, we set off for Quarryside. We walked in silence for a while. As we climbed the top end of Fieldhouse Road, Mike asked me if I'd seen 'After the Storm' yet.

'Nope. Don't go to the flicks much. Can't afford it.'

Mike was putting a stiff pace on; I was fairly fit but I was out of breath.

'Course you can. You eat in cafés often enough; it's only half as much again.'

'Got to eat, though.'

'You can always eat at home or round my place. Costs less than half as much.'

'True enough. 'After the Storm' might be worth seeing, at that.'

'Tomorrow's the last night. Shall we go?'

'Why haven't you gone tonight, with the girls?'

'Tell the truth, wanted a chat with you.'

Silence again as far as Mike's flat.

'Wasn't half damp when I got back here on Thursday. Had to have the fire on all night to get it habitable again. Keeping this place dry costs me a fortune in gas.'

I was about to tell him about Terry's wood fire, but didn't want to have to go into any explanations. It left me without anything to say, and I felt slightly awkward.

Mike cooked a simple but filling meal, and we sat together staring into the gas fire for a time in silence while we ate. I reflected that Terry's wood fire would be better for staring into, but didn't say anything. The silence dragged on; I felt I couldn't say anything and I wished Mike would start talking. Maybe he felt the same; but I couldn't see why.

It wasn't until he'd finished eating that he asked me again if I wanted to go to see 'After the Storm' on Sunday night.

'I'm not sure. I'm not sure I can afford it.'

'Of course you can. You haven't got some other plan half cooked up, that you don't want to talk to me about, have you?'

I hadn't, but I didn't know what to say: the innocent and the guilty both plead not guilty. I protested, and mumbled about money.

'If that's really the hassle, I'll lend it to you; you can pay me back very quickly: just don't eat in the Britannia for a few days.'

Now he was coming close to a subject I really didn't want to talk about; and I could feel myself reddening.

'You wouldn't be much of a liar, Pete. I'm not good enough to know what it is, but I've hit a nerve there somewhere, haven't I? You should see your face!'

'I'd rather not. It'd make it worse. It feels bad enough inside.'

No point pretending it hadn't happened.

'Well, just quit worrying, will you. If you can't talk about it to your best friend, who can you talk to?'

After the gentle, non-intrusive way Terry had opened me up without asking any questions at all, perhaps even without intending to do it, Mike had all the subtlety of a police inquiry; he discovered Terry and Chris, but not Cathie. He concluded that I was depressed and lonely, and that what I needed was a holiday, to get out of the vicious circle of loneliness making me depressed, depression making me unattractive, and unattractiveness making me lonely.

As he talked, it all made so much sense that I was completely convinced. The nagging feeling at the back of my mind that I didn't want to neglect the delicate growth of the fragile flower of a possible relationship with Cathie didn't stand a chance against the persuasive power of unanswerable logic.

But affording a holiday was another matter entirely.

'You can borrow my tent and hitch-hike round Wales or something. You won't spend much more than you would here. Take plenty of cash in case of emergencies, though; and if you do spend it, I'll lend you some to tide you over.'

I said I'd think about it, and I let him persuade me to go to see 'After the Storm' with him.

Then Mike said he'd just got his month's money that day, and why didn't we go down to the Black Swan for a couple of pints? And I observed that it was a bit extravagant, but that maybe we didn't do it very often.

We put our names down for a game of pool, and Mike bought our pints. It was winner stays on, and we were beaten one after the other by a cocky little bastard who, it must be grudgingly admitted, was very good at the game.

The Black Swan was more crowded than I'd ever seen it, and the clientèle classier than it used to be. We realized that our local had been discovered, its atmosphere appreciated; and that very atmosphere was now being destroyed. Soon the very fabric would change, with the money that must be coming in. We wondered where we'd go for our spree next month, and laughed at the idea that we constituted the beginning of the rush to spoil the next pub.

But either the jukebox was too loud, or the local taste in music had deteriorated, and we got fed up of getting hoarse trying to talk to each other long before closing time. We finished the evening off with a couple of cups of tea at my flat.

Chapter 7

Sunday: a bath and a long walk, out to the end of the tunnel. The end had been bricked up, but they'd built a heavy steel door in, and it was hanging off its hinges. I went in, but the light didn't penetrate very far. There were regular drips with various intervals, and there was a glorious reverberation when I shouted and clapped my hands.

I thought it would be good to borrow a torch from somewhere and walk right through. I hoped Mike would come with me. I didn't know where it came out, but I decided I didn't want to know: I'd find out when I emerged. I hoped Mike didn't know either.

Then out again, and up the side of the cutting onto the moor. Fifty yards away I couldn't see the cutting any more, and I could have been in the middle of nowhere, if I didn't look at Quarryside nestling under Rose Hill in the distance. Even that disappeared behind a heathery mound when I sat down on a rock in the sun for a while.

Returning in the early afternoon, crossing the viaduct, I saw dozens of people out for their afternoon strolls around the paper mill and the falls. The magic of Tuesday morning was gone. But the early morning sunshine and the fresh wetness came back to my mind, and I vowed to myself never to take anyone there for the first time except in conditions like those.

Probably Cathie's been there hundreds of times.

That evening I was just finishing eating my fry-up when Mike arrived. We walked into town without saying much. There was a very long queue at the Odeon – last night of a very successful film – but we just managed to get in.

The film was very powerful, and covered a lot of ground. But somehow it left me unsatisfied. I said so to Mike as we walked home.

'Me too. It seemed unreal, as though it was fiction about a different world altogether.'

'And I don't think it told me a single thing I didn't know already – that anyone reasonably well informed wouldn't know anyway.'

'I believe you're right there. The problem isn't informing people, I don't think. It's making them believe it. There are those who know, and who are worried, and those who have heard, and who don't believe it. To them, that was just a cracking good tale.'

'In fact, thinking about it, I think that that film does more harm than good: imagine trying to tell someone about Karen Silkwood[1], who's inclined not to believe. They'll just laugh it off as a story, based on that chap that they bumped off in the film.'

'And those mutants were ridiculous.'

'It almost makes you wonder whether they're all humbugs, saying they're opposed to the Government; whether it's really an enormous Aunt Sally.'

We discussed the difficulties of making a film that would change anyone's mind, and the difficulties one would have getting it shown, or raising the money to make it; and by that time we were home.

After Mike had gone, I realized I'd said nothing about the tunnel.

I signed on rather early on Monday morning. I think they were so surprised at the office that they never thought of making me wait. Then I went into town to buy some food for the evening's meal with Chris and Terry, and to restock the fridge a bit.

Back at the flat, I had a grand tidy-and-clean-up. I cleaned the windows for the first time since I'd been there, and moved the fridge and the cooker and cleaned behind them. When I'd prepared the food for cooking, it was still early; but I couldn't really go out because we'd not arranged any particular time, and they might turn up at any moment.

I played patience for a while, but that just made me even more bored. Then I thought of making a reading list from the

---

1   Karen Silkwood was real. Look her up on Wikipedia!

bibliography in Geothermal Energy, and skipping through it to remind myself of the main areas of interest. That occupied half an hour, and felt much more productive.

I made myself a cup of tea, and lay down on the sofa for a while to think out what preparations I'd need to make for my possible hitch-hiking holiday.

My tea was cold. I was sure I'd not put the gas fire on. There was a smell of cooking in the flat, and a sizzling noise. A suppressed giggle.

'Shh! You'll wake the sleeping beauty!'

'Does he take sugar in his tea?'

'I don't think so.'

'No, I don't.'

'Hark! The beauty wakes!'

'I hope you don't mind us doing the cooking.'

'No, I don't mind. I hope you don't mind being invited round for a meal and then cooking it! You should have woken me up.'

'Seemed a shame to. Anyway, we've been enjoying ourselves.'

'How long have I been asleep?'

'How should we know? Ever since you finished doing the spring cleaning. You shouldn't have done that just for us, you know.'

'Hey, Chris, leave him alone! That was below the belt. Your tea was cold already when we arrived, and we've just finished cooking.'

Chris and Terry were in high spirits, and we spent all evening laughing and joking. We made stupid anagrams of all our names, and all our friends' names.

I said I'd been to see 'After the Storm' with Mike, and Terry asked why I'd not gone with her and Chris; and I told them how much trouble Mike had had persuading me I could afford it. They laughed at that; but it was good-natured and I laughed with them. I told them about the possible double-edge to the politics of it.

Chris said, 'Yes. It weakens your case a lot when someone says, "you got that from *After the Storm*", and it's irrelevant to say that you knew already. And it's so easy for them to say that *After the Storm* is a load of rubbish, 'cause so much of it is. But if it is an Aunt Sally, it's overkill anyway. There's no way that our side could persuade enough people to make any difference.'

But she wasn't pessimistic. She thought that there was at least a fair chance that the war wouldn't happen, and that anyway there was no point worrying about something that we'd absolutely no control over. We might as well assume it wasn't going to happen, because if it did, it wouldn't make an iota of difference what preparations we might have made.

Then we made a huge tower of cards; and we set fire to dangling strips of polythene in the back yard, with wonderful noisy burning droplets streaming to the ground.

I'd not been so happy in ages; but I felt very empty and alone when they left. They'd invited me to tea at Terry's for Friday; and I'd said, 'Provisionally, but I might be away for a couple of weeks.'

I went to sleep thinking up anagrams of 'Cathie Jordan' – the only name that I knew that we hadn't played with together.

On Tuesday Mike turned up early in the morning, while I was washing up the things from Monday's meal with Chris and Terry.

'How do you fancy ten days in Finland?'

Mike is about to go into a long leg-pull. Still, he's come round here specially early for something.

'I know what you're thinking. No, seriously, it's straight up. The little travel agent on Northgate's offering a flight to Helsinki and back, and nine nights in a hotel there, bed, breakfast, and evening meal, for a hundred and thirty-five pounds. You can't miss a bargain like that.'

'It's too much of a bargain to be believable. You're having me on.'

'No, I said, it's straight up. I talked to the old gent who runs the place: he says that what with the depression and all, the hotel trade is desperate for business, especially in Finland. And the exchange rate's in our favour at the moment, and the airlines are flying half empty.'

'Okay, I'll buy all that for the time being. But package tours don't sound my scene at all anyway; and cheap package tours are notoriously unreliable. So where's the particular catch in this one? Is the airline going to go broke while I'm there, or is it the hotel? And now we've just about exhausted the possibilities of this particular leg-pull, what have you really come round here for at this time of the morning?'

'Hey! It's a good job I'm not sensitive or anything. I hope you don't go round jumping on all your friends like that.'

'Sorry. I didn't mean it like that.'

'And it isn't a leg-pull, I keep telling you. It's the only reason I've come round at this time of the morning, to be sure of catching you in. I think you ought to go. I'll lend you half the money, and you can pay me back so much a month. And the hotel and the airline both belong to the Finnish government, so they're not about to go broke. I asked him about that.'

Mike was not to be put off. By the time we'd had a cup of tea my Girocheque had arrived – on time for a change – and Mike came with me to cash it. Then he came with me to the travel agents, 'I don't trust you not to change your mind if you go on your own.'

'I can't change my mind – I haven't made it up yet.'

But either I was particularly gullible that morning, or it was all particularly convincing and definitely a bargain not to be missed. There were places left for only one departure date: that Thursday, two days away. Mike paid a cheque for seventy pounds – he said that that way he couldn't back out of his offer while I was away and leave me penniless when I got back – and I paid the balance in cash. Committed. Two days away.

Then Mike went off to meet Jill. Possibly June too, but he didn't mention her. I was left feeling rather high and dry, and I went down to the Britannia for a cup of tea and a scone, to calm down and think about what I needed to do to prepare myself for my trip.

Cathie was serving. There were a couple of people in front of me, and I was miles away by the time it was my turn.

'Hello Pete! What's up?'

'Nothing. Tea, love, please, and a scone.'

Cathie waved her hand in front of my eyes. 'What's the matter? You're miles away!'

'Sorry, Cathie. It's all so sudden, that's all.'

'What's all so sudden?'

'I'm going to Finland on Thursday.'

'Not for too long I hope. Hey, look, I'm too busy for a chat right now. Will you be in later?'

'I might be. No, yes, of course I can be. Yes, I will be.'

That little exchange put my mind in a whirl again. Cathie was obscured behind a crowd of customers at the counter when I finished my tea, and I left without taking my leave.

I spent most of the afternoon dangling my legs over the canal at the end of my little passageway, chasing my thoughts in circles: Cathie, Finland, Money. I did manage to work out that my trip needed minimal preparations, and that I needn't start yet. But that didn't stop me worrying about whatever it was that I wasn't doing, and I had a sort of vague back-of-the-mind what-have-I-forgotten feeling.

Late in the afternoon I began my economy drive by eating at home. *I'll just have a tea (or two) with Cathie this evening.*

I realized I ought to return my books to Raikeley library before I went away. I couldn't remember the exact times it was open; but I remembered the general pattern, and with an effort I worked out a timetable of the previous week's events, and deduced that Tuesday was evening opening. I went there on my way to the Britannia. It was busy when I got there, and I was beginning to wonder whether I ought to get another tea, when the queue expired, and Cathie made two cups of tea and came and sat with me. No-one seemed to take any notice, although there were still three or four tables occupied. Perhaps they assumed I had something to do with the place.

'You haven't gone and got a contract in Finland, have you?'

'No, just a holiday.'

'How on earth can you afford a holiday in Finland?'

'It's an amazingly cheap package tour. Mike's lending me half the money. I'll have to be pretty frugal for a while when I get back to pay him off.'

'Somehow I can't imagine you on a package tour.'

'No, neither can I. Come here, go there, see this, do that. But this one's just the flights, the hotel room, and breakfast and evening meal.'

'How long are you away for?'

'Just ten days.'

'Have you got anything planned for tomorrow? It's my day off.'

'No, not really. Just got to get everything ready.'

'Then meet me here about nine in the morning. Jenny'll give us a cuppa and a bit of cake. We'll go out for the day together. Okay?'

I couldn't believe my ears. I didn't know what to say. I felt myself going red.

'My dad'll be here in a few minutes. I know you'd rather not meet him in the state you're in. See you tomorrow love.'

'Okay. See you love.'

Chapter 8

Wednesday was the most wonderful day of my life.

Cathie was standing at the counter talking to – Jenny? – when I arrived. She introduced us, and we shook hands. It all felt very strained and strange. Then we caught each other's eyes, and realized the absurdity of it, and both burst out laughing.

There was no one else in the café, and Jenny came and chatted with us over our tea and cakes. After a while a couple of customers arrived and Jenny went to serve them.

'Well, shall we be on our way then, Pete?'

'Okay. Where shall we go?'

'Where do you suggest?'

Somehow I'd assumed that Cathie would have had some idea in her mind already. I hadn't thought about it all. It hadn't been wet, and it wasn't so early, but there was a lovely clear sunshine and I doubted that there'd be many people around the paper mill and the falls yet.

'Do you know the old paper mill?'

'Of course! It'll be lovely round there on a morning like this. Come on!'

'See you Jenny!'

'See you. Enjoy yourselves!'

Cathie had never been on the top of the viaduct before, and I felt great introducing her to it: she loved it. We wriggled out to hang over the edge, and dropped pieces of ballast into the canal. They seemed to take ages to fall, and it was so still that we could hear the little distant rip as they entered the water. Then we threw pieces in great exhilarating parabolas towards the falls.

We went back down to the river, and took off our shoes and socks and paddled about in the pool at the foot of the falls, and splashed water at each other.

We lay down in the sun to dry off, and I put my arm around her, and she snuggled up to me. We lay there in silence, our pounding hearts and breath gradually easing after the exertion.

After a while, Cathie surprised me by producing sandwiches from her bag. We chatted as we ate; I was still full of 'After the Storm' and we talked about politics, war and the media. Cathie hadn't seen 'After the Storm', but she'd been with her dad to an old film called 'The War Game', which had apparently been made by the BBC and then banned. It had eventually been shown quite widely, but more or less underground. It seemed to have had a much less sci-fi ambience than 'After the Storm', to have been much more related to the real world.

When I mentioned the tunnel, and getting Mike to go with me, Cathie exclaimed,

'Why do you have to go with Mike? Why don't we two go, now? I'll borrow my dad's big torch.'

I waited outside while Cathie slipped indoors for the torch, and we went and bought a spare battery just in case.

In the tunnel it was very cold, and we wished we'd brought more clothes; but it wasn't unbearable, and we didn't want to chicken out. We got used to it after a while. At first the going was very rough underfoot, where the sleepers had been ripped up; but further in they'd left them to rot where they lay. Gradually the little rectangle of light shrank behind us, and then disappeared behind the curve of the floor as the incline flattened out. Suddenly there was a rough brick wall right in front of us. A little light filtered through here and there, but we couldn't see out. The possibility that there'd be no door at this end had never occurred to me.

'I never thought of that, either,' said Cathie. She put her arm round my neck and pulled my face down to hers and kissed me. That kiss lasted for ages. We held each other tightly, partly for warmth. But standing still like that, the cold began to seep right through us, and after a while we set off back.

'My mum's not expecting me back until she sees me; what are you doing about eating tonight?'

'I've got a load of stuff in the fridge to use up before I go away. Come round to my place and I'll cook for us both. But I've got to get ready to go sometime.'

'I'll cook while you pack. Knowing you, it won't take you ten minutes.'

It didn't take me ten minutes, and we finished the cooking together. Cathie was surprised how tidy my flat was.

'I expected to find the sink full of washing up.'

'It usually is. I had a big spring clean on Monday. It was a terrible tip, and Chris and Terry were coming round to tea. I gave myself more time than I needed, so it got a better clean than it's ever had.'

It was gone midnight when we kissed each other goodnight on Cathie's front doorstep. Afterwards we noticed a small face pressed against an upstairs window. We laughed and waved, and then he was more embarrassed than we were.

'I hope you're up in time to catch your bus!'

'Don't worry – it doesn't go until half past ten.'

Wednesday had been the most wonderful day of my life. I ran all the way home.

Part II

Chapter 1

Mike woke up early on Thursday morning. He looked at his watch on the floor by his bed and decided to get up: if he let himself go back to sleep he might oversleep and miss seeing Pete off.

It was another fine day and he slipped out to the corner shop for a paper and a litre of milk. Then he had some cereal, washed up all the things from last night's meal with the Js, and sat down to read the paper.

There was an article on the military manoeuvres in China, that gave Mike the feeling that it was a press release from the armed forces, subtly written to look like straightforward, unsophisticated journalism. A public relations exercise; calculated opinion moulding; propaganda of a very sophisticated kind. He wondered how much of it was true; how much, if any, downright false; how much distorted, and in what respects. How well was it related to things people might know, to tie it into people's perception of reality?

Or whether, perhaps, it really was straightforward, unsophisticated journalism. But how would they come by some of the information they presented as bald fact? Perhaps from armed forces press releases.

There had been an aircrash in Turkey. There'd been no Britons aboard, and only a few Americans and West Europeans; it only merited a couple of column inches.

There weren't many jobs: the usual armed forces adverts, and the ads for 'construction work' – shelters – abroad had resumed after the mysterious hiatus of the last couple of weeks. A couple of jobs for trainee technicians at the new power station at Speeton; temporary labourers to help erect overhead lines on the railway; and one for a local delivery driver. Boring.

Mike walked into town via Branch Road to avoid bumping into Pete before they got to the bus station; he didn't know why, but he wanted seeing him off to be a surprise. He got there before Pete, but there was already a motley crowd waiting at the 'Special Coaches' stand. He assumed that they were all waiting for the same bus. The bus arrived; it said 'Glasgow Airport for Helsinki' on the front. It was almost half-full already; maybe it had started at Sheffield or somewhere. Still no sign of Pete, but it was five minutes before the bus was due to leave.

Everybody got on, except a girl who seemed vaguely familiar to Mike; then a family with two small children arrived running, with an impossible amount of luggage, and finally Pete appeared round the corner of Carter's with a small kitbag.

The girl ran over to Pete and kissed him, and said something Mike couldn't hear; Mike didn't know what to do with her there. They came straight over to him, and Pete was saying,

'I've been down to the Britannia to say goodbye, Jenny said you'd come here,'

'Hello Mike, this is Cathie; Cathie this is Mike.'

'I know.' She stretched out her arm to Mike, and pulled them all together into a big hug. 'Look after yourself, Pete love. See you soon.'

Mike produced his camera from his haversack, and said, 'Here, take some pictures for me. And here's a spare roll of film. Hey, I think they want you to get on.'

Pete took the camera and the roll of film, gave Cathie one last kiss, and then the bus was roaring up the hill. They were the only two waving it off.

'I've got to get back to the Britannia – I'm not supposed to have left at all. Jenny's on her own and it's awfully busy. If you've got time, come down and have a cuppa and we'll have a chat if I can get a free moment.'

'I can't see anyone minding you deserting your post for a few minutes every now and then if you're going out on the streets pulling customers in!'

Quick shy grin.

When they got to the Britannia there was a tremendous queue. Cathie apologized for having been so long and began serving beside Jenny. Mike joined the tail of the queue. There were more people behind him before he reached the counter, and his tea was finished before Cathie had a chance to come and sit down, bringing another cup of tea for Mike and one for herself.

'He's a dark horse, that Peter. He's never said a word about you.'

'There wasn't really anything to say until yesterday.'

'I feel a bit awkward talking like this behind his back.'

'You don't need to feel bad. He's not like that. It'd never even occur to him not to trust us both, so he wouldn't be worried what we might say to each other.'

'You seem to know him pretty well for one day! I've known him for years, and I think you're right, but I would never have worked it out so clearly for myself.'

'We spent the whole of yesterday together, but I've known him a lot longer than that. He's been a regular here for ages. He's ever so shy, but you can read him like a book.'

Cathie had to go back to her work after a short time, but not until she'd extracted a promise from Mike to come in the following evening, when she wouldn't be so busy. Jenny too smiled at him as he left a few minutes later.

Well, there's a turn up for the book. Pete's got himself a new girlfriend already. Or perhaps more like she's got him, but he seems very happy. She seems a very nice lass. Very conscious and considerate.

Jill and Mike had arranged to meet in the library; whichever of them got there first would be reading 'current periodicals'. Only a few new issues had come in since he'd last been there, and he'd got right down to 'The Engineer' and 'Sweden Now' before Jill arrived. 'Sweden Now' was more interesting than he'd anticipated – he'd never read it before – with some not-quite-orthodox political analyses backed up with some solid information, complete with sources.

Maybe I should check some of them out. Anyone can quote sources if the're confident no-one will follow them up. But I know I'll never bother – it all FEELS right.

'Hello love.'

'Hello.' There was no-one else in the reading room to mind the noise. 'June's gone to help her Auntie Alice decorate her living room now that the workmen have gone; there's only thee and me.'

'It's a lovely day. Let's get some pies and fruit and go and sit in the sun on Rose Hill or somewhere.'

The market was quite busy. They bumped into Tony and Steve, who chatted to them about nothing in particular for ten minutes; and Pete's upstairs neighbour Timothy, who didn't. He nodded in acknowledgement and hurried on his way.

On Rose Hill they were alone again.

'You won't believe this. You'll never guess who else saw Pete off this morning.'

'I can't.'

'No, I know, I really meant you'd never guess. One of the waitresses from the Britannia, Cathie her name is. They spent all yesterday together and seem quite serious about each other.'

'It's a bit quick isn't it? Doesn't sound like Pete.'

'I don't think Pete made any of the moves. I think Cathie's had her eye on him for a while. And she's quite self-assured.'

'You seem to know a lot about her.'

'She took me back to the Britannia after we'd seen Pete off and we had quite a chat. She seems a very nice girl.'

'Hey, what are we going to do about Pete and June? I'm sure there's no way they're going to get back together, but they can't drive a wedge between everyone else. I've scarcely seen Pete since; and you are starting to lead two separate lives.'

'I wish I knew. Perhaps Pete being away for a couple of weeks is a blessing in disguise: maybe I should introduce you and June to Cathie and all be friends when he gets back.'

'That doesn't sound like such a bright idea to me. He'd feel we'd been plotting behind his back. I could see him getting squeezed out again.'

'Maybe, but I don't think so. Cathie said something very true, that wouldn't have occurred to me. She said... I can't remember exactly, but something about how unsuspicious Pete is. He just assumes his friends are his friends. I know, she said she was sure he wouldn't mind me and her chatting about him with him away.'

'I bet Cathie'd be as embarrassed as hell meeting June.'

'I doubt it, but June might be; but I'm sure I can ask Cathie about meeting you. And if Cathie's game, you can ask June.'

'Mmm.' Doubtful sounding.

A jet trail was progressing across the sky, away over to the east; it pointed out the little silent brilliant speck that was the aircraft catching the sun. It put Mike in mind of Pete, and that by now he'd be in a plane for the first time in his life. None of the rest of them ever had been. He'd be over the North Sea by now, or somewhere over Scandinavia.

Mike thought of the aircrash in Turkey, and then tried to forget about it again.

I cross roads every day without thinking about the old lady I saw knocked down.

When it began to get cold in the early evening, they went back to Jill and June's house, and did a bit of tidying up and made themselves a meal. Old George from next door came round to ask for help with the crossword, and they had a very difficult time with it until they realized that he'd got a crucial clue wrong. Then he got them playing cards until June came in about nine o'clock.

'I'd better be going on home, ' he said, and shuffled out.

It wasn't that June was openly hostile or impolite towards him, but he made her uneasy and he knew it. Mike and Jill took him as they found him, and he felt relaxed with them.

They drank tea and chatted until quite late, but somehow the subject of Pete, and Finland, and Cathie, didn't seem to come up at all.

It had clouded over and was beginning to drizzle by the time Mike was walking home. He wondered what Pete's hotel in Helsinki was like. What would Pete do tomorrow – well, today – in a big city, not knowing a word of the language, and with next to no money? Or, for that matter, what had Pete been doing for the past couple of weeks, in Burnfield, with next to no money?

Mike was confident Pete would find things to do. Though he might get lonely, he'd manage all right. Mike hoped he'd done the right thing pressing him into going. The Cathie question complicated the whole issue, but there was no allowing for the completely unforeseen.

Chapter 2

Bye, Cathie. Just the two of them waving us off.

Rounding the corner half-way up the hill, Mike and Cathie out of sight.

Wish she was with me. Couldn't stay pre-occupied for long – the unfamiliar view of the world from high up in a coach was much too interesting. Pity I was last to get on; not a chance of a window seat. Fellow passengers quite interesting, too. Snatches of conversation.

A few vaguely familiar faces, but no-one I knew, not even vaguely. A lot of young families. Not surprising: no concessions for the elderly or the unemployed, but generous ones for children. A foretaste of the Finnish mind?

Sweeping around the curves of an overgrown model racetrack. A complex intersection. Onto the motorway. Steady drone of engine.

Cuttings, featurelessness. Embankments, putting the world below us, far away, toylike.

Cuttings again.

Steady drone of engine.

Roadworks, mile after mile of pink plastic posts. Half a dozen of them skittle-scattered, bright green dye all over the road where one of them had been a burster to mark the culprit's vehicle. Another burst, orange, a mile or two further on.

Steady drone of engine; rising to a roar, climbing a long gradient. Crawling convoy of heavy trucks. Strange to see so many vehicles, particularly so many private cars.

Tremendous view over small towns in valley to the right, hills beyond.

Steady drone of engine.

Reservoir to the left, our road crossing the dam. Cutting. High, slender bridge over.

Steady drone of engine.

Snatches of conversation.

A baby crying.

The old lady beside me – the only old person on the coach – stands up to take her furs (fake?) off.

'Excuse me, young man.'

'No trouble.'

'Thank you.'

Steady drone of engine.

Big, complex intersection. Slip-roads joining and parting, big blue signs.

Hunks of tyre in the road. Truck on the hard shoulder.

Car on the hard shoulder, bonnet open, small group standing disconsolate staring at the traffic. Woman trudging telephonewards.

Steady drone of engine.

Another long hill. Decelerating. Pulling off into service station. Coach park. Blessed silence, disorientating. Strange sensation of everything moving forward past me from behind.

'We're going to be here for thirty minutes. Don't be late back.' Exit driver.

Isn't he going to lock the coach?

Off the coach. Driver is checking something under a side cover. Locks up and follows us all.

When, if ever, are these places busy?

Rows of shabby video games, solitary teenager playing. Two pool tables in a dimly lit alcove. Light and balls two-fifty for thirty minutes. Deposit ten quid.

Tea. Everything else too expensive.

Terrible tea.

'Do you mind if we sit with you?' Young couple, three small children. From my coach party. Plenty of other tables free; just being sociable.

'Of course I don't mind.'

'You're on our coach, aren't you? We'll be in the same hotel in Helsinki I imagine. I'm Harry. This is Irene, and the boys are Ken, Graham and Leon, in order of size. I hope you don't think we're forward.'

Yes, I do. I wouldn't have thought about it if you hadn't said, though. What's wrong with being forward, anyway? Not that I'd have the guts myself. What do I say?

'Not at all. I'm pleased to meet you. My name's Pete. Harry, you said? And Irene. But I didn't catch the boy's names.'

'Ken, Graham and Leon, in order of size. But don't try to remember them. 'Oy! You! Terror!' is a fine mode of address.'

'Are you on your own? We thought you must be with your grandmother at first, but you never said above two words to each other the whole way here, and then when we got off, you obviously had nothing to do with each other.'

They're two of a pair, these two. She's as bad as her husband. Blunt! But what's wrong with being blunt?

For all she knows, she could be being incredibly tactless.

I bet those boys are revolting brats, with parents like these.

'Yes, I'm on my own.'

Don't know what else to say. Don't really feel like saying anything else.

Half an hour's conversation. Nine-tenths The Blunts, one tenth almost monosyllabic responses from me. Most of what they say in one ear and out the other.

A blessed relief to be back on the coach.

'Would you like the window seat, young man?'

'Thanks for the thought, but I'm all right here. I could see you were enjoying the view.'

'But I think I'm going to nod off now, so it's all right.'

'Thanks'

The old lady really does doze off.

Scotland. I've never been in Scotland before.

Another big junction. Suddenly there is a lot less traffic.

Steady drone of engine.

Desolate moorlands. Not a cloud in the sky.

Police car speeds past, blue light flashing. Quickly vanishes in the distance.

River in the bottom of the valley far below us, swinging from side to side of its bed of gravel, between green meadows. Calm and beautiful. Railway, running parallel, a hundred feet or so below us.

Catch a snatch of strident Blunt voice reprimanding a brat.

Climbing again, engine note changes. Railway disappears into cutting, just a slash across the moor.

Coach coming the other way flashes his lights. Just friendly, or communication of some kind?

Notice the weight of the old lady's head resting against my arm. Feeling sleepy myself.

Cathie, I love you. I'll see you in ten days. Maybe one day we'll go to Finland together. I wish you were here now.

Bonk! goes my head against the window. Sound of coach's horn.

Vision of the viaduct in sunshine. Lying on the rocks by the falls, with Cathie in my arm. Splashing each other in the river.

Bonk! goes my head against the window. Changes of engine note as the driver changes gear. Bonk! again.

Blunt voices pointing out aeroplanes to brats. Funny how the voices you recognize stick out from the general chatter.

There is something particularly strident about Blunt voices. Harsh and loud.

        ... Aeroplanes?

Waking up just as the coach draws to a halt outside a swish modern building with rows and rows of glass doors. The old lady is already awake, and has her furs on.

'Had a good sleep, young man? I did.'

'Yes, thanks.' But I've got a headache now.

Off the coach. Driver unloading cases from under side covers. I start for the glass doors, following laden fellow travellers. I see the old lady struggling with an enormous suitcase.

'Here, I'll carry that.'

'Thank you very much. There's not so many chaps like you about any more.'

I wonder if that's true. I wonder if there ever were.

Actually, I think we're as common as muck. But we don't often notice when someone needs help.

All in a queue. Baggage weighing and check-in. My kitbag goes in the cabin as hand luggage. I could've walked straight past. If I'd known.

Security screening. X rays that don't fog your film. I don't believe that. They don't mind checking my camera – Mike's camera – and spare roll of film separately, by hand.

Departure lounge and duty-free shop. It's a different world from Burnfield.

Wander over to the duty-free shop. Apart from fags and booze, prices are much higher than in Burnfield. The cafeteria prices are loony, too. I hope they feed us on the plane. I think they're supposed to.

Three o'clock. No wonder I'm thinking about food.

Departure board. We are due to board at fifteen thirty. Expected to leave on time.

What a boring place. Thank goodness The Blunts are eating.

Sitting on a low seat, staring at another just like it.

'Flight PIA217 now boarding at Gate Number Five.'

We're next on the list.

But we're not the next to go.

Fifteen forty-five. We're off!

Ten minutes sitting in the plane. Noise of engines. Rolling across the airfield. Five minutes not moving. Another short roll. Three minutes stationary.

'Please extinguish your cigarettes, and fasten your seat belts.'

The sensation of taking off was very strange. The whole environment seemed unreal. My ears hurt. Then the plane levelled off a bit – or perhaps just wasn't accelerating so much. After a bit the pain in my ears lessened. I wished I was by a window.

They did serve a meal.

Is delicatessen the same everywhere? Or is this what Finns eat normally?

It didn't really fill the hole in my guts.

The coffee was better than the tea in the motorway service station.

No, I didn't want any alcoholic beverage. Not even if I had to pay for it.

I was bored. I tried to read the magazine from the pocket in the back of the seat in front, but it was boring. I tried to sleep, but the seat wasn't a suitable shape, at any of its angles. Even worse than the seat in the coach.

I thought of the day before, with Cathie. It already seemed far away and long ago.

I wondered where we were.

'Please fasten your seat belts. Extinguish your cigarettes.'

Surely we're not there already.

The plane started shuddering, and we seemed to be descending steeply. An announcement in a foreign language. Presumably Finnish. Then in English:

'Your attention please. There has been a partial failure in the control system, and we will shortly be making an emergency landing. Please keep your seat belts fastened.'

We seemed to be descending at a tremendous angle for ages, shuddering the whole while. It was really rather frightening.

The air crew obviously realized that many of the passengers were terrified. They issued another announcement in Finnish – presumably – and then again in English:

'The situation is not dangerous. We expect to make a perfectly safe landing in a few moments. Please keep your seat belts fastened until the aircraft is completely stationary.'

My ears were hurting dreadfully, and I had a pain in my sinuses.

Suddenly the plane started levelling out.

Announcement in Finnish, then: 'Please put your head between your knees.'

There was a sudden lurch, pressing me down deeply into my seat. A new, rumbling, roaring sound; and then another, harsher roaring as well, and I was pushed forward against my seat belt for what seemed a very long time. Another lurch.

A great feeling of relief as suddenly everything seemed quiet and still. We were still moving, but the violence had gone. I could feel the plane turning. I sat up. Out of the window beyond my neighbour I could see tarmac, then grass, and in the distance, wooded hills. A small cluster of neat, modern concrete buildings swung across my view. Then a group of about six small aircraft sitting on the grass. They were light blue underneath and blotchy green and olive on top. They had no sign of windows at all. They looked solid and strong, with short, thick wings and sweeping, uncompromising lines, with no irregular curves or bumps.

With a slight jolt we came to a halt.

'Please remain in your seats. Do not light cigarettes. You may unfasten your seat belts. Tea and coffee will be served in a few moments.'

A small, military-looking vehicle sped across the tarmac towards us. It disappeared from my field of view.

Nothing happened in the interval of several minutes before the stewardesses appeared with drinks. The level of excited chatter rose.

I was glad of the coffee. I felt very jumpy.

Nothing happened. I wondered what was going on. I looked round at my fellow passengers. Most of them were talking excitedly. Several were trying to attract the attention of the stewardesses. One man was quietly reading.

I decided to follow his example, but the magazine seemed as boring as it had before, and I had nothing else.

After several minutes, another vehicle came across the tarmac towards us, and again disappeared from sight.

'We were unfortunately unable to reach a civilian airfield, and we have landed at a military base in Sweden. Arrangements are being made to bring a relief aeroplane here for you as soon as possible. In the meantime I'm afraid you will have to remain in this aeroplane.'

The two vehicles went back across the tarmac.

A baby cried for a while.

Another vehicle came out to us. This one stopped in my field of view. Two uniformed men got out. A man in airline uniform went out to meet them. They stood talking for a few moments. One of the Swedes went back to the vehicle and drove off. The other two returned towards the plane.

'The relief aeroplane is expected in about two hours. We apologize for this unavoidable inconvenience. We are shortly going to be towed out of the way. Please remain seated until I tell you that all movements are complete. Thank you.'

The cluster of concrete buildings and the military planes reappeared in the distance briefly. A few moments later we were alongside the buildings. It was very hard to orient myself, but I had the impression that we had been positioned in such a way that the buildings were between us and the windowless planes.

'We do not expect to move this aeroplane again until after you have left it. Arrangements are in hand for a further supply of coffee and tea, which will be served on request until the relief aeroplane arrives, and for a supply of sandwiches.'

Thank goodness for that.

The drinks arrived after only ten or fifteen minutes, but the sandwiches seemed to take forever.

A glaring red sun appeared in the window the opposite side of the plane. It seemed to be moving quite fast. Craning my neck I could see it setting, silhouetting a distant line of trees.

The cabin lights had been on all the time, but they suddenly became noticeable. Outside suddenly looked dark and cold. Gradually everything outside disappeared except the lighted windows of the buildings.

Two hours passed, without any sign of a relief plane. Another hour.

'We apologize for the delay in obtaining a relief aeroplane. The commander of the base has kindly made arrangements for a meal for us in the canteen here, and for us to spend the remainder of our wait there.'

The stewardesses ushered us out of one of the emergency doors over the wing. The descent to the ground was an undignified slide down an inflatable ramp.

The canteeen was very impressive. Everything looked solid and well-made, despite a modern appearance. Everything was spotlessly clean. Nothing seemed to be marked or damaged.

The food was excellent, the helpings generous. Although we'd been served cafeteria-style, waitresses hovered about, clearing away dirty things and offering teas and coffees. I felt comfortably full, and warm, and relaxed.

The eldest Blunt boy appeared, bearing a chess set. 'Hello. Dad said he thought you might like a game.'

Why not? Anything to wile away a little time. I hope the relief plane arrives soon.

'Okay. You be white.'

He wasn't bad, for an eight year old. I let him take the silliest moves back, and made my moves quickly, without following them through in my mind, and we had quite a reasonable game. Half-way through the second game Harry came over to watch. I was astonished to learn that he was able to keep his mouth shut.

Perhaps I wasn't being very charitable. What was it Mike called me? A curmudgeonly old recluse? Perhaps I'd better watch myself!

Then Harry wanted to play with me. Ken watched for a bit, and then wandered off, bored. Harry was back to his infuriating self in moments, commenting on every move either of us made, and how-silly-of-me-ing every time I saw something through one move farther than he did.

I wish that plane would hurry up.

'Would you like another cup of coffee, sirs? Or tea?'

Excellent English. Only a trace of a foreign accent.

'Please. Coffee. White. No sugar. Thanks.'

'And you sir?'

'The same. Thanks.'

'Attention please! We regret to announce that the relief aeroplane will not arrive until seven thirty tomorrow morning. We have arranged for you to stay in a hotel near here tonight. Coaches will arrive to take you there in about twenty minutes.'

Do we get an extra day in Helsinki at the end of the holiday, to make up? Some folk probably have to be back at work the day after. Do we get a discount? Or is a night in Sweden reckoned to be as good as a night in Helsinki?

The coaches were very luxurious. Double glazed, air conditioned, beautifully upholstered. We were treated to a video show. In English. I took the headphones off again; I preferred to stare out into the night. The horizon was barely visible as a demarcation between shades of black.

Then we were driving through forest. The headlights of the coaches made eerie shadows dance down dimly lit files of trees alongside. The journey took just over an hour.

That means an hour going back in the morning. Away at six thirty. Up at five thirty? Or is there another airfield nearer the hotel?

It'd be quite nice to do that drive again in daylight.

Everyone's luggage had arrived ahead of us, and was waiting in the hotel foyer. The hotel seemed brand new, and very up-market.

Not the sort of place we'll be in in Helsinki!

The reception desk was unattended. The wall behind it was an enormous computer screen. A border of pulsating lights drew attention to the message at the top of the screen:

BRITISH HELSINKI PARTY:

YOUR ROOM NUMBERS APPEAR BELOW.

WE WILL CALL YOU AT 5:45 am FOR BREAKFAST AT

6:15 am, UNLESS YOU REQUEST OTHERWISE

(SEE TERMINAL BESIDE RECEPTION).

REFRESHMENTS ARE AVAILABLE AT ALL TIMES.

FOLLOW THE YELLOW FLOOR TILES TO THE

DINING ROOM AND BAR.

PLEASE MAKE USE OF THE ELECTRONIC

TROLLEYS

TO CONVEY YOUR LUGGAGE.

I had a good look at an electronic trolley, even though I didn't need one. It had a keyboard and a screen. The screen invited me to load my luggage onto the platform, and punch in my room number, or F for foyer. I wondered what other messages might appear on that screen, in what circumstances. Or whether a printed plate would have done equally well.

The old lady was looking in puzzlement at a trolley.

'I don't think this one's working.'

I looked at the screen. She had typed her room number; it had appeared on the screen instead of the message. There was a flashing yellow cursor blinking cheerfully just after the last digit.

'You probably need to press ENTER. It's waiting for you to finish your room number; the stupid thing doesn't know this hotel doesn't have any four digit room numbers. Here.'

I pressed ENTER and the thing trundled off, negotiating piles of luggage and people's legs with perfect judgement. It waited for a moment to avoid moving into the path of a speeding child.

The old lady watched it in amazement. I realized that she hadn't understood a word I'd said, and hadn't a clue what I'd done. Not that I'd ever seen anything like it, either. But I had had a little experience with keyboards and screens at school.

It'd be so easy for them to include 'Then Press ENTER' in their message. But would it help? I imagined the old lady typing ENTER letter by letter. *Anyone much younger than her knows. Anyway, why shouldn't it accept ENTER in letters instead?*

'If you follow it, it'll take you to your room.'

But I was wrong. The trolleys had their own tiny lift.

The rooms were very easy to find. I took the lift to L floor. *There's no F floor – F for Foyer.*

A plaque opposite the lift informed me, in about ten languages, that room numbers less than one hundred were to the left, greater than one hundred to the right. I wonder how many rooms there are on each floor? I didn't even count the floors. *It's a big hotel.*

But I had to be up early in the morning, and I didn't investigate any further.

After I'd got into bed I realized that the message on the trolley screens had been in English. A printed plate would've been no use at all. *Tomorrow those screens will be offering a choice of languages before telling you what to do.*

I was asleep a few moments later.

Chapter 3

Mike arrived at the Britannia at about half past eight on Friday. Jill had been a bit put out, but had accepted it as he'd said he'd be there; and she didn't want to go with him, however much he protested that it'd be quite okay. June was still helping her Aunt Alice, and didn't know what time she'd be home.

There were only a few people in the café, and Cathie was reading when Mike came in. 'Cup of tea, Cathie love, please.'

'Oh! Hello Mike. I was just thinking about Pete. Tony Ramsden came in a couple of minutes ago asking if I'd seen him.'

'Does Tony come in here too? Jill and I saw him in the market yesterday. It's odd we didn't mention about Pete going away. Did he say what he wanted?'

'No. He didn't seem too bothered that he couldn't get hold of Pete, but he was more animated than usual.'

Two cups of tea and a table near the counter.

'I wonder what on earth Tony wanted with Pete, anyway? They normally take hardly any notice of each other at all.'

'He must really have been looking for him to come in here. I think it's the first time he's been in here since he split up with Jenny. But I can't begin to guess what it's all about.'

They talked about Pete's state of mind, and unemployment, and money. Holidays in Finland, and labouring contracts abroad.

Customers came and went.

Neither of them noticed the passage of time and they were surprised when Mr Jordan arrived.

'I'll see you soon then.'

'Yes. See you Cathie. See you, Mr Jordan.'

'Cheerio – Mike isn't it?'

'Yes, that's me. So long.'

Mike went straight round to Jill's; he'd not intended to stay so late at the Britannia and he suspected that Jill would be in a pretty sour mood. But June was home already, and they were sitting over mugs of tea with Tony.

'What do you make of this, Mike? Go on, tell him, Tony.'

While Mike got himself a tea, Tony explained how he'd been down near the police station at ten o'clock that morning, and had noticed a good dozen police cars – marked and unmarked – parked outside in Shipton Street.

'Odd, I thought; considering they've got an enormous car park at the back – I've never seen them parked in front at all before. So I slipped round the back to see if they'd got the car park all dug up or something. But no, it was just jam packed full. A lot of police cars, but all sorts of other vehicles too. I suppose a lot of them would be their private ones, but the police recovery vehicle and two Black Marias were out there too. They normally stay inside in the garage.'

'You seem to know a lot about the ways of the police! I've never noticed details like that at all.'

'You should watch the police, you know. Propaganda isn't the only weapon the State's got. Anyway, of itself, that didn't amount to much. But it whetted my interest, so I went up on the embank-ment to watch. You know, the garage doors at the back never opened once in the hour and a half I was there, and all the pigs went round and in the front way, none of them went in through the door at the back at all. Now that is something unusual.'

I imagine this is what he wanted to tell Pete. There's probably some very ordinary sort of explanation, and he's just dramatizing. If it was Steve or Angie telling me, I'd be sure that was the case. But it's not like Tony to dramatize; he must think there's something behind it, and he's more likely than anyone else to know enough to have reason.

They all tried to think what it might mean, and Mike discovered how little he knew about police activities compared with any of the others.

Jill suggested that they should all put in a couple of days of intensive 'copper watching,' and maybe a bit of theoretical study. 'This itself might well be nothing at all, but it'd be good practice. Tony's right, we should be more aware of the strong arm of the State, anyway.'

June observed that intensive copper watching might be a dodgy thing to do, they might spot you and wonder what you were up to. 'I'd feel a lot happier just walking up to the reception desk and asking them why they aren't using the garage.'

'But then they'd be sure to notice you after that, and you'd never be any good for watching. If you're careful, they'll never touch you. Just don't get seen too often with binoculars, or the wrong side of security fences. They've probably got us all down on the files as rebels anyway, but marked down as unorganized and ineffectual.'

'What do Angie and Steve think about it?' Mike asked.

'I've not said anything to them. You know them. It'd all be some big conspiracy, and we'd be the little secret band of heroes who'd uncover it all.'

'And then go around behaving furtively and get themselves caught.'

'Caught doing what? I've not heard anyone suggest doing anything illegal.'

'Poking your nose where it's not wanted may not be illegal, but it's a first class way of getting yourself into trouble if you get caught.'

Walking home in the small hours, Mike had an uneasy thought that the four of them were behaving just the way they'd imagined Angie and Steve behaving. He wondered why Tony and June – it had been them particularly, hadn't it? – had their knives in Angie and Steve so much. Then he realized that he could understand Tony, at any rate: they'd drive him barmy in half the time Tony had been living with them. *Mind, Tony'd drive me barmy pretty quick, too.*

Mike's day of intensive copper watching told him very little; maybe they were behaving strangely, or maybe policemen always behaved like that. Certainly, in the hour he sat watching the back of the police station from the other side of the canal, the garage doors never opened; but he couldn't see if any policemen used the back door, because he'd placed himself where he could see only the top of the big concertina door. He was pleased with that touch, because it meant that his poor view of the station would allay any suspicions. Later it occurred to him that he was in full view of the offices on top of the station, and that from there it wouldn't be particularly obvious that he couldn't see much. But sitting on a wall by an almost disused canal for an hour, reading, didn't seem to be especially suspicious; not even near the back of the police station. And no-one can have known that what he was reading was Moriarty's Police Law – except the people at the library.

It would be sheer paranoia to suppose that they would tell the police every time someone borrowed that. But it would be so easy – and the librarians needn't even know – with that computerized checkout. In fact, thinking about it, it would be such a wonderful way of checking for possible dissidents, just to program the machine to give the police lists of books borrowed by anyone who borrowed certain volumes, or more than some threshold number of certain categories of books. Or the reading list of individuals they were interested in for other reasons. Ouch. And all so completely out of the public eye.

But do they really do things like that? I doubt it.

They gathered that evening at about seven at Jill and June's. They'd each done a stint outside the police station, and the story was the same in each case. Mike gave them his thoughts about the library computer.

Tony thought it was likely that it was being done: 'You can be sure that if you've thought of it, they've thought of it too. It only takes one policeman somewhere to think of it, and make the suggestion. They've probably got people employed full-time just to think up things like that.'

June wasn't so sure. 'But surely there are safeguards against infringements of civil liberties like that?'

'It might be interesting to know what they are.'

'I doubt if they're much use, even if they exist in theory. Who would enforce them? The police?'

'The problem surely isn't enforcing the safeguards – it's exposing the abuses. How does one go about finding out about them – much less proving anything?'

'That's why I think more people should make it their business to keep an eye on the Law. But finding out what links exist between computers sounds like a job for experts, and it probably would involve some spy-thriller type work. Not our cup of tea.'

'I must admit I can't see how we could begin to get into a sys-tem like that – except sort of by observing how it works from the outside – borrow a lot of books that seem likely to be sensitive, and see what happens. And if anything happens, we know we'd have been better not doing it... and we still can't prove a thing.'

'And with them being so keen on identification before you can even get a ticket, we couldn't even do it with a false ticket.'

June thought it unlikely a system like that could be set up without someone involved blowing the whistle; but Tony said that nobody was likely to blow any whistles and risk losing their job. *He might well be right there.*

Tony had found that copies of detailed planning permissions, with architect's plans, were kept in Public Health offices; and that, for public buildings, they were available for public inspection. He'd had a look at the plans of the town hall, but had decided not to draw attention to himself by asking for the plans of the police station.

'I suspect that they might be just the one set of plans that aren't available, anyway.'

'Very possibly. I'd hoped that I might have been able to root through the plans myself, but you have to ask for the particular ones you want.'

They decided to give the main police station a miss the following day partly because they suspected that they'd learn nothing new, and partly because, especially on a Sunday, they might be noticed if they suddenly became regulars on the towpath or the embankment. 'Perhaps we should each walk past Shipton and Quarryside police stations, once in each direction, about an hour apart, as if we were going somewhere and coming back. Just to see if anything's going on that might give us a clue.'

'And Raikeley while we're at it. I can't see what kind of clue you're expecting – I can't imagine why they've closed off the garage at all, less still why it should involve any other stations. But it sounds like good copper-watching practice.'

'Trust you to know that there's a police station in Raikeley! I bet all that's happening is that they're doing some alterations to the building.'

'No – if there was any building work going on, the doors would be in use for the builders' vehicles. They did something like that in there a few months ago, but it's been back to normal again since then.'

They worked out a timetable for the following day, covering each police station at about hourly intervals, between them, throughout the day. They included the central police station as well, in the end. 'Just walking past it two or three times in a day isn't like sitting around near it for an hour.'

Mike's Sunday was mostly a dreary round of police stations and long walks. *What do you look for? If nothing out of the ordinary is obvious, the important thing must be to take careful note of just what is ordinary. Really, you need pen and paper – then you can compare notes with the others as well – but that would draw attention to you. Difficult, but not impossible I suppose, to take down notes a few hundred yards after you pass the place. Shouldn't really stand still to scan the place, either.*

About three in the afternoon Mike walked down Bridge Street. Cathie caught sight of him and beckoned him into the café. She didn't have a single customer.

'Join me in a cup of tea?'

'I shouldn't.'

'On the house, silly. Or are you in a hurry?'

'Not really; thank you very much.'

It's not so important to keep to the timetable. Not important at all, in fact.

A customer came in and she served him first, but then brought two teas and came and sat with Mike.

'Have you seen Tony? Do you know what it was all about?

Should I tell her about the Secret Four? My God, this is ridiculous! The conspiratorial psychology of it is getting to me.

He began to tell her all about it, his misgivings about the attitude and all. After a while, she changed the subject abruptly.

'I wonder how Pete's doing in Helsinki? Do you know anything about the place?'

'Not really. Probably a bit chilly at this time of year. I think it's pretty civilized. A few years ago it wasn't such a healthy place to be with the Americans and the Russians playing cat and mouse with each other's subs all around the eastern end of the Baltic, but that seems to have calmed down recently. I bet language is his biggest problem.'

'I doubt that. He's too shy to talk to anyone anyway!' Laughter.

'Perhaps. But he won't be able to read the notices, or ask his way, or find the right bus.'

'I expect plenty of people there speak at least a little English.'

The customer finished his coffee, got up, and left.

'Sorry I changed the subject like that. I didn't like the way that chap seemed to be listening to you.'

'You know, I hadn't noticed he was. Not that I was saying anything momentous anyway.'

'I'm not certain myself that he was. He wasn't giving us his undivided attention openly exactly. I just had the feeling he was listening with interest.'

'Not that it matters. I'm just as interested in Pete's holiday anyway.'

'Me too. But until he comes back, or we get a card, it's just idle speculation. But the other thing sounds quite interesting. I'll think about it myself, and try to be more conscious of that particular side of the way of the world. But I think I share your doubts about the value of systematic watching, unless you know what you're watching out for. I'd better start cleaning up soon, before the tea-time crowd. But you'll be in again soon, won't you?'

'Of course. But you mustn't keep giving me free teas. Come round and see us out of work hours sometime.'

'One of the few perks of this job is to give away teas to my friends. Grub too if there's a bit left over that won't keep, as long as no-one starts expecting it and spongeing off us. But I'll come round anyway.'

'See you.'

'So long.'

They had a meeting again at the Js' at eight o'clock. Jill had got home early and had a meal ready for them all.

'If we're going to make a habit of this, we'd better all chip in for the grub.'

'Better still, the work as well. But these two will never let us loose in their kitchen, Tony. We'll do a meal round at my place tomorrow if we're meeting again then.'

'I vote we leave this a day or two after tonight. We don't want this to take over our lives. It's not as though we're on to anything at the moment.'

'I'm glad I'm not the only one who feels that way.'

'Let's make it Wednesday round at Mike's then, okay Mike? Social, but we'll talk about this a bit anyway without a doubt. I take it no-one has noticed anything funny?'

'Not really. I don't even feel as though I've increased my awareness of the police, but that's very hard to tell.'

'It is hard, isn't it. You never notice filling in unsurprising details into your world view; but when details change, you do notice. Even if the new details would have been just as unsurprising if it had been them in the first place.'

'I bet you can't say that again, Tony! Quite a little philosopher tonight, aren't you?'

That was uncalled for, June. But he's smiling.

Then the discussion turned to shelters. Mike expounded his theory about foreign labour being used in order to keep the public as much in the dark as possible.

'They do that with bank vaults and the like, certainly. I'm sure you're right. My brother applied for a job 'on a construction site' in France a few months ago. He was turned down. They'd asked him about his qualifications. He'd told them about his 'A' in French, but not his others because he reckoned they'd not want clever buggers. I bet they don't want you to be able to converse with the natives, either.'

'None of the lads working on the sewage project at Wood Lane have a word of English. I don't even know where they come from. Your theory doesn't explain why they should use foreign labour for a project like that at all.'

'Unless it's really a shelter, not a sewage works at all!' Laughter.

'Hey, but seriously: you hear them talk about shelters, but does anyone know where they are?'

'There's one under the town hall in Oxford, and one under the telephone exchange in Bradford.'

'Wonderful. We know where two are in all Britain – maybe one or two others. But where is the nearest one? Is there one in Burnfield? Where?'

'If they were shelters for the general public, the general public would have to be told how to find them. Anyway, there can't be shelters for the general public, or why all the pressure to build private ones?'

'Even if there was shelter space for everyone, not everyone would be within reach of one in the time available...

'What time available?'

... if you were at home, you'd go into your private shelter, if you were in town, you'd go into the public shelter.'

'I'm glad you said 'Even if,' – I don't know how anyone is supposed to know when to go into a shelter at all. Do we all sit in our shelters whenever the situation gets tense? Or do we wait, ears glued to our portable radios, for the four-minute warning, and then rush to the nearest shelter, wherever it might be?'

'In one way, perhaps it's not quite as silly as that. It depends what weapons get used. If you're in a zap zone or right under a nuke, the shelter's not going to do you a lot of good unless it's a hundred feet down and you're in it already. And you don't even get four minutes warning for a zap. But if you're a fair way from a nuke or it's biols, then it's the aftereffects you're worried about, and you've got a little time to get down. But in another way, it's even sillier. You shelter for four weeks while radiation levels drop or the antis are developed, and then come out to die slowly instead of quickly, or to find the biols have mutated and the antis don't work any longer, or there's nothing to eat, or no air.'

'I don't think there's going to be a war at all. The shelter thing is just for the shelter companies to make a profit out of. In which case, presumably, it is a sewage works at Wood Lane. Which brings us back to the question of why they use foreign labour?'

'It could be to do with union-busting. Or maybe they use foreign labour here because it's cheap, and Brit labour abroad because it really is shelters.'

It was late again when Mike and Tony left for their respective homes; Tony had a long walk ahead of him.

'See you Wednesday. So long!'

'Good night.'

Chapter 4

God! What a way to wake you up! Is it really a quarter to six already?

That's no wake-up-it's-breakfast-time alarm. That's a siren.

Fire? In a place like this?

Whatever it was, I was very soon well awake. The room lights had turned themselves on dimly, too, and were slowly brightening.

My God. What a place.

The siren wailed down into silence.

A speaker somewhere in the ceiling came to life.

'Please leave your room immediately. Follow the yellow flashing arrows in the corridor. Do not use the lifts. Do not wait to pack your luggage. Please leave your room...

This place even knows the right language for its guests, room by room...

I was already out in the corridor, moving away from the lifts, following the yellow flashing arrows. My kitbag was in my hand, I'd never unpacked it.

I realized suddenly that I was the only one in the corridor. I was either ahead of everyone else, or behind them. I began to rush, thinking I must be late.

I can't be. I was ever so quick.

People began to appear, and I realized why I was the first. Everyone else had children with them, on this corridor at least. And I seemed to be the only one who'd only thrown a few clothes on carelessly. I had no socks or underwear on, and my shirt was flapping out.

A woman appeared, carrying a baby, walking slowly with a toddler in tow. I picked up the toddler. He started bawling, but his mother looked very grateful.

The yellow flashing arrows led us down a side corridor, and then onto a flight of stairs. People were already descending from higher floors, and as we went down we were joined by people from lower floors. The stairs seemed endless.

The corridors seemed endless, too, on L floor. But it can't have been more than a hundred yards. Adrenalin. Crisis psychology.

What's the crisis, anyway? Surely not fire.

Suddenly the stairs were going down a plain shaft, with no side corridors. Then the walls were plain concrete, and there were no more flashing yellow arrows, but we hadn't missed the way: there was no other way. Then we were at the bottom of the stairs, in a wide, low, bare concrete tunnel. We passed through a set of huge, heavy steel doors that looked like something out of a film set for a space ship. *Why would spaceships have huge, heavy steel doors? Surely they should be as small and light as possible?* Beyond them the corridor was much higher, with walls, floor, and ceiling of shining metal. There were shower heads in the ceiling.

It's a shelter. O God, is this it?

I knew already.

What incredible luck to have been in this hotel.

O God! Cathie!

The toddler was still bawling. The corridor passed through another set of space-ship doors, and was bare concrete again. Then through a set of relatively ordinary-looking solid steel doors, and we were in a vast, dimly-lit hall. There was no direction to go. Everyone was just drifting to a halt, or wandering aimlessly about. I put the toddler down. His mother thanked me. The toddler clung to her leg and looked at me with tearful eyes, but he had stopped bawling.

I looked back at the doors through which we had come. People were still streaming in. I looked around and tried to estimate how many people there were, but with no vantage point it was impossible. The size of the hall was also very hard to estimate in the dim lighting.

The flood of people coming in was diminishing. I walked to the entrance and peered down the corridor. The last few people were all infirm in some way, or had small children in tow.

After the last people had arrived in the hall, I watched to see if the doors would close themselves, or whether there would be someone to do it. The lights in the corridor went out, and I couldn't see the doors at the far end. The doors at the entrace to the hall did close themselves.

Now what? Is anyone going to tell us what's going on?

Apparently not.

It's not very warm. In fact, it's cold.

I rummaged in my kitbag and extracted my jumper and put it on. Then some socks. I wanted to put a pair of underpants on, so I set off in search of a lavatory.

I followed the wall from the entrance. It curved gently, and I wondered if the hall was circular, but after about sixty yards the curving wall ended in a right angle junction with a straight wall. The curving wall was bare concrete; the new wall was polished metal. In the angle, a few inches from the walls, a thick steel hawser rose vertically out of the floor. Above me, it disappeared into utter blackness above the level of the suspended lights.

The lavatories were quite close to the corner, but I almost walked straight past them. The doors had no handles, visible hinges, or engaged / vacant signs at all. They were simply a door-sized area of the same material as the rest of the wall, with a quarter inch crack around them. They opened at a push at the right hand edge. In the dim light, the etched images of a man and a woman were barely visible.

Inside, they were very plain. The door hinges weren't visible from that side either. The door was locked by rotation of a simple handle at the edge, which also served to pull it open. There was a bench at the back with an unlidded oval hole in it. All the surfaces were the same polished metal, which resulted in a disturbing mass of dim, blurry reflections. Just as in the main hall, no ceiling could be seen: everything faded into utter blackness beyond the light, far above.

There was no toilet paper, and no washing facilities.

I looked down the hole, but there was absolutely nothing to be seen. The light didn't reach anything at all.

A small child could fall down there, quite easily.

I wondered what would happen to one that did.

More out of interest than out of any biological need, I peed. The golden parabola disappeared into an abyss, soundlessly.

I put on a pair of underpants and left. I was fascinated to know more about both upward and downward directions, but had the strong feeling I'd have plenty of time.

Back in the hall, things hadn't changed. People were still milling around, talking excitedly, or looking bewildered.

Where are we going to sleep? What are we going to eat? How long are we going to be here? What is happening? Is anyone going to tell us anything? Or is everything going to be like those lavatories, find out for yourselves?

No-one seemed to be organizing anything, and I could see no notices.

There were no announcements.

I decided to continue exploring.

There were five lavatories, all just like the one I'd been in.

Only five? For all these people?

All vacant! People don't know there here. They haven't found them. Some people must be desperate by now.

For a moment I thought of shouting out that they were here, but I decided I didn't want to draw attention to myself.

The next feature I reached was a narrow, open passageway, with a ceiling at about ten feet. It curved sharply, and out of sight from the entrance, was a stout floor-to-ceiling turnstile. I was able to turn it, but it was designed to let people in the opposite direction. Beyond it, the passageway curved back sharply out of sight.

There were four such passageways at about twelve foot intervals, all identical. Coming out of the last one, I met a boy coming in.

'Hey! Mister! Is this the gents? There's no sign, but I can't find one anywhere!'

I explained to him where the lavatories were, and what they looked like. He dashed off.

English child. I wonder how many English people there are here? How many people altogether? I still don't have any idea. Hundreds, anyway.

The metal wall met an identical one at another right angled corner. Another hawser rose into the gloom. I followed the new wall.

Four more curving passageways.

A queue. Beyond the queue, above their heads, I could see the curved concrete wall. There were five lavatories in this corner too, and they had been discovered.

There was no hawser in this corner.

I followed the featureless concrete wall, and was soon back at the entrance.

So that's our prison. A quarter circle, or something like that, maybe eighty or ninety yard radius. Toilets. No other facilities, unless they're somewhere away from the walls. Or down the second lot of curving passageways.

Walking directly back to the passageways, I realized how crowded the hall was. I noticed one family, sitting huddled together in the middle of the floor, all crying. Further on, two young men were arguing about nuclear weapons. In English.

The turnstiles at the end of the other passages wouldn't turn in either direction. I sat down in the end of the last passage I'd tried, to consider, but I didn't have much to go on.

They must make an announcement soon.

I was tired, but it was too cold to sleep.

The other turnstiles turn, but the wrong way. These don't turn at all. Presumably, they're locked, but when they're released, they'll be the way to sleeping, eating and washing facilities, and the other four will be the way back. Then why are they so far apart?

Anyway, I reckon I'm in the right place.

Why is this place such a funny shape? What's going on, anyway? Is it all out war? Or have we been taken prisoner in some bizarre plot? Don't be daft. This is a shelter. There's a war going on, or about to begin I suppose.

What's happening in Burnfield? How are Cathie, and Mike, and Jill, and June? Interesting to see how I do care, quite a lot, how June is.

Pretty much like I care about Mike and Jill.

But the feeling that Cathie was in danger gave me a quite physical anguish.

Two days ago we scarcely knew each other. It seemed an eternity ago.

I had a vision of a small face at an upstairs window, embarrassed at being caught watching me kissing Cathie. *Only twenty four hours ago, or so.*

What is the time, anyway? It was half past four. *How long have we been down here?* I hadn't the slightest idea.

I woke up chilled to the bone. There was a man trying to turn the turnstile. He addressed me in an incomprehensible tongue, when he saw that I was awake.

'I'm sorry. I don't understand. Do you speak English?'

'A little. You think like me, I think, yes?'

'I expect so.'

At that instant there was an audible click. The man disappeared through the turnstile and round the curve in the corridor before I'd really come to.

The turnstile was locked again.

I suppose it is the thing to do. It feels odd, not to say foolhardy, to go through a turnstile without knowing where it goes, without knowing that it's what we're supposed to do. We have to trust the people who made this place, I suppose, though. We did when we followed the yellow flashing arrows; when we allowed the doors to close behind us. But why is no-one telling us what to do now?

The turnstile unlocked after about ten seconds, and I went straight through. Round the bend in the corridor was a straight section, with a hatchway to one side. As I came to the hatchway, a canvas bag was pushed into it from the far side. I looked into the hatchway, but all was shrouded in gloom. I took the canvas bag, presuming it was meant for me, and continued along the passageway. A curve, a turnstile, a curve... and I was out into a vast hall exactly like the first one.

Well, almost exactly like. There were only about twenty or thirty people in this one, and despite the dim lighting I could see the whole room, apart from whatever might be above the lights. The only difference I could see was that the steel entrance doors were almost at the near end of the concrete wall, whereas in the first hall I'd estimated that the doors were pretty well half-way along the wall.

As I gazed about, another man came out of the passageway behind me carrying a canvas bag just like mine.

Everyone in this hall had just such a bag. In fact, apart from the clothes they stood up in, it was all they had. I felt like the odd man out, with my kitbag in addition.

Most people seemed to be investigating their canvas bags. I decided to do likewise. It contained a sleeping bag, of the cheap, zip-two-together-to-make-a-double, nylon and polyester variety; a plastic flask with about a litre and a half of water in it; a plastic box with a clasp-fit lid; and some plastic bags containing what looked like towels.

I opened the plastic box. Inside it were two cartons which could have come from a Chinese take-away, and a knife, fork and spoon.

The food wasn't bad at all. It too could have come from a Chinese take-away.

Without thinking why, I put the empty cartons back in the box. I noticed that it was still warm inside. I looked at the box: it was double walled.

By that time, there was beginning to be a crowd in the hall, all with the same canvas bags; and the passageways were each issuing newcomers at ten or fifteen second intervals.

There has obviously been a general realization in Hall One that it's the way to go, even without any word from Hall Two.

I investigated the packages of towelling. The first one contained a towelling shirt, somewhat large for me; the second a pair of baggy, fly-less trousers with an elasticated waist; the third was actually a towel; and the fourth contained a vest, a pair of unisex knickers and a pair of long socks.

At the bottom of the bag I discovered a small packet containing soft toilet paper, a bar of soap, toothpaste and a toothbrush.

The realization came to me that we were expected to sleep on the floor of the hall. Looking around, I could see other people acting on the same realization. I unrolled my sleeping bag, put my kitbag into my canvas bag, and lay down to sleep, using the canvas bag as a pillow.

I was exhausted, and despite a turmoil of worries about my friends, my family, Cathie, the world in general and the future, I was soon fast asleep.

Chapter 5

Monday passed uneventfully.

On Tuesday morning Mike had diarrhea, and felt a little under the weather. He didn't feel like having an energetic day, so he bought a Guardian and a Times on his way over to Jill's.

Jill met him at the door. 'I'm afraid I'm going to have to leave you to your own devices for a few hours, Mike. After you left last night, Mum popped round and said that Adrian and David had been brought home from camp with a stomach upset, and asked me to come and look after them while she goes shopping, and goes round to see Gran.'

'I'm not so clever myself this morning. Bit of diarrhea.'

'The boys must be a lot worse than that for my mum to want me to see to them while she's out for a bit!'

Jill didn't reappear until the middle of the afternoon. She found Mike fast asleep, with his head on his arms on the paper on the kitchen table. She didn't wake him; she started to make a pot of tea.

Mike woke with a start. 'Hello love, when did you get back? How are the boys?'

'Just this minute. The lads aren't too good, I'm afraid. They've had to go into hospital. Diarrhea and vomiting, and this morning Adrian was shitting blood. They say half the lads in the camp have got it. And we had to wait ages for an ambulance. The ambulance man said they're rushed off their feet at the moment. Proper little epidemic by the sound of it.'

'Is June round at Auntie Alice's?'

'I imagine so. She went round there last night, and didn't come home.'

'I hope Auntie Alice isn't ill.'

'I don't suppose she is. Apparently it's mainly youngsters that've got it, though David said the staff at the camp were as badly hit as the boys.'

'Do they know what it is?'

'The ambulance man said he didn't think that they did. But he didn't hang around. His ambulance was half full, and he had a list to collect before he went back to the hospital.

'There's a pot of tea just ready. Do you feel up to a mug?'

'Now don't you go treating me like an invalid. I'm all right. Of course I want one.'

They exhausted the subject of the epidemic quite quickly. Although Jill was worried about her two brothers, there was nothing they could do, and they agreed that they should try to take their minds off it. They settled down and did all three crosswords in Mike's papers one after another.

'I hope the boys are all right.'

'I expect so.'

'Give us a kiss, love.'

When June came in at half past nine, they were fast asleep in each other's arms, on the sofa in front of the gas fire. She put a fiver in the meter and relit the fire, and put the kettle on. The whistle of the kettle didn't wake them, so she made tea in the cup just for herself. They didn't wake in the hour or so she sat in the rocking chair reading, so she fetched a blanket down from Jill's bed and put it over them before she turned off the fire and went to bed.

Jill and June were talking in the kitchen when Mike woke. He felt much better than he had the previous day, but when he stood up after putting his shoes on, his head reeled for a moment. Then he felt okay again. They heard him going upstairs to the bathroom.

'Morning sleepy-head! How do you feel this morning?'

'Better, thanks.'

'Cup of tea when you come down!'

'Thanks.'

'By the sound of it, you and June have had the same bug. She had a bit of diarrhea at Auntie Alice's, so she stopped there the other night rather than walk home. Then she was asleep on and off all yesterday afternoon.'

'How do you feel now, June?'

'Fine. A bit dizzy when I first got up, but okay now.'

'Let's hope that what the boys have got is just a slightly worse version of the same thing. Shall we go down and see them at visiting time this afternoon?'

'They're only allowed two visitors at a time.'

'Two each. Us three and your mum.'

But at the hospital there was a cordon, and a sign:

IN THE PRESENT EMERGENCY, ALL VISITING IS CANCELLED. PLEASE CO-OPERATE. SERIOUS CASES AND EXPERIENCED VOLUNTEERS ONLY PAST THIS POINT.

There was quite a crowd outside. A few people were arguing with the policeman or the porter at the gate, but most were rather subdued, and conscientiously keeping out of the way of the ambulances, and the taxis that were apparently operating as ambulances.

They found Jill's mother. She had already been to the counter by the other gate, where there was another sign:

PLEASE QUEUE HERE FOR INFORMATION ABOUT RELATIVES OR FRIENDS

The boys were not on the "critical" list.

'There's a danger list?'

'They say that the disease isn't thought to be dangerous, with treatment; but all visiting is cancelled because of the number of cases, and there are always critical cases in a hospital.'

'Don't they know what it is?'

'No, they don't. Come on, let's get out of the way.'

They walked together down into town, Jill's mother on her way to cook lunch for herself and her mother, Mike to buy stuff for dinner for four, the others for company. As they were passing the Britannia, Jill's mother said,

'Let's pop in here for a cuppa. I've plenty of time. I'll treat you all.'

Jenny and Cathie were sitting at a table by the counter. Although it was Wednesday lunchtime, there wasn't a customer in the place.

'Four teas love, please. You're busy today!'

'I think it's the epidemic. Everyone's staying at home, for fear of catching it. Or they don't trust anything they've not cooked themselves. Are you sure you do?'

'If I'm going to get it, I've probably got it already. My two sons went into hospital yesterday.'

'Were they at the camp? My little brother was supposed to go, but he had a bit of a cold and couldn't go, lucky devil.'

'Yes, they were. How did you know?'

'We've been listening to the local radio. There've been a lot of odd cases, here and there, but there've only been two big groups of cases: most of the boys and staff on that camp, and a whole lot of foreign labourers off the sewage project. Apart from them, it's mainly children, but nothing much to connect one case with another. Hello, Mike.'

'Hello, Cathie. Seems as though Pete's escaped at just the right time, doesn't it?'

'I don't know. He's in a foreign country where no-one will understand him if he needs help. And they say there's several other places scattered around the country and Europe that've been hit just like Burnfield.'

'They still don't know what it is?'

'They say not. Hello, here comes Tom Green.'

Jill's mother excused herself, saying that Gran would be wondering where she was.

While Jenny served Tom, Mike introduced Cathie to Jill and June. He told the Js about how Cathie had asked him what was on Tony's mind, and how they'd discussed the copper-watching idea. The epidemic totally overshadowed the whole issue. Jill had two brothers sick with it, and Cathie had been listening to the news every hour: they had a common obsession and were old friends in no time.

Tom couldn't help overhearing.

'I'll drop you a paper in as soon as I get them.'

'Thanks Tom.'

Mike left to do his shopping, and June slipped out a little while later and found him in the market.

'That's the Cathie who's taken up with Pete, isn't it?'

'That's right.'

'You know, I didn't think I really loved Pete any more, but now I'm as jealous as hell. But she seems a very nice person. I don't know what to want.'

'Your're asking the wrong person. I'm glad you like Cathie; I think she's great. And Pete's my best friend, and you're one of my best friends. What chance have I got to be impartial? For what it's worth, I think the sooner you find yourself a really nice boyfriend, preferably one who fits in well with the rest of us, the better.'

'Jill seems to think Tony has his eye on me. I like him, too, but somehow he just doesn't seem to be right. I think he'd send me round the twist after a bit.'

'Funny, that's just how I feel about him, though I can't put my finger on why. But I don't get the impression you fancy him anyway.'

'That's the difficult bit for me. You see, I don't think I ever fancied Pete, either. But I'm sure I loved him. I think I still do.'

'I wish I was certain we all meant the same things when we use words like those. I'm pretty sure I know what you're talking about, but I'm not sure I would if I didn't know you and Pete so well.'

Shortly after June and Mike got to Mike's flat, Tony arrived to help Mike prepare the meal. When the three of them had almost finished, and were beginning to wonder where Jill had got to, she came in dripping.

'I hope no-one minds – I've invited Cathie along too. She'll be here in a few minutes. She's coming via her house to let her mum know where she is. Get the fire on, Mike, there's a dear, while I get out of these wet things. Cathie'll be soaked, too. It just suddenly started bucketing down.'

June helped her out of her wet things. She was soaked to the skin. They found some of Mike's things and she came down-stairs looking like a rag doll. Tony laughed; Jill made a face.

Mike said, 'If you come round here much, you'll see Jill looking like that quite often. She's got quite a collection of my stuff round their place, so I've no problems.'

'Cathie's smaller still. She'll look really funny!'

She was, and she did. Mike wrung out the two lots of wet clothes and hung them up over the bath.

'They won't be properly dry, but they'll be a bit lighter to carry home, anyway.'

Cathie had brought the evening paper with her. She and Jill had waited for Tom to bring it, and it had been a bit late. She hadn't been able to keep it dry, and Mike took it apart carefully and laid it out on the floorboards in front of the fire. Cathie and Jill perched as near the fire as they could. Everyone could see the headline, but Jill read the lead article out for them.

IF YOU'VE GOT IT, GET HELP

But if you have a minor complaint, PLEASE don't bother the health services. Your local doctor's surgery is CLOSED: he is helping at one of the emergency hospitals.

The disease has two forms, or two diseases have both struck widely at the same time. The mild form has diarrhea, sleepiness, and dizziness for about twenty-four hours. DO NOT TROUBLE THE HEALTH SERVICES. The serious form has severe diarrhea, possibly with blood, uncontrollable vomiting and possibly a blotchy red skin rash. Without treatment, several people have DIED from this: SEEK HELP AT ONCE. There is an emergency hospital in every school in the Burnfield area.

If you have any medical experience, please volunteer to assist at your local school.

Tony and June brought in the food, and they ate slowly in silence, digesting the news privately. None of them had 'any medical experience'. Two of them had had the 'mild form' of the disease – or the other disease. How many cases were there, if every school had been converted into a hospital? Pity Cathie hadn't brought the radio; but Jenny would want it at the café.

Maybe they've converted every school, rather than just a few, to make it easy to find an emergency hospital.

Tony finished his meal first, and picked up the front page, dry enough now. 'Shall I read it out loud?'

Chorus of 'mmm's.

There was a list of towns affected. Figures were changing constantly, but at the time of going to press, about four percent of the population of Burnfield was sick with the serious form of the disease, and about half a percent nationwide, 'but this figure is probably less up-to-date than the Burnfield figure.' The differences of age of different reports from abroad made 'comparison impossible', but it was 'evidently a major problem worldwide.'

Then Jill picked up a page with a leader article, which speculated about biological warfare, and questioned the veracity of reports from China of similar problems there. 'Their reports did not begin until some time after ours: perhaps they were waiting to see the precise effects before pretending to suffer in the same way.'

'I think that's pretty unlikely. They couldn't keep that kind of pretence up for very long, and unless they're expecting pretty well a hundred percent fatalities, they'd have some pretty difficult explaining to do later. They'd have foreseen that, if it was a premeditated act of war. For that matter, why should one expect reports to begin simultaneously? It's a funny epidemic that appears everywhere at the same time, and the press is always harping on about the Chinese tendency to secretiveness about internal problems.'

'It is a funny epidemic that appears simultaneously all over the place. That's one of the things that points to biological warfare. It's hard to see how a disease can spread as quickly as this has.'

'There didn't seem to be any rhyme or reason about where it's struck.'

'That's a thought. Pass us the atlas, Jill, and read us that list of towns again, Tony.'

'You're not going to deface the atlas, are you?'

'I don't mind having a bit of history recorded in it!'

Mike marked each town as he found it.

'It's got a pattern. I can't understand why, but it forms three broad stripes. Two of them go through London.

'And the other one?'

'Hull to Liverpool approximately, with a bit of a curve. We're just to one side of that.'

'Let's have a look.

'No, you're right, it looks too much like a pattern to be just your eye connecting up random dots. Perhaps it follows the major transport routes.'

'I suppose that's a pretty obvious way for an epidemic to spread.'

'But it doesn't seem to have spread at all. It seems to have appeared simultaneously along the whole path. That might be hard to tell within a small area like Britain, but over the whole world?'

'But we don't know accurately when it struck anywhere else... hello, there's someone at the door.'

'Sorry to bother you...'

'Come in out of the rain and let's get the door shut... What do you want?'

'I'm a policeman. Not here on official business though. It's just that I couldn't help overhearing your conversation with the waitress in the Britannia the other night. I should have reported it, and we'd probably be watching you all now, but I didn't. I'm probably putting my job on the line, but it's reached the point where I don't care all that much.'

Mike's mind reeled. He didn't know what to do for a moment. *Probably it's true. It could be a very subtle 'in' to our group, but he knows about us anyway, and there's nothing else to discover about us really.*

'We're all here at the moment. Let me hang that wet mac up for you, and come and get warm by the fire – there'll be a cuppa in a minute. What's your name, anyway?'

'Brian. Brian Westover. You're Mike, aren't you?'

'That's right. I won't ask you how you know, or how you know my address!'

'Not the most difficult piece of detective work!'

'I think I'd rather let you tell everyone what you're doing here... Everyone, this is Brian. Brian, this is Tony, Cathie, June, Jill, and I'm Mike.'

Jill put a chair next to the fire for Brian, and disappeared into the kitchen.

'Sugar, Brian? Milk? It's only tea, I'm afraid.'

'Milk but no sugar, ta, love. Tea's very welcome, thanks. Perhaps I'd better wait till – she's Jill, isn't she? – Jill comes back, before I start my story.'

Cathie shot Mike a meaningful glance. 'You were in the Britannia the other night, weren't you, Brian? I'm a waitress there.'

'Yes, I was. That's really how I come to be here. Can I have a look at your paper? I've not had a chance to see what the Press is saying yet. None of you are ill, are you?'

'Jill's two brothers are in hospital. Mike and I have both had the mild form, we think.'

'Haven't you got a radio or a telly here?'

'No. Mike's an ascetic and the rest of us are just poor.'

General mirth.

'I'd be poor too if I wasn't an ascetic.'

'Why do you ask about the telly?'

'I want to know what's happening on the epidemic front. In this kind of thing the paper is hopelessly slow and infrequent. This tells you damn all.'

He threw the paper down.

'It tells you how to tell if you've got it, and where to go. Those are the really important things, surely?'

'But not how it spreads, and how you can avoid getting it.'

'Or even that no-one knows the answer to either of those questions, which happens to be the case.'

'How do you know that, Brian?'

'Superintendent Davies gave us a briefing this afternoon. They haven't isolated the cause, but a lot of labs are working on it. They think it's a virus, but they don't know how it's spread so far, so fast.'

Tony gave Mike a puzzled look, but Mike just smiled enigmatically.

'If they don't know anything about it, how can they treat it?'

'There you have me. Thanks very much Jill.'

'Help me fetch the others through, Mike love.' Then, in the kitchen, under her breath, 'Who the hell is he?'

'He'll tell you, in a minute.'

'Well, I know that the epidemic has a horrible fascination for all of us, and that Jill has an especially charged interest in it; but it's not what I came here for, and now that you're all here I'll introduce myself properly. I'm a detective constable in the Burnfield police force. Mike has obviously decided that I'm straight up, or that I'll learn nothing by coming in here that I couldn't learn easily enough anyway. I overheard a conversation between Mike and – Cathie? –

'That's right. I thought you were listening.'

' – the other night. It ought to have aroused my professional ear, but instead it aroused a sympathetic one, so I didn't report it. I just hope I'm talking to the right people, that, at best, you'll do some good with the information, and at worst, that it won't rebound on me. I don't know who else I could talk to. How Tony managed to stumble on the fact that the garage was out of use beats me; it was assumed that Joe Public would never notice. Without some pretty daring escapades, opening yourselves to some pretty drastic consequences without any very sound reason for doing so, I doubt you'd ever have found out just what is going on. I'm surprised you were astute enough to realize that it was anything significant, Tony.'

'I wasn't sure. I couldn't think of any reasonable explanation, that's all. All the unreasonable ones I could think of sounded so far-fetched, I didn't really believe in them. I was mystified.'

'Well, the real reason is pretty far-fetched. I'm very interested to know whether you'd thought of it. It's an exercise, the first of a series. I don't like the social and political implications of it a bit, and it wants exposing, but I don't know how. I'd be risking my job and my future going to the media. At best I don't think they'd touch it, and sooner or later someone would shop me.'

'I'm touched that you trust us.'

'You seem the best possible people to trust: I know the nature of your interest. If you lot are a set-up to trap me, then the thought police have reached a level of sophistication even I hadn't imagined! You've already stumbled on things, so if you find out more for yourselves and spill the beans, with a bit of luck it doesn't have to involve me.

'The garage and half the cells have been converted into a shelter. It can be sealed completely, biologically, chemically and radiologically. Between exercises the garage and cells can still be used, albeit with a reduced capacity. About a fifth of the Burnfield force are incarcerated in there at the moment.

'They don't know if it's an exercise or the Real Thing. They're in communication with us via intercom, and we are feeding them a prepared story about what's happening outside. We've been thoroughly briefed about the story, and we've got advisers on the spot to help us with awkward questions. A lot of the time there's no-one at our end because "we're too busy". With this epidemic, we really are.

'I was rather surprised that they didn't call the whole exercise off when the scale of the epidemic became apparent, but Davies said that he'd been in touch with the MoD, who are organizing the exercises, and they said, "no, keep them in there, the labs say they want to know if they get any cases inside, it'll give valuable information."

'Of course, we can't ask them, because they don't know about the epidemic – they think things are much worse! – and they haven't volunteered anything; but they might just not want to add to our troubles. But I doubt if they've got real problems, or they'd surely ask point-blank, "if it's an exercise, let us out." Mind you, they've got first-class medics in there anyway.'

'How come none of them realized it was just a false alarm when they were being gathered up in the first place?'

'It was about three o'clock, last Friday morning. I was sitting in my car, watching a house – but I can't tell you anything about that. Suddenly the radio comes to life:

"All personnel! Alpha Alert! Proceed at once to your Alpha location."

'We'd all been briefed about it; Alpha Alert meant war drill, or actual war. All our Alpha locations were the same: Burnfield Central Police Station. Those of us who arrived after the door was sealed were to take over running the station until the relief arrived. I was too late: I'm jolly glad it wasn't the real thing.'

'If it had been, would you still have had to go on running the station?'

'Officially, yes. Unless you've got a private shelter, there's nothing much else to do. The station's as well protected as anywhere; it's filtered air and distilled water that's the real problem. Depending where you are and what weapons are used, you've got some chance of surviving, anyway.'

'Why should the police get a shelter, when nobody else does?'

'Some other people do. But it would be impossibly expensive to provide adequate shelter for everyone. They just figure that it'll be chaos afterwards, and they'll need all the police they can save.'

'And I suppose inadequate shelters for everybody would just make the police to population ratio even worse, while people were taking longer over dying.

'That's about the size of it.'

'But surely any shelter is inadequate, in the sense that the day comes eventually when you have to come out and face the world. None of the big weapons are going to leave the world fit to live in for the foreseeable future, are they?'

'I don't know much about it – probably no more than you lot do. Zaps aren't supposed to have much effect outside the zones, though – apart from pollution from smoke and dust, depending what gets zapped. Obviously if someone zaps a nuclear power station or two things'll be pretty messy.'

'It's another of those things that people like us should be finding out more about – but I suppose that's not an immediate problem. Do the police in the shelter have any instruments to tell them about conditions outside? Are they in communication with anyone outside the station?'

'I don't know the answer to either question – we've not been told. They're obviously not on the public telephone network, any more than they're on the public electricity or water supply. But whether they're in contact with other shelters, or Ministry workers simulating other shelters, I don't know.'

'That's surely a giveaway for them that it's just an exercise: if it were real, there'd be no reason to keep them incommunicado.'

'I think there is: it's a matter of morale. But I shouldn't like to be the briefing officer who told them.'

'That's a neat virtue in their not knowing if it might be an exercise, when it's actually real. The psychology of knowing that the reason you're being held incommunicado may be so that your family can't tell you they're okay is much better than knowing that it's so that you can't share their agony. But there's another thing exercising my mind: I can see how they expected the members of the force to keep it secret. But they'd have to tell their families, and I can't see how they expected them to keep it secret.'

'That's not so difficult. You're obviously not as au fait with police organization as Tony is. I bet he could tell you.'

'Possibly, but go on, I'd only be guessing.'

'For several years now, it's been fairly normal for policemen and women to be called away on compulsory training exercises at no notice. The first the family knows is when a welfare office calls round to tell them they've gone, and ask if the family needs assistance while they're away. There was a rumpus the first time it happened, but it seems that it's been possible under the conditions of service for ages, and they give a big bonus afterwards. We're under strict orders not to tell anyone about Exercise Alpha, not even family. The pre-briefing was quite brief. A lot of questions got cut off with, 'you don't need to know that.' There'll be a bit more information floating about when they come out. They'll have had the full briefing, and a few weeks experience in the shelter. There'll be no stopping them talking to their colleagues. That's when I think it'll be hard to keep it under wraps: civilian staff are bound to overhear something.'

'What did they do about civilian staff during the 'alert'?'

'Didn't tell them a thing. Don't forget, this was at three in the morning. The mechanics were all transferred to the vehicle depot over a year ago; they'll just assume that the building work is still going on. I don't know what they'll do when they have a daytime alert, though. They've got to have them, or if the real thing happens in the daytime, they'll know it's real.'

'But that's not as important as not knowing either way in an exercise.'

'I suppose not.'

'The Ministry of Defence is organizing this, you said?'

'Yes. They've been interfering more and more directly in police affairs over the last few years.'

'No, what I was thinking is that they must be taking the possibility of war pretty seriously.'

'Either that, or they want the police to think that they do.'

'I find it hard to imagine what they'd gain by that.'

'That's not so hard. It could be nothing more sinister than consolidating their own status. If war is a strong possibility, then the MoD is important. They could just be making sure of their jobs.'

'And making a profit for their friends in the shelter trade.'

'Well, you know as much as I do, just about. What are you – or we – going to do? I'm going to have to be going soon.'

'I think we'll need a little time to think about it...'

General nodding of heads.

'... can we contact you if we need you? You can always find us here, or via Cathie at the Britannia.'

'You could leave a message for me to contact you, at my parents' in Raikeley. I share my flat with another cop, and he'd want to know who you are. Only friendly interest, but awkward, so my parents' place is better. Get a bit of paper, I'll give you the address.'

'Before you go; you were saying you'd had a briefing about the epidemic. What did they say?'

'It was mainly organizational: a general lowering of all other priorities, and how to help in organizing volunteer labour, and getting the sick to the hospitals. But he told us a few things that aren't in the paper: at that stage, no-one had died under treatment in Burnfield, and not many anywhere. But no-one had really been cured, either. He thinks that the government will declare a state of emergency soon if things don't improve. But I'd better be going, or Mark'll wonder what's happened to me.'

'Well, thank you very much Brian. We'll be seeing you again, I hope.

'Don't get up, Mike, I think I can find my way out! So long, everyone.'

'See you.'

'There's a turn-up for the book! He's a strange policeman, that's for sure!'

'I'm pretty sure he's straight up though. It occurred to me that he could be an agent provocateur; but now we know what we're looking for, I think we can check his story without any daring escapades. And anyway, if it isn't true, there's still the original observations to explain. They've scarcely shut the garage for our benefit.'

'But what are we going to do?'

'I suggest, for the moment, nothing. It's got no immediate consequences of any significance, and it doesn't radically change our world-picture. We ought to try to find some innocent way of checking it, just in case it's a subtle red herring to keep us off a more significant trail, but I doubt that. The epidemic is the real issue at the moment.'

'But there's nothing we can do about that. It's very frustrating not being able to do anything at all for the boys, but I've thought and thought about it, and there's absolutely nothing we can do. Except worry.'

'We're all thinking about them, Jill.'

'All we can do is keep checking that they're not on the critical list. And what do we do if they are? Worry a bit more?'

'But there might come a time when there is something we can do; so what we should be doing now is keeping as up to date as possible with what's going on. Where can we get hold of a radio, or a telly?'

'We could all go to Auntie Alice's. I'm sure she wouldn't mind. In fact, she'd be glad to see us. I don't think she'll be much bothered that we've come to see her telly, not her. If we all went round without an ulterior motive, she'd be worried what it was! And it's stopped raining.'

'Come on then. And everybody try to think of Tony's innocent way to check Brian's story.'

'It does feel bad, to be so suspicious of Brian.'

'It doesn't hurt him – I think he'd expect it. And it doesn't feel nearly so bad, to be so suspicious of a policeman!'

Laughter.

Auntie Alice was very pleased to see them, and to be introduced to Cathie and Tony. She laughed at Jill and Cathie in Mike's things. She showed off the new decorations, and gave them all tea and cakes.

She's always got fresh cake, even when she's not particularly expecting anyone. Half her diet must be cake when no-one comes round for a couple of days.

Every channel on the telly seemed to be totally obsessed with the epidemic: they didn't have to change channel very often to keep to the subject. But extracting any solid information was like looking for needles in a haystack. In three hours more or less all they learnt was:

The number of sufferers was increasing all the time. Every town in the country was now affected to some extent. Several hundred people had now died despite care, mainly in the London area. The Government had declared a state of emergency, and all unnecessary traffic was prohibited: essential foodstuffs and medical supplies and very little else was to be permitted to travel. Most businesses were obliged to close. Following the observation that many dogs were also becoming sick, all stray animals were to be shot on sight and incinerated.

'That'll keep Brian busy!'

All pets were to be kept indoors, and handed over for destruction at the first signs of illness. No real progress had yet been made towards finding the cause, the means of propagation, prophylaxis, or a cure.

Little wiser, and much more worried, they made their various ways home.

'I'll pick my clothes up sometime tomorrow, if that's okay, Mike. We'll not be opening, I don't suppose, so I've the whole day to kill.'

'Of course, Cathie. See you tomorrow.'

No-one had had another thought about Brian's story.

Chapter 6

When I awoke, it was daylight. Or at least, the lighting wasn't dim. I had a vague recollection of a dreadful dream, but the only thing I could remember was the dreadfulness of it.

My memory of reality, when it came to me, was much clearer, and quite as bad.

It's not so much what I know about reality that's bad, as what I imagine. My own weird environment seems secure enough, if a bit spartan. But what's happening outside?

I'm ready for breakfast. I wonder if the next lot of turnstiles are unlocked yet?

I realized that I was jumping to the conclusion that my new world consisted of three or four halls, divided by turnstiles and serving hatches.

Where the first hall had had two sets of five toilets, this hall had two sets of five showers in addition. There were queues for all of them.

No-one else seemed to be ready for breakfast.

I walked across to the exit passages. I noticed that most people were lying in their sleeping bags, some asleep, many talking quietly to their neighbours. Very few couples had zipped their bags together, but many of those still asleep were snuggled together in their separate bags. In the 'daylight', and with nearly everybody lying down, the hall didn't seem so huge; but there seemed to be an awful lot of people.

'Your watch needs mending, old chap. What time do you think it is? Or don't you understand English?'

'I am English. It's eight fifteen. What are you talking about?'

'Didn't you hear the announcement last night? We move on between nine and ten thirty.'

'I must've been asleep. I was wondering if anyone was ever going to tell us anything. What did they say?'

'Not a lot really. Just that there are four sectors, and that food is issued each time as we move from one sector to another. We move between nine and ten thirty, between two and three thirty, and between seven and eight thirty. If you didn't hear the announcement, or at least hear about it, how did you know to come through?'

'There had to be somewhere to get food, and there was nowhere else to go.'

But that chap who went through just before me didn't seem to have heard. And there wasn't a queue. And I was one of the first through. I reckon they opened the turnstiles, and I was through, before the announcement.

But I didn't say anything about that.

'They didn't say anything about why we're here?'

'That's pretty obvious, surely? I'm Will, by the way. What's your name?'

'Pete. What were you doing here? You weren't on our plane, were you?'

'I'm here for the Swedish Timber Conference. I'm a sales rep for a builder's merchant in Manchester. Don't you know about it? There's about a hundred and fifty of us here, from all over Europe. What plane's this you were on, anyway?'

'We were flying from Glasgow to Helsinki, and had to do an emergency landing not far from here.'

'So you know more about what's happening up there than the rest of us. We were just woken from our beauty sleep and hustled in here without a whisper about why. Not that it isn't obvious.'

'No, no. Our emergency landing had nothing to do with the war. Just something wrong with the plane. They brought us here by coach, to stay the night. They were going to get us another plane for this morning.'

But neither of us wanted to chatter much. We lapsed into a contemplative silence. I sat down with my back against my bag. Visions of Burnfield, devastated, came into my mind. Scenes from 'After the Storm'. Kissing Cathie in the disused tunnel.

The day before yesterday.

Will I ever see Cathie again? Or Mike, or Jill, or June?

At least no-one's likely to zap Burnfield, or bomb it directly. But are there any shelters there? Is there room for everyone? Who will find their way into them, and who won't?

What will the world be like when we come out?

When will we come out?

Queues had formed by the exit passages. Will had gone. I looked at my watch. It was nine thirty.

I looked around. The hall was noticeably emptier.

I joined a queue. I was about fifteenth or so, and it took less than five minutes to reach the turnstile. A paper carrier appeared in the serving hatch, and I took it and went on.

The next hall was different.

To the left, it looked similar. To the right, instead of a continuing expanse of flat polished metal wall to a corner some twenty or thirty yards away, the corner was just past the last of the four passageways. The next wall curved away from me. There was a crowd gathered at the foot of it, so I couldn't see the wall below a level of about six feet. Above that level it looked just the same polished metal as everywhere else. I wondered what had attracted the crowd. I couldn't get close enough to see at first. I walked the entire length of it, and discovered that it was just a quarter circle, concentric with the outer concrete wall, cutting off a small portion of an otherwise identical hall.

Whatever is so interesting at the foot of that wall, can wait.

I investigated my paper carrier instead. It contained a waxed paper carton of water, a smaller one of milk, a plastic bowl, a snap-top plastic tub of sugar, a similar one of marmalade, and several cellophane packets containing salami, rolls, margarine, cornflakes and tissues.

By the time I'd finished my breakfast, the hall was considerably more crowded. The foot of the wall was still obscured by the crowd, so I decided to tour the rest of the hall.

I'm sure it's just like the other two, though.

There was a queue at the toilets, and this corner had no showers.

There was only one other difference: there was no steel-doored entrance in the concrete wall.

That set me thinking again. *There was an entrance into Hall Two. So presumably when we came into Hall One, another group of people came into Hall Two, and now they're in Hall*

Four. There could be three groups moving round like that. In fact, I bet there are. So this is only one third of us!

There was a queue at the second set of toilets as well, and no showers there either. I joined it. I rather wanted to change into my towels, but by the time I reached the head of the queue, many people had joined the queue behind me, and I felt obliged to be as quick as possible.

I had the feeling that queues for the toilets were going to be a permanent feature of life.

We're going to have to change our clothes in the main hall. Any idea of privacy is going to go by the board before long.

How long are we going to be here?

I suppose that depends rather on the course of events on the surface. Why doesn't anyone give us any news?

Back into the hall. From the toilet corner I couldn't see whether the convex wall was yet accessible, so I walked over to it. The crush was beginning to lessen.

I looked back to the entrance passages. No-one was coming out of them. I watched for a few seconds, and still no-one came. I looked at my watch. It was still only ten fifteen, but we all seemed to have come through.

Gradually I worked my way to the wall.

I couldn't really understand why people were taking so long studying it.

Every few yards along the wall, there was a small hatch, with a ramp at the back of it leading up into darkness. Below the hatch, a rectangle of the wall was marked off by a narrow crack in just the same way as the toilet doors. I pushed at it on every edge, but it didn't open. There was nothing else to see.

There was no indication whatsoever as to what it was all for.

By lunchtime I was bored out of my mind. I hadn't felt like talking to anyone, and no-one had approached me, either. I hadn't felt like investigating any of the mysteries of the shelter: I felt there'd be plenty of time, and anyway, I couldn't think how.

I didn't even have a pen and paper to record my thoughts and impressions. I kept thinking about Burnfield, and my life there. How little I'd thought I had there, and how much I missed it.

Two o'clock. A substantial proportion of the people were in the queues at the exit passages. I'd been there some while, and wasn't far from the front.

Funny how we form one queue for five lavatories, all down the wall, yet we form four separate queues for these passages, straight out across the hall. I wonder what the psychology of that is?

Another paper carrier. Hall Four was just like Halls One and Two, except that the steel entrance doors were now in the furthest corner. Like Hall Two, this one had showers.

It was interesting to see the hall well lit but with few people, a combination I'd not seen before, giving a much clearer impression of the place. Still utter blackness above the lights, apart from a few feet of gloomy wall.

There was a book in my paper carrier, in addition to lunch: 'The Orion Crusade', by Anthony Wissall. Flicking through it, I got the impression it was fifth rate SF. *But I expect I'll read it sooner or later. There's nothing else to do.*

A realization suddenly struck me: *It's in English! How did they know?*

They didn't. It was pure chance. Just as I was finishing my lunch, the Blunts appeared.

'Hello, Pete! How are you doing? What was your consolation prize?'

It took me a moment to realize what he meant.

'Hello, Harry. Hello, Irene. Hello terrors. Oh, some SF or other. Not an author I've ever heard of. What did you get?'

'In English? You're the lucky one! We got two books, one in German, and one in Finnish. We wouldn't have known, but a Finn swapped the Finnish one for an English one for us, and told us that the other was German. Ken got a jigsaw puzzle, Graham got a pack of cards, and Leon got a teddy-bear. He's furious, and trying desperately to find someone to swap with.'

So it allows for size, does it? I suppose it has to. I wonder how? I suppose the food and water probably depend on your size, too.

Obviously the clothes did! They may be the sort where size isn't critical, but imagine Leon in the ones I got!

But the psychology of random presents seems right: it encourages us to mix, in search of swaps.

That afternoon I read 'The Orion Crusades' from cover to cover. It wasn't exactly profound, but it was absorbing enough to stave off the boredom.

I suppose there'll be a few like this doing the rounds. I wonder if Harry's got rid of his German one yet?

By the time I'd finished, the hall was half empty. I joined a queue, and was soon back in Hall One, with a bag of supper. Supper was rather more generous than the other meals had been, and I put half of it away in my insulated plastic box, for an early breakfast.

Harry appeared. He had managed to get rid of his German novel. He was very pleased with himself: he'd acquired a travelling chess set.

I decided that the best way to avoid having to suffer his running commentary was to put him off playing chess with me altogether. I studied every move very carefully, without regard for the clock, and made absolutely sure of trouncing him.

Two hours and three victories later, I decided it was bed time. I was one of the first to do so, although a few people were lying in their sleeping bags reading.

Harry'll think I'm the sort of dreadful bore who takes chess much too seriously, can't bear to lose, and doesn't care about his opponent getting bored.

But then, I don't care if he does think that. The idea was to put him off playing chess with me.

But I hope he doesn't spread me a reputation.

I woke in the middle of the night with a desperate need to go to the lavatory. I got up and packed all my things away. It wasn't so much that I was afraid anyone would take anything, as that I was afraid I wouldn't be able to find my little pile again, among so many similar piles. Especially in the gloom. When I'd gone to sleep the lights had been bright; now they were dimmer than I'd ever seen them. In each of the lavatory corners, one was a little brighter. With almost everyone asleep on the floor, I could see the walls all the way round.

There was a queue for the toilets.

Four in the morning. We've been in here just over twenty-four hours, I think. Twenty-four hours ago we were in this same hall. In another twenty-four hours we'll be asleep in Hall Four. Round and round and round. What a life! For how long, I wonder? Three weeks? Six months? Years? Why don't they tell us?

Perhaps they think we're better off not knowing.

Perhaps they don't know themselves.

How long will the food last?

The queue for the toilets wasn't very long, fortunately.

Finding myself a place among the bodies, I noticed that they were clustered in an interesting way: family groups – presumably – all snuggled right up to each other, separated from the next family group by a space just wide enough to walk down. A few individuals with a narrow space all round. *I'll be one of those.* The whole assembly forming a super-group of ten or twenty families, with wide expanses of floor separating the super-groups.

Chapter 7

On Thursday morning, Mike, washing himself, noticed that his hands had red blotches all over.

This I don't believe. I've had the 'mild form' already.

But he didn't have a rash anywhere else, and he had neither diarrhea nor vomiting, so he thought he oughtn't to bother the beleaguered health authorities. He was a bit worried though.

What right have I to be worried for myself? Jill's brothers could be at death's door for all I know.

He couldn't stop himself thinking,

In fact, perish the thought, they could be dead. 'Several hundred people have died, despite care'; 'there is no cure in sight at the moment.'

But at least it's only several hundred, and there's probably a million or more cases by now.

That thought is worth remembering. It might come in handy for reassuring Jill.

He was just making himself his morning cup of tea when Tony knocked at the door.

'Morning, Tony. You're just in time for a cuppa.'

'Thanks. I need it. Just been taking Angie and Steve down to Carr Syke first school. They look awful. I've brought Steve's radio.'

'Let's have it on then.'

'I'm not sure you'll want to. The death toll at the last count was about half a million, but she said they couldn't really say exactly because the figures from some places were several hours old.'

'They're not pulling any punches, are they! I'm quite surprised the government hasn't suppressed some of that kind of information to prevent panic reactions.'

'So am I. But I think everyone's too stunned to know what to do.'

'I know how they feel. I hope they find a cure soon, and I hope Jill's brothers are all right.'

How many cases are there now, if there's half a million dead? My reassuring thought sounds a bit hollow now.

'Hey! Look at your hands! You've got it too!'

'I don't know. I've got no rash anywhere else, and I've not got diarrhea or vomiting. Perhaps this is the second stage of the mild version.'

'The people who are dealing with it might have seen it before, and know if it's serious.'

'They don't know much at all. They can't cure it yet. I feel fine. I don't want to bother them.'

'Mmm. They're still saying this morning that 'there's no cure yet', but the Ministry of Offence labs are supposed to have isolated a virus, and they're hoping to have a cure soon, or at least prophylaxis. It seems that quite a number of people are recovering, but that they're keeping them in for observation at the moment.'

'I'd like to go round and see Jill. She'll be in a hell of a state about David and Adrian. But I'm expecting Cathie to come round sometime to pick up her clothes.'

'I don't know where she lives, or I'd pop them round and then join you at the Js'.'

'I don't know either.'

'Pin up a note for her with the Js' address, and we'll take her clothes with us.'

But the Js were not at home.

'We'd have met them if they'd been on their way to my place. They'll have gone down to the hospital to see about the boys.'

They couldn't see them at the hospital, but there was a fantastic confusion there, and they couldn't be sure. There was a large circle, clear of people, around a dog that was lying in the middle of the road, coughing up blood. Great patches of its coat had fallen out as well.

'I wonder how long before they clear that up? I wonder if there's any evidence that it's any more infective than the relatives and friends that many of these people were living with up to the moment they brought them into hospital?'

'I doubt if it's any worse. But clearing the mess up makes it look as though the authorities are doing something. It's probably reducing a few other health hazards, too.'

'Perhaps the Js have gone round to your place from here – they'll surely turn up sooner or later anyway.'

There was another bit of paper pinned on the door. It was a very brief note from June saying she'd be at Auntie Alice's. They wondered if Cathie would remember where that was. It was one thing to put up the Js' address for all to see, but Auntie Alice might not like it.

They eventually decided to put the address but no name. You can get addresses without names by looking at street signs. But why a note just from June? Where's Jill? Mother's? Asking about the boys? I hope she's not sick!

But she was. They found June glued to Auntie Alice's telly, with a very long face.

'Jill was red and blotchy all over this morning, and feeling sick. Then she suddenly got the runs. I practically had to carry her down to East Park Upper school. At least there wasn't any blood, but there's still no news of a cure. I asked the volunteer who admitted her if Jill would be able to find out how her brothers were, and he said, 'perhaps, it depends whether anyone can find the time.' I found out, but now I can't get a message to her.'

'How are they?'

'Hopefully, recovering. They're both on the 'recovering' list. No personal details, but it apparently means they're probably very weak, but succeeding in keeping food down, no rash, pulse and temperature normal, and not suffering from dehydration. Might still have the runs a bit, but no blood in it.'

'Well that's some consolation anyway. It's nice to have personal experience of someone recovering. Our circle's luck so far has been pretty lousy, unless fifty percent is the current casualty figure. I had to take Angie and Steve in this morning, June.'

'Bad?'

'Typical, by the sound of it.'

'Mike! Your hands!'

'Yes, I know. But nowhere else, and no other symptoms. Perhaps I've got partial immunity from having had the mild form already.'

'I wouldn't take a chance on a perhaps.'

'They haven't got a treatment anyway. All they're doing is taking care of people who are sick. And I'm fine. I'd feel a real fraud, especially when they're so overstretched.'

'Overstretched is the word. There's two and a half million cases now, estimated...

'So we have been pretty unlucky.'

        ... but it's not quite true any more that there's no treatment. They still can't get rid of the disease, but there are various drugs that interfere with the some of the processes by which the damage is done. Then if you survive long enough, the disease goes away by itself.'

'So now the big problem is supply of those drugs. Is there any progress on how it spreads, and how to avoid getting it?'

'Not that you'd call progress. The Americans say they have evidence that it's an accident in a Chinese biological weapons factory, and that the bug has a complex life cycle of about sixty days, and had spread all round the world before it reached the active stage. They say the Chinese should have warned everyone, to give everyone some extra time to work on counter-measures, in particular making vast quantities of these drugs.'

'And the Chinese say, nearly right, except it was an American lab?'

'Possibly, but the BBC aren't reporting that. The Chinese are calling it ludicrous propaganda, and pointing to the fact that they're no further forward in counter-measures than the Americans. They say that the British MoD labs says it's a virus, that they've no reason to disbelieve it, and that viruses just don't have complex life-cycles.'

'And the Americans say, who says you're no further forward in counter-measures?'

'Exactly.'

They stayed glued to the telly for most of the day, and Auntie Alice made lunch for them and plied them with tea and cake. Mike's hands began to itch, but otherwise he was okay.

Just like bad sunburn. I wish I could go and see Jill. I hope she's okay.

Please be all right love.

Late in the afternoon, while Auntie Alice was in the kitchen making the hundredth pot of tea, June suggested that they should leave before Auntie Alice started thinking about what to give them for supper.

'There's been no sign of Cathie all day.'

'Perhaps our note blew away. It's been quite blowy.'

'We'll go to your place first and see.'

'Then what?'

'Jill and I have plenty of food in the house. I'll cook for all of us.'

But the note was still pinned to the door.

'You don't know where she lives, do you, June?'

'No. Pete would, of course. I wonder how he is.'

'There's no telling. I suppose it's not surprising we've not had a card from him, in the circumstances.'

'The post's still working so far, they say. Not that I've had any mail. But he's only been gone a week.'

'He's due back in three days. If he doesn't hurry up he'll be back before his cards get here!'

'At the present rate, I doubt if there'll be any flights. I wonder how he'll cope, stuck over there? I hope the hotel don't put him out on the street.'

'There'll be a whole party of them. They'll do something for them. I just hope he doesn't get ill. God, I wish Jill hadn't.'

'Mike! She's going to be okay! Adrian and David are recovering. She'll be okay.'

'Sorry, June. I hope you're right. I just wish there was something I could do. I just wish I could be with her, that's all.'

'Anyway, what are we going to do about Cathie?'

'I don't know, Tony. Have you still got your key to Pete's flat, June?'

'Yes, of course. But surely he'll have taken his address book?'

'Very likely, and if he hasn't, I won't be able to find it, and it won't have Cathie's address in it, anyway, because I bet that that's on a scrappy bit of paper screwed up in his pocket. But let's try.'

When they got to the house, it reminded Mike about Jill, and June could see the strain in his face again. She got him organized quickly.

'Here's the key. I'll stay here and start cooking, you two go to Pete's. Come back here, and if she's not got here by the time we've finished eating, we'll all go round there together if you can find the address.'

Pete's address book was on the mantlepiece, and Cathie's address was in it.

I bet he copied it in so's he wouldn't forget it, so he'd be sure of being able to send her a card, and then forgot to take his address book.

After they'd eaten, Mike went up to the toilet and Tony whispered to June,

'Mike isn't taking it so well, is he. He bottles it up, but you can see he's pretty upset.'

'I know. He loves Jill a great deal, you know. I don't think we should leave him on his own tonight. What do you say to the three of us sticking together for the time being? You and Mike stay here.'

'I must admit I wasn't looking forward to a house to myself tonight, myself. And I can't see the Benefit Office hassling anyone much at the moment.'

'I'll ask him later on.'

Half an hour later they were knocking at Cathie's front door. Her little brother opened it.

'Hello. Who are you? What do you want?'

'We've come to see Cathie. We've brought her clothes back...'

A woman's voice, in the house, 'That'll be Cathie's friends.' Then, louder, 'Come in, loves, and sit yourselves down.' She sounded as though she'd been crying.

The little boy stood aside silently, and they trooped into the house. As they came into the lighted kitchen, Mrs Jordan jumped up,

'I'm sure you'd all like a nice cup of tea, wouldn't you? Sit yourselves down at the table, and I'll put the kettle on.' Too brightly.

Mr Jordan was staring into the gas fire. He looked up with a start.

'Oh! Hello, Mike. Hello...?'

'June, and Tony.'

O God, what's happened? Where is Cathie?'

Silence.

Five cups of tea.

Silence.

Mrs Jordan put her elbow on the table in front of her, put her head on her fist, and fought back tears.

'She's dead. Our Cathie. Dead.'

I knew it. I just knew it. The moment we came in, I knew it. I've been thinking all afternoon, 'I hope Cathie's not sick; don't be silly there's a hundred other explanations'. But I couldn't stop thinking she was sick. And as soon as we came in, I just knew she was dead. O God.

'O God! I'm sorry, Mrs Jordan. I don't know what to say.'

'She woke up about six this morning, screaming. She was red all over, and she said the pain in her guts was killing her. Jack had to carry her down to the school like a babe in arms. Then this afternoon a policewoman came round...'

Mrs Jordan's voice disappeared into soft sobbing, and the table shook with her erratic breathing. June pulled her chair round beside Mrs Jordan's, and put her arm round her shoulders; Mrs Jordan pulled her close and put her head down on June's other arm, crying.

Mike was as white as a sheet, staring through the table.

Mrs Jordan's voice had been a trembling monotone, not apparently aimed at anyone. Mr Jordan picked up the narrative almost as tonelessly. He was staring into the fire again. 'She says, 'May I come in? Sit down, Mrs Jordan, may I make some tea?', and she makes us both some sweet tea, us wondering what on earth's going on, and half knowing, and then she tells us. After a little while she says, 'I'm sorry, I've got to go, we're frightfully busy at the moment.' We've just been sat here ever since.'

A long silence. Tony was the only one who drank his tea. After a while Mrs Jordan stopped herself crying, sat up, and felt her cup.

'They've all gone cold! Let's have fresh ones, and drink them this time!'

'I'll get them.'

'No, thank you Tony, it's good for me.'

This time they did drink their teas. In silence. Then Mrs Jordan began again. 'We were still up when she came in last night. We were all watching the telly. She made us laugh, wearing that get-up of yours, Mike.'

'Last thing she said, when I put her down in the reception area in the school, was that you'd probably come round for your clothes sometime. She said to give her love to you all, and to tell you she'd see you all soon. That, she won't.' He was staring into the fire again.

'She said she wished Pete were here, too, Jack.'

'Aye, that's right, she did. She might as well have stayed here, with us, for all the good they did her down there.'

'Don't, Jack.'

They stayed at the Jordan's for about an hour and a half, most the time in silence. They said how they'd not known Cathie very long, but had taken to her immediately. They asked that they be let know when and where the funeral would be.

'The policewoman told us we'd not be able to have a proper funeral, because with so many deaths here all at once at the moment, they're having to dispose of bodies in a lime-pit. She said to talk to the vicar about a service.'

Mrs Jordan got Mike's clothes for him, and they left. The clothes were freshly washed and ironed.

'Thank you all for coming. You're welcome here any time. We'd like to see you.'

Pete'll be devastated. I wonder how Jill is? Oh God, I hope she's okay.

Mike was more than glad to stay with June and Tony at the Js' house. He slept on some cushions on the floor, and Tony slept on the sofa; but they stayed awake talking until the small hours.

'I don't like the sound of this lime-pit business. That sounds like the death rate is much higher than they're letting on.'

'I'm not sure. They were saying half a million this morning, and it'll be more by now. When something like one percent of the population dies in a day or so, it's not surprising they run into difficulties. It's something like two hundred times the normal death-rate.'

'Sometimes, Tony, you amaze me. I wouldn't have a clue what the death-rate was.'

'It's only a rough guess, based on an average life-span of about seventy years.'

Chapter 8

I didn't wake again until about ten o'clock. The hall was practically empty, and there was only a handful of us not queueing for breakfast. All the super-group on whose periphery I had put myself down had disappeared.

I needn't have saved anything for an early breakfast at all. Shall I have this now, and save some breakfast? Don't know what breakfast's going to be. Get it first, and then decide what to eat, and what to put by.

But I wasn't in a tearing hurry to get up. I changed into the towelling clothes inside my sleeping bag. The legs of the trousers came half-way down my shins, and the socks reached almost to my knees. Unisize style.

I was just entering a passageway when an alarm bell sounded, followed by an announcement:

'Ten fifteen! The turnstiles will be closing in fifteen minutes! Hurry up or you'll miss breakfast!'

I wondered if the announcement would be made in any other languages; if they were, I didn't hear them. I thought about what would happen to anyone who did miss a meal; presumably they would then be in a following population. All very well provided it isn't a child, separated from its family. Okay if the child is behind; the family stays back next time, it's a safe bet the child would come, it'd be starving. But if the family is behind?

I imagined a child wondering where its parents were, moving on several times before realizing, or being told, that they were in a following population; staying back once, a few moves after the initial separation, only to find them not there either, because they're staying back twice to wait for it. Then the parents arrive to find the child isn't with the people they all started out with, when they finally catch up with them. I imagined people trying to leave messages for each other, but the whole place seemed to be made in a way which made graffiti very hard to make. Anything else would be hard to make sufficiently durable, or sufficiently easy to find.

You could leave messages with the people in each population, of course. You'd have to spread your message around quite widely, to be sure it got through, but that's the solution. I felt quite satisfied with myself.

I wondered how quickly a divided family would reach the same idea. Some of them, immediately. Others, never. They'd ask for help, or spill their troubles, and somebody would suggest it, though.

It might be interesting to stop back myself, sometime, just to meet the other groups. *I've started to build up a stock of food.*

I expect the cross-section of society in the other groups is much the same as in this one. Different individuals, of course, but I've scarcely met any of the individuals in this group yet.

Plenty of time.

Fully half the people in Hall Two were wearing pale buff towels. Breakfast was almost identical to the previous one.

I was just beginning to wonder how to go about approaching people for a book swap, and wondering whether many other people would have finished their first one yet, when Will appeared.

He too had finished his book, and we swapped. But this morning we both felt more like chatting, and we sat with our backs to our bags, books disregarded in our hands.

It didn't take me long to decide that Will and I were going to be friends. He seemed to see things in roughly the same sort of way that I did, to think about the same sort of things.

Not like my idea of a salesman at all. Perhaps he's not a salesman by nature, perhaps it's just a case of 'any job is better than none'.

Perhaps that's the way it is for most salesmen.

I wonder how many salesmen are anything like my preconception of a salesman?

Will waved his hand in front of my eyes. 'A hundred miles away, weren't you?'

'Mmm. Something like that.' *Probably still a bit vacant.*

We talked about the shelter, the probability that there were three circulating populations, the question of what was below us, and above us.

'A lot of rock, apart from anything else. I was too freaked out to judge how far we came down those stairs, but it was an awful long way. This part of Sweden is famous for excavated caverns in the bedrock – apparently the rock is ideally suited for it, and the Swedes have got pretty good at it. The ceiling of the cavern itself will be way above us, a great big arch, but I'll bet a pound to a penny there'll be a false ceiling of some sort somewhere between here and there, otherwise we'd be getting dripped on all the time.'

'And the drips would be contaminated, at least they would be after a little while. I hope the false ceiling's pretty good. If the water the other side of it's radioactive, I hope it's pretty thick, not just waterproof.

'I wonder why it's so far up?'

'It'll be arched too. Easier to make.'

'The walls go straight up, though, for quite a way beyond the lights. If you shield your eyes from the direct glare of the lights, you can see quite a way up them.

'I'd like to know what those hawsers in the corners are for, too. It's almost as if our whole world was hanging from the ceiling.'

'Not really. They're not in the right places. They're not structural at all. Apart from being too thin, their placing relates to the rooms, not the structure. Just making a wild guess, they're something to do with cleaning the place. If you look closely, there's a slightly wider joint in the floor, dividing off a long narrow rectangle, with one of the hawsers in each end of it. I imagine that every so often, between one lot of folks leaving a room, and the next lot coming in, that section of floor is hauled up on those hawsers. Underneath there'll be some kind of cleaning gear. Just guessing, mind.'

He's looked at our prison more closely than I have. I wonder how he happens to know about Swedish bedrock? Knows more about structures and things than I do, too. Not surprising, being in the building trade, I suppose. Wouldn't have thought he'd have had much to do with this kind of place, though. Hawsers and polished metal walling aren't the kind of thing one associates with builders' merchants!

'I'd not thought about cleaning at all. I suppose the place would get pretty revolting pretty quickly without some kind of cleaning. There certainly isn't a sign of any kind of staff.'

'There could be in one of the other populations, of course. But I suspect that the whole place is a hundred percent automated, like the hotel. Everything seems to be designed with that in mind, and those turnstile-and-serving-hatch arrangements are incredible.'

'Somehow, they know your size. They gave books to adults, and toys more or less appropriate to the ages, to the kids. And clothes are more or less to fit.'

'I think they identify you individually, with the hotel records. Even the books are in the right language.'

'No, they're not.' I explained to him about Harry and Irene's experience. We got on to talking about the psychology of encouraging swapping, and how difficult it would be to ensure that everyone remained sane. We came to the conclusion that it was most unlikely that everyone would remain sane; and we wondered what the effect on everyone else would be when someone did crack up.

'That's possibly a very strong part of their reason for automating everything. The staff would be obvious targets for anyone going off the deep end.'

'But I'd like to see the automatic version of a policeman. Well, really, I don't think I would, at all. I suppose they could be programmed to use the 'minimum necessary force' to restrain someone. But would they be?'

'There's a darn sight better chance of programming a machine to use the minimum necessary force than there is of programming a man to – if you could possibly design a robot policeman, which I'm sure is way beyond the wit of man to do really. But I wouldn't be at all surprised to find that policemen are the one kind of staff there is here. Plain clothes. But I suspect it'd take more than one homicidal maniac to tempt them to show themselves. In a closed community like this, you can only blow your cover once.'

'So our hypothetical homicidal maniac would be left on the loose?'

'Oh, I don't know. I suppose it depends on what kind of other contingencies they've considered. Perhaps they would intervene.'

He thought for a moment, then continued, 'But no, think about what would happen if they didn't, or if, for that matter, there weren't any police anyway. Someone would organize something to deal with the situation. Sort of vigilantes. Or perhaps some tuppeny hero would do the maniac in, or something. Anyhow, the situation would resolve itself somehow. There'd probably be all kinds of emotionally charged debate about whether the tuppeny hero did the right thing, afterwards, or even whether he should be done in himself, as a murderer. But I have the feeling it wouldn't be likely to develop into widespread violence.'

'Oh, I'm not sure. Probably not so many people will crack up anyway. They probably won't be homicidal when they do. Or they'll be restrained before they do any harm.'

'Another possibility occurs to me. Our policemen don't have to be plain clothes. They could be living in another part of the shelter, watching us with video cameras, from above the level of the lights.

'Or the policemen themselves could be up there.'

I suddenly had a vision of ladders descending from the darkness above, and cops descending, notebooks at the ready. Then I imagined that the cleaning staff might do the same thing, between one population moving out and the next moving in.

'Go on then, share the joke!'

My vision must have shown in my face. I described the two pictures that had come to my mind's eye.

'You ought to make surrealist films, you ought. Still, it would be nice to have a look what's above the lights. I wish I could think how.'

Eventually our conversation ran dry, and we began to read. I'd gained greatly in the exchange. 'Of Mice and Men', John Steinbeck. I'd read it once, many years before. I almost felt like keeping it; but then I'd not be able to get any others. And I'd be depriving other people, too.

I'd not be able to get any others. There's a thought. Will there be any more books given out? Or have we received our library?

Will looked at his watch. 'Nearly two, Pete. How say you we try to get through first, and count everyone? I'd love to know how many of us there are. There's no chance of counting people in the hall, but if we each watch two passages, we can count them as they come in.'

'Mmm. Good idea. We'll do it this evening, though. There'll be a queue already, and we'd be nothing like the first through.'

'No, come on. No time like the present. We can guess roughly how many are ahead of us – count the queues before we start going through. We don't need to know exactly.'

We don't need to know at all. But I'll pick up the thread easily enough later, and I wouldn't have finished the book before last orders anyway.

'Okay. Come on then.'

There were about a thousand of us. Times three, probably.

Our dinners were cold. The counting had been slow enough to be deadly boring, but too quick, and too erratic, even to transfer the food into the insulated boxes, less still eat any of it.

'I wish we'd thought of doing that at breakfast time. This is awfully greasy.'

'Or counting people out of the last place and getting ours last.'

'If there's really three thousand of us down here, surely we aren't all from the hotel? I'd love to know who everyone is, and what they're doing here. But I don't want to go round asking people, and draw attention to myself. I'd much rather stay anonymous.'

'I don't know. It's an awfully big hotel. But no, you're right, it can't possibly be that big. But the announcements are only in English. That's fair enough for the hotel guests, they're an international mob, and it's the lingua franca; but if there were a lot of locals, you'd expect them to use Swedish, too. Perhaps this lot are the hotel lot, and the other two are locals. I can't think of anyone I met at the conference, who isn't here.'

'If you already knew some people here, how come you singled me out?'

'I thought I'd give you a try, after meeting you when you didn't know what time breakfast was. You didn't seem to know anyone. And to tell you the truth, all the people I got to know at the conference seemed to be proper noddies.'

So he is an odd man out among salesmen. Were all the delegates at the conference salesmen anyway? Wouldn't there have been architects, builders or civil engineers as well? Shall I ask him about it? No, leave it a while. Get to know him better first.

'Have you finished with that aluminium foil dish? Pass it here.'

I passed him my dish. He wiped it cleanish with a bit of tissue, and then pressed it out flat on the floor. He'd already done the same thing to his own. He folded an edge of each over, locked them together, and made a tube out of it. *Dextrous fellow.* He stood up, put the tube to his eye, and stared between the lights for a full two minutes. Then he sat down again, looking disappointed.

'Can't see a thing. Too much light reflects inside the tube. Ought to be made of black card. Preferably with a belled-out end. Can't see them giving us anything like that though.'

'It took me a minute to cotton on to what you were doing. I jut had a thought myself. How about climbing the hawser in the corner? Just to just above the level of the lights. I reckon I could do it, with my feet wedges into the angle of the walls, leaning back with my hands round the cable.'

'You can try. It'd cut your hands to ribbons, though, I reckon. Put your towel round the hawser first.'

We set off for the corner, the one by the outer concrete wall, for extra grip on the concrete.

Disappointment was almost immediate. There wasn't enough tension in the cable. When I leant back, and put my weight against the cable, it pulled away from the corner. Will bent down quickly and looked at the floor near the foot of the wall.

'Mmm. You've not lifted the floor a fraction, doing that. All the give is at the top end. Can you climb it straight up, without using the walls?'

'No, it's too thin, and too close to the walls. Here, look, I've made an awful mess of my towel.'

'Don't worry, they're not going to put it on your bill. It's only shredded, anyway. It's perfectly clean. You can still use it. I'd love to know how we're going to clean anything, though. Maybe they'll just issue us some more stuff in a day or two, and we'll throw the dirty stuff away.'

'Where do we throw things away? I've still got loads of empty cartons.'

'I've been throwing mine down the lavatory. It seemed the obvious thing to do. Don't they smell?'

'Yes, actually, they are beginning to. But I don't like throwing anything down there. I don't know how they work. I wouldn't want to block anything up.'

'I figured they must be designed for it. They'd have to allow for the possibility that someone would throw almost anything down there. And the lack of any other disposal system suggests that that's where you're supposed to sling things. The only reason I considered keeping a few is as materials for making things, like that tube. But the supply seems pretty reliable. I bloody hope it is!'

'So do I! We're very much in the hands of whoever created this place. Did you know the hotel had a shelter when you booked for the conference?'

'No. It might have said in the hotel brochure that came with all the conference bumph, but I scarcely looked at it. It was obviously a pretty classy place, the sort I'd never dream of patronizing, except that the firm were paying. We still haven't worked out who's in the other two groups of people.'

'There's a few things we haven't worked out. I wish we had a pen and paper. We could make ourselves a list of questions, and rack our brains about how to find out about each one.'

'Mmm. My pen was in my jacket pocket. It's still up there in the hotel. There must be somebody down here who's got one, but somehow I don't fancy going around asking.'

'I doubt if they'll part with it anyway. Would you, if you had one? I wouldn't mind lending it to somebody, but we really want one long-term. I don't know why, but I have a feeling that pens and paper aren't going to be on the menu, either.'

We got into another long discussion about what we thought we might get, and why. The psychological study behind the planning of this place must have been fascinating.

If it was done at all. It could have been all purely conjectural.

In fact, it must have been. How do you conduct experiments about things like this?

Like this! Ugh! The thought made me shiver; the notion of us all simply captured, mass-kidnapped, came to me.

'Whatever's the matter with you? Seen a ghost?'

I shared my thoughts with him.

'I've heard of daydreams, but daynightmares are a bit much. It couldn't be done. Too many people, and people back at home know where we are.'

'No-one knows where I am. So far as the rest of the world's concerned, I was on a plane that never arrived in Helsinki. No problem for them there.'

'Well, I suppose if the conspiracy is postulated on that scale, anyone trying to find us conference delegates could arrive at the offices of the firm who provided the coaches from Stockholm, to find them closed down or something. I don't think they said where the hotel was, exactly, in the brochure. And the pictures could have been any modern Scandinavian hotel.'

I began to think again of the people who would be missing me, if it were a kidnap; and then I began to think about what was really happening to them; and that I didn't really know. I decided not to say anything about it to Will; I didn't know who he'd lost. I wasn't sure if I wanted to talk about my old friends or not, but I certainly didn't want to force him to.

He could well be feeling just the same; we might never know that, secretly, each of us was dying to talk about it. That's the shyness trap.

'And the address we were given, to give to our families, could be completely imaginary.'

It took me a moment to reconnect with his train of thought.

'But that would expose the whole thing as a set-up!'

'I never suggested it could be hidden entirely – that's a bit of a tall order, for three thousand people – but knowing it's happened, and finding the perpetrators and the victims – two different things altogether. I'm not suggesting it's very likely, mind you.'

'It doesn't have to be three thousand people – we only surmise that the rest of them are there. For an experiment in social psychology, the other groups aren't actually necessary.'

'All this isn't actually getting us anywhere...'

'Which doesn't really matter much, I don't think.' I regretted saying it as soon as I'd said it. True as it was, it wasn't very polite, and we didn't need untimely reminders of the futility of anything we were doing. But Will took it in his stride.

'Pete, have you noticed anyone smoking?'

'Not a soul. Now you come to mention it, that's pretty odd, in a crowd this size. It's not as though there were any no smoking signs.'

'Perhaps more people than I thought might have realized that smoking in a shelter would be a dreadful waste of good air. Or perhaps most people's fags are in their rooms in the hotel. Or their lighters. It's a lighter I want.'

'Whatever for?'

'I want to set fire to a waxed carton, and drop it down the loo. Then stick my head down after it and see what I can see.'

'I tried that without a light, but I couldn't see a thing.'

'You didn't let your eyes get accustomed to the darkness then. I could see a bit, but only enough to make me wonder what on earth I was seeing.'

'Go on. I'm fascinated.'

'Just some very faint greenish glows. Couldn't focus on them, or anything, so I don't know how far away. I felt as though it was an awfully big open space, but I couldn't bring myself to shout and listen for the echo.'

'Could be very unsettling for anyone in the other loos, anyway.'

'That was something I wondered about. If it is a big open space, all the loos, within each group at any rate, must go into the same place. But I couldn't see light coming down any of the other toilets. I was looking for long enough, someone must've got up while I was there.'

'Which supports your idea that it's a jolly big space. The floor must be too far away for the light to reach. And you don't hear anything hitting the deck, either.'

'Never thought about that. I wasn't particularly surprised not to hear my own, because I was covering the hole, but you're right, you can't hear anyone else's, either.'

We chatted about the structure of the shelter, and how to investigate it, without actually doing anything further about it, the whole afternoon. We didn't take any notice of anyone else, and if anyone else was listening to us, we didn't notice them.

While we were eating our supper, the eldest Blunt boy came and sat near us. I wondered if he was angling for a game of chess, and asked Will if he played.

'Yes, I play. Not very well, mind, and in the ordinary way I don't have the time. But we're not going to be able to fill all our time chatting about how to find out more about this place. Surely you've not got a set down here, have you?'

'No, but Ken there has, and I'm sure he'd love a game. I'll watch.'

Ken played with us alternately all evening. But it didn't stop our talking, and Ken caught on to our way of thinking very fast.

'I'm much lighter than you, Pete. I might be able to climb the hawser. I'll try after breakfast, when it's properly light.' He suggested making a rope out of towels – 'especially if they do issue new ones when they reckon these'll be dirty' – and lowering Leon down the loo – 'my shoulders would be too big' – to have a look. We didn't think that was such a good idea.

He also suggested that we could go on pulling on the hawser, rather than just pull enough to find out that it gave a little at the top, and see what happens. We thought perhaps it might be good to see what was at the top first.

But he did have the useful piece of information that his father had a lighter.

'He keeps on cursing himself for not picking up his cigarettes. They'd all have been finished by now anyway. But I'll have to tell him what I want it for, and then he'll want to join in and watch too. that means occupying four loos, and waiting for the last one to get a place before dropping the paper.'

'Which seems pretty antisocial, what with there being queues all the time anyway. I haven't actually watched carefully, to see if there's any time of day or night when there's no queue. We could all crowd into a couple of closets, I suppose, but I don't really want to draw attention to myself like that.'

'That's something I thought about after we were talking about three circulating populations, and moving from one population to another by staying behind. I don't want to draw attention to myself in this population, but somehow I feel as though I wouldn't care what I did in one of the others. I'd just come home here.'

'I think I'd want to get to know all three populations first, and decide which one to call home. And by the time you knew all three, I doubt if you could bring yourself to make a fool of yourself in any of them.'

'The other thing is, we've been talking as though we'd be the only ones with the key to the magic door from one existence to another. I can imagine that after a while there'll be quite a few people moving from one group to another, and to all intents and purposes it'll all be just one big population in the end.'

'Anyway, we're surely not going to be down here forever! We'll all be together when we come out, won't we?'

'God knows. God knows where there'll be to go when we come out. I can't see us all catching the next bus home, somehow. Unless it is a psychological experiment, of course. Checkmate. Sorry, Ken, old chap. Your turn, Pete.'

'I think I'd better pack up now and go and find Mum and Dad. They'll be wondering where I am. I'll not say anything about the lighter just yet. See you in the morning.

'Do you want to borrow the chess set?'

'No thanks, Ken.'

'Go on, Pete. I haven't played with you yet. All our other chat'll keep. Anyway, playing chess won't stop us.'

'Go on then. Thanks, Ken. Good night.'

He beat me, but not too easily. We only played one game before we decided to turn in.

Chapter 9

In the morning, the three of them went down to East Park; Jill was on the 'critical' list. Mike was distraught; June and Tony tried to comfort him.

'I'm sorry, no, it is not possible to visit a patient at the moment. No, not at any time of the day for the time being. We can take messages for patients, yes, but not from them. It's a matter of what is practicable with the number of patients we have. We're doing everything we can for the patients.'

Mike had the feeling that his message of love and encouragement would be considered too trivial for them to bother to deliver.

They went on down to the hospital. The boys were still on the 'recovering' list.

'Those two lists are awfully big wadges of paper. I'd love to know how many cases there really are.'

'That's just the 'critical' and the 'recovering'. They don't seem to have any lists of all the admissions, or the deaths. And I don't know how many schools there are in Burnfield.'

'It's not long since you were saying that they weren't pulling their punches, letting us know there were half a million dead. Perhaps really they aren't letting us know how bad it is.'

'Let's go and see how Angie and Steve are.'

Recovering.

The general consensus was that they should go round to Auntie Alice's again.

'But she'll feed us again. We'll be eating her out of house and home.'

'She likes feeding us. But perhaps we should get her something.'

'So she can feed it straight back to us? And if we get her more, to put into stock, she'll just think we're extra hungry.'

'We'll get her something else, for herself.'

'Like what? Everywhere's shut except the food shops.'

They decided to get her two quarter kilos of butter, and a pot of her favourite ginger and orange jam.

'We'll end up eating half the butter, but it's still a treat for her; and she'll know the marmalade's for her, 'cause she only eats it at breakfast.'

The till at Longridge's was operated by an unfamiliar man.

'Before you ask, Barry's critically ill. I'm his brother and my firm's shut for the present. Four-forty-five, please.'

They met Jenny coming in as they left the shop.

'Hello, Jenny. Have you heard about Cathie?' Subdued.

'No. What about Cathie?' Apprehensive.

'She died yesterday.'

'I don't believe it! No!' Jenny sat down on a crate, dazed. 'I've known her since we were little girls. We were at school together. I've been working with her for nearly a year now.'

Silence.

'My little sister Vicky, and my dad are sick too. And Lynne – she's the other waitress at the Britannia. Vicky's critical. Why's it got to be all my friends and relatives? Me and my mum's worried silly. I don't even know how to tell her about Cathie. We didn't even know she was sick.'

'The night before last, she wasn't. It started during the night, her dad took her in first thing, and a policewoman came round yesterday afternoon and told them she was dead.'

Silence.

They had to move aside to let some more customers in. Jenny got up and started to go into the shop. She reeled, grabbed Mr Longridge's brother's coat sleeve, and sat down heavily on the check-out table.

'I'm sorry, Mr Longridge... Oh! Who are you?'

'That's alright, ducks. Are you okay?'

She was pale as a ghost and glistening with sweat. Mike put his hand on her forehead; she was clammy, cold.

'Put your head between your knees, Jenny.'

She didn't seem to hear him; he gently curled her over and did it for her. She didn't resist.

'What's up with her?'

'Shock, I think, and then standing up suddenly.'

'Is there anything I can do?'

'No, I think she'll be alright in a moment.'

'I'm okay now.' Starting to rise.

'You stay down there for a bit... Would you mind getting her a cup of sweet tea?'

'Of course not.' He locked the till and disappeared into the back room. He re-appeared a moment later.

'It'll only be a minute. She had the kettle on already for a cuppa for us.'

'Thanks very much.'

Silence.

Teas, not just for Jenny, but all round.

'Goodness! Thank you. We didn't expect that!'

'Don't mention it. You okay now, love?'

'Yes thanks. I felt awful for a minute. I thought I was going to pass out.'

'You nearly did. Are you sure you'll be all right? Do you want us to walk you home? Where do you live? You sit here and tell us what you wanted to buy and we'll collect it for you.'

They prepared Jenny's mother properly: they sat her down, and June made the tea, Jenny telling her where everything was the while. Then Jenny broke the news.

'It kind of brings it all home to you when it's someone you're so close to... God, I hope Vicky's going to be all right!'

And Jill.

There was a copy of Thursday's Evening Echo on a chair in the corner. Tony picked it up and read it. After a period of silence, Jenny's mother got up. 'Have you lot made any plans about lunch? I've a stew on the stove, that I was making for the four of us before Viv and Mark got sick; and Jenny didn't feel like eating last night. I'll just hot it up.'

They were very grateful, and the stew was very good. 'Mum's stews are always the better for being recooked!'

For a moment, laughter; but it reminded them of why the stew had been left in the first place.

'We'd better go round and see the Jordans as soon as we've washed up, Jenny. They'll need all the emotional support they can get.'

'Before we go to Auntie Alice's, let's get a paper. Yesterday's Echo was very thin, but all to the point. They said the

Government's ban on traffic was depriving them of supplies of paper, but that by keeping the paper thin and reducing the number of copies printed, they could keep going to a week. They actually suggested that customers share their papers!'

But there was not a newsvendor to be found, and all the newsagents were closed. They went round to the Echo offices, but there was a notice on the window, **CLOSED DUE TO STAFF SICKNESS**.

'That doesn't look like an Echo notice to me! Neat block type isn't their style: they'd dash it off with a thick felt tip pen. And they'd put it up on the inside of the window, I'd have thought.'

They peered into the gloom in the office: things seemed to have been left where they were in the middle of working.

'Is there anyone about?' whispered Tony.

'Can't see anyone.' *On a Friday afternoon, in the middle of Burnfield!*

Tony tried to tear the notice off the window, but it was well stuck on.

'Now I'm sure this isn't an Echo notice! I bet it's covering up the Echo's own notice; I'd love to know what that says.'

Tony decided that while the others went to Auntie Alice's, he'd go to see Terry Dobson, an Echo reporter he knew. 'I'll see you round at Auntie Alice's later on; failing that, back at your place, June. Are we all staying there again tonight?'

'I should think so. Mike?'

'Yes.' Preoccupied.

Auntie Alice was mourning her cat. She'd kept it indoors since the threat to destroy all straying animals, but it had died sometime in the night. No previous symptoms, nothing.

'I sealed it in a plastic bag and put it in the dustbin. They said not to bury dead animals, but I couldn't bear to hand it over to be incinerated. The bin men are supposed to have been this afternoon, but there's been no sign of them.'

Surely rubbish collection is one of the last services they should cut during a major epidemic. I bet they're not really incinerating dead animals; I bet they're going into lime-pits. But Mike didn't share his thoughts.

They told her about Cathie, without mentioning anything about lime-pits; and that Jill was critically ill. 'And here am I, grieving about a cat that was getting on in years anyway! Cathie seemed such a nice girl, the once I met her. I do hope Jill'll get better soon.'

It's almost as if she hasn't really taken it in.

She was very grateful for the butter and marmalade. 'I know whose idea these were, but thank you both anyway.'

'Thank Tony too. He chipped in as well. He was going to come round later on. He still might if he's not too long at Terry Dobson's.'

They all settled down to watch the telly. Alan Wilberforce was chairing a discussion between various unheard-of celebrities. Coming in on the middle of it, they didn't know exactly who anyone was. A Ministry of Defence spokesperson was explaining away the apparent conflict between their own labs research and American statements. His explanation was being dismantled, piece by piece, apparently very effectively but quite incomprehensibly, by a Professor Lindale – professor of what, or from where, they never discovered.

'So what you're saying, Professor, is that Mr Waterford is a deliberate liar?'

'Or at least that the originator of his statements certainly is. If you'll allow me to ask him a few questions, I can quickly discover whether he understands the rubbish he's been talking, or whether he's merely following a brief.'

'Perhaps first you'll tell me what you think is the Ministry's motivation for hoodwinking the public over an issue like this?'

'I'd rather pass that question over to your political experts.'

'Dr Clarke?'

'May I first check my understanding of their positions? The MoD labs claim to have isolated a virus responsible for the disease. The US Department of Defense claims that a bug – of unspecified type – with a complex life cycle, is responsible, and further, that the bug is a biological engineering product from China, released not as an act of war but accidentally. The UK MoD reconciles these two positions by saying that the bug with the complex life cycle could be a normally harmless, perfectly ordinary inhabitant of the human digestive tract, but that now it is carrying the virus. Professor Lindale says that this is absolute balderdash, and that neither of the original claims have the ring of unadulterated truth about them. The question of whether Mr Waterford is personally responsible for the MoD's lies is surely irrelevant, except in so far as it may imply that we are unable to probe the Ministry position more deeply than his brief goes. Do I have the picture?'

'That is pretty much the picture I have; I think you have clarified this very difficult discussion admirably. On behalf of our viewers, thank you. Do continue; you were going to tell us what you supposed might be the Ministry's motivation for lying to us.'

'I can imagine quite a few possible motives. To help me choose between them, I'd like to ask a few questions.'

Then they were mouthing silently; and then the picture disappeared. A moment later the test card appeared, and a voice apologized for the temporary fault, saying that Alan Wilberforce would be back as soon as possible, and that in the meantime, here was some music.

June got up and changed channels. Astonishingly, there was a Western on BBC1. The other channels all appeared to be in the middle of continuous News. It was all on the same subject. June and Auntie Alice stared in horrified fascination as casualty figures, county by county, appeared.

But Mike wasn't so interested in the details, and he wasn't sure he believed them anyway. He'd been doing a bit of mental arithmetic, and he didn't like the answers. Unless the few pages of 'critical' and 'recovering' lists he'd seen at the hospital and two schools were wildly untypical, or his estimate of the numbers of such pages in each wad was wild, or those three places had ludicrously more patients than the other schools, then Burnfield had far more than its fair share of cases, without counting the dead and those neither critical nor recovering. Casualties within his own circle certainly ran much higher than they were saying in general. But he'd not heard Burnfield mentioned in the news as a particularly bad area.

The news finished with a report about the war in South America, and how disease casualties were now worse than the casualties from the recent fighting. Both sides were 'drawing back and trying to care for their sick.'

Or simply too many of them are too ill to fight.

Adverts.

Whoever is going to go out and buy a keep-fit machine just now?

Channel change. BBC 2, still test card and music. BBC 1, still a Western. Peak, off altogether. By winding the little channel adjusting screw June was able to get a distant independent, but the picture was spotty and the sound was crackling. June tried to tune in better, and then tried to decipher it for a while. Eventually she gave up; it seemed to be something about a remote tribe somewhere who'd been found all dead except a small child. She tried BBC 2 again, and then back to the adverts.

Auntie Alice went to make a pot of tea.

When BBC 2 finally reappeared, it apologized for the loss of Alan Wilberforce's Hour, and went straight into the news. Which told them nothing of significance. They learnt nothing worthwhile all afternoon. Auntie Alice made them supper, and they left about nine o'clock.

By eleven o'clock they were getting worried about Tony. At a quarter to midnight, he arrived on a bicycle.

'Where have you been? We've been worrying you might have got sick and gone in. You are okay, aren't you?'

'Yes, I'm fine. Get the kettle on Mike, and help me find somewhere to put Brian's bike, June.'

'Cup of tea at this time of night? I'm ready to turn in!'

'We'll be up ages yet. I've got an awful lot to tell you.'

'How come you've got Brian's bike?'

'Easy, easy, I'll get to that. Give me time. I could do with a sit down, and a cup of tea.'

'Have you eaten?'

'Not since lunch. Haven't had time to think about it. Now you mention it, I'm starving. What have you got?'

Mike fried Tony a couple of eggs, and made beans on toast. He and June had a small helping each too.

'Last time we saw you, you were going to see a chap to ask about the closing of the Echo.'

'Mmm. Terry Dobson. Well, he's dead. Tim, his flat mate, found his address book for me and marked the other Echo reporters. Most of them are sick and some are dead. Melanie Downs is the only one I could talk to: she's at home in bed recovering from being beaten up by a gang of BNP thugs a few days ago. She's the lucky one. But she didn't even know they'd closed the Echo down, much less why. But she gave me the names and home addresses of some of the other staff.

'To cut a long story short, I was right. That notice was covering up one that Andy put up, which said **CLOSED BY GOVERNMENT ORDER**. Apparently Geoff Haworth, the editor, got himself arrested when the pigs came to tell him that the Government's order to close all non-essential businesses applied to newspapers as well. The rest agreed to go quietly, but please could Andy stay long enough to clean up so everything wasn't ruined? About the only thing he actually did was put up that notice, and take photocopies of some of the stuff they'd been going to print: he was afraid that the pigs would come in and remove it.

'Well, I was beginning to want to know a bit more about some of the briefings the pigs might have been getting recently, so I thought I'd try and track down Brian. I went round to his parents in Raikeley. Brian is dead, too; he died yesterday afternoon.

'Nothing ventured, nothing gained, thought I. I don't know any policemen, but the chap Brian used to share with is at least as likely as any other to turn out to be decent. So I got his address from Brian's dad. Mark, his name is. I thought, telling him Brian'd talked to us can't do Brian any harm now. And even if Mark won't tell me anything, with a bit of luck he won't tell anyone I was asking.

'I was lucky. Mark was at home, and ready to talk. He said I'd got the luck of the devil, he doubted that there were above half a dozen blokes on the force who wouldn't have run me straight in.'

'What would they charge you with?'

'I asked him that. He said he didn't know, but they'd find something down at the station. If necessary they'd make something up. They don't like nosey parkers. And Exercise Alpha is especially secret.'

'Did he tell you anything new about that?'

'Only that the lucky devils don't seem to be getting sick. They still don't know if there's really a war or an exercise. Some of them have lost wives or kids, and they don't know.'

'Seems a very fortunate coincidence from their point of view. All the same arguments about needing a higher police to population ratio afterwards could well apply even though it isn't a war. And nice for them personally, although I bet they wish their families were in there too.'

'It gets a bit much of a coincidence when you discover that Exercise Alpha happened at the same time everywhere. Mark isn't sure, but he thinks it did. It certainly did in several places. Officially, they're not supposed to tell even pigs from other areas when exactly the exercises are, but he's got a friend in the Sheffield force who didn't quite get in in time, like Brian; and his father in Slough was taken away supposedly on a no-notice training course. And he's got various bits of indirect evidence about other places. There's a little group of them who've discussed it, but he says they don't know what to make of it. None of the others would talk to us, he doesn't think, and none of them have any idea why it is.

'And then, on top of that, he says that the casualty rate in the force seems to be awfully high, much higher than the national, or even the local average...'

'Does he have any figures?'

'No. He just knows about an awful lot of individual cases. I told him, so do we. But he seems to know more, particularly in the police force.'

'Perhaps he just knows more people than we do. He must know an awful lot of policemen.'

'I'm not so sure. He was thinking in percentage terms, and saying more like fifty than eight percent incidence, and more like ten than one point eight percent deaths.'

'Eight and one point eight? It was six point five and one point six at eight thirty.'

'Was it? Which channel? They've been varying a lot, according to Melanie Downs. My figures were Independent, at ten thirty.'

'Independent was off this afternoon. And BBC2 went test-card-and-music for three quarters of an hour.'

'I reckon the figures are all eye-wash – or more like whitewash – anyway. If the critical and recovering lists at East Park, Carr Syke and the hospital are anything to go by, even if every case is one or the other, it was nearer twenty or thirty percent incidence this morning. There's no way to find out about the deaths.'

'Short of digging up the pits and counting.'

'Don't, Tony. It's not funny. So, the authorities aren't telling us the truth. That's surely not news. Would it do us any good to know the truth? Would we be able to bring back Cathie, or do anything to help Jill, or even to improve our own chances, if we did know the truth?'

'I don't know about helping Jill, but I think we can do something about improving our own chances. And we could have improved them more if we'd known sooner. If it's not just coincidence, then someone else must have noticed. I wish I knew what it meant.'

'What, for Pete's sake?'

'Being outside isn't good for you. And especially not rainwater. Cathie, Brian, Jill: out in the rain on Wednesday night. Jill not out for as long as the other two, and she's survived. Mike wrings out the wet things, and gets red itchy hands.'

'They've just about cleared up now.'

'Good. Anyway, having noticed this among my friends, I mentioned it to Mark, and he did a mental tally, and it's the same in the police force. The office chaps are doing much better than the others. The same goes for the Echo staff. And right at the beginning, it was all the kids under canvas, and all the sewage project workers. That's why Mark gave me the bike, to avoid me being outside any more than I had to.'

'But why should being outside or getting wet give you the disease?'

'Don't ask me. But if it seems to be so, I'm not going to experiment with my own life to find out for certain.'

'But surely it must just be coincidence, or they would have noticed, and checked with much bigger samples, and told everybody?'

'Like they give us the true casualty figures?'

'And like they feed us a lot of baloney about viruses and complex-life-style bugs, if Prof what's-his-name's right.'

'But I can see why they might lie to us about the true casualty figures: to stop people panicking.'

'I've heard that before. But they admit that two percent of the population have died, and another two or three percent are at death's door, and that there's no sign of a cure. If that doesn't panic people, nothing will.'

'It's a matter of psychology. One madman on the loose with a gun will panic people; he might kill a couple of dozen people or so at most. June's right: they might lie to us about the casualty figures, or having found a virus, to keep panic at bay. The Americans could easily just be trying to score propaganda points against the Chinese. But why shouldn't they tell everyone to keep out of the rain?'

'And why silence newspapers? I don't really follow the argument for cutting non-essential traffic and business activities at all, since the disease seems to be everywhere already. They're not stopping anything spreading.'

'Nationally, no, but within a locality, possibly. Keeping people at home reduces the chances of it spreading on an individual level. Perhaps that argument applies with particular force to newspapers, with their distribution arrangements. But that still doesn't explain why they shouldn't tell people to keep out of the rain. And a disease which you catch by being out in the rain doesn't sound like one which spreads by personal contact.'

'I find it rather hard to imagine how a disease can be caught from rain. Perhaps it is spread by personal contact, but getting wet through gives it a chance to take hold. Perhaps it breeds in wet skin.'

'That might explain why washing doesn't seem to be harmful. But it doesn't explain why being out a lot is bad, or Mike's red hands.'

'I'm not sure about the being outside bit. The kids in the camp, and the sewage workers were very much in personal contact, and might well have been wet a lot. Mike's hands might have got a lot of it that had been breeding on Cathie and Jill, off the clothes.'

'We're doing a lot of speculation with very little to go on. Generalizing from the particular and all that. Did Mark get anything useful out of any of his briefings?'

'Not really. He's only had general briefings, sort of 'This is the Situation, This is what you should do in such-and-such Circumstances.' He's not been on any special operations, to have had special briefings.'

'Maybe they suspect he might tell someone. Did he know what special operations there'd been?'

'No. He didn't even know about the closing of the Echo until I told him.'

'I suppose another interpretation is that he's not telling us, just wants to *seem* to be on our side.'

'That's another thing that bothers me. They shut pretty well every paper in the country down by starving them of paper. One contrives to keep going for a while, so they squash it less subtly. I bet they haven't done that to many ordinary businesses that've defied the close-down...

'I doubt if many have anyway.'

... and on top of that, Independent blacks out for a whole afternoon and BBC2 has a 'temporary fault' which cuts off the only programme trying to explore any real issues involved in the epidemic. If it's censorship, then it's subtle enough to be unsure about, but unsubtle enough to be suspicious. There must be a lot of people wondering by now. What do you suppose they're trying to hide?'

'I don't know. But if Exercise Alpha really did happen everywhere at once, it sounds as if someone at the Ministry of

Offence knew – or at any rate suspected – that something was about to happen.'

'I bet he's in a shelter somewhere. With his wife and kids. If you're right. But there's a lot of ifs about. I grant you there's a lot of coincidences about, too, though. I wish there was something we could do.'

'There might be, if only we knew what. I wish we knew what the situation really is. I don't feel we're getting anything useful out of the telly.'

'You never know when it might say something useful, so one of us ought to keep tabs on it. Or we should keep in touch with Melanie Downs; she's watching pretty well all the time, stuck in bed. We ought to put our heads together with more people anyway. I'd like to see what it was Andy thought the pigs might try to suppress. I didn't have time to look properly when I saw him. I wish the library was open: I'd love to read up something about public health, and epidemics in general. I don't say I'd become a doctor overnight and solve the whole thing when the experts can't, but it might help to understand the situation better.'

'I think it's time we all got some sleep. We can think what to do in the morning.'

Chapter 10

In the morning, Will and I were both awake early. We lay in our bags and chatted until nine o'clock. Few people seemed inclined to move much before then, but after nine the breakfast queues formed rapidly.

There was nothing in my carrier except breakfast. I didn't know what I thought I needed, it just felt like time for another little something.

I suppose there's a lot of books around I've not read yet. Ought to go in search of a swap. Will and I'll get tired of each other's company before long.

Ken arrived before we'd finished breakfast. I handed him his chess set.

'Ta. I had a brainwave. I told Mum what I wanted the lighter for, and I've got it without saying a dickie bird to Dad. She says he's forgotten he's got it, and she'll just slip it back in his bag when we've finished with it.'

'And Mum isn't the least interested herself, I suppose.'

'Nope. I knew she wouldn't be. She's always keen on my showing a sense of curiosity, but she thinks you're a couple of big babies. She said not to tell you she said that, and that Dad's a big baby too.'

Will took the lighter, and collected all our breakfast packaging into one carrier. I went into the middle lavatory. *At least they're still clean. Is anyone or anything cleaning them?*

I put my head in the hole and put my towel around it to block out the light from behind.

Will's taking his time.

After a while Will's green glows became visible. They didn't have any clear form or any detail. I began to think again about magic doors to other existences; there was definitely a feeling of vast space down there, but it didn't seem to be the same vast space as that under the adjacent cubicles.

Perhaps it's just a very deep shaft, with matt black walls.

If so, Will will see when he drops his papers down. Which he must have done, by now. I'd better let someone else in here.

Will was waiting for me.

'Frustrating, isn't it. All this stuff's non-combustible. I bet the clothes are too. Just at the moment, I wouldn't want to part with the books.'

'We could try my towel, it's pretty grotty already. But I wouldn't want to part with my clothes until we know if we get any more. I hope Ken isn't going to wait for a week in there. He surely doesn't really think you're still waiting for a cubicle.'

He appeared almost immediately. When we had found ourselves a space on the floor some way from the toilet corner, he said:

'What happened? Wouldn't the lighter work? But I saw someone's pee. You can't see it until it's gone quite a way, there's something in the way, and after a bit further it disappears again.'

'Quite likely it's just falling out of the shaft of light. I think the air down there is fantastically clear. The lighter worked well enough. But these cartons won't burn. Let's see if you can climb that hawser, Ken. Where's that grotty towel, Pete?'

Ken swarmed up the hawser like a monkey. It was a good feeling not to be frustrated for once. He disappeared from sight.

'Hey! Can you see what you're doing up there? We can't see you any more! Don't go up too far!' *Or fall. God! What would I say to his parents?*

'Don't worry. I'm sitting on the beam. I can't see a lot, but I can see the hawser all right, to climb back down.'

'What beam? Don't worry, don't tell us until you're safely down again. Come on!'

'I'm just having a rest. I want my eyes to get used to the dark first, to see as much as I can, too.'

'Put your hands on your cheeks then, to shield your eyes from the light from below.' *We're beginning to attract a crowd, talking so loud and looking up. Damn.*

But it was too late. When Ken came down, everyone wanted to know what he'd seen.

At least it's Ken who's the centre of attention, not me and Will. We can't desert him, and everyone knows we're with him, but it's his face they'll remember, and they'll just think he's a kid being a kid.

He loves it, anyway.

We'll let everyone else ask him all the questions. We'll catch him later.

Will had obviously had the same thought; neither of us said a word.

How can I get up there? He's seen quite a lot, it seems, but doesn't know what to make of most of it.

This was obviously becoming apparent to everyone; they were drifting away. I was beginning to think we'd got off lightly, when Irene appeared.

'There you are Ken! What's all this I hear about you climbing ropes? What'd happen if you fell? I don't see a hospital round here, do you?

'And you, Pete, you ought to be ashamed of yourself, encouraging him like that!'

Ouch. You could have told me off in private, Irene.

At least you don't know Will.

I felt about two inches tall. I didn't say a word, and I could feel myself going red. Irene stormed off, towing Ken by his ear. Will and I were soon left alone.

'Come on, Pete.'

Will led me to another part of the hall. *He knows how I feel. He thinks it'll be better somewhere else, with people who weren't there.*

I still felt very wretched. I had the feeling that everyone was whispering about us, all around us; knowing it wasn't really so didn't help at all.

'I feel pretty bad myself. He's gone off with your towel, and we've still got his dad's lighter.'

'That means Irene'll be back, before she gets caught borrowing the lighter. I wish I could drop down a hole in the floor.'

'Hopefully she might be a bit less abrasive next time – after all, she knew what he wanted the lighter for.'

'True. Somehow I can't imagine her actually being apologetic though.'

But she was positively conciliatory when she did find us, not very much later. She had my towel in her hand.

'I've got a book, too. It's absolute rubbish. I wouldn't want to inflict it on anyone else. Maybe it'll burn. If Ken was a bit younger, I'd go into a cubicle with him to watch myself, but I'll wait for his report and yours. I wouldn't want to block yet another cubicle.

'I bet Ken told you I called you a couple of big babies. I'm sorry. I didn't mean it like that. I'm a big baby myself. I'd really like to know a bit more about this place too. I bet Harry would as well, really, but I can't talk to him about it because I've no idea how he'll react. He might be fine, or he might go off the deep end. He's so unpredictable.'

Makes two of you, I thought, but I kept the thought to myself. *Maybe I can see the same thought going through Will's mind. Might mention it to him later – if I remember.*

Will was braver than me, or just a bit less embarrassed about the earlier fiasco. 'I think you're right that sending Ken up the hawser wasn't such a great idea, but I'd still love to know what he could see. I've not managed to think of any way of getting to see up there myself. I tried to make a tube to look between the lights with, but the only thing I'd got to make the tube with was those aluminium cartons, and the light reflected inside it too much. What I need is some black card, but I don't suppose we'll get anything like that.'

Irene reddened. 'I'm really sorry about telling you off in front of everyone like that. I really didn't think...'

'That's okay. You were right.'

Daft bugger, Pete. Don't be such a wimp.

'Oh, I know I was right. But I should have done it quietly in private later.'

'That would have been better, certainly. But your reaction was understandable.'

Will's better at this than I am.

'Tell the truth, I'd love to know what he saw, too. But I can't ask him in front of Harry. Harry doesn't even know about it yet. I'm not looking forward to when he finds out. It's bound to crop up in conversation with someone sooner or later. He'll want to know why I didn't tell him straight away.'

'I can understand why very well...'

'I'm sure you can. But he won't. Actually, if Ken hadn't said, "don't tell Dad," I might have done. I'm glad Ken's got that much sense. I'm not looking forward to when Harry does find out, but it could have been ten times worse if I'd told him straight away, while I was still wound up about it myself.'

'With a bit of luck no-one will say anything. Probably most people within earshot were as embarrassed as we were. They were all asking Ken what he'd seen, no-one had thought about the risks until you arrived.'

Maybe they were all embarrassed. But they can't have been as embarrassed as me, surely? It was me she told off. But the idea that everybody else was embarrassed too, if only a little, was quite comforting in a way.

'I hope you're right. Maybe the biggest risk is that Ken will talk about it to Graham – or, even worse, Leon. Whether they would manage to keep quiet, even if they were asked to, is highly doubtful. I'll try to impress on Ken the importance of not telling the two little 'uns.'

'I'd better get back to them all before Harry begins to wonder where I've got to. He's playing chess with Ken at the moment, but even he might eventually notice I've been in the loo longer than usual.'

Well. She might have all the tact of a bull in a china shop, but her intentions are better than one might have thought.

'That's a turn up for the book. I didn't expect her to realize what she'd done at all, much less come and apologize.'

'Exactly what I was just thinking. And that I can be pretty tactless too sometimes – just don't realize what's going on quickly enough.'

'Oh, that happens to everyone. It's a question of how often and how badly. I've not seen you do it yet. She made quite a scene. I can't imagine you doing that.'

'I couldn't imagine her coming and apologizing, either. But she did.'

'True. I wonder at what point she realized it was your towel, not Ken's?'

'He probably told her pretty quick, before they got anywhere near Harry. I think he knows his dad.'

Laughter.

There was nothing to do but chat until lunchtime, and that's what we did. Well, almost nothing. Will realized at some point that the cover of the book Irene reckoned was rubbish was fairly dark, and that if he tore it off he could make a better tube to look past the lights. I wanted to check first whether Irene's assessment of the book was fair. Without reading very far, I came to the conclusion that she was right – or at least we were of the same opinion. That was good enough for Will and he didn't bother to read it at all before he tore the cover off, but he still couldn't see much past the lights.

We agreed we should wait for Ken before trying to drop burning pages down the loo. 'We've got enough to do it more than once, but we shouldn't occupy the loos unnecessarily too often.'

I reckoned it was fairly certain that the book would burn okay. 'They can't have had them specially printed on fire-retardant paper, surely?'

'No, but they could have treated normal books.'

They had, but we didn't discover that for a couple of days, when Ken next sought us out. He told us that his mum had said we should keep the lighter. 'Dad thinks he must have dropped it in the hotel. And you never know when you'll find a use for it. More likely you than me or Mum.'

Chapter 11

June and Tony walked round to Melanie Downs's flat after a late breakfast. Mike took Brian's bike to do the hospital round, finishing with East Park Upper School to give Jill news of her brothers.

Angie and Steve were still 'recovering', so was one of Jill's brothers, Adrian. David had been discharged.

'Does that mean he's a hundred percent okay?'

'Not really. But they'll be able to look after him just as well at home, and we need the space for serious cases.'

'He should be all right in a few days then?'

'No-one knows. The experts think the disease itself is finished in cases like this, but they don't know how quickly the body recovers. I don't know how much they know, but it's not a lot, certainly. It's a new disease, you see, and its full life-cycle isn't known yet.'

Jill was still on the 'critical' list. Mike left her a message about Adrian and David. He was a little puzzled why they didn't transfer the worst patients to the hospital; he couldn't believe that the temporary facilities at the schools were as good.

'Most of the facilities at the hospital are totally irrelevant. We've got all the drugs, and intravenous feeding stuff, and oxygen, here. A few who get complications go to the hospital.'

Mike popped into Longridge's to pick up some food for the three of them, and some milk. But there was no fresh milk, and the sterilized was two ten a half litre.

'They've prohibited the sale of pasteurized milk for health reasons, and only sterilized milk sealed before last weekend is allowed. The dairies have put up the price, and there's not a lot left anyway.'

Mike bought some milk powder instead.

'You know they're saying to boil all your water for three minutes, as well?'

'No, I didn't. Thanks.'

There were no fresh vegetables, either; and the only fruit were bananas and oranges. They looked old, and the price was out of this world.

He was almost at Melanie Downs's before he remembered he'd been going to ask after Mr Longridge's health.

'Let's have the milk then, Mike. The tea's ready.'

'It's only powder, I'm afraid. And you've got to boil the water for three minutes.'

'I did. Melanie told me. But why powdered milk? Milkman sick or something?'

Mike told him the tale, and Tony led him through to Melanie's bedroom and introduced them.

'Melanie says we can use this place as a base, she'd appreciate the company. And she's not only got a television, she's got a telephone as well. And there's another bike here.'

Mike had noticed the bike in the hall; the two bikes made the passage rather awkward.

'The phone's not as much use as it ought to be. Public figures and powerful people are never all that easy to get hold of, even when you know your way around the ex-directory system; but this last week they've been downright impossible, most of them. On top of that, very few people are at work. And on top of that, I keep getting crossed lines, number unobtainable, engaged, or just plain silence. I've not even been able to get through to my sister in Nottingham.

'Perhaps it's not so silly to think someone knew beforehand. Perhaps they're all in shelters.'

'Mmm. I doubt if my sister is. You were telling me about Exercise Alpha, Tony.'

June was on Telly Watch. Only BBC1 was showing a program. The other channels all simply bore a printed message:

BOIL ALL WATER FOR THREE MINUTES.
COOK MEAT VERY THOROUGHLY. MEAT OF
DOUBTFUL FRESHNESS AND ALL DEAD OR SICK
ANIMALS SHOULD BE GIVEN TO HEALTH PATROLS
FOR DESTRUCTION. AVOID UNNECESSARY
HANDLING AND WASH THOROUGHLY AFTER
HANDLING.
IF YOU SUFFER A RED RASH WITH DIARRHEA OR

VOMITING, GO IMMEDIATELY TO THE NEAREST HOSPITAL OR EMERGENCY CLINIC.

'I'd like to see what it was that Andy thought the police might want to suppress, too. Andy'd be a good person to get our heads together with, anyway.'

'I'll go round there now, and invite him round here.' Exit Tony.

'If we're all going to stay here for the present, is there anything you'd like me to fetch from your place, June? If you'll give me the key, I'll get my sleeping bag, and Tony's. I'm going to my place, as well, to see if there's any post, and bring everything out of the fridge, and a few clothes.'

'I'll come too. You'll be hopelessly loaded with the stuff out of our fridge as well, and I'd better get my own clothes. Melanie won't mind keeping telly watch for an hour.'

'I'm used to it by now!'

'But there's only one bike left, and until I hear any other theory with more to commend it, I'd rather we accepted Tony's, and stayed indoors as much as possible.'

'You take the bike to your place, Mike; then you take the bike June, and go to yours. There's a set of pannier bags on the shelf over the door in the loo, Mike. June'll need them even if you don't!'

On his way over to Quarryside, Mike met his first Health Patrol. They had a Burnfield District Council lorry, and a machine for sealing plastic bags. One of the men was carrying a rifle, and they were all wearing plastic gloves and lint face masks. The truck was half-full of plastic bags. A woman wearing yellow rubber gloves was emptying a dish of mince into a bag that was already half full. Another woman was carrying a yowling cat by the scruff of its neck. The man with the rifle produced a pistol-like instrument from his pocket, and put it to the cat's head. There was no sound, but the cat stopped yowling and went limp. It went into the sack.

Mike got back on the bike and cycled on.

No post. *That's no surprise.*

Melanie had seen the humane killer before. 'It's spring loaded. A hypodermic needle shoots out – hardened steel, goes straight through the skull – injects a few millilitres of air under pressure into the brain, and retracts. Kills a cat instantly. Not always as quick with a dog, they say.'

June was back again, and they were thinking about lunch, before Tony got back. He was in considerable distress.

And I thought he was such an unemotional character. He wasn't much shaken – not to show, anyway – even at the Jordan's, when they told us Cathie was dead.

They eventually got his story out of him. There'd been no answer at Andy's, and he'd just been leaving, when he noticed the light was on in Andy's room. Perhaps he'd just left it on the previous night, gone out, and stayed at someone else's place for the night. But it was odd enough to make Tony try the bell again, and then to climb the porch, and along the window sills to look into Andy's room. Andy was sitting at the table, with his head on his arms, shaking visibly. Tony banged on the window repeatedly, but there was no response. At first, he didn't know what to do.

'I decided to try to raise one of the other people in the house, and hope that Andy's room wasn't locked. But no-one answered, and in the end I broke in. There was an awful smell in the room, and Andy wasn't conscious at all. His breathing was very irregular, and he was twitching and shaking. I lifted his head up. It was quite limp. His eyes were shut. Then I saw the source of the smell: he'd had diarrhea in his trousers, it was all over the chair and there was a pool of it on the floor. I had to go to the loo to be sick; when I got back Andy had stopped breathing. He hadn't a pulse either. I tried to give him the kiss of life, but when his pulse hadn't come back after ten minutes I gave up. It's one thing when you hear someone's died; it's quite another when you give them up for dead yourself.'

He'd gone to the nearest school and told them, and they'd said they'd get a health patrol round to clean up as soon as possible. They took a note of the address, but didn't seem to be interested in any other details.

There's going to be an awful lot of 'missing – presumed dead' cases after this is all over.

'I'd washed my mouth out pretty thoroughly at Andy's after trying to revive him, but they gave me a mouthwash of some pretty foul-tasting stuff, and told me to have a bath and change my clothes, and wash them as soon as possible.'

'The switch to put the hot water on is to the left as you go into the kitchen – that's it June. There's a launderette in Alma Road about two hundred yards away. If you don't mind, there's some of my stuff too – it's been festering for a week now. It's in a basket in the bathroom.'

'I'll take them while you bath, Tony. There's some of my things in that plastic bag you can wear until you get your own. Hasn't anyone been looking after you this last week, Melanie?'

'Sort of. Mrs Halstead from downstairs has been coming up to feed me. But I didn't want to put her out too much. She's been a dear, helping me wash, as it is. The poor old lady went into hospital the day before yesterday. I can't tell you how pleased I was to see Tony, even though I didn't know him from Adam. I thought the other Echo staff must've been run off their feet because of the epidemic, when none of them came. I couldn't get through to the office at all – always engaged. Come to think of it, that's odd. When did you say it closed down, Tony?'

'The last issue was Thursday. I don't know when the police came.'

'I suppose that a lot of people might have been trying to ring them yesterday.'

'I'm an idiot! I never thought to look for those photocopies! I'll go back now, while the water heats up.'

He'll get himself all stewed up again. 'I'll come with you.'

'No sense in two of us going in there. I'm going to have a bath in a minute anyway. Don't worry about my state of mind – it won't be any worse than it was before, and I survived that.'

He was back in twenty minutes. 'The clean-up squad wouldn't let me near the place. I'm going back tomorrow when there's no-one there.'

'I'll cook something while you bath. Don't go to the launderette till after we've eaten, Mike, you'll take ages.'

Mike and Melanie watched BBC2 – which had come back to life – until Tony and the lunch appeared, almost simultaneously. Cases, and deaths, were supposedly rising steadily; but they no longer believed the figures at all. They were much too low.

After they'd eaten, June took a bike and went to see how Auntie Alice was. Tony went off to his house to pick up some clothes and any food there was there. Mike left Melanie on Telly Watch, and went and found the launderette. It was empty, but open.

A little girl went by on a bicycle, singing. It gave Mike a better feeling than he'd had for days. He almost felt guilty about it. *I wish I could be with you, Jill. Please get better – soon!*

Then he realized that it was the first child he'd seen out and about since Wednesday, despite the good weather there'd been for the last couple of days. *In fact, it's been pretty quiet altogether, apart from just outside the hospital and the schools. And nobody's singing.*

I wonder what that lass had to sing about? Some kids are irrepressible, thank God.

Transferring the washing to the drier – they'd discussed the merits of hanging it out to dry, and decided not to take unnecessary risks, however intangible – Mike noticed heavy bloodstains, which the washing had failed to remove, on several of Melanie's things.

Tony was in the kitchen making a pot of tea when Mike got back with the dry clothes.

'They weren't playing games when they beat you up, were they, Melanie! Couldn't get the bloodstains off some of the things. And there are holes torn in some of them, did you know?'

'It tells you something about some of the Burnfield police force, that I've got them back at all. If I'd been an average member of the public, and they'd not been BNP thugs, my clothes would've been exhibit B, after the photos of my injuries. But the police say they haven't a chance of catching the bastards.'

'They haven't if they don't look.'

'Exactly. I reckon two of them were casualty cases themselves, or at any rate will have had to see a doctor. I'm sure I bust a nose pretty badly, and possibly an arm, before they got me on the floor.'

'What were you doing to upset them so much?'

'At the time, absolutely nothing. But I've written a few things about the BNP in the past, and put my own name to them, like a fool. I think they'd discovered that I sometimes go for a jar with Tony and Geoff, and that I walk home alone. They'd probably got a spy in our pub. They waited till I was halfway along the alley up from Alma Road, and then came in two from each end. I screamed like mad, but no-one came until after they'd run off. Bloody cowards!'

BBC2, which had been singularly boring anyway, went blank for a moment, and then the printed message reappeared. It hadn't changed. Mike searched the channels. They were all the same.

'If you twiddle the channel tune you can usually get Tyne Tees. Reception's not bad up here.'

The picture was a bit obscured by a herring-bone-weave pattern, but the subject matter seemed most interesting. 'Hey, Tony, come on through! Gordon Waters is talking about viruses!'

'There'll be tea in a moment. If I miss anything, tell me.'

They'd all missed the first part, of course, and some of what Waters was saying went over their heads. The summing up could scarcely have been clearer:

'The cell damage that we've been seeing here at Newcastle University, in tissues from several different species, is very like that caused by radiation or certain kinds of toxic chemicals. So far as anyone here knows, no-one has ever seen this kind of effect from any virus, but they know of no reason why it isn't possible in principle. They haven't been able to find a virus; but looking for a virus is notoriously difficult and slow.

'We've failed completely in our attempts to talk to any of the Ministry of Defence team who are supposed to be working on the virus. The Ministry of Defence intercepts us at every turn. I doubt if I'm supposed to have told you that, but I think it's in the public interest to know.

'In fairness to the virus theory, no toxic chemical has been found, either, nor radioactivity. But this kind of effect can be caused by some chemicals in quantities so small that you cannot find them unless you know what chemical to look for. The nuclear facilities available to us here are minimal, and the Nuclear Physics department is closed nowadays, of course.

'We will be back at five o'clock with a study of what is known about the spread of the this disease.'

Printed message, exactly as before. All channels ditto. Tyne Tees was not back with its epidemiological study at five o'clock, or at all.

'I've rarely seen such blatant censorship in this country! What I'd like to know is, what are they hiding?'

'We wondered about that – but I suppose it could be that sickness among the staff is making program production very difficult.'

'They've not even tried to fob us off with that one. Six channels out of six, on the blink most of the time? If they can't make live programs, you'd think Independent would've snapped up a recording of that Gordon Waters thing as soon as it was finished, rather than just show that wretched card. They're scared for some reason. He dropped a clanger – or a hint – when he said the MoD intercept them at every turn. It'll be the MoD that'll have squashed this epidemiology thing. Why, is another question.'

'Presumably they don't want people to know how it spreads. The only legitimate reason I can think of would be to prevent panic, which suggests that they know something pretty unpleasant.'

'Until you know how a disease spreads, it's hard to interfere with the spreading process. The only really unpleasant thing I can imagine is that they might still know nothing, and that all the advice about water, and milk, and meat, and animals is just to make the public think something is being done. They wouldn't want all that exposed as baloney.'

'I think it's got to be something worse that that, Tony. Tyne Tees wouldn't bother to expose baloney at that level. They'd see that kind of lie as a harmless attempt to reassure the public. The MoD wouldn't need to squash anything. And I'm surprised at you, Mike, talking about panic that way. When governments talk about preventing panic, what they mean is preserving apathy. People like them sneak up to the exit in a crowded cinema before they shout FIRE!'

'And then they shout in code, so only their friends can understand. All right, all right, I know the analogy is getting a bit stretched, but you know what I mean.'

'Alpha Alert. And your friends don't necessarily know it means fire, but they know it means get out quietly. Which suggests the MoD did know ten days ago.'

'And that the possibility existed, longer ago than that. But we don't have anything really significant more to add to the evidence for that theory than we had when the idea first came up.'

'But what would the public do, if they did know?'

'That depends rather on what they knew. Since we don't know, it's hard to tell.'

'Well, what do we know? We may be able to read between the lines a bit more than the average member of the public. Get me that file and that pen off the chest over there, Mike, and let's start a file. Then we might be able to work out what else we want to know. Let's start with some headings. Alpha Alert.'

'Being out of doors. Rain.'

'Milk. Boiling water. Freshness of meat. Sick animals.'

'Stopping freight. Censorship. Closing businesses.'

'Virus. Toxic chemicals. Radioactivity.'

'Ah! That reminds me. When he first mentioned radioactivity, my mind did a somersault, but I didn't say anything because I was too engrossed in the program, and then I forgot. In a novel about nuclear war, I can't remember the title, but I think it was by Peter van Greenaway, I've come across your rain-and-being-outside effect before. It's supposed to make the effects of radiation worse, according to him. And the symptoms are similar, red rashes, diarrhea, vomiting.'

'But they couldn't possibly keep a nuclear war secret! They can't even keep a major nuclear accident secret, much as they might like to.'

'Major nuclear accidents aren't like this, anyway. This is far too evenly distributed over the whole world.'

'Could toxic chemicals have the same rain-and-being-outside effect? And the same symptoms?'

'I don't know. But a big chemical accident wouldn't produce a worldwide uniform effect, either. They wouldn't try so much to hush it up, either.'

'They wouldn't be able to if they wanted to. Too many people would be able to find out for themselves.'

'Even with restrictions on public mobility and the telephone system screwed up? I'm not so sure.'

'It's a pity we don't have a C.B., or a short wave to listen to the Radio Hams. There might be all sorts of things being said on the air, and we just don't know.'

'It's not an effective medium for public discussion, really, anyway. Too easily policed. You never know when the authorities are listening in. There's lots of ways they can shut you up if they don't like the things you say. A short blast of a big signal will blow your receiver up, or they come round and impound your equipment for alleged 'infringement of the regulations', or they just swamp you under a more powerful signal of the banal kind that the whole system is so full of anyway.'

'But you could talk for quite a while before they picked you up on a random check and squashed you. They couldn't stop an idea spreading.'

'The kind of discussion we've been having would only get through to a handful of people like us, and they'd already know who to squash as soon as anything important happened.'

'But they couldn't squash news of a major disaster that was apparent to Joe Public.'

'That's an awful expression! Aren't we all Joe Public? You pick that up from your policemen friends?'

Sheepish looks. *Never thought about it.*

At half past six, Mike was in the kitchen trying to work out what to cook, when June arrived with a child in tow. *That's the little girl who was singing, riding a bike. She's been crying.*

'Hello, Mike. Is Tony in with Melanie? This is Linda. She's got nowhere to go. I was sure Melanie wouldn't mind. Put the kettle on – do you like tea, Linda?'

Silent nod.

'You two had anything to eat? I'm just making supper.'

'No. Linda's had nothing to speak of all day.'

June told them all Linda's story over supper. Linda only contributed odd words. She alternated between an overawed and forlorn withdrawal and a desperate brightness.

June had found her sitting on a low wall by the cemetery, resting her head on her arms on her bicycle, crying silently. It had taken some time for June to get anything out of her, but her need for help had been obvious.

Linda's father had been working in Germany, and had been due home a week ago, before the epidemic had started.

But after Exercise Alpha had begun, thought Mike.

But he hadn't turned up, and no word had come of any kind. Her mother hadn't let her out of the house since the very first illnesses were reported, and they'd argued about it. Linda felt very frustrated being shut up indoors and not seeing her friends. She'd thought that her mother wasn't very well, but her mother had assured her that it was only a bit of an upset tummy. Then this morning her mother didn't get up, and Linda went in to her room to plead with her to let her go and see a friend.

'I didn't even ask her how she was. She just said, "You do what the hell you want, Linda".'

'So Linda went out on her bicycle, singing, suppressing a worry in the back of her mind that her mother was pretty ill. She began to get frightened when there was no answer at any of her friends' houses.'

Mike made a note to ask how many friends houses she'd tried, and how many people there were in each family.

You can't do any useful statistics with non-random samples like this, but it would still be interesting. It doesn't square very well with the official figures. It sounds even worse than our experience. But then, we've not talked to any little girls who weren't crying on a wall.

But he didn't interrupt the story.

Anyway, they don't all have to have been sick or dead. Some of them might just have been out. But not many people are out and about these days.

In the early afternoon Linda had gone home. Her mother still wasn't up, so she went into her room. She was lying in exactly the position Linda had left her that morning. Linda thought she was dead. Linda fled round to the doctor's, but there was no-one there. There was still no-one there when the surgery was due to open. Shortly after that June found her. They went to Linda's house; her mother really was dead. They went to Linda's school and reported the body.

'I hope you picked up some clothes for her. The clean-up squad won't let you go back.'

'I brought my mum's purse as well. I've got to be able to buy food.'

She's got her head screwed on, this one!

'That's a thing! I've not thought about it before, but are banks counted as essential businesses? They've not said a thing either way about it on the telly. I'm almost out of cash.'

'Post Offices too, for that matter. I should have a Giro coming on Tuesday or Wednesday. I've almost run out too.'

'They're not telling us much on the telly, not even basic information like that. They never said anything about the milk ban. There'll just be a notice on the Post Office door. They've not said whether you've got to sign on or not. I bet it's cancelled, but it'll just be a note on the door of the employment exchange. I hope they're still sending giros!'

'If the post's operating at all. Most of my money's in the bank, and I'm not due a giro for a fortnight anyway. We're going to have to go carefully or we'll starve.'

'You're assuming they aren't open...'

'You think they might be?'

'Not really, I suppose. But it's not so bad actually. I've got the key to Mrs Halstead's flat, and she's a regular hoarder. She said I could use anything I wanted and pay her back later.'

'Panic buying is the sort of panic I thought the authorities might be trying to prevent.'

'But that isn't panic. It's good sense. Panic implies irrationality, like rushing off in a car, leaving the environment you're familiar with, without any reason to suppose things are any better wherever you're going.'

'I presume it's mainly tinned stuff Mrs Halstead's got? There's another advantage to that. It won't be contaminated. Whether it's a virus, a chemical, or radioactivity, that's worth something. I'm not normally in favour of packaged food, but it has that advantage just now. Any disadvantage it has is only if you eat a lot of it consistently over a long period.'

'She has things like breakfast cereals, rice, flour, dried beans and fruit as well. But the same argument applies anyway. They been in sealed packs since before all this began.'

'But I thought radioactivity could go through packaging and suchlike.'

'So it can. But that's the rays that the radioactive material gives off, not the radioactive material itself. The rays can kill living things, but they don't do food any harm – in fact you can use them to sterilize it. They don't make the food radioactive.'

'That's not quite the whole story, actually, Melanie. They don't make the food radioactive, but they do change the chemistry of some of the food, producing small quantities of a whole range of toxic chemicals. Any quantity of radiation enough to be really effective against bacteria isn't really safe for food.'

'Is that so? It's amazing the things you know, Tony! Are you sure?'

'Pretty sure. There was a lot of controversy about it twenty years ago; they even did it for a while. They couldn't pin any individual cases on it, but the epidemiologists and the cancer experts said that the number and pattern of cancer cases had changed in a way that statistically proved that it was causing thousands of deaths. The lobby in favour of it wasn't as powerful as the tobacco industry, say, so it was banned. The whole thing was kept pretty low-key at the time, but there's enough information around still if you're interested in that kind of thing.'

'Anyway, how's Auntie Alice, June? When you arrived with Linda, I never thought to ask.'

'She's okay. But I'm not sure whether perhaps all this isn't helping to unhinge her a bit.'

'Perhaps I should come with you tomorrow, June. I'll come when I've done the hospital round.'

'That's fine, Mike. But what are we going to do with Linda? I don't think we ought to take her to see Auntie Alice. And I think we ought to go round to Jill's mum and see how David is, so we can let Jill know.'

I've not seen Jill's mum since Jill was taken ill. She'll think I've forgotten her. But I don't know what to say. I wonder how Jill is, what she's thinking?

Chapter 12

As we entered Hall Three for the third time, we received another towelling suit and towel. Then, in the hall itself, an announcement informed us that if we threw our old suit and towel into the hatches in the curved metal wall, another suit and towel would come down the ramp above the hatch. It was only announced once, when only a few dozen of us had entered the hall. Everyone else had to find out by watching or being told.

Neither Will nor I ever got to see beyond the lights, but talking with Ken we did manage to work out a bit about what he'd seen. The 'beam' he'd been sitting on seemed to have been a curved track with a little trolley carrying a winch that could pull the hawser. We guessed that there was another winch – which didn't need a track, but which might rotate a quarter turn in a horizontal plane – to pull the other hawser, but Ken couldn't see that past all the lights. Will was fairly sure that his idea about cleaning apparatus must be correct.

Ken had seen that the lights hung from gantries several feet higher, and that there were catwalks higher still. The walls all continued straight up for a considerable distance, and he couldn't see a ceiling at all, just blackness beyond the catwalks – themselves so dark he could only see them after letting his eyes get accustomed to the darkness, shielding them from the lighted scene below.

We decided to stay back to watch the cleaning process, and saved a bit of food to keep us going; but it wasn't to be. A couple of days later, we ignored the fifteen minute warning that the turnstiles would close. Then there was a ten minute warning. By this time there were just four of us left: Will, me and two big, burly blokes whom we'd seen around but never taken any notice of. Finally, there was a different warning at five minutes, 'Turnstiles will close in five minutes. Do not attempt to remain in this hall during cleaning. Danger of death.'

We decided it wasn't worth the risk. The two strangers were the last out of the hall. They never spoke a word.

Will and I wondered whether they were self-appointed guardians of our group, or whether they were plain clothes officers, but didn't talk about it until later. We decided that they must be official. Would anyone else have stayed back and heard that warning, and then decided to protect everyone else from themselves? And wouldn't self-appointed guardians have said something?

We decided it probably wasn't a good idea to try to talk to them later, ask them about their role: we'd already drawn more attention to ourselves than we liked.

Chapter 13

On Sunday, Mike and June went round to Jill's mother's house about eleven in the morning. David answered the door. He'd lost a lot of weight and looked pale. 'Come in both of you! Cup of tea?'

'Please! How are you?'

'I'm okay, I suppose. But Mum had to go into hospital yesterday evening. She wasn't so good at all.'

'Which hospital is she in? We'll go and see how she is.'

David looked puzzled. 'Which hospital?'

Mike did a double-take. *My God! He doesn't know about the schools being converted into emergency hospitals. Which means that he doesn't know that Jill's at East Park Upper School. Does he know she's ill at all? Hasn't his mum told him?*

Jesus! does she know?

'June, have you seen their mum since (*quick think*) – Thursday? Does she know about Jill?'

'Christ! I bet she doesn't. I've not told her.'

'What about Jill, for Pete's sake?'

'She's critically ill in hospital – at East Park Upper School. I took her in last Thursday morning.'

They explained all about the emergency hospitals at all the schools, and a hundred and one other things he'd missed while he was in hospital. He was shocked to hear the scale of the epidemic, and more shocked still when he heard of all the cases, and deaths, that impinged on them personally.

'I've had a close call, it seems. I hope Ade and Jill and Mum pull through.'

'Are you going to be all right here, on your own...'

'Mike! You can't go offering space in Melanie's flat without asking her first!'

'I suppose not. But I was thinking that we ought to help look after David. He doesn't look very strong yet.'

'Don't worry about me. If you pop in and let me know how Ade and Mum and Jill are every day I'll be more than happy. There's plenty of grub in the house for just one of me.'

He's putting a brave face on it. But he's only a kid. And he looks like death warmed up.

'I'd say we should all stay at the Js', except that we can't move Melanie. And of course we can't move Auntie Alice, either.'

'Now there's a thought! I bet Auntie Alice would be as pleased as Punch to have you round there, David. It would do her no end of good to have someone to pamper.'

'We'd better ask her first, but if she says yes, I'll come back up here and take you down on the cross-bar. I'll come back either way and let you know what's going on.'

'Whose bike is it, anyway?'

That was another long story.

On the way to Auntie Alice's, June suddenly said, 'We ought to go and see Jenny, and the Jordans, you know, sometime.'

'Mmm.' *June's very conscious of people's emotional needs. I'm sure she's right. It's good for us, too – keeps us busy – keeps our minds off morbid thoughts. I feel so impotent, unable to do anything constructive. Not even reduce the risks for ourselves, never mind help Jill or anyone else.*

Auntie Alice was delighted to have David. Mike went to fetch him, and filled the pannier bags with food to boost Auntie Alice's larder. Then he set off on his round of the hospitals.

Jill was still critical, and her mum was critical too. Fortunately she was at the hospital itself, and Mike didn't have to go searching round the neighbouring schools.

June and Mike stayed to lunch with Auntie Alice and David, and then cycled back to Melanie's. The streets were absolutely deserted. Tony, Melanie and Linda were playing Monopoly and watching the telly.

'Every channel is showing old films now, with a break every five minutes or so to show you that bloody card. Beeb one broke off for five minutes to show us white coated scientists hard at work in a lab, 'working on a vaccine'. Not a word about how long it might take to develop a vaccine, or how long it would take to manufacture it in quantity. They didn't even commit themselves as to whether the agent had been isolated yet.'

'I think they're just playing at covering the epidemic. It was just thrown together without any thought at all. The footage could have been shot anywhere. It could easily have been library stuff, years old and nothing to do with it at all really.'

'We're thinking of going round to Jenny's, and to the Jordans. Would you like to come, Linda? They're likely to be a bit sombre, because they've both got death or disease in the family, but they're nice people and there's a little boy about your age at the Jordan's.'

But there wasn't a little boy at the Jordan's; he and his mother had both had to go to hospital. Jenny's little sister Vicky was back at home, but as weak as a kitten and feeling cold all the time, even swathed in blankets in front of a blazing fire.

I bet they're only guessing who's infectious and who isn't. But it would be inhuman to treat her as untouchable, and there's no evidence at all that she's more infectious than anyone else. An awful lot of people have picked it up without any contact with the sick.

Except when asked a direct question, Linda scarcely said a word at either house. But cycling from house to house she was very happy. She'd never been so far on her bike before. Even tagging along with two grown-ups she obviously felt an exhilarating sense of freedom.

When they got back to Melanie's, she told them that Tony had gone round to Andy's on foot, to see if he could get hold of the photocopies. She was expecting him back any time. Mike cooked a meal for the five of them, and Tony was back just in time to eat with them.

'The pigs had been there before me. They'd turned the place over really thoroughly. Not a sign of any of his papers. They didn't care who could tell it'd been done, either.'

'Not expecting anyone to go looking. Anyway, so far as anyone who didn't know what was missing is concerned, it could've been the clean-up squad.'

'Not on your life! The clean up squad had scrubbed the floor and sprayed some foul-smelling chemical. The pigs had emptied all his bookcases, files and drawers, all over the freshly scrubbed floor. I'd have thought it was burglars except that they'd left the sort of things burglars might have been after, and I couldn't find the papers anywhere.'

'I'd like to talk to Mark – that's his name isn't it – about an operation like that. I would imagine it must mean that they've already raided the Echo office and found something that they wanted to disappear. It must've been quite something for them to go out to Andy's on the offchance he might have copied it.'

'I wonder. I bet they've not left a mess at the Echo office, even if they've been there. Think of the stink when we reopen if they have.'

Mike was beginning to wonder whether it was a case of 'if the Echo reopens', but he didn't say anything. *I wonder how many of us are thinking the same things, and not saying anything? The telly is obviously making do with a very thin skeleton staff. Have they been sent home as 'non-essential workers' – censorship – or are they all sick? Or dead.*

Still – our immediate circle hasn't suffered any more casualties recently – cross fingers.

But Tony had to get up during the night, several times, with diarrhea. He had no rash, and he wasn't vomiting, but he felt nauseous and lethargic. In the morning Mike walked down to East Park Middle School with him, wheeling the bike so he could cycle on to ask about all the others.

'Let's got to East Park Upper instead, where Jill is. Then you can check on both of us at once.'

'Don't be daft, Tony. It's no hassle for me to go to one extra place. It's no distance on a bike. But you're in no fit state to be walking at all, never mind further than you need to.'

In the end, they had to walk to East Park Upper anyway, because they couldn't raise anyone at East Park Middle. They could hear someone – a child, they thought – coughing inside, but no amount of banging got any response at all.

The volunteer receptionist at East Park Upper appeared to be in a total daze. She directed Tony towards a door along a corridor, and seemed surprised when Mike was still there when she turned round again. She looks as though she's been on duty for about three days.

'I wanted to inquire about another patient you've got here. Jill Warley. Admitted last Thursday.'

A few moments scanning lists.

'Last Thursday, you said? She should be on the recovery list by now, or on the critical list. W – A – R – L – E – Y Warley, you said?'

'That's right. She's been critical for a couple of days already.'

A dreadful feeling was going through Mike. He felt nauseous and weak.

The receptionist asked him, 'You're sure she hasn't been discharged?'

She'd wonder where we all were! There's no-one at her mum's place, or her place, or my place. She'd be desperate!

She can't have been discharged.

'She was still critical yesterday morning, so she can't have been discharged already, surely?'

'It's possible. I'll check. We're so desperately crowded we're sending people home as soon as we possibly can.'

But the dreadful feeling persisted. *She's dead. I know it. The police gave up trying to tell anyone when there was no-one at her place or her mum's. Jill!*

'She was discharged this morning.'

Mike collapsed.

The next thing he knew, he was lying on his side on the floor with a blanket up to his neck. A man was squatting in front of him looking at him.

'Back in the land of the living, eh? How do you feel? Like a cup of tea?'

Mike felt chilled to the marrow. He nodded weakly.

'Sit down, Ruth. I'll get it. You look as though you could do with one too.'

The man disappeared. Mike started to sit up.

'Don't try to get up yet. Just relax for another couple of minutes.'

'I'm freezing.'

Ruth helped him into an armchair, wrapping the blanket all around him on the way. She sat down on the desk. Mike realized where he was; he was sitting behind the reception desk at East Park Upper. *Jill's been discharged!*

'You did say Jill had been discharged, didn't you? How is she?'

'I don't know. She's just on the discharge list, that's all. Dr Wells might remember her, though. Here he is now.'

Dr Wells appeared bearing three steaming mugs.

'Hugh, do you remember a Jill Warley – that's the name, isn't it? This chap came in to ask about her. Sorry, what's your name?'

'Mike Shaw. Yes, Jill Warley, that's right.'

'Yes, I remember Jill. She'd been unconscious for days, I didn't think she'd live. But she hung on, and came to last night. This morning she was very perky and insisted I discharge her. I had the devil's own job persuading her to have an ambulance to go home. You must've only just missed her.'

Mike started to disentangle himself from the blanket.

'I'd better be going then. There's no-one at her place. She'll try to walk to her mum's, and even if she gets there, there's no-one there either.'

'You sit down and finish that tea. If you start walking anywhere in the state you're in, you'll collapse again, and won't do her any good at all.'

'I've got a bike outside.'

'Even worse. Can you drive?'

'Nope. Couldn't afford the lessons. Why do you ask?'

'Never mind. Just a thought.'

'Goodness! It's just come to me. I ought to tell you about East Park Middle School. We went round there first, and couldn't get an answer. There was someone coughing horribly inside, but the door was locked, and there was no answer to all our banging.'

Hugh and Ruth looked at each other, puzzled.

'I don't understand that at all. The door was locked, you said? No, I can't fathom that at all. We'll send Geoff round to have a look as soon as he gets back.'

'I really had better go and try to catch Jill in a minute. I feel much better now. But before I go, is there anything I should know about looking after Jill? Is she out of danger?'

'I think so, but it's impossible to say, really. We know very little about the disease yet. We can't even tell who's got it and who's got something else, we've no lab test for it. Was it you who brought that chap Tony in?'

'Mmm.'

'He's a case in point. For all I can tell, he's just got good old-fashioned gastro-enteritis. But about Jill: make her rest, keep her warm, and feed her well, fresh fruit and veg if you can get any. I'd give you a chitty for a course of vitamin tablets, but you can't get any for love nor money at the moment. Here comes Geoff now – he might as well take you to find Jill, I'm not going to discharge anyone in the next hour. You can come back with him for your bike when you've got her settled.'

'But what about picking up patients to come in?'

'Our phone isn't working. We couldn't get an engineer to come and fix it: Geoff went down to the hospital and tried to ring for one, but there was no answer on any of the operator service numbers. They've got plenty of drivers down there, so they let Geoff stay here to run people home, and run errands in general.

'Hello Geoff. Two runs: take this chap and find Jill Warley, that you took home this morning. There's no-one at her place, or her mother's apparently, and Mike here is going to take care of her. When she's sorted out, bring Mike back for his bike, and then nip round to the Middle School and find out what's going on there. It's all locked up and no-one's answering the door, but there's people inside, Mike could hear someone coughing.'

Mike and Geoff found Jill half-way to her mother's, sitting on a doorstep having a breather.

She's lost a lot of weight. In four days! She didn't have any to spare, either. She's all skin and bones! Still, it's good to see her.

'Mike!' Jill stood up, and Mike caught her as she tottered. He held her to him. Tears streamed down his face. She kissed him on his cheek. 'I love you.'

'I love you too. O God, it's good to see you.'

While Geoff drove them to Melanie's, Mike explained to Jill about her mum being in hospital, and how they were all staying at Melanie's flat.

'Who is Melanie? But anyway, how are the boys?'

Mike told her that David was at Auntie Alice's, and that Adrian was still in hospital. He told her about the closing down of the Echo, and Tony's search for Echo staff, how some were dead and others were incommunicado in hospital, and how Melanie had been beaten up.

He took Jill into the flat.

June looked up, startled. 'Jill! You're a skeleton! How do you feel? Sit down, I'll put the kettle on.'

'Confused! And a bit weak, but okay.'

'June, you do the introductions, I've got a lift waiting to take me back to pick the bike up.'

'Bike?'

'Oh goodness! You explain, June!'

By the time Mike got back with the bike, Jill had caught up with the broad outline of the dreadful events of the previous few days. June and Melanie were discussing money and food. Linda was luxuriating in being able to understand the grown-ups' discussions, and being encouraged to take part, and having her contributions taken as seriously as anyone's. Jill was listening, half-dazed, the reality of the situation just beginning to sink in.

They had a cup of tea, and then June went off to see about signing on, and investigate Post Offices and banks. Linda went with her for the ride.

'She's fantastically good, considering she found her mum dead in bed the day before yesterday.'

'Is it really as recently as that? She seems to have been here forever. Almost as long as the rest of you.'

'We only came on Saturday, too. Just a few hours before her.'

'I just can't take all this in. I've lost the last four days altogether, and the rest of the world's crammed a hundred years into them.'

Every channel on the telly carried only the same old printed message:

BOIL ALL DRINKING WATER FOR THREE MINUTES,

etc.

'Turn the wretched thing off. We'll try again in a couple of hours.'

They talked about what they could do. They discussed trying to get in touch with people by telephone, but the only friend or relative any of them had who was on the phone was Melanie's sister, who was still elusive.

'Even if we could get through to anyone who's investigating prevention or cure, we'd only be distracting them from their work, and we've no information or original ideas to offer.'

'We ought to ring round the hospitals rather than you riding round them to enquire about people. We should leave a message for everyone about where we all are, to avoid what happened to Jill happening again.'

'I'll have to visit Tony, though, because East Park Upper School's telephone isn't working. They can't get hold of an engineer. Something strange has happened at East Park Middle School too. I hope we can get through to all the others.'

Mike told them the story of the locked up hospital. They worked out the messages to leave at each place, and then rang round. They got through everywhere.

Jill's mother was now said to be 'recovering', instead of 'critical', but otherwise there was no change in anyone's condition. They couldn't trace Mrs Halstead; she would most likely have gone to East Park Middle School. Melanie suggested to Mike that he ask the driver, the next day. 'It'd be silly to go down there again now. I expect you and June'll be going over to see Auntie Alice and David later. You're spending more than enough time outside, if there's any truth in the being outside theory.'

'What's this 'being outside' theory?'

'It's something Tony noticed. The first cases had all been out of doors a lot, and the worst cases had either been out a lot, or had been caught out in Wednesday night's rainstorm.'

'So we do have an idea to offer if we manage to get through to any research people.'

'We did think at one stage of trying to suggest it, but we came to the conclusion that if there was anything in it, it would be fairly general, and they'd pretty certainly have noticed.'

'But from what you've said, they might have been barking up the wrong tree epidemiologically, looking for infection from people, or animals, or food and drink. That pattern you made, Mike, of the towns affected early on: could that have been a weather map?'

'They'll have been barking up every tree they could find. Gordon Waters mentioned radioactivity and toxic chemicals, and anyone thinking about them would surely think about weather conditions. But what's this map Mike made?'

'Perhaps I ought to get it on my way to Auntie Alice's. In one of the last issues of the Echo, there was a list of towns affected – this was way back in the days when it hadn't hit everywhere. I marked them on a map in the atlas, and they formed a clear pattern. But of course we only had a list of the towns affected at one particular time.'

'Not even really at one time, because the reports they'd collated would all have been different ages, and things were changing pretty fast. I imagine they still are, only no-one's telling us. But anyone doing an epidemiological study would have a whole series of maps like that, corrected for the times of the information. I imagine they'll have compared them with weather maps, but you can't tell.'

'Nor can you be sure they'll have been able to get any information on the exposure of individual victims to rain and sky. Perhaps we ought to try to ring Newcastle University labs.'

'We could try to ring Tyne Tees, and get in touch with Gordon Waters. He'd probably know if anyone was already on this track, and save us distracting the real workers.'

'Hey! You remember what Waters said about the Ministry of Defence intercepting them every time they tried to talk to anyone in the MoD labs? He's the chap to tell about Exercise Alpha!'

They could get no answer from Directory Enquiries, or any of the operator services. Melanie tried the local Independent offices, in the hope that they might have Tyne Tees's number on file, but there was no answer there, either.

'There's a complete set of directories for the whole country at the office, but I don't know where Mrs Rushton lives, and she and Geoff Haworth have the only keys. I've been trying to get hold of Geoff since Tony came and told me the Echo was closed, but there's no answer at his house.'

'You know he was arrested when the police came to close the place?'

Tony didn't know when he came here in the first place, of course.

'I'd gathered. But I can't imagine they'd have held him for long. Anyway, I'd expect his wife to be at home sometimes. I've got a horrid feeling they're ill.'

'Is there no-one else on the staff you could ring who might know where Mrs Rushton lives?'

'Or failing that, someone I could visit on the bike?'

'No, I don't think so. The only people who's home addresses I know are Geoff, Andy and the reporters.'

'Do any of the others have really unusual names, so we can find them in the directory?'

'There's Fiona. Her name's Tyzack. But I bet she's not on the phone.'

There was one Tyzack in the book, but it wasn't Fiona, or anyone related to her.

'Well, at least someone answered! I was beginning to wonder if your phone had been tampered with!'

Mike left Jill and Melanie to try to work out some way of contacting Gordon Waters, and went into the kitchen to investigate food stocks. They had quite a lot, but it was an odd assortment.

'I can make some sort of a meal for supper today, but I'm going to have to go shopping sooner or later. I think I'll pop out now and see if I can get some fresh stuff.'

'The sooner you go, the better chance there is of getting fresh stuff, I guess. I can see it being like gold in a few days' time.'

'It already was, on Saturday.'

'It'll be food of any kind next, then. Don't spend the earth on a few fresh things. I ought to have thought of this before. Go down and fetch up Mrs Halstead's stuff and we'll make a list of what we've got. Then we can work out what to spend our money on. We'll spend the lot this afternoon, before prices start going up – or before they go up any more. The key's on the mantlepiece. That's it.'

Mrs Halstead's hoard turned out to be enormous. Mike was still ferrying it upstairs when June and Linda arrived, and they helped him finish.

'How are we ever going to know how much we owe her?'

'It doesn't matter exactly. Make a rough guess what it's worth, and I'll pay her fifty percent above that. I can afford it; she'll try to say it wasn't worth so much, but'll really be pleased as punch; and in the present circumstances, it's a bargain.'

'I don't know how I could even guess what it's worth. I'd have to guess item by item and add it all up.'

'I'll do just that, while you fix a meal, Mike.'

'Would it be easier for you, June, if I make a list of what there is, and then you do it from the list?'

'Thanks for the thought, Linda, but it seems to make an awful lot of work for you without saving a great deal for me.'

'No, let her, June. Then Jill and I can work it out sitting here, and work out this afternoon's shopping strategy at the same time.'

June had discovered that signing-on had indeed been cancelled 'until further notice'.

In other words, you've got to go and look every time. But what else could they do? Apart from telly announcements, which wouldn't reach everyone.

'Giro payments will continue normally'.

If the post delivers them.

The Post Office had a notice saying that local food traders and chemists would cash Giros for regular customers, and that supermarkets would cash them on production of 'satisfactory evidence of identity'. Banks were closed too, but with no indication of alternative arrangements.

'If I could get down there, I could use my cash card. You don't have one, do you, Mike?'

'No, they won't issue them to claimants.'

'My mum's is in her purse. Bother! I'm going to have to start counting the pilchards again!'

'But none of us could do her signature. Anyway, that'd be a criminal offence.'

'That'd be the least of my worries, June, if I thought we could get away with it. I'm much more bothered by the moral offence of the banks preventing Linda getting at her mum's money.' *I hope that doesn't precipitate an argument about innocent side-effects of the bank's 'duty to protect its clients', 'Linda would get the money eventually' – 'yes, when the solicitors have had their unfair share' etc. etc. When will I learn to keep my mouth shut?*

'I can do Mum's signature quite well.'

'But the machine doesn't look at the signature, Linda love. It analyses the movements of your hand while you're writing it. That'd be very hard to copy; I'm not sure it would be possible at all.'

When they'd eaten, Mike and June set off on the bikes, to spend all the money on food. It had turned out that they had plenty of protein, carbohydrate and fat; but very little in the way of vitamins, and a slight shortage of fibre. *I'd never thought about it before, but I suppose that's the nature of pre-packed and preserved food, on the whole.*

There was very little fresh food of any kind to be had anywhere. What little there was was ludicrously expensive. They bought none. At first they kept to the collective decision not to buy very much in any one shop, to avoid being the spark to light the dry tinder and start the fire of panic buying; but they realized that they were too late for that. After the first few shops, seeing the bare state of the shelves, they gave up, and bought entire stocks of especially desirable items.

Each time they filled the panniers on Melanie's bike, Mike rode it back to the flat while June scoured the shelves of another shop.

Several shopkeepers tried to increase prices on items Mike and June wanted a quantity of, but it wasn't long before they knew better than the shopkeepers what items were genuinely in short supply, which gave them a telling bargaining advantage.

They eventually ran out of money. The pile in the kitchen looked as if it would feed an army for a year, but calculation suggested that it might feed the five of them for about a month. They didn't know whether they might have to contribute something to Auntie Alice's larder if things got worse; and of course there was the possibility that some of their friends might be discharged and need feeding.

'If I do get a Giro tomorrow, we'll go and spend it all straight away.'

'Do you really think it could be a month before there's food in the shops again?'

'Nobody knows, Linda love. I expect it'll be a lot longer than that before things get back to normal properly.'

They never will for Linda. I wonder what's happened to her dad? They'll never get back to normal properly for anybody. I suppose they'll reach some new semi-stable condition that we'll call normal.

While June and Mike had been out, Melanie had managed to get a Newcastle University microbiology lab's number, from a pathology technician at Burnfield hospital. She'd talked about their suspicions about being outside, and rain, to a research worker at Newcastle, who said that she wasn't aware of any work on those lines going on; epidemiology wasn't her speciality. She said she'd mention it to her colleagues. She also looked up Tyne Tees's number for Melanie.

Tyne Tees's phone was continuously engaged.

Mike and June went round and spent the evening playing Monopoly with David and Auntie Alice. They cycled back to Melanie's flat after midnight.

Auntie Alice was absolutely right. It was good for us to forget about our troubles for a few hours. I wonder what Pete's up to? He'd be back by now, if it wasn't for the epidemic. I hope he's okay.

The streets were deserted, and the town had a desolate feel about it. Scarcely any houses had lights on, and there were more street lights out than usual.

I suppose that's because no-one's fixing them at the moment. I'd never realized that it was such a continuous job.

A rat scurried across the road just in front of them.

Melanie heard them come in, and called to them softly from her room, 'Shhh! The other two are fast asleep; but do put a kettle on, there's dears.'

Linda was in bed with Melanie, snuggled up to her good side. Melanie used her right hand to hold her cup, for the first time since her rib had been broken, so as not to wake her up. It hurt a bit, but she managed.

'Poor Linda's got an awful boil between her legs. It began to bother her while you were out on the bikes this morning, June. She's a brave little lass. She never said a word till Jill tried to find out what was wrong with her when she couldn't get to sleep. It must've been rubbing horribly on her saddle.'

'That's a shame. Auntie Alice said to take her round there tomorrow. She was half cross we hadn't taken her before. It'd be good for both of them, too.'

'We could walk round there. We can't hide indoors all the time.'

'You're scarcely hiding in doors much at all! Anyway, I think walking that far would hurt her quite a bit.'

'I could carry her easily enough.'

'If she wants to come, I don't see why she shouldn't ride on the pannier carrier. There's no traffic, and I can't see the police stopping us.'

Not like June to be the first to think of breaking the law, even in a minor way like that. She's right, of course.

'I've not seen a police car on the street for several days.'

Jill semi-wakened as Mike crawled into his sleeping bag on the floor next to her. She snuggled up to him.

Mike was wakened in the small hours by the sound of coughing. He could hear whispering from the other room, but he couldn't make out what was being said. Then there was a padding of small feet – that must be Linda – and a line of light appeared round the door. Mike wanted to get up and see what was going on, but Jill was sleeping peacefully, with her head on his shoulder and his arm around her, and he didn't want to disturb her.

The coughing became less frequent, and eventually Mike realized that it had stopped. Then the light went out in a further episode of padding, and finally the whispering died away.

It took Mike ages to get back to sleep. Jill never stirred. Mike noticed the rhythm of her breathing: a long period of soft gentle breaths; a sudden, sharp, deep inspiration; deep, slow breathing becoming shallower and less slow progressively over a few cycle and merging imperceptibly into the next period of gentle breathing.

Does everyone breath like this when they're asleep?

Chapter 14

The days dragged on. One day blurred into the next, and I lost track of them. Writing implements never featured in our thrice-daily packets, and if anyone in our group had one I never found out. If anyone had a fancy watch with the days of the month or even the week on it, I never found out about that, either. I don't know whether anyone really knew exactly what day it was after a while.

At some point, I realized that I'd not seen the old lady who sat next to me on the coach to Glasgow, and wondered what had happened to her. *I saw her in the hotel, she didn't know about pressing ENTER on the luggage robot. Was she in a different part of the hotel, and ended up in one of the other populations? I thought Will and I concluded that the other populations must have come from some other source, that the hotel couldn't have been so big? If so, did she fail to make it down to the shelter at all? I wonder what's actually happening up there now? What's already happened? Nothing I can do about it, anyway. Poor old girl.*

Chapter 15

Linda, June and Jill were up and about when Mike woke in the morning. He dressed inside his sleeping bag and emerged, dishevelled but decent, just in time for a cup of tea and a bowl of porridge.

'Powdered milk in the porridge, of course, I'm afraid.'

'It's a treat to have porridge at all. Who was that coughing during the night?'

'Melanie. A real horrible chesty cough. Made her rib hurt dreadfully, you could tell, though she didn't say much. She thought that what brought on the coughing was lying in one position all the time, trying not to disturb Linda. The coughing woke Linda up, and she came in my bag with me to give Melanie a chance to change position, which certainly seemed to help.'

Melanie still hadn't woken up by the time they'd planned the day's movements. June was to take Linda to Auntie Alice's, then go and check the house for the possible arrival of her Giro – generally considered unlikely – followed by a visit to Jenny and her mum before returning to Auntie Alice's. Mike was to go to see how Tony was, visit Mr Jordan, and join June and Linda at Auntie Alice's. If June had a Giro, they would set out on another shopping expedition. Jill was to stay wih Melanie, and was expecting at least one of them back early in the afternoon. She'd ring the other hospitals when Melanie woke up.

Ruth was on duty at East Park Upper School. She looked even more tired than before.

'Hello, Ruth.'

'Hello...?' She seemed to be puzzled as to who he was.

'I'm Mike. I was here yesterday.'

'Oh. I've seen hundreds of people in the last few days – Oh! Of course! Mike. You're the chap who fainted, and who told us about the Middle School.'

'That's me. You look whacked. When did you last get any sleep?'

'I don't know. I've lost track. I've been dozing here, on and off.'

'Haven't you been relieved at all?'

'Not since Penny was admitted on Sunday morning. I don't want to go home to an empty house anyway, I'd rather sleep here. Geoff takes a turn on the desk every now and then. He's asked at the hospital for another worker for here, but they're short there too. No-one's volunteering any more. But it's not so busy any more, either.'

Why ever not? Are admissions at last beginning to diminish? Are people not coming to enquire? I don't understand.

'Why's that? I've not heard anything about things improving.'

'I've no idea. I've heard no news for days. No-one's told Hugh anything new about treatment, though.'

'How's Tony? Tony Ramsden.'

Ruth couldn't find him on any of her lists. 'That means he's okay, not really getting better yet, but not serious either.'

'Hey, look, I don't have any medical experience, but I could sort out your paperwork for you. Make an alphabetical list of all the admissions and mark up the current status of each.'

'But that's a tremendous job, keeping proper patient records! That's why we only made these lists in the first place.'

'I don't know what a 'proper patient record' is. I was just thinking of putting a letter by each name, corresponding to your categories of Critical, Recovering, Discharged, plus one for dead. At the moment, you can't tell, if someone's name isn't on any list, whether they've never been here, or they're new admissions that aren't on any list yet, or whether they're dead. And your lists must be a substantial proportion of all admissions by now.'

'I don't think they are, actually, but I can't say for sure. A lot of people came in on Saturday and Sunday, and most of them aren't on my lists yet, I don't think. But it's not worth bothering anyway. Very few people are coming to ask about anyone. I think they're just sitting at home trying not to meet anyone who might infect them.'

'There's no evidence that it's infectious anyway, is there?'

'Not just by meeting people, anyway. They seem to think it spreads by contamination of food and water, to judge by the precautions they suggest. But I think people are scared.'

'What had happened at East Park Middle?'

'Oh! Goodness. Geoff went round there, and sure enough, every door was locked. He climbed up onto the window sills and peered in here and there, and there were classrooms full of patients, just like here, but no sign of any staff. Hang on a minute, here comes Geoff now.'

Geoff came in carrying a child. 'Can you take this little mite down to Hugh, Ruth? I've another one out there.'

Both the children looked very sick, pale, with sunken eyes.

'They belong to that woman I took home just now. Her husband isn't well, either, but he wouldn't come in. I couldn't persuade him that there was any point. He knows there's no cure, and couldn't understand that we could do any good just by treating symptoms, as he put it. He said he'd stand the pain, and his wife needed him to look after her.'

Geoff finished the story of the locked school. He'd been on the point of breaking in when a car had arrived with the missing receptionist and a couple of other people that Geoff didn't know.

Early that morning the poor receptionist had begun to wonder why she hadn't seen the other staff for so long. She wasn't overly worried, because she assumed that if anything was wrong, one of the others would have come to tell her. It had been so long – she didn't know exactly, but she thought several hours – that she went to look for them.

She found the doctor, collapsed in a corridor, apparently dead. At first she couldn't find Mary, the nurse; she became frantic, and looked everywhere, in the most ridiculous places. Eventually she thought of going back into a classroom and asking a patient, if she could find one awake. She found Mary semi-conscious in bed, just another patient with an intravenous drip.

She tried to ring the hospital, but the phone was dead. She was expecting the taxi-driver allocated to them to turn up for the day about eight o'clock. She waited for him, getting more and more worked up about the delay in attending to the doctor, if by any chance he might still be alive. When the driver hadn't turned up by half past eight, she set off on foot for the hospital.

'Pity she didn't think to drop in here,' Geoff concluded.

'Our phone was as dead as hers, and you weren't here anyway.'

'Was the doctor okay?'

'No. Stone dead. He'd had a heart attack, presumably on his way to ask Rose to ring for a relief nurse.'

Mr Jordan wasn't at home.

Mike arrived at Auntie Alice's before June returned. He found the old lady and the two children absorbed in another game of Monopoly. Linda was winning convincingly; Auntie Alice was almost bankrupt.

'You take my place, Mike, and I'll get a kettle on.'

'No, don't worry, I'll do it.'

'No, I'll do it. I've got some things in the oven I ought to have a look at, too.'

Mike was bankrupt before the tea was made, and he and Auntie Alice discussed the state of the world while the children battled on. David had done particularly well out of Mike's bankruptcy which gave the game a new lease of life.

June arrived just in time for lunch. She had bad news: Jenny was ill, and Vicky was dead. Their mum was all alone, and in a dreadful state. The news brought Linda back to reality with a jolt. She curled up in her chair and wept silently. She couldn't be comforted, and wouldn't come and eat her lunch. Auntie Alice put it under a bowl in the still-warm oven, and they left her to her private grief while they ate.

They'd discharged Vicky. She didn't seem a bit well, but they discharged her. She didn't seem on the brink of death, either. Jill! Don't die, Jill.

Get a hold on yourself, Mike. The odds must be very much against what happened to Vicky happening to anyone else.

By the time they'd finished eating, Linda was ready to be cuddled. She let June slide down beside her in the chair. They put their arms around each other, Linda's head on June's breast, and she broke down into proper sobbing.

After a while she looked up, and asked to borrow a handkerchief. Auntie Alice produced a box of tissues. While Linda dried her eyes and nose, Auntie Alice asked, 'Would you like your lunch now?', and Linda nodded, with a wan smile. She was so unsteady that she almost spilt it down June and herself, and the meal eventually was a co-operative effort, June holding the dish in her free hand, and Auntie Alice spooning the food into Linda's mouth. None of them could help laughing, Linda through her still plentiful tears.

June had not received a Giro, and Mike went back to Melanie's leaving June to do a little shopping for Auntie Alice before bringing Linda back.

Jill was sitting on Melanie's bed, talking on the telephone, when Mike arrived.

'That's Mike home now. We'll talk again another time. You did get our number, didn't you. Goodbye for now.

'Oh, Mike!'

She stood up, buried her head in his chest and burst into tears. He put his arms around her and kissed the top of her head. 'What's up, love?'

Jill looked up and started to speak, but choked on her words, gave up the attempt, and just held him tight and shook with sobs. Melanie answered for her, 'When I woke up, we rang the hospital. Adrian's dead.'

'Oh God.' Mike bent down and kissed Jill's head again. 'I'm sorry love.'

Jill squeezed him tighter for a moment. He picked her up gently and sat down with her on his lap. They all sat in silence for a while.

Eventually Melanie said softly, 'Angie died last night too. Jill's mum's back on the critical list, and Steve's critical too, now.'

'Our news is bad, too. Jenny's sick and Vicky's dead.' Jill pulled herself together enough to ask about the Jordans.

'I don't know. There was nobody there. I'll go round again later on.'

'Stay here, Mike. Mr Jordan doesn't need you; if he's okay, he must've gone to see someone himself. I wish you didn't have to go to Auntie Alice's. I wish she was on the phone. Don't leave me again, Mike. It doesn't do him any good for you to ask about him, and I'd as soon not know how he is, if it means you can stay here with us. He knows we're here if they discharge him.'

God, how the world's changed in the last week. Not, 'when they discharge him' but 'if they discharge him'.

Then, *Will we be here, anyway?*

Another long silence.

'Who was that you were talking to on the phone when I came in?'

'Roland. Roland Metcalfe. I know, you've never heard of him. Neither had we. It's a long story. You tell him, Melanie, while I put the kettle on.'

'Don't be daft, love. You stay there, I'll make the tea. The story'll keep five minutes, I'm sure.'

'I've been making teas all day.'

'I don't doubt it. Time you had a break. You're in no fit state to be out of bed.'

Tea for three. Melanie had just begun to tell Mike that they'd tried the telly, and found nothing on any channel, not even a printed message, when June and Linda arrived. Mike stretched the tea out with some extra hot water, while Jill brought them up to date with the dire news.

Linda had another fit of weeping; but she allowed June to hold her, and went to sleep in her arms after a while. When June was sure she was well away, she whispered, 'She's got two more boils, one each side of her tummy, just where her belt rubs them. I'll get her to change into a dress when she wakes up.'

Melanie told them how Jill had gone down to Mrs Halstead's flat to see if she could get anything out of her telly, in case it was simply Melanie's telly that had packed up. Nothing doing.

They'd tried to get Tyne Tees on the telephone again. Still continuously engaged. Directory Enquiries: no answer.

After trying every channel of telephone communication they could think of, they'd hit on the idea of trying random numbers, with city codes from the book. They got a lot of 'number unobtainable' tones, and a lot of unanswered ringing, but eventually got through to an old lady. They explained what they were trying to do – only really working it out in their own minds by having to explain it to someone else. The old lady wasn't interested.

Roland Metcalfe was their second contact. He was only too pleased to talk to someone. He'd been wondering if he was the last man on earth. He was an old chap living on his own in an isolated house at the end of a long straggling village near Hebden Bridge. He'd been ill, and none of his neighbours had come on their usual two-or-three-times-daily visits. When he recovered sufficiently to walk down to the next house, he found nobody there.

There was no-one in the next house either.

'By that time, he was too tired to face the walk back up the hill, so he sat down in his neighbour's armchair, and went to sleep. He didn't wake up until after dark, and still no-one had returned. He made himself a cup of tea and put the telly on. He was shocked to find only one channel working, and that displaying the printed message we all know and love. It was the first he knew about the epidemic. He tried to ring the village shop, and friends in the village, because he was running out of food at home, but there were no replies. In desperation he tried the doctor's surgery and the police, the operator, and finally 999. No replies at all.

'Eventually, after a period of panic followed by a period of despair, he decided to investigate his neighbour's larder, and estimated he'd got a couple of weeks' food if no-one came home.

'We rang just as he was beginning to despair again. He's going to continue with our random ringing policy, and hopefully we're going to start a network, all giving each other any contacts we find.'

All that afternoon they tried random numbers. They made a few contacts, and talked briefly to a few people who weren't interested. They worked out a standard introduction, with a short series of questions which elicited a little interesting information even from some of those who didn't want to remain in the network. Linda slept in June's arms the whole while.

'Hello. My name's Melanie Downs. I'm trying to find out a bit more about the epidemic, and I wonder if you'd mind answering a few questions?'

'Are any of your household sick, at home or in hospital?

'When did they fall ill?

'Oh, I am sorry to hear that. Do you have any neighbours to help look after you?

'I'm sorry, there's absolutely nothing we can do from here. We're just a group of friends in Burnfield. We've no transport except a couple of bikes.

'Yes of course we'll ring again. You can ring us anytime too. We can put you in touch with a few other people by phone, too.'

Early that evening the phone went dead.

'I rather doubt if we can get it fixed until all this is over!'

'First the telly, now the phone. Try the telly again, Mike. Let's see if it's come back on.'

But it hadn't.

'It'll be the electricity next, I suppose.'

'That's a dismal thought. Half the food we've got'll be useless if we can't cook it. And there's a fridge full of stuff that'll go off.'

'Linda's asleep, isn't she, June?'

'Mmm.'

'I'm wondering whether you and I should do some careful looting, June, before the rush starts. And the backlash. Not so much food, as a gas stove and come cylinders. I bet not a lot of people have thought about the 'lecky going off yet. I'm sure it will soon.'

'Mike! Don't leave us!'

'It could be that or starve, love. There'll be two of us, to keep an eye on each other. Don't worry. Are you game, June?'

'I think you're right anyway, whether I'm game or not. I'd love to know how one loots carefully, that's all. While we're out, I reckon Jill ought to fill every available container with water, too. I dare say the water's not so likely to go off, but we'll be really stuck if it does. Ought to cook everything from the fridge that'll keep better cooked, too. Are you up to that, Jill?'

'Perhaps we should do that before we go, June. I'd rather go later in the evening anyway.'

'You mean you're a bit afraid, Mike. I reckon dusk is the best time. It's the hardest time for anyone to see. With the street lights still working, night-time's not so good, and with no-one about to speak of, daylight's hopeless. But you've got to work out what you intend to do before you go. I think we ought to leave it twenty-four hours, and hope that every Tom, Dick and Harry hasn't had the same idea by then.'

'Where do you intend to get a stove and cylinders, anyway? Carter's and Oakenshaw's will both have alarms, probably linked to the cop-shop. I haven't a clue who else would have any.'

'All the shops'll be alarmed. With luck the link to the police would be out of order, courtesy of British Telecom, but I wouldn't like to rely on that. I was thinking more of finding someone's caravan.'

'You'd get a stove like that, if it wasn't too thoroughly built in. But I bet you'd find the cylinder was in the house.'

'Probably empty anyway.'

They talked in circles for a while, then decided to get the water drawn and the cooking done. When they looked at it, there wasn't a lot that would keep better cooked than raw – they didn't have a great deal of fresh meat. They made a strange meal composed of the most perishable items.

They woke Linda to eat it. Her boils were troubling her dreadfully; one of them had burst. She was a bit dopey with sleep, pain and tears. June took her to the bathroom to dress the boils and change her clothes for something more comfortable.

Mike had a brainwave. 'They'll have stoves and cylinders down at the sewage project at Wood Lane. And I bet there's no guard dog any more!'

'They'll have damn big cylinders, too. You'll be a bit obvious carrying one, if you can manage it at all, all that way. I suppose they might have some smaller ones for some portable equipment, that might have the same connections. It might be our best bet, at that.'

They didn't think of anything better that evening. Mike, Jill and June went off to sleep quite early, leaving Linda and Melanie playing cards on Melanie's bed.

During the night Melanie was coughing again. It woke Mike. He was conscious of Jill's breathing again – the same pattern as the night before. Was that a hint of a wheeze on the deep breath? It was there next time the deep breath came round, just as slightly, but now he was sure.

He moved his shoulder a little to try to improve her airway, hoping not to wake her up in the process. A little pain jabbed him in the muscle under his armpit, making him start slightly. Jill stirred, coughed slightly, and settled down again. Mike felt sore under his armpit.

Chapter 16

Harry and Irene had a very public blazing row, and split up. Whether it had anything to do with him hearing about Ken's exploits, I don't know. Maybe Will knows, but he and I drifted apart after a week or so, and he, much to my surprise, took up with Irene. Harry studiously ignored them for a few days, and tried to chat up just about every unattached female he could find, apparently without success.

Then he took it into his head to accost Will. At first Will ignored him, then when Harry got louder and more aggressive, he laughed at him. A circle of watchers formed. Irene and the kids tried to melt into the crowd, and when Harry shouted at them to come back, they refused. Will told him to calm down. Harry completely lost it, and threw a punch at Will.

I saw the two big burly chaps, who'd been standing at the back of the crowd, start to react; but only for a moment. Will hadn't mentioned to anyone that he was a black belt in some martial art or other. I still don't know whether he actually is, but however it happened, Harry found himself flat on his face with his arm behind his back.

'Try that or anything like it again mate, and next time I'll break your arm. Or your fucking head.'

He turned to the watching crowd. 'I hope no-one thinks I'm wrong to say that, because I mean it. In this place we can't afford to have nutcases running amok.'

Chapter 17

The next time Mike woke it was broad daylight. He could hear June and Jill in the kitchen. He had a splitting headache. He was still sore under the armpit. He investigated with his other hand. It came away sticky with what seemed to be a mixture of blood and pus. There was a bit of a mess in his sleeping bag, and on the edge of Jill's. He went into the bathroom and cleaned himself up. He couldn't see properly in the mirror, it was too high. He went into the kitchen in his trousers, and got Jill to look.

'It's just a boil. Burst. I'll put you a plaster on it.'

'I've not had a boil since I was a kid! And I've got a whopper of a headache.'

'Linda woke in the night. Her boils were troubling her. She's got a whole crop more coming, by the look of it. She's fast asleep now, though.'

'When you've finished dressing that, Jill, don't let me forget to give our bags a clean. It's made a bit of a mess on them.'

June went round to Auntie Alice's on her own. Mike's headache wasn't getting any better, and Jill didn't want him to go.

'None of us should be out more than we have to be.'

Linda and Melanie slept on. Mike and Jill had a cup of tea – electricity and water both still going – and then sat, Jill on Mike's lap, in the big armchair. They kissed, and then Jill put her head on his shoulder and wept.

Mike didn't know what to say.

After a few moments Jill started coughing, a phlegmy, bubbly cough deep down in her chest. Suddenly it became violent. Jill looked up at Mike with terror in her eyes, and then there was blood all over his chest. The coughing stopped, but the terrified staring didn't. She tried to say something, but nothing came. She went rigid for a moment, then as limp as a rag doll. Her eyes closed.

'Jill!' *My God, she's dying!* 'Jill!' *She's not breathing!*

All he got for his pains was a mouthful of phlegm and blood. He couldn't find a sign of a pulse. He kept on trying, desperate.

A sleepy looking Linda was patting him on the arm.

'What's the matter, Mike?'

Tears were streaming down his face.

'Linda!' Breathe. 'Wake Mel!' Breathe. 'I'm going,' Breathe. 'To take,' Breathe. 'Jill,' Breathe. 'To the,' Breathe. 'Hospital.'

Linda went back into Melanie's room. Mike heard her crying and shouting.

Then he was in the street, Jill in his arms. He was trying to run, and ventilate Jill at the same time. He knew there was no hope.

He made it to East Park Upper School.

The face looking down at him was familiar, somehow. His head throbbed. He felt as if his lungs were going to burst. *Where am I? I was doing something frightfully important. Mustn't give up! What was it?*

'Jill! Where's Jill?'

'Shh! Don't jump up! Are you warm enough?

'Where's Jill?!'

'Easy, easy. There's nothing more you can do now. Are you ready for a cuppa?'

'Where is she? How is she?'

'You did everything you could. More. Quite...'

He tried to jump up, but found himself tangled in bedclothes.

'Where is she?'

Ruth was sitting on the bed, beside him, holding him round the shoulders with her left arm, trying to rearrange his bedding with her right hand.

'Calm down, Mike, and I'll get you that tea. The kettle's boiling, I can hear it. How far did you run? You practically killed yourself, you know. You must've known it was hopeless.'

Mike came back to earth with a bump. He went quite limp and cried like a baby. Ruth went off to get the tea.

She came back a few moments later with two mugs. Mike tried to take his, but he wasn't steady enough, and she put it on a trolley by the next bed.

'You'd better let it cool for a minute, anyway.'

She sipped at her own, sitting on the foot of his bed, eyeing him worriedly.

Mike looked at her. She looked exhausted, haggard. Her clothes were crumpled, dirty, bloodstained. An angel.

'She's dead, isn't she? Don't tell me, I know. Where's the doctor?'

'Hugh? He's in that bed over there, directing operations during his periods of consciousness. He's incredible. Not that there's a lot of directing to do; I know the routine. It's hopeless, anyway. It's quite a pleasure to have someone like you, worth some effort. Physically, there's not a lot wrong with you, I don't think.' There were tears in her eyes.

'Geoff?'

'I don't know. He went into town yesterday afternoon to try to get some more glucose. I've not seen him since.'

Mike looked around the room. Many of the beds had intravenous drips erected by them, on makeshift stands of various designs. Not a single patient showed any signs of life. There was a dreadful smell in the room.

It must be frightful, for me still to be able to smell it after all this time exposed to it.

'Here, are you ready for that tea? Don't let it go cold!'

It was very sweet. *Jill! Jill! Jill! O God!* Mike's head throbbed. He forced himself to think about something else.

'How's Tony?'

'I don't know. What's his full name?'

'Tony Ramsden. I brought him in the day before yesterday, in the morning.'

Christ. Only two days ago. It feels like a lifetime. It is a lifetime. Only two days since Jill 'recovered', and she's dead now. Oh Jill, Jill!

'Oh, him! The lively one. Do you want to talk to him? I'll find you some of Hugh's clothes. I think you'd be okay to get up in a minute. I don't know if Tony's awake, but he's all there when he is. He'll be on an IV drip before long though, the way his bowels are. And if I can't get some more glucose, it'll be pure saline.

IV – ah, intravenous. Saline? Salt? I suppose so.

'Clothes? What's happened to mine?'

'I hope you don't mind. I slung your shirt away. It was foul. You were only half-dressed anyway. I thought you might be suffering from exposure when you first arrived.'

Tony was wide awake. Ruth disappeared to get him a cup of tea.

'Hello, Mike! Has she started allowing visitors? How is everyone?'

'Jill's dead. She died in my arms this morning. I brought her in here, but it was hopeless. I...' Mike broke into uncontrollable sobbing.

'O God! I'm sorry, Mike.'

Tony got out of bed unsteadily, sat on the bed beside Mike, and put his arm around him.

Mike put his head on Tony's chest and wept. Ruth found them like that a few moments later. She untucked the blankets from the other side of the bed and wrapped them around the two young men.

'Cup of tea, Tony,' she whispered.

'Ta.'

After a few moments Mike pulled himself together.

'June and Linda and Mel are okay, Tony. June's fine, gone off to see Auntie Alice and David. Linda's pretty miserable with her boils, and Mel's got a bit of a cough, but they're okay. Oh, and I've got a boil, too. Oh Christ, June doesn't know about Jill. Jill was fine when June went this morning.'

'Hey, Ruth, it's not doing me any good being here, is it? I might just as well spend my last days out there with my friends, mightn't I?'

'Tony! Don't talk like that!'

'It's true though, isn't it, Ruth? What's the prognosis? What can you do for me that they can't do at home? How much longer can you go on, anyway? Once I get on an IV drip, what are my chances? One in a hundred of a two-day reprieve, like Jill?'

'I haven't a clue, Tony. No-one has. You're right, I'm not going to last forever. I've had no solids for days.'

'And no sleep either, I bet. How many patients have you got? Couple of hundred? And you're on twenty-four hour duty as doctor, nurse and receptionist?'

'Reception's no bother. You're the first person I've seen since Geoff went yesterday. And I don't have anything like that number of patients. Most of them are dead.'

'You mean there are dead bodies in the beds?'

'What's she supposed to do, Mike? On her own. She can't lug them all off to the bins. She's enough on her plate, coping with the living.'

'Hell, at least I could do that for her!'

'Don't bother, Mike. No-one's collected them since Monday. They might as well stay where they are as go to that stinking pile. Anyway, there are dozens of them.'

Now that I look, the sheets are pulled over the faces of at least three-quarters of the patients. My God, perhaps it is going to be a hundred percent mortality! Perhaps it is biological warfare! And the bloody authorities know, and aren't saying! Exercise Alpha!

Don't jump to conclusions, Mike. How many people have recovered? How many haven't even been sick? Still, I'd like to talk to Tony about it if Ruth leaves us alone later on.

'Was Geoff removing the bodies? Right up until yesterday afternoon? All these have died since then?'

'No. I mean, yes he was, but he was well behind. It's hard work. He was exhausted.'

I hope he didn't crash his car yesterday. But what has happened to him? Chances are it's no better than a car crash anyway.

'I'd better go round and look at my patients. I've not been round for ages.'

'Is there anything I can do to help?'

'Probably not. I'll come and get you if there is. I'll probably only be fifteen or twenty minutes.'

Mike told Tony about his thoughts: a hundred percent mortality, biological warfare, Exercise Alpha.

'I thought about that myself. Exercise Alpha makes it look awfully much as though someone knew it was coming and how bad it was likely to be, whether it's biological warfare or whatever it is. I wish we'd been watching telly regularly since before it all started. I'd love to know whether many VIPs have stopped appearing on telly since Alpha Alert. And which ones.'

'Your ordinary copper didn't know what exactly was going on, obviously. Just got shunted underground, ignorant.'

'He may have been told since, of course. Or fed some cock and bull story. Depends on what the truth is, whether they'd want him to know. It's worth remembering they're not underground, too. Just in a sealed fortress. And when you think about it, it seems likely that someone not only got wind of the whole thing in time to call Alpha Alert before it was too late, but had oodles of warning and set up Exercise Alpha especially.'

'Granted, it's possible. But it's stretching the available evidence a bit far, isn't it? Setting up Exercise Alpha doesn't seem a particularly strange thing for the Ministry of Offence to do anyway. Then, when they get wind of the impending epidemic, they call Alpha Alert.'

'Okay, fair enough. But it's a bit odd that Exercise Alpha had only just been set up. It was the very first Alpha Alert. Not one drill. And I've never been very happy about the idea that the whole shelter thing is to boost MoD status with the public, and line the pockets of shelter builders. Public awareness of their uselessness in the face of nuclear weapons is too great, little as it is. I'm sure it does the MoD's image, and the Government's, more harm than good.'

'I'm not so sure. I think you might be overestimating the awareness of the public. Anyway, they chose their course when public awareness about nuclear matters was even less than it is now. The loss of face to change tack would be enormous.'

'The daft thing is, some of the shelter designs could well be very effective against the most likely biological agents. They scarcely ever mention that. I've never seen it in the popular press, only in scientific journals, and in shelter ads in the upper-crusty mags.

'I read them sometimes, in the library,' Tony added, almost apologetically.

'What do you mean, the most likely biological agents?'

'The sort that hit hard over a short period, don't spread quickly, and don't survive long in nature. They don't backfire on the aggressor that way. Or something you can immunize against; but that's dodgy. An intelligence leak may mean your intended victims turn out to be immunized. Immunizing whole populations quickly is a major undertaking and very hard to keep secret, and it commits you to a continued immunization programme for a while at least.'

They talked about biological warfare for quite a while. They decided that whatever the epidemic was, it pretty certainly wasn't biological warfare.

'It hasn't hit hard, or fast, enough. There's been plenty of time for a counter-strike.'

'It's hard to imagine a biological agent that could hit hard and fast enough. Even if death was almost instantaneous once the agent got to you, the spreading would be slow. You'd have to deliver it with an absolute blanket of little bombs.'

'Which obviously hasn't happened. Nor did I see a fleet of small planes spraying. Anyway, it didn't hit hard or fast enough. It seems to me biological weapons are only any use to a major power trying to wipe out people incapable of hitting back – a very poor country, or tribespeople, or insurrectionists.'

'Underdogs, you mean. Um. I think so. Ruth's been gone a while, hasn't she? Go and see if she's okay, Mike.'

Mike found her in a crumpled heap on Hugh's bed. Hugh was awake. He put his finger to his lips.

'Shh. She's okay, just asleep. She needs it. She'll kill herself, going on the way she is. How are you? Are you up to a bit of work?'

'Me? I'm fine. What do you want me to do?'

'Shift the body out of the next bed, and remake it. There's fresh linen in that chest over there. Then put Ruth in it. She'll be well away by that time.'

'Where shall I put the body?'

'Just put it in the next bed with the body that's already there. No point taking it any further. The best we can hope to do is to keep them off the floor so's not to encourage the rats, and keep 'em covered to keep the flies off. Give yourself a good wash when you've covered them up. Staff toilet's the door opposite. That's it.'

Ruth didn't weigh a lot. Mike took off her shoes, laid her on a fresh sheet and then covered her with another, and a couple of blankets.

'She'd finished her round before she came to chat to me. I'll get up in a couple of hours to do the next one.'

'Are you fit enough to get up at all?'

'Fitter than she is. We're both exhausted, and washed out from the diarrhea. But I've not started to get dehydrated yet. Sugar and salt solution seems still to be getting through to me. I'll last a few more days, as long as I don't overdo it. You know about sugar and salt, do you? If you're diarrhea's really bad, dissolve a tablespoonful of sugar and a teaspoonful of salt in a litre of water. Drink it in sips not long gulps, but get through at least a litre a day. Glucose is better than sugar if you can get it.'

'Ruth was saying about that. Geoff went to get some sugar or glucose yesterday afternoon and never came back. Should I go and get some? Where should I go?'

'The hospital. They've organized a central distribution point there. All the major stockists in the area have been cleaned out. People with no food were turning up at the hospital. They're running a soup kitchen there.'

But Hugh was out of date. There was no soup kitchen. There was chaos. People were hurrying away with bags and packets of food. There were scuffles going on here and there.

Mike was glad he had the bicycle. He didn't try to get anything. After a moment of immobility, he recovered from his surprise and fled. He had the impression that he'd left only just quickly enough to retain the bicycle.

He hadn't particularly noticed the car, on the other side of the road, as he'd coasted down. Passing it, going slowly up the hill, he glanced in through the driver's window. A body was slumped sideways in the driver's seat, one arm through the steering wheel, and the head in the passenger footwell. It registered in Mike's mind that the clothes were familiar looking.

It's Geoff.

It was. Mike opened the door, and reeled with nausea as the smell hit him. Diarrhea. Mike picked up the hand from the wheel and felt for a pulse. Nothing. A horrible coldness.

He's dead, quite dead. Quite certainly, quite dead. God, is there going to be no end to this? Jill! O God!

After a couple of minutes Mike forced himself to compose his thoughts, at an uncomfortable realization.

I'm not very far from the mob at the hospital. It's not really very safe here.

Then:

Pointing this way, Geoff had presumably already been to the hospital. Hopefully the stuff's in the boot.

The boot was locked. Mike cursed himself for a fool and went back to get the keys out of the ignition.

He filled the panniers, and relocked the boot. He locked the car as well before setting off back to the school.

'Now I really wish you could drive, Mike. How many pannier loads do you think there are in the boot?'

'Only three or four. But I feel really vulnerable on the bike, especially going back and forth and stopping at the same place again and again.'

I wish June could drive. With a car, we could fetch big cylinders from Wood Lane.

'Can Ruth drive?'

Why do I suddenly have the feeling I'd trust her with our thoughts of going looting? To the extent of asking her to help?

'I don't know.'

He thinks I'm only thinking of getting the supplies up for here. God, I'm getting confused! Of course he only thinks that.

Christ! How circumstances alter cases! Never mind trusting Ruth. How long have we known Melanie? We've been discussing looting with her!

Talk about double standards! What was my reaction to the mob down at the hospital?

The difference is that we weren't going to hurt anybody.

Really? What would happen if anyone accosted us? Anyway, most of the people at the hospital weren't being violent. There's still a difference between stealing from a functioning hospital and stealing from a defunct building site.

But what would happen if any one...

'Hey, Mike! Are you okay?'

'Mmm. A million miles away, that's all. Even if Ruth can drive, is she fit to?'

'After a rest, I expect she would be. How far away is the car? I'm not so sure about her being fit for the walk.'

'If she perches on the pannier carrier, I could take her down on the bike.'

'We'll see when she wakes up.'

What about June and Melanie, and Linda? I ought to go and tell them what's going on.

But I ought to help Hugh and Ruth. They really need help. Tony's here too.

Jill didn't want me to come here today at all. 'Stay with me, Mike.' O Jill, my love! Who should I stay with now? Does it matter? Does anything matter? Hugh and Ruth need help. What for? To keep a few vegetables alive a bit longer? To wear themselves out and kill themselves a bit quicker?

Is there any chance that they might save Tony? Or if they took it easy, might they have a chance of surviving themselves?

Is anyone going to survive?

Not Jill!

Snap out of it, Mike! As far as I know, there's nothing wrong with me, or June, or Auntie Alice, or Linda, or Melanie – apart from ordinary, transient, things – and David has been out four days and seems okay. Ought to go and remind Tony of that – silly sod talking as though he's only got four days left! Remarkably cheerful about it, though. Doesn't he take it seriously? He can't actually be confident of surviving anyway. Can he? Not unless he's losing his marbles.

'You look as though you could do with lying down for a bit yourself. It'll be a while before Ruth's ready to do anything.'

'No. I want a word with Tony. Then I'd better go home and tell my friends what's going on. I'll be back in a few hours, and we'll see about fetching the car up.'

'Hello, Mike? That is you, isn't it? How is she?'

'Hello, Mel. Yes, it's me. Just let me get a kettle on.'

'Linda, you go and make us all some tea, there's a love. Mike, let Linda make the tea. You come in here.'

Mike sat down on the foot of Mel's bed, and burst into tears. He tried to speak, but couldn't. Mel shushed him.

Linda came in with three teas. She gave Mel hers, and then sat by Mike, silently, with big round eyes. After a couple of moments she put the two teas on the floor, and put her arms round him, her head on his chest, and hugged him. Mike looked down and smiled at her through his tears. He put his arm round her and squeezed. She looked up. She was crying too, but they laughed at themselves and squeezed each other again.

Mike looked over at Mel and started to speak, but Mel interrupted him.

'It's all right, Mike. Don't say anything. I know already. I can tell. I'm sorry.'

There were tears in her eyes too.

June wasn't back for lunch. Mike made a meal for the three of them. In the middle of the afternoon he cycled back to the school.

Ruth was just pulling a sheet up over someone's head.

'Hugh and Tony are both asleep at the moment, but they're okay. This old lady walked in just after I woke up. How she managed it I'll never know. I'm surprised she was conscious at all. She couldn't put two words together. I put her straight on a drip, but she's lasted less than an hour.'

'Christ, this is depressing.'

She sat on the end of the bed. She looked up at Mike with an exhausted, forlorn expression. Tears welled up in her eyes.

Don't crack up, Ruth. You're the shining light, the angel that never says die.

He sat down beside her and put his arm round her.

'Thanks, Mike. But don't worry about me. I'll be okay.'

While you live, maybe. How much longer will that be?

'Shall I get you a cup of tea?'

'No, not at the moment. Just hold onto me a bit longer, then we'll go and get Geoff's carload of stuff. We'll have a cuppa when we get back.'

Balancing the bike with Ruth on the back was much harder than it had been with Linda, but Mike managed.

I'd get used to it if I had to do it much. I'm glad it's all downhill, though.

Mike felt uneasy when they stopped by the car. *I think it's mainly the way I felt the last time I was here. Logically I ought to be equally afraid anywhere, I think.* He didn't follow the thoughts through to any logical conclusions.

They dumped Geoff's body into the gutter. It felt dreadful, but there was nothing else they could do. Mike thought about rifling his pockets. It seemed the logical thing, but he couldn't bring himself to do it with Ruth there. *I wonder if I could anyway?*

Ruth solved the problem for him. She just slipped Geoff's wallet into a pocket without looking inside it.

'I don't actually have a driving licence. I don't think it matters in the circumstances. I only had a few lessons, years ago, but I expect I'll manage somehow.'

She wiped the worst of the mess off the seat with Geoff's jacket, and then threw it over his body.

Her progress up the road was slow and erratic, with much revving and clutch slipping over the gear changes – steering control going a bit wild the while. *I don't suppose I could do even so well myself. It's all very well understanding what's going on – it's another co-ordinating it all in practice.*

Mike arrived at the school not long after her. He tried to make her sit down while he unloaded the boot. She had the tea ready by the time he'd finished. Tony and Hugh were both still asleep. None of her other patients were conscious.

'There's only fourteen left altogether. Including Tony. I'm pretty sure they're all terminal anyway. I barely know why we bother. Still, what else is there to do?

I wonder how many were discharged earlier on – just what proportion of admissions have survived? He couldn't bring himself to ask. *How many of those discharged have died since? Jill, Jill!*

Ruth saw the tears welling up in his eyes, and the anguished look appearing in his face. She leant over the table and put her hands over his.

Mike couldn't bring himself to suggest that she help him to steal a stove and a bottle of gas. *She's worn out just from that short drive.* But he knew his real worry was broaching the subject of looting. *Yet she didn't think twice about taking Geoff's wallet.*

It wasn't until he was cycling back to Mel's flat that another possibility occurred to him. *With a car, we could probably move Mel to Auntie Alice's. Hers is a gas stove.*

How long will the gas keep going?

June still wasn't back. Mike cooked for the three of them again.

'I hope there's nothing wrong over at Auntie Alice's. Perhaps I'd better pop over if June isn't back soon.'

Auntie Alice was surprised to see him, then worried when she heard why he'd come. 'No, all's well here apart from David's boils. But June left, oh, a couple of hours ago. I wonder where she's got to?'

David's got boils too? Are they really something to do with the epidemic, not just coincidence? But where is June?

'Was she okay when she left here? Did she say anything about going anywhere on the way home?'

Perhaps she's gone on a hospital round, now the phone's dead. But she'd have told us, surely?

'She was fine. She said she was going straight home.'

'Have you any idea which way she'd go?'

A horrible thought had entered Mike's head.

'Not really. But she said she wasn't going to go past the hospital on the way back. There was half a riot going on there this morning, apparently, when she came past.'

Thank goodness for that, anyway. But where is she? And which way would she go instead?

'Yes, I know about the riot. I saw it too. I didn't come that way this evening, either. But there's a few other ways she might have gone.'

Mike cycled slowly back to Mel's a different way, with his eyes peeled. No, she hadn't arrived home in the meantime. Then he went back and forth along the various alternative routes without seeing anything.

Just as he was starting up Alma Road, someone called out, 'Hey, young fellow! Are you looking for someone?'

Mike looked all around, and couldn't see anyone. He was a little afraid to get off the bike, but it was the voice of an elderly lady. As he stopped, she called again.

'I'm up here.'

Mike located her. She was at an upstairs window.

'Yes. A tall girl, on a bike. She should have been home about three hours ago.'

'She your girl friend? Yes, I saw her. Come inside. I'll get a kettle on.'

She disappeared from the window before Mike could say that June was just a friend.

Anyway, what's happened to June? The old girl's not saying straight off, thinks I need a cup of tea. God, I hope June's okay.

'Here, bring your bike into the hallway. That's it. Just sit yourself down in the lounge a minute. I won't be a minute making the tea.'

She ushered him into the lounge and disappeared into the kitchen without letting him get a word in edgeways.

There was a gas fire blazing, and the room was warm. It was a homely, old fashioned room, cluttered with dark, polished wooden furniture, ornaments and pictures. It reminded him of the digs Pete had had when he first came to Burnfield.

What's happened to June?

The old lady came in, with two teas.

'What's happened to June?'

'Here, drink your tea. A tall girl, you said? Riding a bike? Jeans and a blue sweater?'

'Yes, that's her. Where is she?'

'I think she's down the side of my house, probably. Take it easy, young man. Put your tea down, that's it. No, don't jump up. Let me tell you, and then take your time before you do anything.'

'Is she hurt? Can't I do anything?'

'No. You can't do anything. She's as dead as a doornail. The little bastards! I'd hang, draw and quarter the lot of them!'

She was suddenly animated, in sharp contrast with her previous perfect composure.

O my God!

'What happened?'

'I went to the window when I heard her screaming. I didn't dare go out, there were four of them. They all raped her right there, on the pavement right in front of my garden. Then they sliced her belly open. She was still screaming then. They were laughing. Then something seemed to put the wind up them. One of them pelted off on her bike and another shoved an iron rod in through her eye, and drove it in with a brick. She stopped yelling then. They carted her off down the side of my house, and disappeared over the back gardens.'

Mike buried his head in his hands. He couldn't believe it. *This morning Jill. This evening, June. The epidemic isn't enough for them, they have to murder her.*

I suppose I'd better go to the police. For all the good that'll do. Christ, how am I going to tell Auntie Alice? I haven't even told her about Jill yet!

And this old dear watches it all, cool as a cucumber. Like a telly film. 'I'd hang, draw and quarter the lot of them!', and then sit back and watch the next gory episode. Ugh! He suddenly hated the old lady.

He jumped up and stormed out. She couldn't stop him. Extracting his bicycle slowed him down, and she came out into the hallway.

'Do take care, young man. Don't try to catch them. They left hours ago. I'm sorry.'

What else could she do, or say to him? Poor old thing must've been scared out of her wits.

'I'm going to go down to the police.'

He couldn't bring himself to look down the side of the house.
Not a lot of point anyway.

There was no-one on the desk at the police station. Mike
waited for a couple of minutes. They seemed an age to him.
Nobody came, and he started to yell.

'Is anybody here? There's been a murder!'

The deathly silence returned.

He tried yelling again. No response.

He saw a telephone on a desk, behind the counter. An idea
occurred to him. It took him only ten seconds to work up the
courage. He clambered over the counter, and picked up the
phone. He was rewarded with the dialling tone. Nine, nine, nine.

No response. Ringing, ringing.

*A pity I don't know Mel's number. Her phone might still be
working for incoming calls. On second thoughts, I'd be better
telling her in person anyway.*

He put the phone down. He was conscious again of the eerie
silence. He was at a loss what to do. He sat down on the desk
and put his head in his hands. Images of Jill passed through his
mind. He remembered the day the four of them had met at the
baths, after Pete and June had split up. How Pete had felt
awkward and gone off after only ten minutes.

*Jill and June are both dead now. What are the chances of
ever seeing Pete again, for that matter?* He thought of Cathie.
*Dead nearly a week now. It seems an eternity ago. Pete doesn't
know.*

There's no-one here, is there?

He went through the double doors at the back of the foyer and
found himself in a corridor. *There's no-one here. I'm not going
to get caught. If I do meet anyone, I can explain that I've come
in search of a policeman, there was no-one on the desk. What
does it matter anyway? What does anything matter any more?*

The end of the corridor seemed to be approaching terribly
slowly, so he began to run. The sound of his feet reverberated
along the corridor eerily. He was suddenly conscious of being
very, very alone. He reached the double doors at the other end of
the corridor. Beyond them was a staircase. He bounded up it two
steps at a time. Suddenly one wall was glass. It was pitch dark

outside, except for the distant line of street lights on Station Road, at the top of the embankment. From two floors further up, he could see their reflections in the canal.

What am I doing? Why? He became aware of a terrible sense of unreality. He reached the top of the stairs. The doors were locked. He peered through the wired glass. He could dimly see another corridor, like the one on the ground floor. There were no lights on.

Suddenly he wanted to see Melanie. He ran down the stairs. Through the doors at the bottom.

Something was wrong. He was lost. This wasn't the corridor that led to the foyer. This corridor was different. Menacing, oppressive. Cold.

Get a grip on yourself Mike. Calm down. Think straight.

It really is cold here. It really isn't the same corridor. The floor and walls are bare concrete, that's why it feels oppressive. I've come done one flight too many, and I'm in the basement, in the cells.

God, what a stench!

He walked along the corridor. He peered in through the little barred opening in a heavy steel door. There was no light in the cell. He moved his head back and forth to let some of the light from the corridor in, but could see very little.

Then he realized that this corridor was not silent. There was a sussuration and a steady thrumming noise as of a big ventilation system. And a low, human-sounding moaning.

He located the moaning. It was coming from one of the cells. He couldn't see into this cell any better than he could see into the first, and the voice just moaned without reacting to Mike's words. He tried the door, but it was locked, of course. He felt terrible leaving the poor soul.

The corridor was much shorter than the one above it.

I wonder if that's just a trick of my state of mind. The other one seemed endless.

The doors at the end were broken. The lock had been prised out of the frame. Mike pulled, and the door swung open, the lock gripping thin air. Only inches behind it was a heavy steel door. The paint had been chipped off in several places, as if someone had been trying to force the lock, or the hinges.

In six-inch-high letters of sprayed paint, were the words:

YOU JAMMY BASTARDS!

Mike's bike was still where he had left it, leaning on the glass windows outside the foyer. The desolate world outside seemed positively homely after the police station. He was completely drained. He cycled slowly back to Mel's flat.

'Hello, Mike? Any joy?'

O God, what can I say? Joy?

'Hang on a moment, I'll put the kettle on, and I've got to go to the loo.'

'Hey! Are you okay?'

'Not really – but I'm healthy enough, if that's what you mean.'

'God, Mike, you look awful! What's happened?'

'Here, drink some tea. I feel awful. Jesus, it's good to see you.'

'It's only a couple of hours since you were here. You have your tea too. Take your time.' She put her hand on his knee and squeezed.

Mike looked at her and smiled. Tears came into his eyes. He took a few sips at his tea, and then started to speak, but he didn't know where to begin, and got confused.

'Finish your tea first. Then start at the beginning, from where you left here last time.'

He told her about his search, and the old lady, and the old lady's story. Melanie just lay there and stared.

'I went down to the police station. It was deserted. I went right inside, in search of someone, anyone. I got lost, and ended up in the cells. Found the entrance to the shelter. Someone had tried to break in. And someone had sprayed 'You Jammy Bastards' on the door.

Mike couldn't sleep. He kept seeing Jill's terrified face staring up at him; the old lady getting excited and saying she'd 'hang, draw and quarter the lot of them'; a cold, desolate, ill-lit grey concrete corridor, with steel doors with tiny barred windows.

It all merged imperceptibly into dreadful nightmares. Old ladies chased him up endless staircases, with the starry sky all around him. Then he was chasing the old lady. He cornered her in a grey concrete corridor, and as he drove an iron spike into her eye she became June. She was laughing horribly. Then she was Jill, looking at him with terror in her eyes, and he was trying to resuscitate her, but the old lady was chasing him on a bike, and he couldn't get his breath.

Linda was shaking him. The light was on.

'Mike! Wake up! Are you all right? Is there anything I can do?'

The scream died in his throat.

'Linda! Thank God you're okay!'

He still had a terrifying sensation of being chased, but his head began to clear.

'Oh, goodness. I'm sorry Linda. I've been screaming, haven't I? I hope I've not woken Mel. I'm sorry I woke you. I've been having such dreadful nightmares.'

'I don't think Mel woke up. I'm cold. Where's June?'

She's only been sleeping with June a couple of nights. The cold is mainly psychological, I'm sure. She knows something's wrong with June. O God! I can't tell the kid the whole story!

'She's dead...'

'But she wasn't sick at all! Do people just die just like that, without any warning? You won't die suddenly, will you, Mike? Is there going to be anyone left at all?'

'Chin up, love. Come into my sleeping bag and get warm.'

She snuggled in beside him and was soon fast asleep. Mike found her presence comforting, too. Only later did it strike him how strange it was to have her there. *To all intents and purposes we're family. I've known her four days!*

Chapter 18

After Harry's meltdown, everything was quiet for a few days. One young woman, who'd previously given Harry the cold shoulder, maybe felt sorry for him and chatted with him, and their sleeping bags were side by side the next few nights, but I think only side by side. I didn't investigate!

Then maybe he tried to go further than she wanted to, or maybe she just got fed up with him. Whatever, Harry found himself alone again.

A few days later, he caught Irene on her own while Will was in the loo. They were still arguing when Will returned.

'Leave her alone, Harry.'

'She's my wife, dammit!'

'Not once I get a divorce lawyer I'm not.'

'I don't suppose you'll find one of those in a hurry. There's plenty of time to change your mind.'

Irene looked daggers at him, then looked at Will, as if expecting him to say something.

'You've burned your bridges mate, there's nothing you can do now.'

'Don't call me "mate", you bastard!'

Irene said, 'Calm down, Harry. It'll be a lot easier for all of us.'

Harry punched her in the face before Will could react, but was face down on the floor again a moment later.

Will turned to the crowd that had gathered, 'Shall I break his arm this time, or give him one more chance?'

Blood was pouring from Irene's nose.

One of the big blokes spoke up, 'Don't break his arm, mate. Just hold him there a minute, I'm coming. I'll take charge of him.'

Then he turned to Irene, 'Will your nose be all right, young lady, or should I call a doctor?'

So he is some kind of official. And now he's blown his cover. Does that matter to him?

'I think I'll be okay. He's done it before. The blood'll stop in a minute or two, and I'll have a sore face for a few days, but there's no need for a doctor.'

'He's done it before? So that's twice he's hit you, and once he tried to hit this chap? Silly little man. Like this chap said before, we can't afford to have nutcases running amok in here.'

The big man led Harry away to one of the turnstile exits, then returned without him.

Irene was concerned. 'What will happen to him?'

'Don't worry about him. As long as he doesn't try to hit anyone else, he'll be okay, but none of us will see him again for a while. Maybe never, I really don't know.'

Irene asked the question Will and I had decided we didn't want to ask. 'Who are you? And how much do you know about what's going on?'

'You must have guessed by now that I'm a security guard. We knew that couldn't remain a secret forever, but your man made me come out of hiding sooner than anyone expected. I have to admit that I tossed up in my mind whether to let his arm get broken, and decided that revealing myself was the lesser of two evils. I hope I was right – it's up to all the rest of you now to prove that I was.'

Well. You can't get much more straightforward than that, I suppose. And he's obviously a good deal brighter than the stereotypical security guard – maybe quite a lot of them are, really – and better trained.

Irene still wanted to know how much the security guard knew about what was going on, but either he didn't know much or he didn't want, or wasn't allowed, to tell us much. 'I know how to call for a doctor, or reinforcements, a few things like that, but that's about it.'

I wondered whether he was being as straightforward as he'd been before – and where the doctor and the reinforcements were, and how long they'd take to get to us.

Has Harry simply been moved into a different population? The security guard must have had some special method to open the turnstile at the wrong time. He's presumably warned the security guards in the other group that Harry is on his way.

Maybe that other group is staff, including all those 'reinforcements', the doctor or doctors, and so on. Probably technicians to maintain this incredible place. There could be two groups like ours, and bad boys – or girls – could be sent backwards from the other one just as Harry seems to have been sent forwards.

Or maybe the three groups are all similar, and sending someone into a different group is the only punishment they've got. At least the security guards in that group will know who Harry is, but he won't know who they are. They can only do it twice, though. And although no-one but the security guards will know anything about Harry, quite a few people might realize he was a new arrival, and wonder how, or why. Or maybe not – would I know if someone here was a new arrival?

Maybe he'll even find himself a girlfriend, who knows? He won't have a history working against him.

I'd have shared these thoughts with Will, but I didn't know when or whether we'd have another conversation. I didn't have anyone else to share them with.

Chapter 19

On Thursday it rained all day. Mel persuaded Mike not to go out in it. 'For my sake, and Linda's, and Auntie Alice's and David's, if not for your own.'

'But I've got to tell Auntie Alice about June. And about Jill, too, for that matter.'

'Not at the risk of your own life! It doesn't matter much anyway: she can't be imagining anything worse than the truth.'

They tried to play cards for Linda's sake, but Linda's heart wasn't in it any more than theirs were. They gave up very quickly, and gave in to their depression. They reminisced despondently about better days. They drank a great deal of tea, and had frequent snacks, but no real meals all day.

Linda's boils were getting worse, and Mike's was still producing a lot of pus. Mel's cough wasn't improving, and she had a pain in her chest.

Quite early in the evening Mike brought his sleeping bag into Melanie's room. He put himself to bed on the floor, and propped his back up against the wall. None of them had much to say, but they didn't go to sleep for ages.

Mike woke at first light. Sometime during the night Linda had wriggled in with him again. She hadn't woken him up, but somehow his arm was round her. She was fast asleep. He lay still and listened to the wind, and Melanie's breathing.

It's stopped raining. I must see Auntie Alice today. If Mel's game, perhaps we should all move over there if Ruth'll drive us.

If Ruth is in any fit state. Is she still alive, even?

Ruth was very glad to see him.

'I was scared something had happened to you when you didn't come yesterday. Hugh died last night. I've only five patients left, and only Tony is conscious. I've not been out of this place for days, except for that trip to fetch the car. I didn't see a soul then. Is there anyone about at all? It feels like the end of the world.'

Mike couldn't bring himself to tell her about June. He told her that he'd not been out the day before, but that on Wednesday he'd seen quite a lot of people.

Tony was awake, and feeling much better.

'How is everyone?'

O God! Now I've got to tell the story. He opened his mouth to speak, and had to think what to say. Visions of the old lady came into his mind. And an empty police station. A corridor of cells. A steel door. *You Jammy Bastards.*

'June's dead.'

It was all he could say. He sat down on Tony's bed and wept. Ruth slipped away. Tony stared at him.

'But June was perfectly okay two days ago!'

Mike nodded, but couldn't say anything.

Ruth reappeared. 'I was going to make us all a cuppa, but there's a power cut. You'll have to wait a bit.'

Mike's turbulent mind focussed. 'I'd be surprised if it comes back on at all. We were going to ask you, Ruth, if you could drive the car for us, to move Melanie over to Auntie Alice's. Auntie Alice has a gas stove. Ours is electric.'

Ours? Melanie's! How many days have I been there?

'You don't think it'll come back on? What am I going to do for distilled water for the IV drips?'

'Can you remember anything from your school chemistry, Tony? If I break into the chemistry labs, do you think you can tell me how to set up a glassware still with a bunsen burner?'

'Of course I can. But I'm not so bad now, I'll come myself.

        ... Goodness! I feel unsteady. I'll be okay though, just let me hang onto you.'

'Sit down, Tony. I'll come back for you when I've found the labs and got in. I expect I'll have to break into the cupboards too. I'm sure they'll be locked.'

'I'm not thinking. There's a key cupboard in the staffroom. I'll show you.'

The cupboard contained the key to the laboratory, but no keys to the apparatus cupboards. They found the laboratory, and the cupboards were indeed locked. The keys were in the drawer of the teacher's desk.

Mike went and fetched Tony. It took Tony half an hour to set the still up and get it started, a steady drip, drip, drip into a glass beaker. It took Mike back years. Tony was pale and sweating. He sat down on a stool.

'All you've got to do is keep topping that flask up with water, through that funnel, and keep taking the distilled water away. If there's more than you need for the drips, it'd be better to drink than tap water. The phone and the electric have gone off, with no-one to look after them; I don't think the water will go off for ages, but it may not be as safe as it used to be.'

'They've been telling us to boil water for three minutes for ages.'

'Of course they have. I was forgetting. I'd better set you up some more bunsens for boiling water, and for cooking.'

'Nobody here takes solids, anyway, Tony. Just one for boiling water's quite enough. I'll go and get the things to make the tea if you'll put some water on, Mike.'

As soon as Ruth had gone, Mike told Tony all about June. He managed to maintain his composure, more or less. Tony was thunderstruck. Ruth came back with the tea things before the story was finished.

There was an awed silence.

Then Tony said, in a hushed voice, 'If someone had told me about the overall situation, and I'd thought about it, I'd have guessed that that sort of thing would start happening. But you don't think of it in those terms. You don't imagine it happening to your friends.'

Ruth agreed to move Melanie. Mike cycled off to check with Auntie Alice, and tell her about Jill and June. She was inconsolable. David went to make tea for the three of them. He was totally blank.

Coming back with the teas, he said, 'I wonder how Mum is? There's only me and her left. O God! And Gran! Has anyone been to see her since Mum went into hospital?'

O Christ! Poor old lady! She won't have seen a soul in a week! She'll barely have had a thing to eat, I doubt.

Seriously, I'd be surprised if she's alive.

'I'd better go round there straight away, before I get Ruth to move Melanie.'

The clean-up squad had been, probably several days before. Someone had obviously reported the old lady's death.

Ruth had a look at Linda's boils while Mike loaded all the food from Melanie's flat into the car. Then Mike helped Melanie down the stairs and into the car. They were both breathless by the time she was settled into the back seat.

'Do you remember the way, Linda? Or had I better come in the car and come back for the bike later?'

But Melanie knew where Holly Ridge Road was anyway. Mike followed on the bike. He arrived at Auntie Alice's to find Melanie still sitting in the back of the car. Linda and David were ferrying food into the house.

Mike helped Melanie out of the car and into the house. Auntie Alice was ministering to Ruth, who looked exhausted. Melanie started coughing as soon as she sat down. Her face twisted with pain and she clutched her chest. She gasped for breath between fits of coughing. Mike didn't know what to do. He remembered Jill's last moments.

Did I do right to move her? I hope I've not killed her! Please don't die, Melanie!

Ruth doesn't look any too good, either.

But eventually Melanie's coughing stopped, and gradually her breathing eased. Auntie Alice persuaded Ruth to lie down on the sofa for a while. She was soon fast asleep.

Auntie Alice tried to organize a game of Monopoly, but it didn't work. The game started slowly and got slower. Linda began to cry. A deep sigh from Melanie started her coughing again, but it didn't last long.

Auntie Alice admitted defeat. She left the game and went to make some tea. The days of plates of cakes were over. She was pleased to have the stale bread Mike had bought, to make a pile of pilchard-in-tomato-sauce sandwiches.

Ruth didn't wake up until late afternoon.

'You should've woken me! I'm hours late for my round!'

Five minutes after she left, she was back.

'Can you take me down to the school on the back of your bike, Mike? I only got to the end of the road, and the car conked out. Out of diesel. It was nearly full before. I think someone must've syphoned the tank.'

Tony was fast asleep. Two more of Ruth's patients had died.

I wonder if anyone came here while we were away? Unlikely. What are other people doing these days? What are they thinking?

Mike got the still going again, and Ruth used the last of the previous batch of distilled water to make up some IV solutions.

'I wonder how much longer I'll be doing this? I hope Tony gets better.'

They prepared several beakers of distilled water, and covered them with glass dishes. Dusk became darkness. They left the bunsen burning, and sat mesmerized by the flame.

The sound of coughing aroused them from their reveries.

'That must be Tony awake. Getting there's going to be fun, in the dark!'

They held hands and groped their way through the corridors.

'I wish we had a torch.'

Getting back to Auntie Alice's with all the streetlights off is going to be well nigh impossible. Oh for a moon! I couldn't possibly do it on the bike. I don't really fancy walking. I'd be terrified of every shadow and every sound. Especially pushing a bike. Too desirable. But I can't leave it here. I'll need it tomorrow.

'How are you going to get home?'

Telepathy.

'I was just thinking exactly that myself.'

Not surprising really.

'Ow!' Simultaneously.

'I'd forgotten these steps.' Again in absolute unison. They sat down on the steps and laughed.

They both tried to climb one more step than there was and almost fell. They started laughing again.

'What's so funny?'

'Nothing. Just trying to get about in the dark. How are you feeling?'

'Pretty rough, to tell the truth. I'm glad you've come, Ruth. My bottle's full.'

'That's a good sign. You're still absorbing water if you're still passing it.'

'I know. I shouldn't complain. Most people seem to be a lot worse off than me.'

'You'd better stay here tonight, Mike. I don't fancy the idea of you groping your way all that distance.'

'I think you're right. I should have realized earlier and gone before dark. They'll be worried silly at Auntie Alice's.'

It was no easy matter preparing a bed for Mike in pitch darkness. Manhandling a dead body was even less pleasant than when he could see what he was doing. Mike groped his way to the toilets to wash. By the time he came back Ruth had remade the bed with fresh linen.

'You know, we've been wasting our time distilling all that water and making up IV solution. The autoclave's electric too. I can't sterilize anything.'

'What that comes down to is, which is the greater risk?'

'They're dead either way. Seriously speaking, they're dead anyway, even if we could sterilize everything. What are we going to do?'

'Stop worrying about them. There's nothing we can do. There must be millions of people dying at the moment. You can't shoulder that kind of burden. Worry about yourself.'

'In that case, I should leave here, logically speaking. But I've nowhere to go.

... God, we'll be sleeping in a morgue! I want to get out of here!'

'Hey, Ruth, calm down!'

Mike found her in the darkness and held her tightly. She started crying.

'You should come and stay at Auntie Alice's with the rest of us. I hope Tony's fit to take on the bike tomorrow. There's nothing you can do here.'

Mike cycled to Auntie Alice's at first light to let them know he was okay. Then he went back to see how Tony was.

Tony was awake when he arrived, but very groggy and obviously in no fit state to be moved by any means, least of all as a passenger on a bicycle. Ruth picked up his hand to take his pulse. Tony seemed unaware of it. He was looking at Mike with a puzzled expression on his face.

'He feels really cold. His pulse is ever so fast, but very faint. I don't know why I'm bothering, I've no doctor to tell. The only symptom I've been shown how to treat is dehydration, and he doesn't seem to be suffering from that. Without the autoclave, I couldn't put him on a drip, even if he was.'

Tony died quietly as they stood there. Ruth pulled the sheet up over his face. Mike remembered Jill's last moments and shuddered.

'Now what?'

Ruth's voice startled Mike. *Now what indeed. Back to Auntie Alice's, both of us. Is there anything useful to take from here? Tea, sugar, glucose, powdered milk, salt.*

'Come on.'

He dragged her out of the room. He took the bicycle into the staffroom and filled the panniers from the cupboard. He led her out of the school. They mounted the bicycle and rode back to Auntie Alice's. They were the only things moving, as far as they could tell.

When they arrived, Melanie was coughing again. Auntie Alice was busy with Linda's boils. She'd already dressed David's.

Mine's still awfully sore. Better get Ruth to have a look.

'God, Mike, this is a mess! It's not healing properly at all. There's a big scab over the whole area, but it's all cracked and it's raw and bloody in patches. I don't know what to do with it. Alice, have you any dressings suitable for a mess like this?'

Alice looked at it, and pronounced the opinion that he ought to see a doctor. Melanie had stopped coughing, but was gasping horribly for breath.

'Even if I could find a doctor anywhere, he wouldn't thank me just now for showing him a boil that won't heal. Just smear it with antiseptic cream and tie me up in a bit of cloth. I'll be okay.'

Suddenly Linda, who had been lying back across two chairs for the boils on her tummy to be attended to, jumped up.

'Somebody help Melanie!'

Melanie was clutching her chest, looking wildly about, and breathing very fast. Short, shallow, hoarse breaths. Before anyone got to her, she slumped forward.

She had stopped breathing altogether. Her pulse faded away from racing to nothing as Ruth held her wrist.

'She's dead.' Ruth's voice was a monotone.

We've lost our capacity to be shocked any more.

'But she didn't have it at all! No diarrhea, no vomiting, no rash!'

'I expect she's had a lung infection, secondary to the broken rib. I should've wondered when I heard her coughing so much yesterday. I never thought, though – a big, strong, fit girl like her shouldn't succumb to infection so easily.'

Auntie Alice and the children were just staring in horror. Mike realized that somehow he had to get rid of Melanie's body.

God, how things have changed. All I can think of is that I've got to get rid of her body. No calling the hospital, the police, or the undertaker. No telling friends and relatives. Where can I put her? There's no clean-up squad or health patrol any more, I don't think.

This is really it, then, isn't it? If we survive at all, we'll just be savages, scavenging amongst the ruins.

Mike found Melanie's body quite hard to carry. He left her in the gutter forty yards down the road. He wondered vaguely where other people were leaving bodies.

Perhaps they're digging graves in their back gardens. I haven't the energy. Perhaps they're just lying there, dead in their beds.

Linda was shaking him. He looked at her. His eyes went in and out of focus for a moment. She was saying something, but he couldn't make out what. He discovered he couldn't remember much at all. Dumping a body in a gutter. Walking into someone's house. Waking in bed, in darkness.

He was in bed now. Linda was shaking him. He looked at her. His eyes were out of focus.

Jill! Jill! Jill! Don't die, Jill!

　　– 'You must've known it was hopeless.'

Suddenly Linda's voice got through.

'Mike! Wake up! You're the only one left!'

He tried to say 'Linda', but his voice wouldn't work.

The pain under his arm was gone.

He didn't wake up again.

Chapter 20

Ellie was the young mother whose toddler I'd carried when we first entered the shelter. Since Will and I had drifted apart, she and her friend Sharon had taken to coming and chatting with me every now and then, but we'd not discussed issues like these. We'd talked about my life in Burnfield, and theirs as army wives. Their husbands had been going to come with them to Finland, but were called away on an exercise at the last minute.

'You go anyway love,' Sharon's husband had said. 'And don't worry about me, it's only an exercise.' I assumed Ellie's husband had said much the same thing.

Sharon wasn't sure about the exercise. 'They used to tell us honestly when our chaps – and some lasses, of course – were sent on missions, but now they'll as likely as not call a mission an exercise, and we don't really know whether it's an exercise or a mission until they get back. We're not supposed to know even then, but we can tell. We could tell even if our men didn't tell us themselves. They're not supposed to, but of course they often do.

'And even if it was originally an exercise, they'll have been dragged off it for active service by now, with a war on.'

I didn't tell them about Will's and my idea that there might not really be a war at all, and that we might have been kidnapped for a psychosocial experiment. It had seemed almost credible while I was talking with Will; it seemed preposterous now. *But Will is really such a down-to-earth fellow. Doubtless it only seemed* almost *credible to him, too. In fact we'd actually said as much to each other, and probably meant it. I don't think we were just covering ourselves against seeming to each other to be conspiracy theorists.*

Anyway, even if it was credible, it would be tactless to talk like that with Ellie and Sharon. I think.

Sharon also had a toddler, Donna, who had quickly decided that I was her friend, and was often fast asleep lying with her head on my lap. One evening Sharon and I found ourselves chatting late into the evening. That night, Sharon and I ended up lying side by side in our separate sleeping bags, still chattering, Donna sharing her mother's sleeping bag. *Everyone else probably thinks we're a couple.*

In the middle of the night I woke to find Sharon's shoulder under my armpit, her head on my shoulder, and my arm around her, inside her sleeping bag. I thought of Cathie, and wanted to extract my arm, but I didn't want to wake Sharon or Donna, who was behind her mum.

The next time I woke, the lights were just beginning their morning brightening. Sharon was sitting cross-legged next to me, with Donna on her lap, playing and laughing. I lay there looking at them for a little while, until Sharon noticed I was awake.

'Morning, sleepy-head! Donna says you're her Daddy now, did you hear her?'

Blimey. I thought Cathie was a bit forward, but that takes the biscuit. Blame Donna, would you? At least when Cathie chose me, we were both single! But how did my arm end up round Sharon during the night? Surely she didn't do that herself? I must have at least played a part. I think.

'And what would your husband say?'

'Just carry on snoring, I expect. Anyway, the chaps don't realize all us wives know the barmaid at the camp bar. Or maybe they think she's deaf or daft or something. But she hears their chatter, and we get to hear all their stories. We know what they get up to when they're away – or what they tell each other they get up to, anyway. Half of it's probably exaggerated or completely made up. Whether it's true or not, he can't say anything without me saying something much worse back. Anyway, he might be dead for all we know.'

The thought doesn't seem to bother her much. Cathie could be dead too, perish the thought. Cathie, I love you! What should I do?

Actually, I knew what Cathie would say. *She's too sensible.* 'I might be dead for all you know. We spent just one day together, and yes, I love you too, but we might never see each other again. Forget me. If I were in your shoes, I certainly would.'

And she'd mean it, too. Whether if she were in my shoes she really would forget me I'm less sure, but she'd mean it when she said it. What should I do?

'You're thinking about your Cathie, aren't you? If we ever get out of here and she's still alive, she need never know what happened here. Same with my Bernie. Live for the day, it's all we can do anyway.'

It took me a couple of weeks to accept the situation, but Sharon was patient. Eventually we ended up in a zipped-up pair of sleeping bags.

One thing we don't get in our thrice-daily packages is condoms. Or at least, I never have, and no-one's ever offered to swap one for anything. Do the ladies get any other sorts of contraceptives? Or are there contraceptives in the food? Or are the authorities hoping that half the younger women will be pregnant by the time we come out? If so, why?

I didn't find it an easy subject to raise with Sharon, but she was less reticent. 'You're worrying I'll get pregnant, aren't you? Well, don't. I've got a coil in. In fact, I'm more worried about who'll take the damn thing out for me when I want another kid! I can see the world being a very different place when we come out.'

If there's a world worth coming out to at all. Even if we come out to a survivable world, will it be one I'd want to raise a child in? I wasn't sure about that at all, but I didn't say anything.

Part III

Chapter 1

It was about three months before we got out of the shelter. The shelter had obviously been designed for a siege at least that long: all the supplies kept coming on schedule, no problems. I still wonder whether the duration of our incarceration was determined by the design of the shelter and its supplies, rather than by exactly what was going on on the surface.

Unless someone had made extraordinary preparations before the war began, people had been hard at work on the surface for some while before we came out. We only knew we were coming out a couple of hours before we actually did: there was an announcement from the speakers in Hall Two – as I'd thought of it ever since arriving in what I thought of as Hall One – and we finally left through the big steel doors in Hall Two.

As at the entrance to Hall One, there was a shower area between two sets of massive doors, and beyond that a long, bare concrete tunnel. But this tunnel ended not in a deep shaft with a series of staircases, but in a garage where several coaches were waiting for us. They looked just like the coaches that had brought us from the airfield to the hotel, and could well have been the same ones.

The coaches were wet, and I wondered whether it was raining outside; but as we left the garage, we passed a massive version of a car wash, and a coach just arriving was being washed down. Powerful jets of water were playing on the underneath of the coach as well as all over the upper body. It had obviously already passed through a set of huge rotating brushes that were dripping foam.

Decontamination. We're going to pass through a contaminated area. I wonder if it's radioactive, chemical or biological contamination? Presumably our coach will get decontaminated again before we arrive wherever we're going.

We must have been a mile or two from the shelter by the time
we surfaced. It was night. I was sitting with Sharon, and Donna
was fast asleep flat out across both our laps.

*So the people who started in Hall Two probably arrived by
coach from somewhere – probably the nearest town. They
probably arrived after things had kicked off, and knew
something about what was going on. As long as they got into the
coaches before anything happened, they could have driven in
through areas that were already contaminated.*

We drove for a couple of hours, and then our coach went
through a decontamination wash. It was just getting light, and I
could see a high steel mesh fence stretching a few hundred yards
in each direction. After the decontamination, we went in through
a huge steel gate in the fence.

The coach pulled to a halt under a canopy alongside a large
building, and we all tumbled out with our canvas bags. Mine
still had my scruffy old kitbag in it. Armed men in military
uniforms ushered us into the building, which housed a large
room with, I estimated, about two hundred seats.

*Does that mean there'll be half a dozen sittings, for just the
people from our group? And then another half dozen for each of
the other groups? Or aren't we all coming to the same place?*

*How long will we be in here? How long will it take for all the
coaches to arrive?*

We weren't in there long at all, and it was actually the
decontamination that was the bottleneck, not the briefing.

We were addressed by a man in military uniform.

He told us that the fenced area had been cleared as clean, and
was expected to remain so because the immediate surroundings
were clean – but that anywhere more than a few hundred metres
from the compound could not be guaranteed clean at present.

'As far as is known, the only survivors almost anywhere in
the world are those who took refuge in competently constructed
shelters.

'Efforts are ongoing to find additional clean areas, or to
decontaminate others, and the enclosed area will be extended
whenever it is safe to do so, or additional enclosures may be
established into which groups of you may move.

'There are enough huts for everyone as long as no-one expects a hut to themselves. Meals will be served in here between seven and eight thirty in the morning, between twelve and one thirty, and between five and six thirty. There is sufficient land here to grow all our own food. We have seeds, chickens and goats. Training in farming will be provided. If everyone shares the work fairly, it won't be onerous.

'Essential services will be organized on a rota basis, and everyone will be expected to pull their weight.

'It will be up to you to organize yourselves for any other activities.

'I'll see you at breakfast later. Now go and find huts for yourselves. The next coach load is ready for their briefing.'

And we were ushered out of the building by different doors.

I think it's three coach loads per briefing, actually.

'Concentration camp, or what? I wonder how long we'll be here? No suggestion of any possibility of trying to get back to England, not yet awhile, anyway. Farming? They think we'll be here for *years*.'

Sharon seems upset, but remarkably accepting of the situation. I'm not sure how I feel about it.

'Why the big fence, though? Are they afraid we'll try to escape? If it's true that large areas around here are dangerously contaminated, why would anyone want to escape? And if it's not true, what's going on?'

'This can't be the only place like this. Is there going to be any coming and going between them? Perhaps we'll be able to migrate home gradually, from one concentration camp to another, a step at a time.'

'I doubt that. I don't think they're going to be running coach services between the various sites, somehow. They'll be afraid of some sites ending up without a sufficient labour force, and others getting overcrowded.'

'So we're slaves, basically.'

'Looks that way, for the present, anyway. All we can do is hope our masters are benevolent.'

'That'd be a first.'

'Pessimist.' *But she's right, really.*

Ellie found us, and we agreed to share a hut – three adults and three small children. The hut seemed plenty big enough for us. *No wonder they don't want anyone to have one to themselves. Even a couple would be being a bit greedy.*

Sharon wondered whether all three groups from the shelter would be in our camp, or whether there were other camps in the area. 'I'm not sure I fancy the combination of Will, Irene and Harry together again.'

'We've got armed guards here though, not just a couple of unarmed security guards.'

'A couple? I thought there was only one.'

Then I had to explain how Will and I had tried to change groups, and discovered the two suspected guards, one of whom was subsequently confirmed.

At breakfast, we were given cards with our timetables on them, all different – or at least, quite a variety of different ones. Sharon asked to be given one that was the same as mine, but was told, 'They're from the same batch, so there's a lot of common timing. But yours is a lady's card, and his is a gent's card. There's bound to be a few differences.'

Rolls and butter, slices of ham and cheese, and a cup of coffee.

Over breakfast we studied our timetables. There was indeed a lot of common timing – we were together for farming training, and most of our leisure time coincided – but Sharon had kitchen and creche duties, which I didn't, and I had more time doing 'labouring as detailed'.

'So. Not just slaves, but gender-stereotyped slaves. I suppose it was to be expected.'

'Even in Sweden?'

'Hmm. Apparently.'

We were encouraged to leave the hall as soon as we'd eaten, to let another group use our table, and on our way out we were told, 'The timetable doesn't start until tomorrow. Please use today to familiarize yourselves with the camp, and make sure you know where each of the locations mentioned on your timetable is.'

So they call it a camp, too.

We did as we were told. Familiarizing ourselves with the camp was unexceptionable, and we agreed that the timetable was probably a good idea too, really. 'Obviously everyone has to pull their weight, the whole situation would be hopeless otherwise.'

We weren't happy, but so far everything seemed to be reasonable, and as fair as could be expected.

'But I bet the senior officers don't do their fair share of the less pleasant duties!'

'No, I don't suppose they will.'

'Not so different from normal life, really – except that we're all semi-employed, rather than half of us overworked and the other half left on the scrapheap. All play and no work is as bad as all work and no play – maybe worse, when you've barely enough money to keep body and soul together.'

'You sound as though you speak from experience.'

Sharon got in before I'd worked out what to say, 'He does. He told me all about it.'

'At least in normal life people get a choice of how they earn their living.'

'You think so? Not a lot, in most cases. Most folks just get any job they can, if they can.'

'I suppose that's true. Geoff didn't really want to be a soldier, but what else is there for a man with no qualifications and a pregnant wife who'd rather like to have somewhere to live?'

'That's pretty much what Bernie said. He's got decent A levels, but where's that get you without a degree? Trainee shop manager? Draughtsman? For the lucky few, and he wasn't one of them. Anyway, the pay's lousy. We weren't badly off in the army – not great pay, but at least we got decent quarters at a sensible price.'

She's talking past tense. Which is probably the sensible way to see things. Oh, Cathie, where are you? What's really going on in the rest of the world?

Donna was riding on my shoulders. Maybe she sensed my momentary detachment. However that may be, she decided to put her hands over my eyes, 'Who is it?'

'I don't know. Sharon? Billy? Tom? Ellie? I know! It's Donna!'

I swung Donna round off my shoulders and into my arms. She was giggling like a loon.

Sharon laughed. She was carrying Tom in a makeshift sling, and Billy was riding on Ellie's shoulders.

We explored the middle of the camp first.

The hall where we'd had our briefing and our breakfast seemed to be a converted barn – and not very much converted. There were two coaches under the canopy, which had perhaps been designed to shelter farm trailers while they were loaded or unloaded.

Just two coaches? There must have been fifteen or twenty to bring us here, we weren't brought in shifts. Well, our group wasn't. The other groups presumably didn't come at the same time as us. In fact, have all three groups arrived yet at all?

There was a large farmhouse, which was apparently occupied by senior army officers and their families. Several outbuildings had been labelled up so we could match them with locations on our timetables. There was a large, apparently new, prefabricated block that seemed to house ordinary soldiers and their families, and there were rows and rows of huts very like ours.

The huts seemed to be new, kit-built, and as far as we could see identical apart from their numbers and the colour of their roofs and paintwork. Ours was K3, quite close to the old farm buildings, with a light green roof and blue and white paintwork. Like all the others, it stood on four wooden legs on concrete slabs on bare, levelled, gravelly ground.

We didn't bother to wander all up and down the rows of huts, but decided to set off across the rough, tussocky grass up a hill that overlooked the farm. There was a rocky outcrop on the top of the hill, but it was easily climbed. Even Billy and Donna, who were walking at that point, managed to scramble up onto the top.

We seemed to be the only people who'd taken it into their heads to go up there – for the time being, at least.

From the top, we could see almost the whole extent of the camp. As far as we could see, the perimeter fence formed a rough circle, perhaps a couple of miles or a little more in diameter, centred on the old farm.

The hill we were on wasn't far from the fence at the northern edge. Between us and the fence was a steep slope down to a boggy area, then the ground rose again before the fence. Beyond the fence the ground continued to rise, a couple of hundred yards of rough grass and then dense conifer forest.

Around us, the land appeared to be rough pasture, but we couldn't see any animals grazing. Generally, it sloped fairly steeply down to a wide, more-or-less level band running across the middle of the camp, then in the far south of the camp the ground fell away below our line of sight, and we couldn't see the southern edge at all. Much further away to the south we could see what seemed to be more farmland, with wooded hills beyond.

The huts occupied a rectangular area maybe half a mile by a quarter, to the east of the farm buildings. I thought I could count eighteen rows of them, and about forty huts in each row, but it was difficult from that distance and at that angle.

By the time we got down to the buildings again, it was almost the beginning of lunch time. We went back to our hut for a wash and to change Tom's nappy, and then went and had lunch. Then Ellie went back to the hut again to wash out the wet nappy, and Sharon and I took all three children for another walk. With the two toddlers walking, we were pretty slow, but we had the whole afternoon. We wandered along the gravel track to the gates, and had a look through the fence at the decontamination unit. I noticed that the drain from it ran into a ditch only just outside the fence, and then parallel with the fence for quite a way.

I hope nothing they're washing off the coaches ends up blowing about and into the camp. They actually seem quite blasé about it. Surely it's not all just theatre?

We followed a well-trodden path just inside the fence, that was probably originally made by the soldiers who constructed the fence.

'The fence is newish, but it doesn't look as though it went up in just the last couple of days. They kept us underground at least two or three weeks longer than the soldiers, so the camp could be ready when we came out. I wonder whether they were in one of our three groups, or whether they were in a different shelter somewhere else?'

'I reckon they must have been in our shelter. Thinking about the number of huts and the number of people, I reckon there were two groups of civilians, and one rather smaller group of soldiers and their families, and so far there's one group of civilians – us – and probably all the soldiers.'

'I've not seen Harry. You think he's in the other civilian group?'

'Probably. Unless he was held with the soldiers, and he's still under arrest.

'Another thing exercising my mind is this: they just asked us to find huts for ourselves, implying there were plenty. Well, with just one group of us here there's more than plenty – but surely they wouldn't have put up so many that there'd still be more than plenty when everyone else arrives. As far as I know, none of them were locked, and they didn't say any of them were out of bounds, so when everyone else arrives, will we find some of us have to take in extra housemates?'

'Hmm. I think we're safe enough from that, with six of us in there, even if three of them are rather little. But I can see some clever psychology there – trying to force the two groups to mix a bit. Of course that could backfire horribly.'

'Especially if the other group is locals who got bussed in from the nearest town, wherever that it. All Swedes in Sweden, while we're nearly all foreigners from all over the place.'

'Large contingent of Brits, in fact. I think our plane had about a hundred and eighty, and Will said practically a third of the timber conference people were English.'

Ellie caught up with us. 'I hope to God I can dry nappies faster than he uses them. I've only got five – seven if I tear one of the towels in half.'

'I suppose it's quite impressive that they've got water in all the huts, and sewers. No electricity, but that's not surprising. They must have a generator at the farm, but it couldn't supply all the huts, not even for lighting. And I'm sure as hell there'll be no other electricity supply. Not sure what we'll do for drying come winter.'

'Perish the thought. I can see those huts getting pretty damn cold, too.'

'So can I. Judging by the thickness of the walls and floors, they've got loads of insulation, but with no heating at all they'll still get bloody cold.'

'Maybe they're hoping to get more power before winter. And get some wiring done.'

'There must be all kinds of equipment and materials lying around unused now, if everyone from the locality who wasn't in the shelter is dead and gone. It's only a matter of going and fetching it. There's plenty of soldiers – and civilians, for that matter – to do the actual work.'

'It's probably not really just a matter of going and fetching it. A lot of it must be contaminated, if everyone's dead. Decontaminating the outside of a coach is one thing, decontaminating random bits of equipment is quite another.'

'I wonder what really happened? If the contamination is radioactive, most of it might have decayed away by now, and any that hasn't can be detected with radiation meters, so you know what needs decontaminating, and you know whether you've succeeded or not. If it's biological or chemical, it's much harder to know what's contaminated and what isn't – but the biological stuff is reckoned to have a very limited life in the general environment. It's no use killing all your enemy's population if you leave their country permanently uninhabitable.'

'That's the official story, Sharon. I wish my friend Tony was here though. He's very sceptical of the official story, and knows enough about stuff to back his scepticism up. In particular, I remember him saying that it's actually very hard to detect modest levels of radioactive contamination with some particular long half-life isotopes. If there's enough of them to be an immediate threat, they're detectable all right – but there can be enough to cause a lingering death months or years later without them being detectable at all with anything you'd find outside a nuclear research lab.

'And biological agents that are designed to self-destruct after one or two generations are all very well, but when you're dealing with the kind of massive quantities you'd need to kill whole populations, there's a big risk that some of them somewhere will mutate so as not to self-destruct, and then spread; or that some of the stuff will be contaminated with non-self-destructing bugs during manufacture. And biological contamination, particularly novel stuff, is even harder to detect than radioactive contamination.'

'Cor. If that's your layman's simplified version, I don't think I want to meet your friend.'

You never will. I doubt if he's even still alive. Unless Sweden got hit a lot harder than England, and I can't imagine why that would be. Oh, Cathie!

'Pete – you okay?'

'Oh – yes, well, no, but yes, I'm okay. Just thinking about England, that's all, and whether my friends have any chance at all of still being alive.'

Or my family, for that matter. London and Sheffield? Surely not, big cities like that haven't a hope if rural Sweden is dangerously contaminated. Funny how it's Mike and Jill and June – and especially Cathie – that I think of first, not my family. Even Tony, that I avoid half the time.

'Pete. Come here. I'm here. Donna's here. You're Donna's New Daddy, remember? You can't keep living in the past. Maybe your friends are okay, maybe they're not, but it'll be a long, long time before you see them again even if they are. Give us a cuddle, we need it as much as you do.'

We all ended up in a group cuddle, because Billy wanted to get involved as well, and then Ellie joined in too. Then we were all crying and laughing together.

With three adults and the two bigger children riding shoulders again, we made better time, and completed the circuit of the southern half of the fence, then trudged back across unkempt fields to the far end of the rectangle of huts.

The fields inside the fence look just like the fields outside, which isn't surprising. In fact, the fence must go right across the middles of the old fields. In a year's time it'll be growing crops in here, and bigger and bigger weeds out there. Forests, before long.

It was nearly time for dinner. Tom's nappy was wet again, and the last one wasn't dry yet.

'At least the weather's dry. I want a line outside, though. It's all very well leaving the door and window open with stuff on a drying horse, but an outside line would be better in this weather.'

'At least there is a drying horse. They've done pretty well, considering, I reckon.'

'True enough. I wonder whether things will get better, or worse, as time goes on?'

'Better in some ways, and worse in others, I expect. That's pretty much inevitable, I think.'

'But you wouldn't care to guess what'll get better, and what'll get worse, I don't suppose!'

Laughter.

'Not in general, no. A few specifics, possibly.'

'Don't bother. We'll find out soon enough.'

Chapter 2

Sharon was right about the other group. They arrived just after breakfast the following day – in time for their own breakfasts. Their meal times were immediately after ours and only an hour long, as Sharon discovered because her kitchen duties two days a week turned out to include serving their breakfasts.

They were mostly Swedish families, almost all of them young mothers with small children. There were scarcely any fathers, and there were quite a few young women of East Asian appearance who seemed to be au pairs.

I wonder how that particular cross-section of the population happened to end up in the shelter? Thursday afternoon: all the men at work. Where were all these families, that they managed to get on the coaches?

Maybe they were having a trip, and got diverted? Hundreds of them? Odd.

But it turned out that that was exactly what had happened. They'd been headed for a summer camp in Lapland.

It took us several days to find that out, and to learn that there had only been about seven hundred in the Swedish group, more than half of them small children. Mostly they had managed to find huts easily enough, but there had had to be some reshuffling to make room for the last few. Many of the parents and most of the au pairs spoke reasonably good English, and there appeared to be a policy on the part of the authorities to conduct everything in English.

Harry wasn't in that group, either.
"He'll be okay as long as he doesn't hit anyone else."
Did he hit someone else, and if so, what happened to him?

My timetable had two one hour slots per week for teaching. The first two slots we spent discussing who would teach what to whom, and I was detailed to help teach English to some of the bigger Swedish children, who had already started to study

English in school. I was to assist Lisbet, the Danish wife of one of the Swedish soldiers, who had been a teacher before leaving to start a family. Her own two children were still tiny, but would be in one of the creches while she was working. We got on very well.

Lisbet's English was excellent – with a fairly strong accent, but clear, accurate and with good use of idiom. She was an excellent teacher, too, and I learnt a lot about teaching from her.

Four of the people who'd been detailed to do teaching had to give up after just a few lessons. I never discovered whether this was because they themselves found they couldn't cope, or because the more experienced teacher they were working with decided they were useless. My teaching load was doubled to four hours a week – but I didn't get any time off anything else. I simply lost two hours a week of leisure time. But I wasn't complaining: I was quite enjoying the teaching, and I was still only working nineteen hours a week altogether.

My additional hours weren't with Lisbet. Lisbet obviously reckoned I was ready for a more independent teaching role. One of the other novice teachers had also had her teaching hours increased, and we were to work together with some of the younger children. Her name was Persie – Perseverance Nguyen, an engineering graduate from Vietnam, in Sweden as an au pair. Fluent in Vietnamese, French, English and now Swedish, absolutely lovely with the children, and with a smile to melt a heart of stone. What it could do to a heart of butter like mine was another matter. I was smitten, but kept my feelings to myself.

Sharon could tell something was amiss, though. Eventually she accosted me, 'It's that Chinese girl, isn't it? You fancy her, don't you?'

I couldn't deny it, and didn't try to. 'She's not Chinese, she's Vietnamese. I've not touched her, and I don't think she knows how I feel. I wouldn't dream of saying a word.'

'You should. I don't want a man who fancies somebody else. Not somebody who's actually around, at any rate. I can cope with you fancying a ghost.'

Cathie's not a ghost. Or is she? All in all, the likelihood is she really is dead, and even if she isn't, what are my chances of ever seeing her again? And if I do, what are the odds she'll have found another boyfriend by now, thinking that I'm *dead?*

But I didn't feel the same physical anguish that I'd felt before. *I'm getting over her. Something to do with Persie?*

But what about Sharon? "I don't want a man who fancies somebody else." What can one possibly say to that? Do I still fancy Sharon anyway? Or do I just feel committed to her?

I didn't know.

Nearly every day, two parties of soldiers went out in the coaches, and came back a few hours later with loads of tinned or packaged food, or tools or building materials. *Basically, raiding parties, but is it stealing when the former owners, and all their conceivable heirs in title, are dead? But are they? How many other shelters are there in this area? Surely at least some of the rest of the population is alive somewhere? Are the military simply commandeering everything from everybody regardless?*

They decontaminated the outsides of the coaches, and there were a couple of sealable suits in each coach for soldiers to wear while checking places for contamination, that could be washed down when necessary using a portable decontamination set. All very professional-looking, but I was beginning to suspect that it was mostly just theatre. The portable radiation meters they had looked pretty perfunctory, and the idea of any biological or chemical monitoring was laughable.

Sometimes, when they'd found particularly useful but large building materials, they took a tractor from the farm, pulling a huge trailer. The trailer had a tarpaulin, which made it possible to wash the whole combination down in the decontamination unit slightly more effectively than would have been possible with an open trailer, but it still looked more theatrical than effective.

So what is the score? I wasn't sure, but I suspected the senior officers were taking the view that a few extra cancers a few years down the line, or one or two soldiers dying mysteriously, wasn't such a big deal, and that the risks weren't really all that great. The raids were probably essential anyway.

A one-in-a-thousand risk to someone else's life is a lot more tolerable than the same risk to your own, of course.

What were the risks to people who weren't in shelters during the war, though? Were they really a thousand in a thousand? Or did they have a chance?

Probably depends where they were. Did the far north of Scandinavia escape unscathed, perhaps? If they did, what are people there doing now?

Sometimes one of my labouring jobs would be to help unload things – generally when it was building materials rather than comestibles.

One day one of the coaches arrived back with, amongst other things, several cases of various alcoholic drinks, chocolates, crisps, peanuts and the like. Party!

It wasn't for everyone. I'm not sure *exactly* how they chose who to invite, but the general picture was fairly clear. Most of the au pairs were invited, as were most of the young mothers whose husbands were absent; but so were Will and Irene and various other couples, and even a few single men. Neither Sharon nor I were invited, nor Ellie. We didn't know which soldiers were or weren't invited, but it was basically organized by the soldiers.

A lot of those young mothers are probably recently widowed – and don't know one way or the other. How many of their husbands made it into some other shelter? Maybe the camp they're in isn't even all that far away.

Persie was invited, but told me that she wasn't going. 'I know what that's all about. I'm sure you do, too. I really, really am not interested. They can all get drunk and disgusting if they like, but they can do it without me.'

Ingrid, the lady she worked for, was going, so Persie had the excuse that she had to look after the children. She was still a little worried that some soldier or other would come round to seek her out. 'Would you come and stay with me? I'd feel a bit safer if you were there.'

'I'm no match for any of those soldiers. How about you bring the children round to our hut – then you'll have Sharon and Ellie to look after you as well. And the children can have a real party.'

'I don't even know them. And I'm sure Sharon is jealous of me, anyway.'

I couldn't escape that. 'There's no denying that. She knows I fancy you. You knew too, then.'

'Of course I knew. How could I not? But you're a perfect gentleman, and you never said a word before, so I never had to tell you. I think you're a lovely man, Pete, but I'm afraid I really don't fancy you. I'm sorry.'

She put her hand on my forearm and looked me straight in the eyes. I couldn't help it: I couldn't hold the tears back.

'Should I ask them anyway? You really would be safer there than in your own hut.'

'I've got a better idea. I'll arrange with Ingrid to let me hold a children's party in our hut. Then Sharon and Ellie and their children can come, and we can have a few more girls and kids round. We'll stuff the little hut full. You can come to help, everyone knows you're good with the little ones. I can even demand some of the crisps and peanuts and chocolate for the children's party. They can't refuse.'

'That does sound like a better plan. The only trouble is that the adults' party will go on long after the little ones have run out of steam. Everyone will want to take them home.'

'True. That could be bad for quite a few of the girls. I know quite a few who've been invited who don't want to go. I don't fancy the idea of them making their way home in the middle of the other party.'

'Perhaps we'd better be honest with the senior officers, tell them our worries, and ask for a secure place for mothers and children for the night.'

'But they could be some of the worst offenders. In fact, I think they probably are.'

'They've all got their wives here!'

'You think that makes any difference?'

'Ah. Maybe not.'

'Why do you think there are a few young hunks invited?'

Ow. No doubt she's right. Where does that leave us?

'So what can we do? Like I said, I don't think I'm any match for any of those soldiers.'

'Maybe the best idea is to invite as many of the girls as can possibly sleep in one hut, and all stick together for the night.'

'Especially the ones who've been invited and don't want to go.'

'Maybe. But Amazons like Ellie and Sharon would be useful, too. Most of the girls I know who don't want to go aren't much bigger than me.'

Amazons? They're average size women.

Ah. Average size in England.

'I hear your friend Will is quite a handy fighter.'

'Yup, but he's going to the party. I don't think he wants to let Irene go without him, somehow. Not that he and I talk much these days. How did you know we were friends?'

'Oh, the grapevine. You know Harry's in solitary in the soldier's accommodation block?'

'I didn't. I did wonder what had happened to him. Did he attack someone else, then?'

'You didn't hear? Oh, I suppose you wouldn't have. Everyone wondered where he'd come from. Nobody told us anything, and he was being as nice as pie. Some of the girls saw he was all on his own, and spent time chatting with him. Gradually his version of the story came out, but a couple of blokes expressed doubts about it, saying it was obviously just one side of the story, and that since he was the one who'd been moved, it seemed likely to be a bit short of the whole truth.

'Well, that got him annoyed, but he didn't hit out. I think he realized that the chap who'd questioned his truthfulness might be another security guard, and might be more than capable of dealing with him. But later on, he tried to get frisky with my friend Merly, after they'd been chatting well into the evening. She screamed, and he whacked her in the face. The security guards – two of them – had heard Merly scream, and were there within moments of him hitting her. That's when he got taken into the soldiers' group.'

'I wonder what they're going to do with him in the end? It sounds as though there's no future letting him out at all.'

'Oh, I don't know. Surely that fence is going to come down one day, and we'll spread out into a wide empty world to make our own ways. This camp might not be big enough to lose him in, but the world surely is.'

'Sounds a bit unfair to someone – or several someones – who do eventually come across him. Can you see him ever behaving himself?'

'So what would you do with him? Leave him in solitary forever? Just get rid of him, kill him? There's people on the loose around the place who've done much worse than he has. Well, maybe there aren't any more, but there used to be. Where do you draw the line, though?'

'Difficult. At least it's not my problem!'

'It might be better if it was. Do you trust the authorities we've got?'

'It's nearly time for my labouring stint. What's next on your timetable?'

'I'm free now. I'm going to see about organizing that girls' sleepover. I think I will invite Sharon and Ellie. It might be easier if it comes straight from me, rather than from you. Sharon'll still be jealous of me, but at least she won't think I'm using you.'

'Good luck. If I think of anything, I'll pop round.'

'I might not be in, of course. I don't think you know my timetable, for one thing, and for another I'll be doing organizing in my spare time. If I don't see you before the party, thanks for your help, and see you next lesson.'

Persie's sleepover was a complete success. Sharon and Ellie spent the night in Persie's hut, and so did several other young women. Several young soldiers turned up during the evening to try to persuade Persie to come to the party, but by the time the women wanted to go to sleep, word had got round that they were being met by Ellie brandishing a dirty nappy.

At first Sharon wanted me to come too, but Ellie had a better suggestion: they could get more of the young women into

Persie's hut if as many children as could be persuaded stayed with me in our hut instead. I ran a children's party. We had a high time, and then I put them all to bed all over the floor. A couple of them woke up crying for their mums in the middle of the night, but fortunately I was able to calm them down and they didn't wake the whole party. I didn't get a lot of sleep, but considered that a price well worth paying.

Persie and Sharon apparently had a good chat, too – albeit maybe not very privately! Sharon told Persie that she really ought to change her mind about me, but Persie wasn't having it. 'He's your man, Sharon. Now I've told him I don't fancy him, he'll probably accept it. He's pretty straightforward.' It was Ellie who reported this conversation to me, but she complicated my thoughts by suggesting that maybe Persie was only saying she didn't fancy me because she thought it was wrong to steal Sharon's man. I wasn't sure whether she realized what she'd done saying that. The possibility had occurred to me anyway, but hearing it from Ellie made it seem much more plausible.

Will wasn't so happy. Irene went off with the one senior officer who had lost his wife. 'I can't compete with a senior army officer in a situation like this. Once I get over it, I know I'll actually be better off without her. There must be some much nicer young ladies around if I only look.'

He's got his head screwed on really.

The party precipitated several changes around the camp.

Ingrid took up with one of the soldiers, who soon moved in with her. Persie was a little scornful. 'I don't think she actually fancies him at all, but I think she reckons she's got better prospects with him.'

Persie moved in with Merly and the family she worked for. 'Ingrid wanted me to stay, but that chap gives me the creeps. I reckon he'd be all over me too if he got half a chance. The children will miss me, I know, but what can I do?'

Sharon asked me to leave. 'Will's on his own now. You could move in with him. I might do an Ingrid if I get the chance – she's probably done the sensible thing really.'

She meant what she said about not wanting a man who fancied somebody else – or she wanted the best for me, and reckoned there was a better chance of me getting together with Persie this way.

Will was happy for me to share his hut. But Persie didn't say anything, and neither did I.

I found I missed Donna and Billy and Tom as much as I missed Sharon. We still saw quite a bit of each other, but it wasn't the same as sharing a hut.

Will and I didn't talk very much. We shared our stock of observations and deductions about the situation, but exhausted the subject fairly quickly. Neither of us liked the situation, but couldn't see anything we could do about it. We began to get on each other's nerves, but neither of us had anywhere else to go for the time being.

We were increasingly convinced that all the decontamination theatre was just that: theatre. 'The actors probably don't realize it's theatre, but the director, whoever and wherever he is, surely does.'

We thought about trying to escape and make ourselves independent lives. 'Just you and me? How is that better than just being here? On our own? That's probably even worse. Even if there really is no serious contamination anywhere, how would we survive?'

'I don't think survival would be much of a problem. There wouldn't be much competition for resources, and there's plenty of everything out there. The only reason they're trying to get the farm going again is because they're looking to the more distant future. For the number of people there are now, existing stocks of tinned and dried food would last for donkeys' years, and there'll be plenty of bottled water and gas cylinders and everything else you could want.'

'Apart from fresh or frozen food, or electricity.'

'Electricity if you want it, no problem. Find a generator, there'll be plenty of fuel around.'

'We'd be in competition with the soldiers out on their raids.'

'Unlikely ever to cross each other's paths. Anyway, they're interested in big shops or warehouses. We'd be quite happy raiding corner shops or even private homes.'

'Sounds a bit ghoulish.'

'Sure. But it would be survival, and in some ways better than in here. Independent.'

'Lonely.'

We discussed various possible methods of escape, but none of them sounded entirely credible, and anyway, did we really want to swap society, however uncongenial, for lonely independence?

Conversations with Persie and Merly were much less fatalistic. They were both getting increasingly worried about the behaviour of some of the soldiers. 'There's a lot more women than men in here, but I think some of those young soldiers think they're entitled to harems.' Persie and Merly decided that they really did want to escape.

One of my ideas was to stow away in the rear luggage compartment of one of the coaches. It wasn't designed to be opened from inside, but I'd worked out how I could jam it shut without letting the bolts catch, and then push it open from inside. But we'd have to get out somewhere before the coach arrived wherever it was going, and there was no guarantee that the bus would be going slowly enough anywhere to get out safely, or we might misjudge how far they were going and still be in there when the coach stopped. The side compartments would be even worse: the soldiers might very well notice us getting out.

Will had circumnavigated the camp and inspected the fence all the way round. It was out of sight of the village – as we'd come to call the cluster of buildings at the centre of the camp, together with all the huts – for quite a stretch in the south, and for a hundred yards or so behind the hill in the north. In the south, the ground was hard all the way along, and the bottom of the fence ran right along it; but the boggy patch behind the hill ran under the fence just before the point where the fence became visible from the village. Will had investigated, and sank up to his knees in it close to the fence. 'I reckon you could lie on your back floating in the bog, and scrabble your way under the fence. You'd get completely soaked and filthy, of course, and have to hold your nose for a short while actually under the fence, but it's doable I reckon. If you could get hold of some of those plastic sacks they got something from the builders' merchants in, you could take all your clothes and a towel through dry, then dry off and put on dry clothes.' I told Persie and Merly about the idea, but they didn't like it much.

'I doubt if they've put landmines in the area outside the fence, but I wouldn't be a bit surprised if they've got trip wires to alert the soldiers to any escape. They might even be conscious of the one place such an escape looks feasible.'

'I doubt they think anyone will try it, but you'd certainly have to watch your step for a fair way outside the fence.'

Persie had another idea. We all knew that there was a big generator providing electricity in the farmhouse, and that they'd recently acquired a couple more generators and had wired the soldiers' quarters and all the buildings except the huts for lighting.

'Even if they manage to find enough generators to supply enough power for heating all the huts, it'll be almost impossible to maintain a fuel supply for them all. I can see winter here being a really hard time. I'm fairly sure that we ought to be able to find a hydroelectric power station we can get going again somewhere within a reasonable distance. It only needs to be a small one. The grid already exists to connect it to the farm, but we'd have to cut off the rest of the grid to stop all the power draining away uselessly in all sorts of odd equipment all over the place. But it ought to be possible to identify the necessary connections and cut the rest off before restarting the system. They'd be doing it already if they knew how. I'm sure I could organize it, if I could get the officers to agree and supply the labour force for me. And even if I couldn't, I could pretend to – which gives me an excuse to be out of the camp. If I give you a bit of coaching, we could pretend you were an engineer too, Pete, and that your presence on the team would be worthwhile. I reckon we could steal a vehicle while we were out of camp, and get a long way away long before they could walk back and raise the alarm.'

'I can't drive. I know in theory what to do, and I suppose with a bit of practice I could manage somehow – especially with no traffic to worry about, and not caring much about a bit of superficial damage to the vehicle or anything else – but making a rapid getaway sounds harder.'

'You wouldn't have to. I can drive. I've never driven a coach or a tractor, but I don't suppose I'd find it hard. Especially, as you say, if it doesn't matter if it gets a bit battered.'

A bold plan. It might even work.

But it was still just an idea, and we didn't actually do anything about it.

If we don't do something soon, it'll be too late. No sense getting out after winter's already begun.

Chapter 3

One night, in the middle of the night, there was a desperate sounding knocking on our hut door. I was at the door before Will was out of his bag. 'Don't open it, Pete. Not until you've found out who it is.'

But I already had, and it was Persie and Merly, in a terrible state.

'You've got to help us, Pete. I've killed him.'

'Who have you killed?'

'One of the soldiers. He broke into our hut, and was trying to rape Merly. I got on his back, got my arm round his neck, and crushed his windpipe in the crook of my elbow. I didn't let go until he was dead.'

'Where's Birgitte?'

'Huddled up with the children. She says she'll just stay where she is as long as she can, and not alert the other soldiers until she really has to. She says she can explain what happened, and isn't worried that they'll blame her.'

'They won't like it that she didn't tell them straight away.'

'No, but she says she can pretend to be in shock. Really, I don't think she's much affected at all. I think she's been half expecting something like this to happen sooner or later. We all have.'

The only possible escape at short notice was Will's method. Persie and Merly were very keen that Will and I came with them, and I immediately agreed. Will dithered a bit and finally decided to stay behind. 'When they find you've gone, they'll wonder why I didn't tell them, too. But I can just say that Persie came asking for you and that it never occurred to me that there was anything much amiss.'

We didn't have any plastic sacks, but we managed to throw a bundle of all our clothes and towels over the fence a little way up the hill from the boggy patch. Getting under the fence was very unpleasant, but as Will had thought, doable. *It's amazing what you can do when the occasion demands.*

Merly spotted the trip wires – there were two, deep amongst the weeds, running more or less parallel with the fence, just a few feet away from it – and we stepped over them without difficulty. *Lucky our bundle of clothes didn't land on them!*

We kept our eyes peeled for more. It wasn't easy in the moonlight, but we were fairly confident that we hadn't trodden on any by the time we reached the edge of the woods. It was too dark in the woods to look, but we didn't think there was any real risk of there being any there anyway.

We dried off and got dressed amongst the trees, well back from the edge of the wood. We couldn't see in the darkness whether we were leaving an easily followed trail, but assumed that we were.

Well. We've committed ourselves now. The first thing we want to do is put a good distance between us and the camp, and if possible find a motor vehicle. Thank goodness Persie can drive! Then it'll mainly be a matter of finding things to eat. Year after year after year. And hoping we're right about contamination.

Should we be heading in any particular direction? We don't even know where we are.

I knew we were all thinking the same thing. It was hard going in the woods, but the only way out of them that we knew was towards the camp, so we just kept on up the hill, hoping to come out of the woods at some point.

The slope got steeper, and soon there were boulders amongst the trees. The trees were smaller and less densely packed, and more light filtered down through them.

Thank goodness for Sweden's short summer nights. It's still long before people will be stirring in camp, and it's getting light already. It's a pity it's past the height of summer, though.

We decided to skirt the hill to the right, rather than just continue upwards. As far as we could make out, that would take us further away from the camp than skirting it to the left, and away from the camp's approach road. The hillside curved until we were heading more or less north again, which suited us well for the moment.

We heard the waterfalls before we reached them. To continue northwards, we had to get across the cataract somehow, but it was steep, slippery rocks everywhere. Upwards to the left looked pretty much impossible, so we struck downhill back into the denser woods, always watching for a place where we could cross the stream, but without finding anywhere. Eventually we came out of the woods onto rough pasture, much the same as we'd crossed between the camp and the woods.

It's a pretty damn obvious place for us to end up for anyone who knows the geography. Hopefully they're not looking for us yet, or if they are, they don't know their way about.

The stream was easy to cross just below the edge of the woods. We barely even had to get our feet wet. We considered heading back up the slope in the woods, but decided we'd make better time on the grass and that that was worth more than staying under cover.

There was still no sign of anyone following us when we reached a farmstead about an hour later. It was still quite early in the morning, and we hoped that neither Birgitte nor Will had found it necessary to say anything to anyone yet.

'I wonder if there's a car here? If there is and I can start it, I think we're far enough away from the camp that they won't hear anything. At least the road heads reassuringly north!'

There was a car. Persie was confident of hot wiring it, but needed tools to break the steering lock. 'I doubt we'll find the right torx driver to dismantle it, but a drill down the keyhole would do fine. Or I could probably do it with a hammer and chisel.'

We went in search. It felt very odd kicking the door in, but it was the obvious thing to do.

We came across one canine and two human corpses, but didn't investigate closely. Merly found a bunch of keys, which proved to be the right ones for the car. The battery was flat, but the car was on a slope. Persie rolled it a little way and bump started it at the first attempt. We hadn't even needed to push it. We were motorized. According to the fuel gauge, the tank was almost full.

'I wonder whether the battery will hold its charge, or whether you'll have to bump start it every time we stop?'

'I'll park on a hill if I can, until I'm confident of it.'

We decided not to search the farm for anything else useful. 'Better to put more distance between us and the camp first. There'll be plenty more places to raid.'

She's very blasé about it. She seems to have almost forgotten the events of the last few hours – or blocked them out, maybe. She was pretty wound up when she arrived at our hut, but she seems to be on an amazingly even keel now. Long may it last.

We drove past two farms, without stopping, before we came to a junction. There was no signpost, but it seemed clear which was the more major road, and it was still heading away from the camp, a little west of north. Not very much further on we reached a proper major road. Persie turned right, which seeming to be the direction away from the camp.

'I'm a bit more worried now. We don't know whether this might be a road to a town where the soldiers go to raid. I wouldn't want them to see a moving vehicle.'

'We'll keep our eyes skinned, watching the road behind, and you just keep going as fast as you dare. If we see a coach following us, we'll yell and you can get up a side road as quick as you can, and out of sight of the road. They're not usually on the road this early, though, so unless they've started looking for us, I think we'll get beyond the distance they usually go before they set off at all. And if they are looking for us, surely they won't think we're motorized.'

'I hope you're right. I think you probably are, but the situation makes me nervous.'

Me too, and I'm sure that goes for Merly as well. But all things considered, we're not doing badly. I wish I'd taken a bit of notice of the sign at that junction. It probably told us the distance to towns in each direction. I'll see if I can see anything next time we pass a side road.

But Persie was driving as fast as she dared, and the signs flashed past much too fast for me to read. I couldn't even catch the distances.

'It's a strange feeling, being absolutely confident there's nothing coming the other way. I can use the whole road, which means I can take bends quite a lot faster. I don't think one of those coaches could keep up with us anyway.'

'They do have the advantage of height. They can often see over hedges and walls where we couldn't, so they often know what the road does further round the bend than you do.'

'Do you drive, too, Merly?'

'Not really, I never had a chance to learn back at home in Hong Kong. Since I came here, Birgitte's given me a couple of lessons so far, that's all. But I've heard her husband talking about it. He's a truck driver. Or was, most likely.'

'One other thing bothers me. We don't know how many other camps like ours there might be, and whether they're in contact with each other. We might meet raiding parties from other camps, and they'd be just as dangerous as raiding parties from our own camp.'

'True. There's even an outside chance of meeting one of them on a blind bend.'

'I'm not slowing down. Not yet, anyway. For one thing, I doubt any raiding parties from any camp'll be on the road yet, and for another, the other side of them being able to see the road further round the bend than we can is that we can see them coming, too.'

'I think the risk of us meeting any raiding parties must be pretty small. They couldn't do it at all if there were any significant numbers of survivors from private shelters. My guess is that private shelters must have been totally ineffective against whatever was used. That probably means that a lot of public shelters were fairly useless, too. The people running our camp must know that. Or at any rate, they're obviously working on that assumption.'

'It always seemed to me that most of the shelters were just profiteering scams.'

'There's a rabbit!'

'Where?'

'Gone. You missed it.'

'Alive? Makes me think. I don't think I've seen any animal life since we left the camp.'

'There were a lot of flies in the place we got the car.'

'Oh, yes. But have you seen any birds? I haven't. Any animals apart from insects? But yes, that rabbit was alive. They don't run as well as that when they're dead.'

'So whatever it was killed nearly everything, but left at least one rabbit. Maybe there'll be a few people around somewhere.'

Farms, villages. The road went on. 'We're obviously beyond the range of our camp's raiding parties by now. They drive to wherever they're going, load up, and are back again in not much longer than this. I vote we try and find something to eat.'

'I expect any farm will do. They'll have some tins in a cupboard. And a tin opener. And some cutlery. Clean water might be a problem.'

'I'd quite like to get off the direct road from the area our camp's in first. You never know, they might send out a search party at least on the main roads.'

'Fair enough. You're in the driving seat.' *Literally.*

We reached an even bigger road – signed Karlstad in one direction and Oslo in the other.

'Let's go to Oslo!'

'I wonder what the border formalities will be like!'

Laughter. *But seriously, it's not completely impossible that there could be formalities at the border. Pretty unlikely though.*

There weren't. There wasn't a soul in sight, any more than there had been anywhere else.

'How's the fuel doing?'

'Still half a tank, if the gauge is to be believed. No reason to doubt it, it's been going down gradually the way I'd expect. I suppose we ought to think about stopping somewhere though. I'll head off the main road fairly soon.'

Persie chose a side road with a sign showing a couple of places at distances of twelve and thirty kilometres. 'At least we know it's not just a short dead-end.'

We stopped at a farm a few miles up the road, and went in. The door wasn't locked. There was a corpse just inside, in an advanced state of decay. We sidled carefully past it. *We're going to have to get used to this.*

In the larder, there was a good range of tins, cheese, cured meat, dried fish, a couple of unopened bags of flour, and two more of sugar. We didn't open the freezer, knowing there'd be nothing worth having in there. 'It'd stink to high heaven.'

We ate some cheese and meat, and loaded the rest into the car. There seemed to be absolutely nothing to drink.

Merly tried the tap – and it worked. 'I expect it's a spring off the hill. It'll be as safe as anything else we can find to eat or drink. I'm thirsty.'

She found a cup, rinsed it out, and drank. Persie and I did likewise.

'I hope there's no dead sheep in the spring.'

'Don't. There's dead sheep everywhere.'

'I had noticed.'

'Whatever they died of is unlikely to be infectious – now, even if it was before. But what else has been breeding in the dead bodies, who knows?'

'That's the chance we're taking. We knew that all along. What's the alternative?'

'Well, exactly.' Persie looked very serious again. *She's remembering.*

'Actually, surely it's unlikely anything particularly pathogenic is breeding in the dead bodies. Surely dead bodies are cold, breeding grounds for cold-adapted organisms, not organisms that would thrive in a warm body?'

'That's not a theory I'd like to rely on. And they could certainly be breeding grounds for things that produce deadly toxins, like botulism. I wouldn't even want to eat those dead sheep cooked.'

'Live rabbit wouldn't be a bad idea though, if we can find a way to catch one.'

'We've only seen one.'

'I'm happy to stick with what we can find in people's houses, if this house is anything to go by. But I'd like to find a few tools, and we need cutlery and stuff.'

We found a tin opener, knives, forks and spoons, plates, bowls and mugs, and loaded them into the car.

'What are we going to do when we run out of fuel? There won't be many petrol stations open. Do we just abandon this car and pick up another one?'

'I've been thinking about that. We do at least have the keys to this one. There's no guarantee we'll find the keys to another so easily. Has anyone seen any car keys here, for example? There's a car outside.'

'Actually, it's a better car than we've got. It's a lot bigger, and it's four wheel drive. It's a lot newer, too – more likely to be reliable. And it's a diesel – not so good if the battery's knackered, but otherwise better. We've got a much better chance of finding a gravity feed diesel tank at a farm, than getting hold of petrol in quantity. We've got plenty of time. Let's find those keys.'

Persie found them. They were in a trouser pocket of the corpse.

'Yuk. Not my favourite game. But worth it. I can wash my hands. And the keys.' Which she did.

'I still feel filthy. Horrible. Much worse than trying to drown in that bog.'

'Definitely worth it.'

The Jeep started on the battery. It didn't sound at first as though it was going to, but it did.

'I'll leave it running to charge the battery while we search the place for anything else useful.'

'How much fuel has it got?'

'Plenty for the moment, but I'd like to get more. I don't want even to consider swapping this one.'

We found a good range of hand tools. There were electric tools, too, but without electricity what use were they? But we went back for them later after we found a generator, which started with the first pull on the cord once we'd discovered the priming button.

There was a tractor, but we didn't want that.

'Not just now, anyway. Maybe we will want one one day, who knows?'

'Maybe. I don't think we'll have any trouble finding one anywhere, though, do you?'

The best find of all was a big tank of diesel, two big jerry cans, and funnels.

How full the big tank was we didn't know, but there was more than enough to fill the Jeep's tank and both jerry cans, and the straps for the cans were loose in the back of the Jeep.

'At least we don't have to have the jerry cans inside. They'd be horribly smelly.'

We found a pair of huge gas cylinders at the back of the house.

'I bet the cooker in the kitchen runs off these. They're not big enough for central heating. We can cook!'

'There's an oil tank for the central heating just behind the big barn. I saw it as we were arriving.'

'I wonder whether we should stay here for a little while – tonight at least. I don't see any special need to move on now, do you? There'll be comfortable beds – even if we have to move corpses out of them and remake them with fresh linen. I'm sure there'll be some of that around.'

'You really fancy moving a corpse out of a bed and then sleeping in it?'

'It might be the only way of getting a comfortable bed.'

'I think I can stand uncomfortable beds for a few nights. We'll find beds without corpses in them eventually.'

The cooker did work, and we had a good meal. We felt a bit silly fetching things back from the car.

'I'm glad there were no corpses in the kitchen.'

'Me too. But I think we'll probably get used to just dragging them out of the way and getting on with life.'

'We certainly can't bury them all.'

There was a corpse in one of the beds, but there were three more bedrooms, and the beds in all of them seemed perfectly clean.

I had dreadful dreams, but I didn't tell the others. I suspected that theirs were even worse, but they didn't tell me about them.

Chapter 4

'We could stay here. We've got comfortable beds, a functioning cooker, water, and central heating when winter comes around.'

'The central heating won't work without electricity.'

'It doesn't need much. We've got a generator. We don't know how much heating oil there is in the tank though.'

'We'll probably find plenty of places like this, but worth remembering where it is to come back to if we want to. I'd rather explore a bit more. I'd quite like to work out a bit about what really happened, and whether it's really as dead as this everywhere.'

'We need a map to mark places on. Next time we see a petrol station let's pick up some maps.'

Persie picked up on the other point, 'You're still thinking about your friends in England, aren't you, Pete? Don't. You're still hoping things aren't as bad there. I don't see much chance of getting across the sea. We could probably get to the French ports, but there won't be any ferries.'

'You're right, of course. We could probably find a small motorboat and get across if we chose a still day. I've never driven one, but I'm sure we could work it out.'

'If it's like it is here all the way to the French ports, it'll be like this all over Britain, too. I don't think there's much doubt about that.'

'The camps might not be so militaristic. People might even mostly be on the loose, like us.'

'That's a lot of might be. We'll go exploring, okay. But don't get your hopes up, Pete. Even if England is full of people on the loose, as you put it, it's unlikely your friends would be amongst them – sorry to be so negative – and lots of people on the loose might actually be quite nasty, anyway.'

'Ow. I'm sure you're right, really, though.'

'I'm not really looking forward to meeting anyone, although it might be fine as long as there's only a small group and they don't feel threatened. I'm most worried about meeting raiding parties from other camps now. I'm really hoping that there aren't many camps, awful as that sounds.'

'I suppose somewhere near Oslo is a fairly likely location. Perhaps we'd better not go there.'

'My feeling exactly. Big towns could be bad news for us. Places like this are much more suitable – and if this place is anything to go by, we'll be fine for the foreseeable future. It seems likely to me that this is pretty typical.'

'I'm going to get the corpses out of the house. Let's have a bit of a clean up. If we're thinking of coming back here later it'll be a lot nicer if they're not still around. They'll be even more disgusting by then than they are now.'

'Sounds like a good idea – if your stomach's up to it.'

I found some rope. Holding one end each, Merly and I managed to work the rope under the downstairs corpse. Then I tried to drag it along, but it just came in half. I felt sick, but remembered seeing a wheelbarrow and shovels. I shovelled the unfortunate man into the barrow, and went in search of a suitable dumping place. Down the track, over the road, and into the ditch. Not a dignified grave, but I wasn't going to dig one. *We could spend the rest of our lives digging graves.*

What's that, just down there?

It's another corpse, already in the ditch.

In fact, it's several. Some of them look like children.

The upstairs corpse was even more of a problem. I tried to pick it up in the sheet, but the sheet was completely rotten underneath it, and it just came apart. I went and found a bucket, and took the mess down to the wheelbarrow a bucketful at a time. The mattress was rotten through the middle too, but I couldn't shovel it; rusty springs got in the way.

I was getting pretty blasé about the mess. *I'll have a bath afterwards.* I dragged the mattress to the top of the stairs up on its edge, and slid it downstairs, then dragged it down the track and over into the ditch. *At least it covers the bodies a bit.*

By the time I got back, Merly and Persie were busy with buckets of water and scrubbing brushes. They'd found some bleach, too.

'I'm surprised there were only two of them.'

'There weren't. There were about six, including at least a couple of youngsters. The two in the house had already dumped the others in the ditch, pretty much where I've just dumped them.'

'So they didn't all die at once, and there was no-one to help bury them by the time they did.'

'Yup. It must have been hell. I wonder how long it all dragged on?'

'And we think we've got problems.'

'I want a bath.'

'We all will. I think it'll have to be cold water though. I suppose we could boil a few kettles in the kitchen to knock the chill off, but that's about the limit.'

'After that bath yesterday morning, even a cold bath will be a luxury!'

I had my bath first. *I hope there's not a tank on the hill with just a trickle filling it. I hope there's enough water for all of us.*

Persie and Merly had the same thought, and shared a bath. 'It wasn't half as bad for us as for you.' I wasn't so sure about that, and as it turned out there was plenty of water anyway. Not having anything else important to do after a very nice lunch, we took a walk up the hill and found the tank. It was huge, and the spring that fed it was still flowing well, despite the long dry spell we'd had.

We checked the heating oil tank. It was just under half full. 'I wonder how many months' worth that is? If we stay here over the winter, it might run out. I think we need to make ourselves a list of suitable places to stay for a while if we can find them. We can't move heating oil from one place to another.'

'Unless we can find a heating oil tanker with some oil in it. I've never driven anything big like that, but I expect I'd manage. And I'm sure we can work out how to fill a tank from it.'

She's nothing if not self-confident.

'One problem I've realized is that the generator is petrol, not diesel. We've got half a tank full of petrol in the car, and I expect I can find a bit of tubing to syphon it with, but after that we're stuck. We'll have to syphon out of every car we can find. We won't be able to get petrol out of a petrol station.'

'Drilling the petrol tanks would be better than syphoning. Petrol's not good stuff to get in your mouth, even a mouthful of the vapour's pretty bad.'

'I don't want to drill the tank on the car we've got. If we do find a heating oil tanker, I'd rather drive to it in the car and leave the car, than have to take the tanker back to get the Jeep.'

'Could we take the generator to a petrol station, break open the pump and hook the generator up to it, and run the pump? It might be better to use the jerry cans for petrol if we can do that.'

'I don't know. Depends on the design of the pump. Worth a try, definitely.'

We'd got enough food for several days, so we decided to take it easy for the rest of the day. We were pretty confident of finding food, and we thought we'd got plenty of time to go looking for petrol stations and anything else we decided we needed. 'The rest of our lives, probably.'

That's quite a thought. Back in Burnfield, I never really thought about "the rest of my life", I just assumed it would be fairly much like other people's lives, and took it as it came. It would have been a luxury to plan anything, a luxury I couldn't even dream of. *Now it really is a necessity.*

Persie had a sudden realization.

'I hope they don't search for us with a helicopter.'

'They'd have to have done that pretty quickly, before we got so far away. We're a needle in much too big a haystack now. Anyway, they haven't got one.'

'Are you sure? They could be in contact with other camps that might be much better equipped. But as you say, they've missed that chance anyway.'

'I don't think they can know about anyone better equipped, or they wouldn't be having to improvise so much. In fact, that's something that puzzles me a bit. They were obviously well prepared with fencing, those huts, and the prefabricated buildings, and they had the skills to put all that together pretty damn quick. Even goats and chickens hidden away somewhere.

Okay, they didn't need to get the electrics and a generator up and running as quickly, but you'd have thought they'd have the materials lined up for the job, all planned.'

'Maybe they do. They just hadn't got round to it yet. No hurry, it's weeks before it'll start getting really cold.'

'I don't think they do. The raiding parties seem to be pretty opportunistic. Having found a load of big insulation panels, they've started to insulate that big shed, and they've picked up a couple of big generators. Much bigger than anything we'd be interested in, but nowhere near big enough to run electric heating in all those huts.'

'You could run the exhaust from the generators through ducts through the shed, and keep it warm and still have the electricity for heating other places. But that shed isn't big enough for everyone. Imagine spending a winter in there with hundreds of other people.'

'Even if they had a helicopter, I don't think they've got anyone who'd know how to fly it.'

'You need a lot of ground support to keep helicopters in the air. And what for? To chase a few runaways who won't be any trouble to you at all, even if they survive? I don't see it.'

'But you'd have thought they'd have some folks with more technical nous than they seem to have.'

'I dunno. It's perhaps a bit random who happened to be in the shelters.'

'I can see that for the civilian population. But you'd have thought the military would be more prepared.'

'That gives me another thought. Perhaps the bigwigs and the technical experts are still underground. We were sent out to test the water, as it were. Maybe they'll come out in time to fix up heating for all the huts – get a stripped down electricity grid going like you were suggesting, Persie, or something like that.'

'Ouch. That sounds horribly credible, and could make things much more uncomfortable for us in a few months' time.'

'Or maybe even quite soon.'

'That wasn't exactly a cheap shelter we were in.'

'No, but if the bigwigs have one designed for them to stay in longer, it'll be a lot fancier.'

'And the first tranche of guinea pigs, the people in their private Kr10,000 shelters, died in them.'

'I don't think we should use any artificial lighting at night. That's the one way we could be spotted from a distance.'

'If they don't have aircraft of some sort, that's pretty unlikely. And if they do, they could spot a moving vehicle. With infrared sights, they could even spot the heat of the engine for a while after we turn it off. Or the heat of our cooking.'

'I think you're worrying about nothing. They don't have aircraft. They're struggling just running the camp. They'll have forgotten about us by now. Well, not forgotten and definitely not forgiven, but given up thinking about us.'

'I'm sure you're right. For the moment. If the bigwigs really are still underground, the situation could change dramatically in a little while. Any time, in fact.'

'Maybe we should put ourselves as far out in the sticks as possible.'

'Like where? The far north? Easy to search for lights up there in winter, and we'd need them. Much harder for us, too. This area is probably as good as anywhere.'

'We won't know when the bigwigs come out, if they do. We shouldn't use lights at night, and maybe keep driving around to a minimum, too.'

'Pete wants to explore, though.'

'I want to survive even more. And you were right about not trying to get to England. It'd be easier to get to Hong Kong or Vietnam.'

'Not really. No sea to cross, certainly, but a hell of a journey. And a huge risk of not managing to find any fuel at some point. Probably nobody hassling you like there'd have been if you'd tried it a year ago, but nobody helping you, either.'

'I wouldn't even be confident of nobody hassling you. We don't know that it's been like this everywhere. We've only that briefing officer's word for it, and I'd trust him as far as I could kick him. Maybe not that far.'

'He was only telling us what he'd been told to tell us. He didn't really know whether it was true or not. Just a pawn, like us.'

The next day, we walked to the next farm, which was within sight from "our" farm. The front door was locked, and we decided to take a look to see if we could find a better way in instead of breaking it. There were no open windows, and the back door was locked too.

We decided to break into the shed first, and found a ladder. I worked out what I thought was the best way to get in. I forced a small upper opener of one of the upstairs windows, and reached in and opened the lower one. I climbed in, went downstairs, and opened the back door, which fortunately had the key in the lock.

At first we were surprised to find no corpses, but realized that there wasn't a vehicle – apart from another tractor – here anyway. Presumably the last survivor had managed to dispose of the other bodies, and then driven off before dying somewhere else.

Whether the first casualties had been taken right away, properly buried nearby, or just dumped in ditches, we didn't discover.

There was quite a bit of usable food here, too. And lots of tools. And a big tank of diesel, working water supply, working cooker and oil fired central heating with half a tank of oil. And a diesel generator. It was bigger than the petrol one we already had and wired into the house wiring, but it wouldn't have been difficult to detach and it wasn't too big to move.

'That's a good find. If it works.'

It did.

'We should have brought the car, to take all this lot back.'

'What for? This is as good a place as the other.'

'Better. No corpses.'

'There's none there any longer.'

'That bedroom is still pretty foul, really. Okay, we don't use it and the door's shut, but still.'

'We don't know how many corpses there have been in this house.'

'No, but if there were any, we do at least know they were removed before they rotted.'

'This place is a bit further from the main road, too. Only another mile and a bit, but still.'

We went back, loaded everything into the Jeep, and moved house.

'We can go back there when the heating oil runs out here.'

'If we haven't found somewhere better in the meantime. We're going to have to go looking for more food before long anyway.'

We left the little car where it was. 'No point bringing it. We know where it is, we can get it any time. It'll pretty certainly bump start down the track.' Persie had parked it facing down the track when we first arrived.

We emptied the Jeep into the new house. We didn't want to carry everything about with us all the time, and anyway we wanted room to load anything we found later.

'We should keep the little generator in it, and some tools, for when we find a petrol station.'

'No. It'd be smelly carrying the generator around. We can come back for it when we need it.'

'Maybe we don't even need a petrol station. We've got a diesel generator now, and quite a lot of diesel. And I expect we'll find lots more diesel in tanks like these two.'

'I still want a petrol station for maps.'

The third farm was in sight from our new home, and we walked there.

'We've got three tractors now.'

Laughter.

There was another tank of diesel, another diesel generator, another tank of central heating oil, another cooker with two big gas bottles, and another functioning water supply. Again, there was a fair stock of food. We ate a meal, and took the rest of the food back to our new home in a wheel barrow.

We didn't want to move house again: this one had a corpse, which we didn't bother to move.

'What if we want to move here when the heating oil runs out in the other two places?'

'It won't be any worse to move then than it is now. And "then" might be "never" anyway. It could be frozen solid, that'd be easier.'

I thought that in reality it might be harder, but kept quiet.

It seemed we would have no problems finding everything we needed, for as long as we had the world to ourselves. Of all our supplies, food was the least plentiful, and even that seemed to be several days' worth per farm.

'There's an awful lot of farms in Norway. And we've not found a shop yet. Then there's Sweden and Finland. The world is our oyster really.'

'We might not be the only independent survivors. We've no idea how many there might be, in fact.'

We did minimize our driving a bit, and we didn't use lighting at night. That was easy enough in summer, with short nights, but we knew it would get harder in winter. We wondered whether to move south, and realized that that meant going closer to the camp, and that we wouldn't be able to get beyond the southern tip of Sweden anyway – unless we went all round the Baltic, and we didn't fancy that.

'Maybe early summer next year, if we're still alive by then.'

Persie's so matter-of-fact. It's true, we might not be. That's always true, of course, but in the present circumstances, even more so. Worse still, one or two of us might still be alive, but not all three. Not a happy thought.

A few days later, we went for a drive. We found a petrol station on our side road, just a few miles further on, on the outskirts of a large village. It had a small shop, but the door had already been forced, and the shelves were mostly empty. It didn't have any maps.

'I hope that doesn't mean we've come across other independent survivors already. Hell, I've left the keys in the car.'

Persie ran back, got the keys and locked the car. 'We'd be unlucky if they happened to be around at the moment, but you can't be too careful.'

But on closer inspection, it was actually clear that the door had been broken months earlier.

'I reckon this happened during the war, and the people who did it are long dead. We already know it was a long drawn-out process, it's not surprising there was some looting. Some of the last survivors wouldn't have had any other means of survival. A lot of good it did them.'

'I still want to know whether we could pump petrol – or diesel – out of their underground tanks. We certainly don't need any at the moment, and we might never, but I'd still love to know.'

'We know where this place is now. We can come back whenever we feel like it. But I'd rather explore the rest of the village, rather than going back for the generator right now.'

We drove into the middle of the village. There were two shops. Both had been looted, and there was no food in either of them.

'That's not a good sign. There could be a lot less food around than we thought, if there was a lot of looting during a long drawn-out dying.'

'I don't know. The shops are pretty obvious places to loot, and the looters might have died with a fair stock of food still in their houses. None of the farms we've been to have been looted. The houses here in the village might be full of food. Let's go and see.'

Persie was right.

At first we tried to get into houses non-destructively, as I had at "our" farm, but after the first couple of houses we realized it really didn't matter. We'd got a sledgehammer in the Jeep, and it was much quicker just to let ourselves in through the front doors with that. *We must be the noisiest housebreakers ever.*

The villagers had hoarded more than the farmers had. After only half-a-dozen houses the back of the Jeep was half full.

How much the empty shops are due to looting, and how much to panic buying before the looting began, who knows? Either way, most of it never got used, and it's still here for us.

Without really looking for them, we found car keys in several houses. In each case, they fitted a car parked outside. We wondered what the best thing to do was.

'One day we might find another car pretty useful. But unless we take notes, we could waste a lot of time trying keys in cars we don't even have the keys for.'

'The ones we've found already, we can just leave in the cars. It might save us some time in the future, and it's highly unlikely to do us any harm.'

But we didn't bother to go back and replace the ones we'd matched up already.

We'd encountered several corpses, some in houses and a couple in the gutter where they'd probably been dumped rather than fallen, but overall there weren't as many as we'd imagined. *For a while at least, there must have been some attempt to dispose of them properly.*

In one house, we found a newspaper on the kitchen table. It was dated five days after my flight – four days after we were shepherded into the shelter. None of us knew Norwegian, but Persie and Merly both knew Swedish. 'We'll take it home. Our spoken Swedish isn't bad, but we both struggle a bit with reading Swedish, never mind Norwegian. I don't know how we'll get on with this, but it's worth a try. I'm very interested to know what was really going on – or what people were being told, anyway.'

'Four days after the beginning of the war, and still lying on the table. I wonder what happened to the person who was reading it? I wonder if we can find any more recent ones?'

A couple of houses later we found another copy of the same edition, but that was all. After a few more houses the Jeep was pretty well loaded, and we decided to call it a day. We'd barely started on the village, and we had food for months.

'I wonder whether we're doing right staying at the farm, rather than finding a house here somewhere?'

'We've got water, heating and cooking where we are. And electricity when we need it. We've not checked, but I bet we'd have none of those here. Good place to raid, but surely we'll stay at the farm. Or some other farm.'

Back at the farm, Persie and Merly pored over the paper. They became increasingly puzzled.

'I'm sure they're talking about an epidemic, not a war. But I can't make it out at all. They seem to be suggesting that people should boil the water, and that you should get help if you're ill. That suggests that four days after we went into the shelter, people still didn't know there was a war on. But our coach driver got a message from his control centre to divert us to the shelter, and you folks in the hotel got a siren, so the authorities knew it was war. Very strange. I wish I could really read Norwegian, though.'

'Boiling the water is quite a point. I'm sure it's normally fine to trust the water in a place like this, but we probably ought to have been boiling it in the present circumstances. We've got the facilities.'

'But we don't have an unlimited supply of gas. We've been drinking it a week now and it's not made us ill yet. I don't think there's any point starting now.'

Chapter 5

We had planned to take the small generator down to the petrol station the following day, to have a go at getting the pumps going. Then we were going to do a bit more raiding, and see if we could find any more newspapers – older or newer editions, or different papers. Anything. But Merly and I were awake half the night coughing, and were miserable with sore throats in the morning.

'Sore throats aren't likely to be anything to do with the water, anyway.'

'I hope this isn't the beginning of the end for us three as well.'

'Don't be daft. It's just an ordinary sore throat. Anyone can get one of those any time.' I wasn't completely sure I believed that myself, but it seemed like the right thing to say. *We've not been in contact with any living being to catch an ordinary sore throat from.*

Neither Merly nor I felt like going anywhere. We didn't really want Persie to go off on her own either, but she insisted that she'd drive to the next village in the hope of finding a shop with some cough mixture. 'It won't cure you, but it ought to relieve the symptoms. Don't worry, I'll drive carefully. I don't expect I'll have much trouble with the traffic.'

She set off quite early in the morning. 'The shops all open really early these days. I'll be back in plenty of time to make lunch. You two get a rest.'

But she wasn't back for lunch. By the middle of the afternoon we were getting really worried, imagining all kinds of dreadful scenarios, and wondering whether to set off on foot in search of her, or whether we should walk back to the first farm and see if I could work out how to drive the other car.

Then we heard a truck in the distance.

'Oh God. They've caught her, and now they're coming for us.'

The truck turned up the track to our farm, and we wondered whether there was any point trying to hide. But it was Persie at the wheel.

'I'm sorry. You must have been dreadfully worried. Bloody Jeep!'

'What happened?'

'Wait a minute. I've got cough mixture for you. Choice of half a dozen different brands. Here. Have some and I'll tell you the whole story.'

'Found the next place, no problem. It's not a village, it's a small town. There's another couple of petrol stations and all sorts of things. Found a pharmacy and picked this stuff up. Raided a couple of other shops too...'

'They'd not been looted?'

'Looks like only food shops have been looted. Wait. Set off back here. Halfway between the town and the village, damn tyre burst. There's a spare, and all the right tools to change the wheel were in the vehicle, but can I shift the wheel nuts? Not a chance. Maybe you'll be able to, Pete, or we might manage with a big socket spanner instead of that stupid little wheel brace. And I've seen another of the same model we can nick a spare wheel off. Or five.'

'So where did you get this truck?'

'I thought I was still closer to the town than the village, so I set off back to the town, to find some keys and a vehicle. That's what's taken me so long. For one thing, I'd judged the distance wrong: I was much closer to the village, so I walked much further than I needed to. Then I broke into several houses to search for keys. I didn't have the sledge hammer, either, so it wasn't quick.'

'How did you do it?'

'You're right, I can't kick them in the way you did.'

'I was lucky. That door was old and rotten. So what did you do?'

'Found a good size chunk of stone in the garden. No nice handle like the sledgehammer though. I still couldn't open the door. But it made a good hole in a window. I had to chuck it pretty hard though – it just bounced off the first couple of times.'

'You climbed in through a broken window? I hope you didn't cut yourself!'

'Safety glass. Just turns to glass pebbles when you break it. I just pushed all the bits out and climbed in. Scratched myself a bit, but no real cuts. No problem, although the front door method is easier if you've got a sledgehammer. Found a set of car keys, but they didn't fit the car outside. Went back in to look for more, but couldn't find them.

'The next house had a car outside, too. Eventually I found the car keys. In a corpse's pocket, upstairs. No water to wash with. Carton of orange juice. It's a bit strange with soap, and makes an awful mess of the towel, but the owner didn't seem to care. The car keys fitted, but the car wouldn't start. Not enough slope on the road to get it rolling at all, never mind bump start it.

'Found a sloping road, tried to find keys to one of the cars parked on it. By the third house where I couldn't find any keys, I was getting pretty frustrated. Then there's this truck in someone's drive. Corpse right next to the driver's door – keys in his hand!

'Can I drive a truck? Well, I can now! Actually, it's brilliant. You get a great view of the road. I thought I wouldn't be able to reach the controls, but it's no trouble at all. It adjusts better than a car. You can move the seat forward and down to the pedals, and then adjust the steering wheel to suit. If I did that in a car, I'd scarcely be able to see over the dashboard, but the truck windscreen comes really low. The visibility is great. And there's room for both of you beside me, nobody has to sit in the back.'

'So why bother going back for the Jeep at all?'

'Well, we ought to get the stuff out of the back of it, but maybe there's not a lot of point in it otherwise. This must use a lot more fuel, though.'

'I don't think that's much of an issue for us, really. And if we can find some more jerry cans, we can carry a lot more fuel with us anyway. There's loads of room on the back, and no problems about smell.'

'We'll have to work out some straps, or they might bounce out. They could get damaged just bouncing about.'

'So what other shopping did you do?'

'Stuff for me and you, mostly, Merly. Pete'll have to come into town next trip to do some shopping for himself. It's still all in the Jeep anyway. I didn't want to spend any time transferring things when it was already so late. It'll be all right there until you two are feeling a bit better. I only stopped long enough to pick up the cough mixtures.'

'What sort of stuff, though, Persie? You're being so mysterious.'

'Oh, some stuff from the pharmacy. You can guess what. And clothes. This towelling stuff is all very well, but it's a bit like prison garb, and it's not always the most practical, either.'

'And if we do ever meet anyone, it's a dead giveaway that we're runaways, not independent survivors.'

'Independent survivors might be a contradiction in terms, by the looks of it. And anyone who's actually got a description of the runaways is going to be a bit suspicious of an off-white Englishman with two East Asian women, anyway.'

Laughter, but it hurt our throats.

'I've never thought about it before, but where *did* your ancestors come from?'

'Most of them, from England as far back as anyone knows. But my mother's father, God rest his lovely soul, was from Jamaica.'

'God? Who's that?'

More throat-searing laughter. Both Merly and Persie were educated in Roman Catholic schools, so each of them had a strange cultural mix in their upbringing, but it hadn't succeeded in making either of them religious.

The cough mixtures helped. At least we slept that night. The next day, Persie had the sore throat, too. *I really do hope this isn't the first symptoms of the Big Death.*

We had pickled eggs, pickled onions, and salami for breakfast.

'We don't have to worry about upsetting each other with smelly breath!'

Don't make me laugh, Merly, it hurts.

Black tea. With sugar. *I wonder if we'll ever get any milk again? We might find some UHT, condensed milk or powder. They'll eventually start getting goats' milk in the camp, I suppose. Maybe the officers already are.*

We got the generator going. It was powerful enough to drive the washing machine, but only on the cold wash setting. We tried the television, and weren't surprised to find that not a single channel was on air. We didn't have enough power for the kettle, but we were boiling water in pans on the cooker anyway. *I wonder how often they had power cuts here, back in the day? All three farms were obviously prepared for them – but the folks in the town don't seem to have been. Is that just relative wealth, or were they less frequent in the town?*

It was four days before we felt like venturing out. *We don't actually have to venture out for months, if we don't feel like it. But life could get to feel a bit pointless if we just vegetate.*

The Jeep was still where Persie had left it. We loaded the shopping into the cab of the truck, which had a fair amount of space behind the seats. The tools went loose in the back.

Merly wanted to look what Persie had got, but Persie told her to wait until we got home.

'We ought to find – or make – some kind of a box to put things in in the back. The sort of stuff we're looking for doesn't really want to be bouncing around loose in the back.'

'No, I don't see us needing to do any building work in the near future.'

'Not in our lifetimes, anyway.'

I wonder what on Earth she means by that.

We could have dressed ourselves to look like a million dollars, but what we really wanted was practical clothes, including some really warm ones for winter. And some decent, tough shoes. And boots.

All just for the taking. And plenty of spares.

'It almost doesn't seem worth taking more than one spare set, they'll still be here when we want them. But there's plenty of room at the farm, or in the truck if we want to move, and it saves trips.'

'To search the back of this shop properly, we're going to need a torch.'

That wasn't a problem.

'Batteries might be. There's a good stock here, but they won't last forever.'

'We'll find a rechargeable one somewhere, I expect.' And we did. It was more powerful than the first little torch we'd found, too.

We went looking for some sort of box to put in the back of the truck, but what we found was a transport company, with a yard full of trucks. Persie backed one corner of the truck against the middle of the gates, and pushed. The lock burst and the gates swung open. *Even easier than the sledgehammer.*

All the truck keys, neatly labelled, were hanging on a board in the office. Persie was almost bouncing up and down.

'I love this truck we've got, but it's pretty rough really. We can have the pick of this lot!'

She found a big walk-through van, nice and clean inside, with the same design of cab as the truck she'd already taught herself to drive.

'The tyres are in better shape, too. I hope it'll start.'

It did, no problem. Manoeuvring it out of the yard was another matter.

'It'd be easier with that one out of the way.'

But that one wouldn't start.

'I'm going to bash something before long, I'm not sure I can get it out at all.'

'They must have a rope somewhere. We could use the truck we've got to pull that one backwards.'

It took ages, but eventually we got Persie's favourite van out of the yard. Unscathed – which was more than could be said for the one she'd towed. *Not that anyone will ever care about that one.*

'We'll never care about our tail lights, but come winter we might want the headlights sometimes. Perhaps we ought to find some spares.'

Persie's thoughts had clearly been running along similar lines to mine.

'We might want our headlights I suppose, but it's probably best to avoid using them if possible. It would be just our luck that that was exactly when someone comes out of hiding who does use aeroplanes.'

'Are we really going to spend all those long nights in winter in complete darkness? If we can't use headlights, logically we can't use house lights either.'

'We could. Black curtains.'

'Well. We've got clothes, and a better truck. There's really only two more things I'd like to find, and that's a tanker full of heating oil, and a stock of bottles of cooking gas.'

'And more food. It'd be good if we'd got enough to last the winter at least.'

'Plenty of time. I vote we call it a day for the moment.'

It was a couple of weeks before we found the cooking gas supplier. Breaking in was harder than it had been at the transport depot, but we managed. It's amazing what you can do when you've got a truck and some rope handy, and you don't care how much noise you make or how much damage you do. *Just be careful not to risk damaging yourself or the truck...*

We reckoned that a van load of bottles would last several years, but we knew where to get quite a few more after that.

We also found an almost full heating oil tanker, but we couldn't start it, not even by trying to bump start it, towing it behind our van. That could have been my incompetence in the tanker's driving seat. I knew exactly what to do in theory, but I'd had no practice driving, and I was scared I might hit the back of our own van if I wasn't careful. We knew we wouldn't be able to manoeuvre it into position to fill the tank at home even if we towed it all the way, so at first we were at a loss what to do –

until we found a place with a stock of jerry cans. Not wanting to stink our new van out, we retrieved our old lorry to take twenty-five full twenty litre jerry cans. Three times. Two trips with five hundred litres almost filled the tank, and we kept another five hundred litres in the jerry cans in the barn. We considered filling the tanks at the other two farms as well, and decided it wasn't worth the trouble. The tanker would still be there when we wanted more, and there were still thousands of litres of oil in it. We'd spilt a little filling jerry cans from it, but not a lot, and what did it matter? *A little bit of nothing compared with the mess five billion people were making a year ago...*

One house we raided for food had a rather fancy radio, which we took home. It was capable of receiving pretty much any signal. Unless it was faulty, there weren't many stations on air – nothing except occasional long-wave transmissions in languages none of us could understand or even identify. Persie thought one of them might be Russian or Polish, 'but they could be from anywhere in the world. There could be short wave or FM stations too far away for us to receive, but there's none around here.'

Persie said that she'd be able to build a long-wave radio transmitter if we found a place with electronic components and some equipment, 'but we don't want to give our location away. We might find ready-made CB gear if we're lucky though. That would have been useful that day the Jeep tyre blew up.'

'We should only use it in emergency, though. Someone might pick up the signal.'

'Not very likely. It's not got much range. And who's listening? But we'd only want it in emergencies anyway.'

We've never found any CB transceivers.

We found more newspapers – nothing newer than the one we had already, but some from the previous couple of days.

We found a bookshop. Of course nearly everything was in Norwegian, which was very frustrating. There were a few books in English, but they were things for Norwegian children learning English, and not interesting at all – apart from a huge Times

Atlas. We took that and a globe, just because we loved them, and some maps of our area of Norway and southern Sweden, and one big and one small Norwegian-English-Norwegian dictionary.

'I really would like to make more sense of those newspapers.'

Persie found some undergraduate level physics and chemistry textbooks. 'I can't read the text, but there's a lot of tables of data I'll be able to make sense of.'

We weren't sure why she wanted to do that, but if she wanted them, why not?

We found a school. It had been turned into a temporary hospital. Temporary? It wasn't going to be a school again, but it wasn't a hospital any more either. Every classroom – every one we looked in that is, we gave up quite quickly – was full of beds, and almost every bed contained a corpse. Many of them had sheets pulled up over their faces, but many didn't.

They must have died after there was no-one left to cover their faces. And before that, they were so understaffed that they couldn't remove the corpses. And before that, they probably had removed a lot. I wonder where to?

I didn't fancy finding out.

We knew already that the whole situation must have been absolute hell.

Persie wanted to find the physics and chemistry labs. They hadn't been converted into wards. Persie took various bits of equipment from the physics lab.

'There's no radiation monitoring equipment at all!'

'We used to have some at my school in London, but they got rid of it all when they had to dispose of the radioactive sources. Too dangerous to have them in schools, they said.'

'Pshaw! Tiddly bits like that? Feeble excuse!'

'I rather suspected that.'

'Did they think someone was going to grind the cover off one and eat it?'

'Or feed it to someone else, I suppose. You wouldn't notice it in your sandwich.'

'There's no shortage of ordinary poisons that would work more quickly and reliably.'

The hospital itself was much the same as the school. 'If we ever need any medical equipment, or oxygen bottles or anything, we know where to come.' But we didn't actually take anything.

We saw our first live rat at the hospital.

Persie and Merly studied the newspapers, and with the help of the dictionaries thought they'd pretty much worked out what they were saying. We couldn't make sense of it. We couldn't reconcile the story the authorities had been peddling to the general population with the fact that we'd been shepherded into the shelter. There was no mention of the war in the papers as far as Persie could make out.

'The accidental release from a bioweapons research establishment theory is complete eyewash. There must be a lot of people who know that. How would it spread so widely, so fast?'

'Were they suggesting that? Even I know enough to realize that's nonsense. Was it just some journalist talking off the top of his head?'

'No, it doesn't look like it. There's exactly the same thing in three different papers. Exactly the same wording, if fact, so it comes from some common source.'

'Still could just have been a journalist. Do we know the papers were independent publications? Even if they were, the common source could be a news syndicate or a freelancer. Especially since they might well have been understaffed by then.'

'Fair enough, I don't know much about newspapers.'

'The authorities are perfectly capable of generating deliberate disinformation anyway, we'll never know one way or the other.'

'The authorities had plenty of motivation to generate a lot of deliberate disinformation, if they were trying to hide the war from the people. But why would they do that? And how would they explain the disappearance of everyone who'd actually got the warning, and made it into shelters?'

'There's nothing in the papers, as far as I can see, about anyone being in shelters anyway. Weird.'

'Everyone we know who was in a shelter was supposed to be away from home anyway. But that can't have been true for everyone. What about everyone in private shelters?'

'I'm beginning to think that there can't have been anyone in private shelters at all. There'd surely be people around if there had been. We were in our shelter a lot longer than private shelters are designed for – they'd have starved or had to come out, and then died of whatever killed everyone else. If the authorities sent us inside knowing how long we'd be there, they might not have wanted to put people in the private shelters at all. Maybe they didn't want to tell everyone else about the war to minimize the amount of damage done by people who knew they'd no chance of survival.'

'How horribly cynical. It's looking increasingly like the only explanation though. But there's still the question of *how* you hide the fact that a lot of people have gone into shelters.'

'Maybe not that many, really. A few bigwigs and technologists who are in on the secret, and have cover stories arranged for them. And a few people like us, staying in a remote hotel, for serfs. Probably a few more like that here and there. Then, even if they were supposed to have come home or anything, the confusion of the "epidemic" explains why they're not home yet. Distressing, but no suggestion of them being in shelters from a war you don't know is happening.'

'As far as I can make out, the symptoms could be radiation sickness, but it would take an incredibly organized operation to distribute such a huge quantity of anything so uniformly that people were dying almost everywhere, without there being hotspots where everybody dropped down dead in minutes. It would have to be something with a long enough half-life to let you distribute it before it had all decayed, and short enough that people could come out of shelters within a few months, and it couldn't be contaminated with anything with a longer half-life – not at any significant levels, anyway.'

'If it was going to be enough to kill nearly everyone on the planet, surely the people handling it in quantities in the first place would drop down dead on the spot? You could shield it at the place it was manufactured, but there'd have to be a distribution system and you couldn't have heavy shielding everywhere.'

'I'm not sure. If it was an alpha or beta emitter, they're easy to shield. They're only dangerous if tiny particles get inside you. I think I can see ways that could have been achieved. Nasty.'

'But surely people would have been able to detect it once it was released?'

'A bit late by then, but yes, a few people with the right equipment could have done. Maybe they did. Maybe some of them were in shelters already, and others were known cranks. Maybe in some countries it was common knowledge, just not in Norway.'

'Or maybe not common knowledge, but just one barmy conspiracy theory amongst many. But every explanation looks like a barmy conspiracy theory. It didn't matter much what anyone thought anyway, they all died. Apart from a few oddballs like us – maybe only us – nobody who's survived is going to know anything about what they were thinking.'

'The soldiers on their raiding parties might find newspapers. But what they'd make of them, who knows? Would they even bother to read them? And would it really make any difference anyway?'

'It might, if it resulted in disaffection.'

'Deliberate release of a bioweapon seems to me the most likely – or a combination of various weapons simultaneously. With a bioweapon, you wouldn't get hotspots – as long as everyone gets enough to kill them, it wouldn't matter if some areas got a lot more. It wouldn't kill them any quicker, so it wouldn't be noticed.'

Persie, you would have got along with Tony Ramsden like a house on fire. Or maybe not. Likes sometimes repel. And anyway, this side of you isn't all there is to either of you. There are big differences.

Aren't there just. Tony's knowledge is – was? – all theoretical. Persie's is very practical, too.

Would Tony have known how to deal with the soldier who was trying to rape Merly? I doubt it.

Oh, and so many other differences.

'It's almost as if the shelter was designed to house people whose disappearance wouldn't raise any significant alarms until everyone else was dead. Why? And if that's true, did the people who designed it really know how quickly everyone else was going to die, and that the mortality was really going to be a hundred percent? And surely they'd have been in the shelters themselves?'

'They might have been. Just not the same shelter we were in. In fact, I bet they were. Either they're still underground, or they're just not anywhere near here.'

'Was it even a war at all? If it was, it seems that both – or all – sides lost.'

'They always do, surely?'

'Not usually on quite this scale.'

'I'm almost tempted to wonder whether it wasn't so much a war, as a cull. Kill off nearly all the population, all but your own friends and family and just enough of the rest to provide the labour you need to support your way of life.'

'If so, it's gone spectacularly wrong for them.'

'Conspiracy *and* cock-up, you mean.'

'Actually, has it gone so wildly wrong? We don't know what's happening in the rest of the world. The people who arranged it could be living the life of Reilly somewhere, with a few pleb camps elsewhere just to maintain a bit of a gene pool.'

'I don't suppose we'll ever know. In fact, if that's the real situation, I hope we never do know.'

'They'd have had to have co-operation between the prime movers in all the major powers. Even if you called that a war, it'd really be a cull in all but name. The only way you could deliver the weapon, whatever it was, would be from aircraft, and you couldn't get away with that over enemy territory.'

'Not if they knew you were doing it. But civilian aircraft fly – well, used to, anyway – all over the place all the time, and the equipment might have been disguised as something innocent. It could even have been something genuinely innocent diverted to this alternative purpose. I wouldn't be a bit surprised if there are systems to feed tiny quantities of something into fuel lines, for example, but that would only be any good for radioactive isotopes. Chemicals or bioweapons would be destroyed in the engine.'

'If it was war, we don't know that the enemy – whoever it was – isn't simply biding their time, waiting to take over the rest of the world when the agent, whatever it is, is thoroughly gone.'

'They might have started doing it. They just haven't got here yet.'

'I don't think so. I'd expect more activity on the radio if that was the case.'

'I'm not sure about that. I don't think there's been all that much activity on long wave for a long time, and all the rest is relatively short range.'

But all that was just speculation. Pawns aren't privy to the thinking of the players. There was nothing we could do with the information even if we had it.

Chapter 6

We've never encountered another soul, and we've never been bold enough to go back and investigate what's happening at the camp. We've often wondered whether Will, who knew how we'd escaped, had eventually decided to escape himself.

'Maybe they worked out how we escaped, and blocked the route. Or maybe, perish the thought, he didn't see the trip wires.'

'I wonder what they'd do to anyone they caught trying to escape? I doubt they'd do anything much worse than fetch them back, really. As long as they hadn't killed anyone first, of course.'

'Or maybe he'd got his eye on some woman or other, and was hoping to escape later, with her. He'd have been worried about them blocking the route though – maybe that's why he dithered so much. He wasn't generally a ditherer.'

Unlike me. I didn't dither then, though. Hmm.

'I doubt if we'll ever happen to bump into him, even if he has escaped.'

'There's no car at the first farm he'll get to – assuming he chooses the same route we did, which seems quite likely. It's quite a walk to the next one – and who knows whether the car there will start. I don't actually even remember whether we saw one there.'

'I don't remember, either.'

'If he'd got his eye on one of the women with children – and that's most of them, apart from the au pairs like us – it'd be difficult to persuade them to drag their kids under a bog. Most of the au pairs would probably think he was a bit old for them, although there is a bit of a shortage of men in the camp, and beggars can't be choosers.'

'Some of the soldiers seem decent enough sorts, but most of them are pretty revolting. There's not nearly enough of them for everyone anyway.'

We took a trip down to the coast one day, mostly to see whether shellfish had suffered like mammals and birds, or whether they'd survived, like insects – and spiders. They'd obviously suffered a huge mortality, but we did see a few live winkles.

More impressively, looking down from the harbour wall, we saw lots of fish. We found a shop full of fishing gear, and tried our luck, but we didn't really know what we were doing, and caught nothing.

Further out onto a headland we saw lots of dead seals, but not a single live one. There were a few seabirds, but nothing like what there would have been before the Big Death.

Persie collected a lot of seaweed. We took it home, and she cooked it. 'Makes a change from tinned, dried and pickled stuff.'

It was really delicious. She knew exactly what to do with it.

We had everything we needed, and little worry about finding more when we ran out. The only thing Persie was a bit concerned about was vehicle batteries. We'd found a place with a stock of new ones – the same place we got the jerry cans – 'but even unused they've only got a finite shelf life. Eventually we'll have to start carrying a portable generator and a booster charger around with us if we go far from home, where we're not sure of finding places to park where we can bump start things.' With a stock of unused batteries that was years away, but Persie wanted to be sure we'd be able to do it. We went back to the place we'd got the jerry cans and the batteries, and found a powerful booster charger.

'This'll deliver enough current to start the engine on its own, no need to charge the battery first at all. And the generator's big enough to power it.'

The only really portable generator we'd got was the petrol one, so we went down to the petrol station. It took Persie a while to work out how to get the pumps working, but she managed. We had access to thousands of gallons of petrol – and a lot more diesel, too.

'We could do with some more jerry cans. I expect we'll find some somewhere eventually. No worries about heating oil ever now. Diesel's just as good, and there'll be plenty more petrol stations when we've emptied this one.'

Life was actually quite easy.

I slept in a big bed in one room, and Persie and Merly slept in two separate beds in another. One night I heard them giggling in their room. Then they came padding through to my room in their bare feet. 'It's not going to happen, is it?'

'What isn't?'

'We've been waiting for weeks for you to get so desperate you come pleading to one of us.'

'Pleading for what?' I was sure I knew, but I didn't want to say.

'You know, you rotter. Sex, of course.'

'But you don't fancy me. I know that.'

'It's an important principle with me not to fancy someone else's man. You were Sharon's man.'

'Not after I moved to Will's hut, I wasn't.'

'Oh, I knew why Sharon kicked you out. You were still Sharon's man, even if you didn't realize it. You're our man now. Definitely.'

'I thought maybe you two were lesbians.'

'Oh, we wouldn't deny we've dabbled in that. But variety is the spice of life, isn't it?'

'I'm not sure. I've never fancied sex with any man, however friendly we've been.'

'Anyway, there are three of us. It's not fair for someone to get left out.'

'You don't want to get pregnant, do you?'

'Not just now, no. Probably one day. We don't want to be lonely in our old age, do we? But for one thing, that's not the only kind of sex. And you remember when I raided the pharmacy for cough mixture? That's not all I found.'

'So you found some kind of contraceptives, then.'

'Condoms. We've got one thousand, four hundred and forty of them, to be precise. I only brought one carton, but there's loads more when we run out.'

'That might be a year or two! I hope they don't go off.'

'They've got a use-by date, but it's a fair way away, and I expect they're actually good for a lot longer than that anyway.'

'I thought you'd brought sanitary pads or tampons when you said you'd got something for you and Merly.'

'Well, I got those too, of course.'

'You mean you've been waiting for me to weaken ever since then?'

'Well, I wasn't positively waiting at first. But I wouldn't have turned you away. Merly wouldn't, either. You mean far too much to us to want to upset you.'

Matter-of-fact, or what?

After that, we all slept in the big bed together.

Persie helped both Merly and me learn to drive – not expertly, but well enough to manage on the empty roads – so we didn't have to leave a vehicle behind every time we wanted a different one. We ended up with quite a collection in the road outside the farm.

'That bothers me a bit. It could be a bit noticeable from the air, if there's ever a spotter plane.'

'I don't think so. Who would know it wasn't something that was going on during the Big Death? They wouldn't have before and after pictures.'

The fear that some victorious enemy would arrive, or that bigwigs with technically competent assistance would emerge from longer-term shelters, gradually faded from our minds, and after a couple of years we were pretty sure they didn't exist – or if they did, they weren't interested in us, or our area of Norway, at all.

I was worried about my dearest friends giving birth without proper medical support, but Persie and Merly laughed at me.

'How do think humanity managed for most of its history?'

'Yes, I know. And some of them died.'

'You can't live without risk. And we've got big advantages over wild people, even if we don't have a health service.'

But they made sure they didn't have babies at nearly the same time, so they'd be available to help each other, and not rely entirely on me.

We've got four lovely children now – Persie has Fiona and Sidney and Merly has Gregory and Anna. Persie and Merly insisted that they should have English names. I suggested lots of possible names, and they picked the ones they liked.

They're planning to have one more each. We're hoping that we'll meet some more people before the children grow up, or the next generation is going to be a little bit inbred. We've taken to exploring more widely – all over southern Norway – in the hope of meeting people, but so far we've found nobody.

We even considered approaching our old camp, but decided that they probably still consider us outlaws, and we're surely of no particular value to them. The question of whether any other camp would know about us hasn't arisen, because we've never found another camp. We've even become brazen enough to explore around Oslo, and there's no sign of people from any camp doing any raiding there.

The Y chromosome never gets mixed and matched anyway, and we do at least have a little bit of variety of everything else.

More for the fun of it than anything else, we taught ourselves to drive the tractors. We knew that if we tried to farm the land, that would be noticeable from the air, and at first we refrained, but eventually we grew bold enough to try. It hasn't been easy, but we're making some progress, especially since we decided to move to a different farm nearer the coast. We got seed from an agricultural suppliers in town, but it was several years old by the time we started trying to farm, and that could have been part of our problem. We've also tried getting our own seed from crops that had gone wild, which has had a higher success rate in terms of germination, but the quality of the crops hasn't been wonderful.

Even at our new place, much of the land is grazing land at best, and we've no animals, so that's all going a bit wild. We're a bit envious of the camp's chickens and goats.

Higher up on the hill, there are lots of bilberries, which are very welcome in season. We've found lots of preserving jars, and nowadays we pick enough bilberries to keep us supplied all year round.

We'd only seen one rabbit that first year, but we're overrun with them now. We've got rats, too, but not all that many, and a few birds – mostly gulls, but Merly thought she saw a skua the other day. What wildlife has survived elsewhere, who knows? Maybe eventually something else will arrive here, gradually spreading out from some remnant somewhere, but nothing else has got here yet.

Neither Merly nor I ever thought we'd fire a gun, but Persie had had some training. We raided a gunsmith's. The alarm wasn't working, but we wouldn't have cared about a little thing like that if it had been. We've become reasonably good shots. At first we found it easier to use shotguns, but now we use rifles. It was a lot of trouble picking the pellets out during the butchering, and we got fed up of finding pellets in our dinner even after my best efforts. It's harder to hit the rabbits with a rifle, but missing a few isn't a big deal. The shotguns are good for rats, which we don't want around the farm. We don't eat them, although Persie says they're perfectly good meat.

We all shoot, but I do the butchering and Merly and Persie do the cooking. Back in Burnfield, I knew people who'd have had something to say about that, but we've fallen into various roles without worrying about it. They're not all exactly stereotypical, but to a large extent they follow the stereotypes. Biological, or learned? Who knows? Most likely a bit of both, but that's pure speculation. I'm aware of it but don't worry about it, and neither Persie nor Merly have mentioned it. I think they would if it bothered them. We'll see what happens with the children.

We make occasional trips down to the coast. There are more seabirds than there were on our first visit, but still not the huge numbers there used to be, and whether all the old species are present we don't know. There's still no sign of any marine mammals. The freezer – which was pretty nasty to clean, but is fine now – is full of seaweed and fish, which we've finally learnt to catch. And rabbits, of course.

We sometimes wonder about moving right down to the coast. We don't really want to abandon our faltering first steps in farming, but we know that eventually we, or our descendants, will have to manage without motor vehicles, firearms or electricity, and we think that might be easier on the coast.

The roads are beginning to deteriorate, but the four wheel drive vehicles and the trucks should still be able to negotiate them for a good while yet.

We've even considered moving much further south, by migrating right around the Baltic since we wouldn't be able to get across from Sweden to Denmark. The possibility of meeting other people on the way excites but also scares us, particularly if they're large organized groups.

We're doing our best to give our children a good education. Persie in particular is determined that technological competence should not die with her, although with no functioning industrial base a lot of it is likely to be of no use to anyone beyond the medium term.

'But is there an industrial base? The camp we were in seems to specialize in farming, but even with wide ranging raiding, all their equipment won't last forever unless there's an industrial base somewhere. Maybe there are other camps somewhere training their serfs in running essential industries.'

'You'd think the industrial serfs would realize that food stocks wouldn't last forever without farming.'

'You'd think the agricultural serfs would realize that machinery wouldn't last forever without industry. We never heard anyone talk about it, but that doesn't mean they weren't.'

'At least farmers can survive without machinery. Industry's completely knackered without agriculture.'

'Surviving without machinery will be damned hard. They've not even got horses or bullocks to pull their ploughs, unless some other camp somewhere had the big animals in their shelter. Come to that, where were the chickens and goats while we were in the shelter?'

'Some other part of the shelter, or their own shelter somewhere. Who knows?'

Speculation leading nowhere again. It would help us to prepare for the future if we'd some idea of what the organized camps were up to. But how the devil could we find out?

Language is another strange issue. Persie and Merly are both polyglots, but apart from a little very poor French, I only know English, which Persie and Merly both know very well, and which is what we always use. Should they teach our children any other language? The only other language Persie or Merly could teach them that has the slightest possibility of being useful is Swedish. Even in the camp in Sweden, with a Swedish military regime, the language in general use is English. Probably the fact of the existence of other languages is all that's worth our children knowing.

I still owe Mike seventy quid.

About the author:

Clive K. Semmens was born in London in 1949, and grew up in Yorkshire and then Hertfordshire, in England. His wife hails from a remote village in central India. They have two grown-up children.

Clive is a multi-talented man with vast knowledge and experience of various countries. Above all, he is a humble person. He knows French, German and Hindi well enough to be useful, but in his own words "would certainly not describe himself as fluent or accurate in any of them."

He describes his hobbies as travel, photography, reading, writing and innovative DIY (anything from microelectronics to major building projects).

He's particularly interested in people and their lives, trying to see things from the point of view of people from very different backgrounds, to avoid as far as possible making errors of judgement arising out of the unconscious assumptions of his own background.

Clive is also very interested in the world around people and is well versed in the issues surrounding energy production and consumption, resource consumption, and environmental pollution.

In 1967, he gained a scholarship from the United Kingdom Atomic Energy Authority to study Nuclear Engineering, a course intended to lead to a career designing nuclear power stations and associated infrastructure. His studies and experiences in the nuclear industry led him to the conclusion that nuclear power generation is a very bad idea, and he changed course.

Since then, Clive has had a wide-ranging professional career in engineering, education, technical writing and academic publishing.

He first visited India in 1983. He rapidly got involved providing technical advice for a charity, and met his future wife. He spent six months in India on that occasion, and again a year later. Since then, he and his wife have visited her relatives in India about once every couple of years.

Today they are retired and live in a small English town. They still travel, and take part in political, technical and cultural discussions and he writes essays and novels.

Don't miss Clive K Semmens's first novel –

The Reminiscences

of Penny Lane

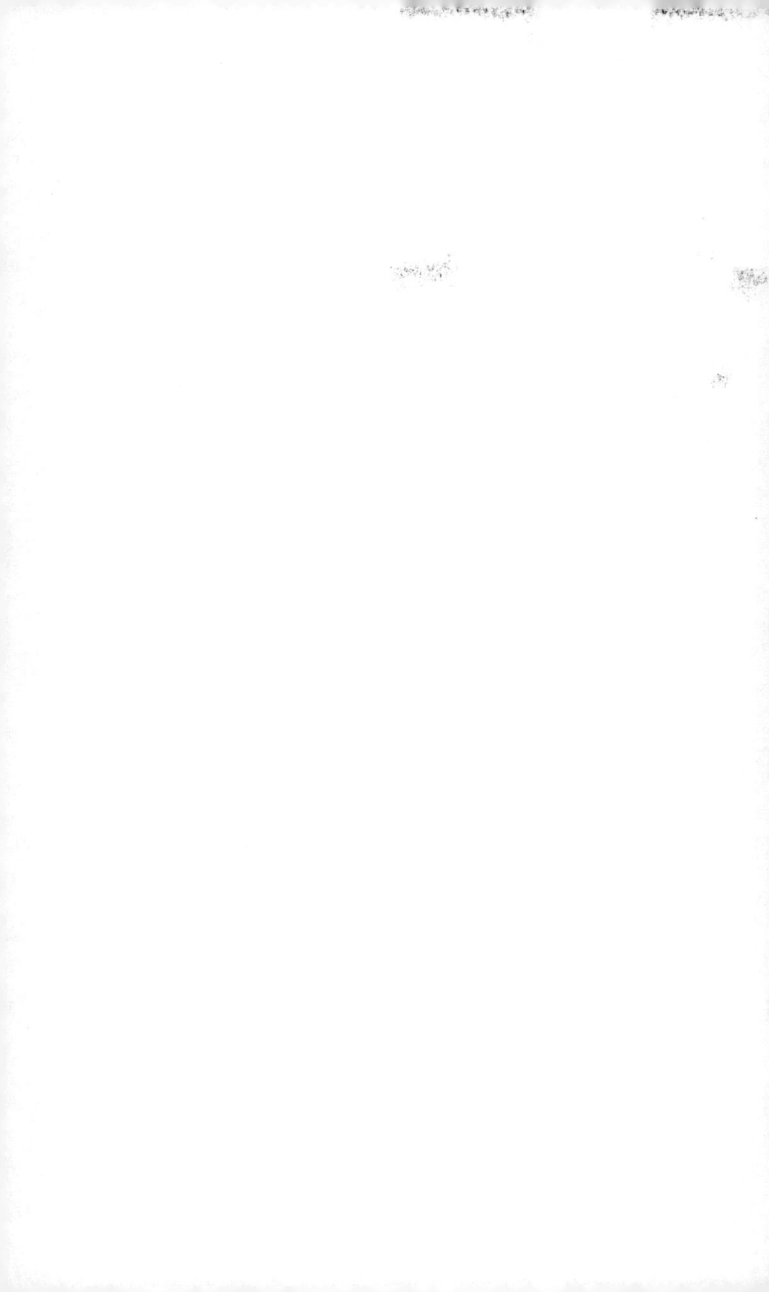